A KILLER
KIND OF
ROMANCE

ALSO BY LETIZIA LORINI

Desserts for Stressed People

The Wedding Menu

Riding the Sugar High

With a Cherry on Top

A KILLER
kind of
ROMANCE

LETIZIA LORINI

G

GALLERY BOOKS

New York   Amsterdam/Antwerp   London
Toronto   Sydney/Melbourne   New Delhi

G

Gallery Books
An Imprint of Simon & Schuster, LLC
1230 Avenue of the Americas
New York, NY 10020

For more than 100 years, Simon & Schuster has championed authors and the stories they create. By respecting the copyright of an author's intellectual property, you enable Simon & Schuster and the author to continue publishing exceptional books for years to come. We thank you for supporting the author's copyright by purchasing an authorized edition of this book.

This book is a work of fiction. Any references to historical events, real people, or real places are used fictitiously. Other names, characters, places, and events are products of the author's imagination, and any resemblance to actual events or places or persons, living or dead, is entirely coincidental.

First Gallery Books trade paperback edition January 2026

GALLERY BOOKS and colophon are registered trademarks of Simon & Schuster, LLC

Simon & Schuster strongly believes in freedom of expression and stands against censorship in all its forms. For more information, visit BooksBelong.com.

For information about special discounts for bulk purchases, please contact Simon & Schuster Special Sales at 1-866-506-1949 or business@simonandschuster.com.

The Simon & Schuster Speakers Bureau can bring authors to your live event. For more information or to book an event, contact the Simon & Schuster Speakers Bureau at 1-866-248-3049 or visit our website at www.simonspeakers.com.

Manufactured in the United States of America

10 9 8 7 6 5 4 3 2 1

Library of Congress Control Number: 2025947989

ISBN 978-1-6680-8235-5 (pbk)
ISBN 978-1-6680-8236-2 (ebook)

Let's stay in touch! Scan here to get book recommendations, exclusive offers, and more delivered to your inbox.

To that teacher who said I'd never use my criminology degree.

Bet you feel silly now.

author's note

Hello there! Thank you for picking up *A Killer Kind of Romance*.

As you might've guessed from the title, this is a romance with a dash of murder. Don't worry, it's all pretty cozy—well, as cozy as serial killer stories can be. It's a book meant for adults, not only because of the murder-y bits but also because of the steamy scenes. Expect detailed, in-depth descriptions of sexual encounters alongside all the twists and turns.

There are also mentions of grief, custody battles, and physical and mental abuse (happening in the past, off-the-page), as well as stalking, threats, and violence (some very much on-the-page). You'll encounter crime scenes, gore, and even a hospital stay before the happily ever after makes its appearance.

A small note before we dive in: I'm bisexual and proud. Just like one of the characters in the book, I have been on the receiving end of harassment and bullying, also because of the gender of the person whose hand I was holding. Gays, lesbians, trans, and queer people are my people.

That said, one of the villains in the book holds bigoted and homophobic views. Unfortunately, this type of thinking is a reality in our society.

Let me be crystal clear: I do not, in any way, condone or encourage the attitudes and actions expressed by this character.

Don't be that person.

The villain *always* gets what's coming for them.

act I

[structure]

---

like a prelude, it sets up the quirky backstories, the awkward
meet-cutes, and the inevitable "will they or won't they" tension

0

the action-packed flash-forward

[trope]

when the story leaps ahead to a future filled with epic
showdowns, high-stakes drama, and enough adrenaline
to give a caffeinated reader a heart attack

Hunting down a serial killer isn't as glamorous as one might think.
But I have to admit, if I wasn't preparing to face a cold-blooded
murderer, I'd appreciate the ambience of the library at night. The still-
ness, the quiet, the way the moonlight filters through the tall windows, casting soft, silvery beams on the worn wooden floors. It smells
like old books and dusty wood, like evenings made for studying and
days filled with reading.

Silly of me to choose my favorite place for the showdown that
I might not survive, though I guess there's a certain poetry to it. I've
spent my life around books—might as well die surrounded by them.

I tiptoe between the towering bookshelves, clutching my pink
Taser like it's a medieval sword. My heart is doing an anxious tap dance.

I know he's here. I *led* him here. But now that I'm actually about to face him with a Taser, I can't help but think . . . maybe luring him into a deserted library was a bad idea. Especially with a weapon that looks like it belongs in Barbie's Dreamhouse.

A faint rustling sound catches my attention, and I freeze. My breath hitches. The noise comes again—somewhere in the far corner of the library. For a moment, I wish it could be a mouse or someone sneezing outside.

No, Scarlett.

This is it. Tonight it all ends.

I inch forward, weaving through the shelves, my steps quiet, as though caught under a librarian's disapproving glare. My palms are clammy around the Taser's handle, and my breathing feels obnoxiously loud in the silence.

Then I see him. He's there, at the end of the aisle, all dark and brooding, with his old leather jacket and that stupid, soft, infuriatingly perfect hair.

I duck behind a desk and take a deep breath. *Okay, Scarlett, you've got this. You're a strong, capable woman. A strong, capable woman with a Taser and zero experience in confrontations that don't involve passive-aggressive emails to customer service.*

I peek out from behind the desk. He's still there, silently waiting like he has nowhere else to be. Meanwhile, I'm pretty sure I'm about to faint.

I grip the Taser tighter, reminding myself of its presence. *Just sneak up behind him, give him a little zip-zap, and boom—hero status achieved.* Easy, right?

I move forward, inching closer and closer until I'm right behind him. My heart's hammering, and I can almost feel the electricity of the Taser pulsing in my hand. One more step . . .

My hand is poised to strike, but just as I'm about to make my move, he turns around with startling speed. His speckled gray eyes lock onto mine, and recognition flickers in them. His hand moves in a blur, pulling a gun from his jacket and pointing it directly at my forehead.

He has a fucking gun. And it's not pink.

"Really?" I mutter, blinking at him. "You *had* to bring a gun?"

He arches an eyebrow, a half smirk that would be incredibly attractive if I wasn't so busy internally screaming. "Were you planning on . . . *stunning* me with that?" He gestures to the Taser in my hand like I've just brought a rubber duck to a knife fight.

I glare at him, desperately trying to retain some level of dignity while simultaneously trying not to wet my pants. "I promise it won't feel as pink as it looks."

His eyes sparkle as he chuckles. *Chuckles*. Like this is all some grand joke. "You know, I had you pegged as smarter than this," he says, his chin jerking down. "You lead me here and show up with that? What did you figure would happen next, exactly?"

I narrow my eyes at him, trying to stand taller, even though I'm currently staring down the barrel of a gun. At this point, my entire strategy has boiled down to *don't pass out*, but he won't hurt me, right? Without me, he's done. "You're here, aren't you?"

"Yes, I'm here. And you're coming with me now." He tilts his gun to the right, his eyes flicking behind me. "After you, Freckles."

I hesitate, considering for a moment whether I can make a run for it.

There's no point. I'm fucked.

With a muttered curse, I turn around and begin walking. "This is *exactly* why I don't do romance."

two weeks earlier

the inciting incident

[trope]

the moment in a romance novel when fate decides,
"let's shake things up"

"Rooo."

"Shut up," I croak. Sherlock's version of a *meow* is the last thing I want to hear after two hours of sleep.

"Rooo."

"I said shut up."

Sherlock's tail tickles the tip of my nose, then his butt is on my face. "Rooo!" he insists.

"You can't be *that* hungry." I push him off my face, then blink one eye open and find his yellow-green eyes staring back at me, unimpressed. I scratch the back of his neck, my fingers sinking into the black fur. "I don't care—too tired."

I close my eyes again, but I can feel him staring in that judgmental way only a cat can manage, so with a groan, I drag myself up into a seated position. I guess I'm also late for work, so I can't resent him *too* much.

I grab my phone and scroll through the notifications. Nothing. I stumble out of bed, pulling on yesterday's shirt. Sherlock brushes against my leg, yowling as I head to the kitchen. Once he's fed, I fumble for the coffee machine, only to find it blinking "low water."

Great.

I fill it, waiting impatiently as it burbles, then pour myself half a mug. I grab my phone again and check through the notifications I've gotten in the last ten minutes—none. Maybe I should text him.

Yeah. You know what? I can. I *will*.

I open up my conversation with Ethan and stare at the screen. The last bubble is green—sent by me—and so is the one before. The last message he sent reads "Bet," which left me puzzled for a good five minutes. It's like he's learned a new language since he turned fourteen. I hesitate for a while longer, then type.

> **Scarlett**
> Hey! It's been a while. How's school?

Nah. He won't answer that. I glance at the haphazardly hung poster that reads, "Dysfunction: Just another word for family," with a doodle of a crooked house, then study the screen again.

> **Scarlett**
> It's my birthday! I'd love to talk if you have the time.
> Maybe after school? Or we could grab dinner. Or lunch.
> Or anything, really. If you're free! No pressure. Love you!

I run a hand over my face, delete almost everything and send:

> **Scarlett**
> I'd love to chat if you're free!

Sherlock lets out a disapproving "Roo," his eyes trained on me as I shuffle to the bathroom, tripping over my half-zipped pants and dodging the piles of laundry lining the floor. I stuff my phone and keys into my purse and bolt for the door, praying I remembered deodorant.

The warm summer air carries the sweet scent of blooming flowers and freshly cut grass. The sun kisses my cheeks, making me loosen my cardigan as I descend the steps. But the peace of the suburbs is quickly interrupted by the neighbor across the street.

"Scarlett!" Mrs. Prattle—Brattle, actually, though everyone knows her as Mrs. Prattle—calls as she hurries over. Despite her age, she's as spry as ever, with her short silver hair pinned back and deep wrinkles that crinkle when she's gossiping. "Did you hear about John Gray, dear?"

Looking for my car keys in the impossible mess of my oversize handbag, I side-glance at the Grays' place, right beside mine. "Hey, Mrs. Pr—Brattle." Keys in hand, I point at my car. "Sorry, I'm late for work."

"I would have *never* imagined," she says, reaching my side with a determined step. She falls into pace with me as I walk to the car, her foldable shopping cart rattling behind her. "You know, Maria—the hairdresser with the tattoos—said she saw him the day before. Looked as healthy as a horse, she said."

"Uh-huh." I open the car door, then check the time on my phone. "Really, Mrs. Brattle, I—"

"Did you see the undertaker? Handsome fella, huh?" she continues, turning to my old gray Toyota.

"Undertaker?" I freeze. "You don't mean . . ."

"Oh, John Gray passed last week, darling. They just found him dead in his home yesterday."

What? "I'm so . . . sorry," I say almost automatically. Truth be told, I must be the only person in town who never liked that man. It always felt like his affable smile was nothing more than a mask.

Still, he's been my next-door neighbor all my life.

"I wonder if his son will show up for the funeral," Mrs. Prattle says.

My shoulders stiffen instantly. "He won't." Noticing the curl of her lips, I casually flip my hair off my shoulder. "I mean, I don't know, of course, but he hasn't been around for so long that . . ."

Her eyes glimmer, the unmistakable sign of gossip being detected. "I didn't know you two were close."

"We weren't," I rush out. "We never even spoke a word to each other." Okay, that might be suspiciously exaggerated. "Besides 'hello' and whatnot."

"Huh."

"Anyway, I'm—" I point at the car.

"Go, dear. Go," she says, though she doesn't move to leave. Instead, she lowers her voice, leaning in closer. "But don't think I didn't notice what day it is." She takes a small envelope out of her bag and hands it over.

"Mrs. Brattle," I half-heartedly complain.

"I know, I know. You don't celebrate your birthday. But it's just a small gift, and I won't tell anyone."

Pretty sure that means the whole town already knows.

She waves off my thank-you, and I drop onto the seat, then check my reflection in the rearview mirror. *Good God.* My bangs are a brown tangled mess, and yesterday's eyeliner is smudged.

I run my fingers through my hair, trying to tame it into some semblance of order. Setting the envelope down, I take out my concealer and mascara.

Once I'm as presentable as I can manage, I start the car and pull out of the parking spot, the old piece of junk creaking as if it can barely sustain its weight.

I turn on the stereo system and connect my phone. It's Friday, which means the latest episode of my podcast aired last night. I open Spotify, and my shoulders relax as soon as the familiar intro music plays.

One episode a week for half a decade, and this feeling doesn't get old.

Welcome to Murders & Manuscripts, *the podcast where we delve into the darkest corners of crime fiction. I'm your host, Scarlett Moore, and today we're unraveling the chilling tale of* The Thornwood Butcher *by Cameron Slate, a story that will send shivers down your spine and keep you on the edge of your seat.*

Thornwood is a quaint village, the kind you'd see in postcards—peaceful, picturesque, and seemingly perfect. But beneath this serene facade lies a dark, twisted secret waiting to be uncovered.

Our story begins with a grisly discovery: Dr. Margaret Fairchild, a respected historian who had been kidnapped during a stroll with her dog, is found dead in her cottage. Her body is a horrifying sight—tied to a chair, her mouth filled with dirt and wildflowers, her throat slit, and her eyes replaced with small wooden animal figures. Scattered around her are blood-spattered manuscripts and artifacts. On the wall, a message written in blood: "The past never dies."

My phone beeps with an incoming text, which causes the Bluetooth connection to stutter, so I give the stereo the usual swat.

—shocking murder has rocked our small town of Willowbrook, Connecticut.

I lower the volume, cursing the Jurassic car for switching to the radio, before I register the words of the host.

Catherine Blake, a professor at UML, was found dead in her home late last night. Details are still emerging, but police sources describe a scene too gruesome to believe.

A murder? Here?
I turn up the volume, my curiosity piqued.

Blake was last seen walking her dog. When her daughter called and received no answer, she went to her mother's residence and found her body.
        Police are urging anyone with information to come forward. This murder has sent shock waves through our small community, and everyone is advised to stay vigilant.

When someone honks behind me, I realize the light has turned green, and I resume driving, thoughts still scattered.

There's hardly any crime in Willowbrook. A town with only five thousand people, where we all know one another, isn't supposed to have murders. This will affect the community—the sense of safety that's always been so strong here, the way neighbors leave their doors unlocked and let their kids play outside until dusk.

I drive all the way to the office, hardly aware of what's around me until I pull into the parking lot and turn off the engine.

After fetching my bag, I enter the building and check my messages, unable to help the slight disappointment that settles in my chest when I notice it's *not* Ethan.

> **Paige**
> Free tonight? We could use an extra at the Single Mingle event.

"Liar," I mumble as I wave at the receptionist, then rush into the elevator just before the door closes.

> **Scarlett**
> That so? And it's not a ploy to get me to celebrate my birthday?

> **Paige**
> Omg, that's true! Happy birthday!

"The worst liar in the world," I say at my phone. She does this all the time—drags me to one of her parties with the promise of work, then insists I have fun instead. It reminds me of why she's one of only three friends I have: friends are a lot of work.

> **Scarlett**
> Fine. Send me the address. Since it's not a birthday party, I'll show up in sweats.

> **Paige**
> Sounds great. See you tonight.

Liar.

I walk up the stairs and enter Booked It headquarters, where the air hums with energy and the faint scent of coffee lingers. The host of *Space & Storycraft*, Sarah, waves at me from behind her desk, cluttered with sci-fi books and a half-empty coffee cup, and in the recording studio, the soft glow of monitors peeks through the open door. Damien, host of *Wizards & Words*, looks up, and as my gaze narrows to the farthest corner of the room, I notice my favorite sound engineer—and the only one I know—Theo.

I move on to Celeste's office, the last door on the right.

"Celeste?" I ask as I knock on the half-open door.

"Yes?" I open the door to see Celeste's sleek dark hair, cut in a sharp bob, as she bends over her computer. "Scarlett! Come in, come in."

I enter the cozy, cluttered room, with shelves crammed full of books and folders stacked haphazardly on every available surface. "Sorry I'm late, it's been a crazy—"

"Wow, you look terrible."

"Thanks," I say flatly. She's always impeccably dressed, today in a tailored charcoal suit. I don't know how she does it—not with a husband and two kids—but she always finds time for makeup, too. If you showed anyone in town a picture of thin black-rimmed glasses and bold red lipstick, they'd say it was Celeste. "Didn't sleep much."

She hums. "Someone interesting keeping you up at night?"

"Four men, actually." I take out *The Midnight Gentlemen* from my bag. "Murderous but distinguished."

She laughs, turning slightly in her chair. "Don't worry. Love will come when it's time. And then you'll wish it had taken longer to find you."

I'm *not* worried, but I'm tired of pointing it out. "Everything good at home?"

"Oh, absolutely. Steve is my rock." She turns to the floor-to-ceiling windows that offer a panoramic view of the town center, then to the bookcase, locating the mug she's abandoned on a top shelf. "Last night's episode was your best yet. *The Thornwood Butcher*. Couldn't agree more with your review—we need more voices like Slate."

"Best book I've read in a while," I offer, fidgeting with my hands. "So, hmm . . . you wanted to see me?"

"Yes, right," she says as she focuses her attention on me. I've known her my whole life, but under her scrutiny, even my hands turn clammy. "Twenty-three, huh? Can I say happy birthday?"

Oh God. Seriously? "Mrs. Brattle already wished me a happy birthday and gave me an envelope filled with cash I'm *sure* the whole town contributed to. So . . ." I stand, motioning to leave.

"Wait—I want to give you a raise!"

I turn to her, eyebrows skyrocketing. "Oh." I walk back. "In that case . . ." I say as I slump back into the chair.

"Here. How does this sound?" she asks, holding out a paper.

I read through the contract, my mouth opening as I notice this is far more than a raise—this is twice my current salary. Does this mean . . .

"I know you've wanted to come on full-time for a while now, but what I said remains true," she rushes out. "We can't afford more weekly episodes of *Murders & Manuscripts*. You know the podcast hasn't exactly been thriving for the last couple of years."

"Okay," I say, excitement dampened. "Then why the raise?"

"Because I have an opening, and I'd like you to consider it."

I watch as she walks to the big bookshelf beside the desk, then returns and drops a thick folder in front of me. Reading the words scribbled on it, I shake my head. "No. No way."

"Scarlett, wait—"

"*Romance books?*" I squeal. "Do you want to kill me?"

"*Passion & Pages* is our best-performing podcast. And now that Tanya is leaving, I'll need to hire someone else."

"So do it. I don't—"

She leans forward over her desk and grabs my hand. "You have a mortgage to pay, Scarlett. And I know that you've been picking up odd jobs around town." She points down at the folder. "Is romance really worse than that?"

It probably is. I honestly can't tell, because I've never read one. "Look, Celeste. This isn't just about whether I *like* it. I don't know the first thing about love."

She leans back in her reclining chair with a dismissive gesture. "Well, it's not like you're a murder expert."

No, but I'm the daughter of a cop and an assistant district attorney. Other kids got fairy tales while I begged my dad to tell me about how the police caught the San Francisco Strangler one more time. I read my first crime fic when I was ten, and I never stopped. I've watched all the documentaries, listened to every single podcast out there.

You know what I've never done? Watched rom-coms. Listened to love songs or daydreamed about boys.

I'm *not* the right person for this job.

But the money, a tired little voice in my head says. How can I say no to stability? Celeste is right: I have a mortgage to pay. And it's for a run-down mess that could be turned into a house if I had some money to invest in it.

"Look, why don't you try it out? A couple of episodes—just to see how you do. And if it doesn't work out"—she makes a decisive gesture through the air—"we forget all about it."

I'm pretty sure I'll regret this, but I can't say no without even trying. I owe it to my back, destroyed after five years of on-and-off waitressing. "Okay."

Celeste claps. "Oh, thank God. This will be amazing, you'll see."

"Your expectations worry me."

"You'll do *great*, Scarlett."

Slapping my thighs, I stand. "Okay, well, it sounds like I have a podcast to study."

"You do. I'll make sure your salary information is updated." She smiles. "Oh, and Scarlett?"

"Yes?"

"Make it ten times better than Tanya's, please?"

I ignore the dread gripping my throat. "I'll do my best, boss."

I walk out of the office, hand already wrapped around my phone. In the main room, I expect to be hit by the usual activity, but instead of the crowd buzzing from one side of the room to the other, all my colleagues are clustered around Damien's computer, their faces tense and focused.

Theo, standing a little apart, offers me a hesitant wave. His glasses are slightly askew, which always makes me smile, and a mop of curly blond hair falls just above the frames. "All good with Celeste?"

"Yep." I check my latest notifications. Nothing from Ethan. "Did you know Tanya is leaving?"

"She told me yesterday." His shoulder bumps against mine. "Hey."

Happy birthday, his expression says. With a smile of my own, I thank him. Which reminds me . . . "Is Paige planning a surprise party?"

"Huh? N-no."

I was wrong. Paige is a terrible liar, but Theo is definitely a worse one. "Theo?" I insist.

He sheepishly looks away, then shrugs one shoulder. "She's planned that event for tonight. Single Mingle."

"Which she wants me to *work* at?"

He holds on for about four more seconds before finally folding. "No. She just wants you to have a good time."

There. I knew it. That doesn't mean I get to skip it, though. I can't stand the inhuman pitch of Paige's voice when she's disappointed. "Single Mingle? Good God." I drop into the closest chair. "Are you going?"

He watches me through the thick lenses. "Do I have to?"

"Hell yes, you have to. Single Mingle sounds like hell, but one built specifically to bring *me* down. I could use a friendly face."

He squints. "Not ready for love yet, then?"

After I make a "hmph" sound, my gaze drifts to our colleagues, still gathered around Damien's desk. "What's going on?"

Theo turns. "Oh, yeah. I still can't believe it. There's been a murder in town." He gestures toward the computer. "The *Willowbrook Whistle* just ran their story."

I stand and walk to the desk, leaning in over Damien's head to read the article's headline on the screen: "Police Respond to Horrifying Murder in Willowbrook."

Stomach tightening, I quickly scroll through the text, grasping bits of information here and there about the victim's background, until I get to the details of the murder.

> In a shocking turn of events, Catherine Blake's body was found tied to a chair in her home, her throat brutally slit and disturbing cuts surrounding her eyes. Authorities believe the horrific attack may have occurred once she came back home from work.
>
> The victim's body was littered with flowers and dirt, and a chilling message was scrawled in blood on the wall. Investigators are now exploring the possibility that Catherine's murder was ritualistic, potentially linked to a local religious cult.

My blood runs cold as I absorb the details. Is it me, or . . . a slit throat, flowers and dirt, a message written in blood on the wall? Either I'm losing my mind or this is almost exactly the murder that happened in *The Thornwood Butcher*, the book whose review aired on my podcast last night.

Straightening, I look back at Theo, lips parted. "What the fuck?"

2

the secret identity

[trope]

a plot device wherein a character hides their true identity,
usually causing a domino effect of catastrophic mishaps,
mistaken assumptions, and revelations so dramatic they
could induce a collective gasp from the entire cast

Paige has rented The Oak for tonight's Single Mingle event—
Willowbrook's very own pub, bar, café, *and* the closest thing to a
club there is in town. I often wonder why someone else hasn't opened
another pub-bar-café-club, or even only one of those things, but I
guess everyone's too loyal to The Oak. To Quentin, who runs it. And
to John Gray, who opened it thirty years ago.

"Wait, what?" Paige squeals over the faint hum of music from
the adjacent room, where people are already arriving. Her voice cuts
through the noise as she places a tray of champagne flutes on the
counter. "You think someone reenacted a murder from a book?"

I glance around the kitchen, bustling with servers and catering staff putting last-minute touches on hors d'oeuvres, then tuck the phone away. Ethan's just not going to answer, I guess.

"It sounds *suspiciously* similar," I murmur.

"And you *just* recorded an episode about it."

"I'm not saying the two things are connected," I explain, catching the hint of mockery in her voice. "That book's everywhere right now. Though you've got to admit it's . . . eerie."

She shoots me a look as she rearranges the flutes. Her auburn curls are pinned back, but a few loose waves fall around her face, catching the soft kitchen lights. "Scarlett, you know I love you—"

"*Buuuut*," I interject, dragging out the word for effect.

She rests both hands on her hips. "Don't do that. You know I hate that. And you can't deny you have a tendency to see corpses everywhere."

"I do not!"

"Oh, really?" She arches a perfectly shaped eyebrow. "How about Professor Lowell?"

I groan. She always brings up Professor Lowell.

"You thought he was running a prostitution ring, Scarlett."

"Only because we saw him driving around town with all those girls!"

"Yeah, well." She snickers. "That sort of criminal and volunteers at the Center for Abuse have that in common. And remember your weird colleague?"

"Damien?" I roll my eyes. "Okay, point taken. Turns out he's not a terrorist, but in my defense, he *does* have a suspicious amount of wires and circuit boards lying around."

"Look, I know you mean nothing bad by it," Paige insists, nudging me to step aside as she walks around me. "It's just . . . murder is all you think about. All the time."

I pout, finally conceding. "Well, not anymore. Now I'll have to think about romance, too."

She removes her apron and smooths her dress. "It'll be great for you. You'll see—romance will change your life."

"I just hope it doesn't get me fired."

"You'll be *fine*."

I slump against the counter, feeling the weight of the deal I made. "I will most certainly *not* be fine. Didn't you hear what I said? I have to read . . . *romance*."

Her laughter is light and infectious as she pulls me upright. "Oh, come on. This is bordering on offensive."

"I'm sorry," I say, thinking of the stack of clinch covers always sitting on her bedside table. "It's not just about the books. You know I'm bad at love."

"Aw, Scarlett." She touches my arm reassuringly. "You can't be bad at something you've never done. I'm not a bad mechanical engineer—I've just never . . . *engineered*."

I slump again, my elbows pressing into the cool countertop. "I'm a twenty-three-year-old woman who's never been in a long-term relationship. What would you call that?"

"Honestly? I call it exciting. You have everything ahead of you." She shrugs. "The first big crush, the first dates, the first 'I love you.'"

I feel my eyes crinkle at the corners. Typical Paige, isn't it? Falling in love at the drop of a hat, getting her heart broken, and doing it all over again without losing hope. There's nothing she loves more than falling in love.

She laughs softly, probably noticing my look. "I know, I know, I'm basically romance's biggest fan and biggest cautionary tale."

She heads to the door to peek into the event room, then turns back. "Honestly, this Single Mingle thing couldn't have come at a better time. How can you judge romance books if you've never experienced romance yourself?" Before I can interject, she claps her hands. "I can feel it. Your love life is about to change."

I cross my arms. "Yes, I feel it, too. It's switching from nonexistent to miserable."

"*Scarlett . . .*"

"And besides, romance books aren't exactly like real life," I protest.

She glances over her shoulder to her girlfriend, Vanessa, who she's been going strong with for almost a year. "Actually, when you meet the right person, love feels exactly like a romance book."

I hum. "That's . . . sweet. And a little gross."

She throws a balled-up piece of paper at me.

"Paige, falling in love is what everyone expects of me, and every time I can't get there, I feel like something's wrong with me."

"Don't say that," she chides softly, walking back to me. "There's nothing wrong with you."

"Sure there is. Everyone dates, has sex, falls in love. And I'm just watching from the outside."

"Okay, look. If you're swearing off love, I won't mention it again. You're done with sex? I'll get you the finest vibrator money can buy. And, hey, if you decide you're aromantic, you know I'll support you—hell, I'll plant a flag on my front porch."

"*Buuuut?*"

Again, she mock-glares. "I don't think that's it, Scarlett. I think it's hard for you to open up. To be vulnerable." She gives my arm a gentle squeeze. "And you're protecting yourself from heart-break by keeping enough distance from everyone. *That's* why you feel nothing."

I exhale, then give her a curt nod. "Okay. So let's say you're right—"

"I am."

"—and that I'm open to changing that—"

"Of course you are!"

"How would I do that?"

Her eyes widen, the green in them shimmering against the light. "Oh, I'm *so* glad you asked." She walks to the chairs where the work-ers have abandoned their jackets in a heap and reveals a black clothes bag. "Happy birthday, Scarlett."

Ignoring the usual lump in my throat every time I hear those words, I take the bag. "What is this?"

"Opening the present usually answers that question."

I unzip it, and . . . *wow*. My fingers brush over the fabric inside the bag—a striking, vibrant red. As I unzip it further, the dress is revealed in its full, breathtaking glory. It's a bold shade of crimson, with intricate lace detailing that winds down like a cascade of flow-ers. It has that high-fashion edge that feels completely foreign to me, like it's supposed to turn heads in a room full of strangers—which is perhaps exactly what Paige intended.

I glance up, speechless, and see her face lit with excitement. "Thanks, Paige," I say breathlessly. "I'll definitely wear this when I'm finally invited to the Met Gala."

She laughs. "You do that. In the meantime, that's the bathroom." She points at the door behind her. "Put this on and get out there.

I guarantee you'll have men begging you to fall in love with them within ten minutes."

"*Yay.*" Though the prospect of wearing this dress makes tonight slightly more exciting, knowing people will *see* me in it dampens all my enthusiasm. I hate parties—let alone being the center of attention at parties. And that dress . . . that's not going unnoticed.

At least this day is consistent with the last five miserable birthdays I've had.

My phone pings, and when I enter the restroom and check the latest notification, the breath is nearly kicked out of me.

> **Ethan**
> Happy birthday, big sis.

I bring the phone to my chest and close my eyes, smiling. "Best birthday ever."

"Mask on."

I glance up into the masked bouncer's eyes and blow out a breath. "No, I know the party planner—she's my best friend." He blinks. "I'm just here to support her." Another blink. "Seriously?"

He gestures behind him with a tilt of his head, where I glimpse inside The Oak. Everyone is, indeed, sporting one of these silly black masks and wearing something red or black. "Fine," I grumble, turning the mask in my hand, feeling the velvety texture and the rhinestones clustered like tiny sparks at the center, thinning out toward the edges and the angled eyeholes.

I pull it on and enter the small, dark hall, handing my ticket to another bouncer. Then, past the curtained entrance, I step into the dimly lit bar—and immediately feel like I've stumbled into an entirely different world.

A wash of sultry red lighting and moody jazz music hits me, blending with the faint, spicy scent of roses. The room is draped in rich velvet curtains, shadows pooling in every corner. Most nights, this place is just a casual hangout where the biggest thrills are karaoke and fried food. It's hard to reconcile that laid-back charm with the lavish spectacle Paige has created tonight.

Still, I'd rather be at home, cozy with a blanket and a good book.

Reluctantly, I step farther in, weaving through the crowd as guests laugh in hushed tones and slip into shadowed nooks. In the center of the room, the dark polished bar glows from below, and the bartenders, dressed in sleek black, are mixing drinks with names like "Sinful Kiss" and "Eternal Flame," each one deep red or dark purple with absurdly ornate garnishes.

Paige, now wearing a mask of her own and her hair curled at the tips, pops up beside me, wrapping an arm around my neck in a half strangle. "So? What do you think?"

"It's amazing, Paige." I take in the dramatic red lights and the velvet-draped walls. "If I hadn't driven here, I wouldn't know we were at The Oak."

"Thank God. My boss has been on me about tonight." She pulls out her phone. "Do you like the dress code?"

"Yeah, I love it." Of course, no man given the choice of red or black went for the red . . . except for one, actually. The man standing in the back of the room dressed in a scarlet suit—bordering on ridiculous but somehow working for him.

He's taller than most people around him, and he glances around like he's fully aware of the attention he's drawing and reveling in it.

Once the red light hits his face, I freeze.

The sharp lines of his suit contrast with his unruly dark hair, which looks as if someone tried to tame it with gel before it rebelliously resumed its windswept state. His black mask has faint silver accents along the edges that catch the dim light, and his mouth curves in a faint, almost lazy smile as he talks to a woman.

I'll never forget that smile.

"Do you see that?"

"That guy?" She looks over casually. "Oh, I see *him*. Definitely."

"No, I mean . . . don't you recognize him?"

"Did I sleep with him?" She squints. "Did *you* sleep with him?"

"No—"

"Then I don't care."

"It's Rafael," I insist. "Gray?"

"Shut your mouth hole." Paige gasps, whacking my arm. "No freaking way. He's back?"

Well, apparently so. And he looks plenty chummy with the woman holding his arm, leaning in close. A breathtaking blonde with flowing hair that cascades down her back, framing a face that could belong in a magazine. Just his type.

"Are you sure? I mean, how can you even recognize him? He's wearing a mask, and we haven't seen him in . . ."

"Five years," I say, a little more sharply than I intended.

Paige studies me with blatant curiosity. "That long, huh? Since the, uh . . ."

"The Incident," I confirm.

"Are you okay?"

Of course I'm okay. So the boy next door is back—except he's a man next door now. We barely interacted when he lived here; we likely won't interact more now that he's back. "He must be here for his dad's funeral."

"Could be. He hasn't been back once—I honestly thought he was in prison."

Prison? "Why would you think that?"

"Because of the way he left?" She scoffs. "And everything he did while he lived here?"

Sure, Rafael Gray was anything but a golden boy. Fights, smoking, underage drinking, driving without a license—since he's been able to walk, he's been making bad choices. But I always had a feeling that it wasn't his fault—that John Gray had something to do with why his mother had left them. With why Rafael looked so miserable. Seeing him miss Christmases and birthdays for five years straight confirmed my suspicions.

"Anyway," Paige says, smacking her lips, "does anyone look good?"

Oh God. "I agreed I would wear the dress. Didn't say I would actually mingle."

"It's implied, Scarlett."

"My very first case of miscommunication."

She grabs my arm, her face suddenly serious. "Find someone you like for some horizontal gymnastics, or I swear to God . . ."

"You know, you're basically asking for me to get murdered," I say, crossing my arms. "'Meet a stranger! Let your guard down!' Next thing you know, I'm a case on *Dateline.*"

She blinks, her eyes narrowing in that terrifying way that always makes me fold.

"Fine."

"Great!" She hesitates. "And if that someone were Rafael Gray—"

"It's not."

"But if you wanted to—"

"I don't."

She rolls her eyes, waving me off. "Have fun, Scarlett."

Why does that sound like a warning?

My palms are suddenly clammy. I look weird just standing here. Maybe I should spend some money I don't have on a drink I don't even want.

A group of masked women rush past me, forcing me to press against the wall. Relieved, I draw a deep breath. Some people don't like to be in the background. Wall holders. Supporting cast. Luckily for me, that is where I thrive.

"I only wish I'd brought my book," I say, my words getting lost in the crowd.

Unable to do much else, I people-watch. Or, rather, Rafael-watch. He's still with that same woman, standing closer than I'd feel comfortable with. Even when he was a nineteen-year-old kid and lived here, he got around, so it shouldn't surprise me that he's still a flirt.

For some reason, it does.

I guess I imagined that he'd left for some tragic reason, and I just kept picturing him being miserable since. Not that I pictured him often—only as much as the average person wonders about someone who mysteriously vanished. His departure was just . . . sudden. And surprising. And the talk of the town, I'm sure, though at eighteen I wasn't privy to adults' gossip.

Suddenly, as if he knows I'm watching, he glances over and catches my eye.

Fucking busted.

I whip my head around, heartbeat rising, then decide that's probably not enough and walk past a wall of people until I'm on the other side of the room, awkwardly hovering next to the small alcoves.

But I look even more out of place here, so I dive into the crowd again, coming out at the bar. I watch over my shoulder and make sure Rafael is nowhere nearby. When I don't see him anywhere, I exhale.

This is stupid, right? This town is too small to allow for avoiding people, and I'm sure The Incident is not at the forefront of his thoughts, especially with his father's passing.

I check my phone, deciding two hours is a perfectly acceptable amount of time to spend here before going home. A long, excruciating amount of time, but at least Paige won't be complaining.

One hour and fifty-three minutes left.

One hour and forty-eight minutes.

One hour and forty-four.

I tuck the phone away and turn around, then stop dead in my tracks, my heart giving a startled thump as I find myself face-to-face with *him*.

Up close, he's even more of a presence, tall and broad-shouldered, the deep red of his suit catching flecks of light that make it shimmer. It's perfectly tailored, fitting him like it was made for his body alone, the fabric stretching just slightly over his chest and shoulders. I can see now that the suit jacket has faint patterns woven into it, subtle swirls that seem to shift as he moves.

His eyes, framed by the mask, are as piercing and intense as they were five years ago. They're an unsettling shade of gray, stormy and unreadable, and his jawline is sharp and severe, with a faint shadow of stubble. A small silver nose ring catches the light—subtle, but impossible to miss.

He looks like the devil.

He *is* the devil.

The devil is standing in front of me.

3

the meet-cute

[trope]

the magical moment when two future lovers collide, often as if
they've never used basic motor skills before; followed by flirty
banter, dramatic eye contact, and at least one ridiculously
timed rainstorm

"Are you going to run away again?" Rafael's voice is low and smooth, and the corners of his full lips are lifted in a hint of a smirk, as though he knows exactly what effect he's having on me.

A sweaty, sticky, nervous effect.

"E-excuse me?"

"You were staring at me. When I caught you, you gasped and ran away." My cheeks heat as the subtle scent of something warm lingers around him. "About ten minutes ago. Remember?"

Fuck me, this is *mortifying*.

"I wasn't staring."

"Oh, okay." His brows draw together in mock concern. "Then what's with the running?"

"I'm not running, I'm . . . looking for my friend."

"Hmm." He points behind me. "She's over there."

I turn around, finding Paige in the crowd. Does he know who I am? Or did he see us talking when we came in?

"The only reason you didn't find me staring back at you is that I was saying hi to an old friend."

Startled, I turn back, his face much closer than it was before. He looks the same as when I saw him last but also completely different. Older, more manly. There's a quiet confidence in the way he stands, like he owns the space without trying to. Maybe hardened by time and experience, but also lighter, as if instead of being miserable, he spent the last five years thriving. He's definitely looking at me differently from how he used to. "Wh-what?"

"I've hardly taken my eyes off you since you got here."

God, his lashes are even longer than I remembered. "What?"

Wait, I already said that.

He chuckles, the deep sound rattling all the way to my stomach. "I'm flirting with you. I'm implying you're so beautiful that I noticed you the second you entered The Oak."

Is he? Why? He didn't think I was beautiful five years ago, and I haven't changed much. My hair's still neither curly nor straight, brown but not the vibrant sexy kind, and my skin is plagued with freckles all over. If anything, now I have stuff like cellulite, which I didn't have back then.

"Do you like dancing?" he asks, giving me some reprieve by taking a step back.

Dancing? Me? I shake my head.

"Then can I buy you a drink?"

"I don't drink."

He hums, eyes drifting away for a moment. "So what do you do at parties?"

"I, uh . . . make sure the walls stay upright."

One corner of his lips twists, as if it sounds terrible. Makes sense, because Rafael Gray has always been the soul of the party. "It looks like they're standing just fine by themselves. Want to sit somewhere?"

Okay, *what* is this dress made of?

His brows rise. "You don't talk a lot, do you?"

"Sorry." I watch the amusement play out on his features and realize I should add something. "I have to go."

Before he can say more, I walk.

"Wait, *wait*," he says, blocking me as I try to sidestep him. "Okay, let me be completely honest." He discreetly nudges his head back. "See those two guys over there? Back of the room?"

Behind him, two men are watching us. Dave Mitchell and Lucas Barrett, maybe? My lips twist. "Yeah."

"We have a bet going on. They said I couldn't get your number."

I look back at him, mouth hanging open. So *that's* why he's talking to me. It's not the dress, not that he knows who I am—it's because those two *idiots* bet him he couldn't hook up with me. Because his friends, who haven't changed a bit since high school, are making a joke out of me. God, this somehow just became *more* mortifying. "Goodbye."

When I try to step around him again, he raises his hand with an awkward chuckle. "Whoa—okay. You don't like them, do you? I hear you, but how about you take my phone, type in your name and number, and help me keep my two hundred bucks?"

Two *hundred* bucks? I glance at his phone. "And why would I do that?"

"A random act of kindness?"

"Kindness? Toward a man who's placing bets on me?"

He opens his mouth, then closes it. I'm not a dancer, but I might just start now. *That's right, Rafael. I'm no longer the younger next-door kid who's had a crush on you since she knew what having a crush meant. I'm no longer under your spell.*

And you're still the same douchebag.

"I'll see you," I say before walking past him.

"We have something in common, you know," he calls.

With a groan, I turn to him. I highly doubt party animal, girl magnet Rafael Gray and I share a single thing. "Really? Like what?"

"I hate those guys, too."

"Is that so?" I ask. "Then why are you here with them?"

"Because I just got back into town, ran into them, and they made a scene about not being notified I was back." He waves a hand around. "They dragged me to this party."

My irritation wavers as Paige swoops in like a whirlwind, flitting from table to table to adjust napkin holders and making sure everything's perfect. When she spots me, she gives me a double thumbs-up like I've won some kind of personal growth award. I turn back to Rafael.

"Okay," I say. "How about this: I give you a *fake* number, and we leave this place together."

His brows rise. "And where do we go?"

"Nowhere," I spit out, like the thought alone is insulting. "*I* go home, and *you* . . . well, you do whatever, but you can't come back here."

He leans in, eyes trained on me. "And why would you want to do that?"

"Because there's an excellent book waiting for me at home." And Paige can't possibly argue about me leaving if I'm with him.

A slow smirk spreads over his lips. "Counterproposal. You give me your *real* number, and we leave this place." He pauses, then adds, "But we actually do something."

"Something?"

"Together."

So I'd be swapping one awkward night with a hundred strangers for an awkward night with Rafael Gray? Hell no. Once upon a time, that was my *dream*, but I know better now. Rafael is just an arrogant prick who doesn't even realize I exist, even though we lived next door to each other most of our lives.

Why does he want my number? So he can add it to his infinite roster and *never* use it?

"I don't think so."

He stops me again as we do our little step-forward-step-backward dance, bringing a hand to his chest like I just harpooned it. "Oh, come on. Spending time with me can't possibly be worse than a party you don't want to be at."

And yet somehow I know it is.

"You don't even have to smile. You can keep frowning at me the *whole* night." When I hesitate, he gestures at my face. "You look pretty when you're offended."

"I'm not offended."

"Then I guess you're just pretty."

I glare, though I can't help the warmth bursting in my stomach. That was so cheesy it *almost* worked. But if I'm to partake in this charade, I'm not walking away without a cut.

"*Fake* number. And I get half the money," I say.

His brows shoot up over his mask. "You want me to pay you for your time?"

"I'm helping you win two hundred bucks."

"Last offer." He squares his shoulders, the fabric of his shirt stretching over his chest and showing a sliver of golden skin. "*Fake* number, and we spend the money tonight. Two hundred dollars, no holding back. Together."

One night with a full budget? Oh, I know exactly how I'd blow it: dinner at La Belle Vue, a place with breadbaskets that come with their own little dipping oils; then the Soothing Spot on Maple Avenue for a massage that's half relaxation, half torture. And after that? Definitely a double scoop at Sweet Cream Dreams.

But I have a feeling his idea of fun is . . . different.

"Who decides what we do?"

"We take turns." When my mouth twists, he adds, "You pick first."

"Dinner at La Belle Vue."

His dark brown curls swing over his forehead with the light tilt of his head. "You had that ready to go, didn't you?"

Damn it, I didn't mean to agree. I got distracted by the thought of the dipping oils.

Before I can take it back, he says, "You got it. La Belle Vue." He holds his phone out, and I type in a random number, saving the contact as "Maybe After the First Date."

He glances down at it. "Cute. I'll be right back—don't go anywhere."

He heads off to Dave and Lucas, who, after peeking at his phone, groan, obviously annoyed. Rafael seems a little too pleased for someone who's scored a fake win, but who am I to argue?

Though it's about a decade late, I get my birthday wish.

A date with Rafael Gray.

"All right." I tap the menu for emphasis. "Let's start with the truffle arancini. Then the heirloom tomato bruschetta and the lobster ravioli, sauce on the side." I glance up at the waiter, who's throwing a disgruntled look at my masked face. "And for my main, I'll take the filet mignon, medium rare, with the black garlic butter on top. Oh! And can you add a side of those duck fat potatoes?"

The waiter blinks, clearly taken aback. He recovers and scribbles furiously. "And for you, sir?"

Rafael sets down his menu, and my eyes catch on the tattoos stretched across his knuckles—black letters spelling LUST in sharp strokes. Between the words, smaller designs creep along his fingers: a tiny dagger, an eye with lashes like rays, and a cracked heart inked just below one knuckle. Silver rings gleam at nearly every finger—one shaped like a coiled snake, another thick and weathered with tiny skulls etched around the band, and a square-cut black stone that catches the light like obsidian.

Over the edge of his mask, his gray eyes glint with humor. "I think someone's trying to get rid of me quickly."

"Nope. Just hungry." Apparently, my attempt at blowing all our budget at once isn't as unsuspicious as I thought.

"Really? You're going to eat all of that?"

I shrug, but he must see right through me, because he turns to the waiter and says, "We'll share."

"All right. I'll be back with your wine soon."

The waiter disappears into the dimly lit interior of the restaurant, leaving us alone at our small table nestled by a window. Candlelight flickers between us, creating soft shadows over the glossy red walls adorned with vintage posters and tiny gold-framed mirrors.

I fiddle with my napkin, suddenly hyperaware that the man across from me is basically a stranger, his masked eyes steady on mine. The silence feels loaded, like neither of us is sure what to say next. Under the table, I cross my ankles. Maybe feeling awkward around a hundred strangers is better than this.

"So," he says, breaking the silence, "we're keeping the masks on."

"Yes, we are," I reply, trying to sound casual as I sip my water.

He hums. "Why's that?"

"This is a small town. Only five thousand of us."

"I'm aware."

"Well, I know a lot of people."

His mouth twitches. "You don't want to be seen with me?"

"I don't want to be seen with *anyone*. People talk, and I'd rather not give them a reason to. Or . . . *more* reasons." I glance around, imagining the gossip mill working overtime if anyone spotted us together. "I have a no-dating-in-Willowbrook policy in place."

More like a "no-dating-at-all" policy, but anyway.

"And you broke your rule for me." He mimics a bow. "I'm flattered."

"You're *wrong*, you mean. This isn't a date."

"Isn't it?" he asks, just as the waiter glides over, then sets the bottle of wine down with an exaggerated flourish. Fair enough—this feels a little date-y.

"If it were, I'd probably be okay with us taking the masks off."

Rafael tilts his head as if to say "Touché," then silently fills his glass halfway. Once I point at mine, too, he says, "I thought you didn't drink."

Two strangers who probably share little except an awkward dinner *need* wine.

"Turns out I just wasn't motivated enough."

The waiter comes back with different types of bread and beautiful, glistening dipping oils. They smell spiced, and the bread looks crispy. I swear, even if I did end up on *Dateline*, this would still be worth it.

I quickly break off a piece of bread and dip it in the oil, then bring it to my lips. My stomach growls on cue, reminding me this is the first thing I've eaten the whole day. And God, it's delicious. "Wow." I point at the small pot. "You need to try this."

He stifles a laugh, taking a piece of bread from the basket. "Can I at least know your name?"

"I don't think so."

"Really? We could be cousins—us being on a date could get weird."

I go in for a second dip. "We're not cousins."

Smug, he grins. "So this *is* a date."

Before I can retort, the waiter strides over again and sets down the plate of truffle arancini, the golden-brown balls glistening under the dim restaurant lights. Next comes the heirloom tomato bruschetta, stacked like miniature towers of vibrant red and green.

"Enjoy," he says, his tone flat, before turning to leave, a whiff of truffle oil leaving me momentarily speechless.

This is *exactly* the type of delicious, pretentious food I pictured.

"You look pleased."

I smack my lips. "Still not a date."

"Fine. In that case, give me all the gritty, nasty details." He holds out the plate, waiting for me to grab an arancino. "You know, the way nobody does on a date. Really let me see what I'm *not* missing out on."

"The worst I have to offer?"

"Exactly." His hair, a dark brown so deep it almost looks black if it isn't hit by direct light, keeps falling over his eyes, but he doesn't seem bothered. My hand itches to tuck it back. "Why should I be glad this isn't a date? The floor's yours."

I fill my plate with bruschetta, realizing I am really and truly starving.

"I'm a mess," I say, though I probably give it away by speaking with my mouth full. "There isn't one corner of my house that isn't constantly infested with socks. I forget to eat and drink, have never ironed a single shirt in my life, and my fridge looks like it hasn't been cleaned out since the last ice age. Because I also don't know how to cook."

He nods thoughtfully. "Life's messy. No point in being put-together."

"Right." I bite into the arancino, barely stifling a moan. Am I having a *food*gasm? "And I have a weird cat that I'll always love more than any man."

He shrugs. "I'll never love anyone more than my pet tarantula."

My eyes bulge. "Pet *what*? You're kidding, right?"

"Hairy Houdini—may he rest in peace."

I exhale in relief. "Oh, it's dead."

He sets his fork down, his lips pressed into a flat line as he playfully glares. "Insensitivity. Another quality people don't exactly elbow their way through crowds for."

"I'm also broke. I have a job that I *adore* but that will never make me rich."

"Hmm. You must be an artist."

I've never thought of myself as one, but I guess I am. "Yes."

"The messy bit makes sense, then. Artists can't tolerate reality."

"Or survive it."

He seems to be hanging on my every word, holding a bruschetta but not eating it, as if he can't afford the distraction.

"I'm a bookworm. Parties aren't for me. Conversations aren't exactly my strong suit, either. I work alone, live alone, and function best *alone*."

He leans back, setting the platter down. "So, your ideal night is spent in a nest of socks, avoiding human interaction, reading until you forget to eat?"

"Exactly," I say, shoving the remaining half of my arancino into my mouth. "If that's not the dream, I don't know what is."

He laughs and, noticing my plate is empty, holds out the arancini platter again.

"Your turn," I say.

"Hm? Oh. I believe everyone with good taste should date me." Watching my unimpressed gaze, he drinks a sip of wine, then sets down his glass. "Fine. Let's see, uh . . . I'm stubborn. I've been told I could argue with a brick wall and come out convinced I won." He shrugs like it's a point of pride. "And I have no patience for fluff. I'd take blunt honesty over polite nonsense any day."

"Would you?" I ask. Then, with an overly polite tone, I add, "Spiders are gross, and I'm glad your tarantula is dead."

His eyelashes flutter dramatically. "I'm lovestruck."

"Come on," I insist. "Give me something good."

"Okay, okay. Let me think." He leans in, drumming his fingers against the table. "You really don't want to talk to me before my coffee."

"So, part-time grumpy and stubborn. Anything actually terrible?"

"I hog the blankets. And I'm not sorry about it. It's a survival instinct."

"Seriously?" I giggle, which is unfair, because he's not playing along. "Forget about it. You're a cheat, Gray."

He swallows whatever he was about to say, his eyes softening. "*Gray?*"

Shit. "Like your eyes," I blurt. "You have . . . gray eyes."

He knows the color of his own eyes, Scarlett.

"Right." He clears his throat, and for a moment, I'm sure he *knows*. That I know him. That we've met before. But then I realize, even if he's caught on that *I* know who *he* is, he doesn't know who *I* am. Not yet, at least. "Okay. You want the dirt?"

Distracted from my spiraling discomfort, I nod. "I want the *filth*."

"Fine." The waiter comes to take our plates and, after depositing the lobster ravioli between us, leaves again. "The reason you should never, ever date me is . . ."

I wait as he breathes out, not sure if I'll get a genuine answer or another deflection. But then he looks up, and as his gaze meets mine, a shiver runs down my spine. "That I'm trouble, Freckles. The kind of trouble you don't walk away from."

4

the slow burn

[trope]

---

a romance technique involving two people who clearly belong
together but enjoy dragging out shit for no reason; characterized
by lingering looks, accidental hand brushes, and enough
unresolved tension to give anyone a headache; usually
ends with the audience screaming, "about f*cking time!"

"Favorite movie?" he asks as we stroll down the main street.

I take a long moment to think it through, adjusting my mask
over the bridge of my nose. "I don't know . . . uh, *American Pie?*"

"*American Pie?*" He looks at me, horrified. "You think *that's* my
favorite movie?"

"Well, not anymore."

He narrows his eyes, pretending to sulk. "A douchebag—that's
what you see when you look at me, don't you?"

I flippantly brush my hair off my shoulder. "I plead the Fifth."

He slows his pace, noticing that I'm lagging a bit thanks to these
ridiculous heels Paige forced me into. I think he knows I'm teasing.

Yes, he is annoyingly smug but also . . . attentive, staring at me like he actually cares about every random word that falls out of my mouth. It's refreshingly rare. And fun. Something I hate about dating—which is *not* what we're doing—is the awkward silence. The forced conversations. There's been none of that during our three-course dinner.

"Okay, let's see," he says, studying me head to toe. "Favorite color . . . yellow?"

"Black, actually."

He hums thoughtfully, as though this black revelation is a clue to my innermost soul. "I can see that." He claps his hands. "Okay, this next one's crucial, so please, try not to screw it up."

"Hit me."

He steps in front of me, clasping his hands as if praying. "My guilty-pleasure song."

"Oh, easy. Backstreet Boys, 'I Want It That Way.'"

He grimaces, shaking his head dramatically. "Are you kidding me? That song is a certified masterpiece. No guilt required."

I give him a long, appraising look, then cross my arms. "'Mambo No. 5'?"

He recoils, turning his back on me. "Wow." He holds one finger up. "Last chance. Don't blow it."

I bite back a laugh. "'Barbie Girl'?"

He doubles over in laughter, shaking his head. "You know what? Close enough. 'Call Me Maybe.'"

"Oh my God. Are you serious?"

"Yes. I had a pet tarantula, and I walk around whistling Carly Rae Jepsen. I'm layered and eclectic."

"I'll bet," I say, grinning. "Well, I'm expecting full honesty here."

"Of course," he says, crossing his heart.

"My favorite movie?"

"*American Pie.*" I narrow my eyes. "Kidding. *The Silence of the Lambs.* You totally had an Anthony Hopkins poster on your wall at some point in your life, didn't you?"

I didn't, though he got incredibly close. I must have watched *The Silence of the Lambs* a million times. What exactly about me screams Hannibal Lecter? Does he know I distractedly noticed all the places we've walked through where either of us could have murdered the other and stashed their body with no witnesses?

Not that I would *ever*.

But seven.

"I'd expect you to be better at a game you suggested," I say.

"Bet you I'll guess your favorite ice cream flavor."

"Like you're obviously a pistachio guy?"

He juts his chin forward, towering above me a good ten inches. "You wish, mint chip girl."

My laugh is cut short as the back of my shoe digs into my ankle for the millionth time tonight. When I put these on, it was under threat—and most important, after I was promised I wouldn't have to walk anywhere.

"I'll never understand how people manage those torture devices," he says with a frown before bending down and pulling his shoes off.

"What are you—"

"Despite your cruel judgment of my taste, I am, at heart, a gentleman." He extends his hand toward my ankle, staring up through his mask and the usual rogue curls. "May I?"

When I nod, he slides off one of my shoes, leaving my foot throbbing in grateful relief as I balance myself with a hand on his shoulder.

His broad, strong shoulder.

He slips his shoe onto my foot, then does the same with the other, leaving me in his slightly oversize oxfords, while he holds my strappy heels like they're fragile glass slippers.

"What about you?" I ask, gesturing to the blue socks on his feet.

"I'll put my socks to good use." He looks around like he's just realized he has no idea where we are. We're surrounded by a dark electronics store, a closed shoe-repair shop, and a tiny bookstore with all the lights off. "And anyway, we're here."

"Here?" There's nothing here.

"Uh . . . huh," he says, eyes suddenly lighting up as he spots something behind me. "There. That's where we're going."

I turn around to see a blinking LED sign, its purple neon letters screaming "Psychic" under a set of worn velvet curtains. "Oh my God . . ."

"I don't need to remind you of our deal."

He does not. We get to choose one activity each, and it's his turn.

"Nor that this won't cost more than twenty bucks."

Which means I'm stuck with him for another round of this. Though I expect the same sense of inconvenience I felt earlier tonight, there's a warm eagerness in my stomach. I guess tonight isn't going as badly as I'd pictured.

"Okay. Let's go waste your money."

He clicks his tongue. "It's *our* money, actually."

I walk, thankful that though his feet are bigger than mine, I can still walk in his shoes without tripping over my own feet, and enter the shop.

The smell of incense and dust violently surrounds us as we step past the velvet curtains hanging from the ceiling. Crystals and tarot cards line every available surface, and a bead curtain rattles as we enter to find a woman with a long shawl and a cascade of necklaces looking up.

"Welcome," she says in a low voice, doing a double take when she notices our outfits and masks.

"Hi. We'd like a reading." Squeezing me into a side hug, Rafael adds, "We're on our first date."

My eyes roll so far back I might just see into another dimension, but I don't argue—he didn't when I dragged him to the fanciest restaurant in town.

"Ah, love readings," she says, eyeing me with a glint that feels a bit too personal. "My specialty."

Why do I have a feeling her specialty is whatever the current client asks for?

She takes a seat at a small table in the corner and motions for us to sit across from her. I slide into the chair, bracing myself, while Rafael flops down with far too much enthusiasm, his knees knocking into mine under the table.

With a deep breath, the woman closes her eyes and reaches for a deck of tarot cards. Glancing at Rafael, then at me, she shuffles slowly. "Hold hands."

"Hold what now?" I blurt.

She looks up, waiting. "For the reading to be accurate, your energies must be aligned."

I glance at Rafael, who's biting back a laugh.

"Gotta align those energies, don't we?"

He reaches over and takes my hand, his grip firm but warm, the cool brush of his rings sending a shiver up my arm. His skin is calloused at the fingertips, like that of someone who's lived a little hard, but his thumb moves gently across my knuckles. A little tingle sparks through me, impossible to ignore.

Just how many times have I dreamed of Rafael Gray holding my hand? Never in a million years would I have imagined it'd be inside a psychic's shop.

The woman spreads the cards before her, face down, in a fan. She gestures for Rafael to pick one, and he reaches out dramatically, then selects a card. Once I pick one, too, she flips the first card over—the Lovers.

Of course.

She raises her brows, looking between us. "Ah. A powerful card, especially for those seeking connection."

I try to keep a straight face, but Rafael, of course, is practically glowing. *I'm not seeking a connection with you!* I yell with my eyes.

The psychic turns my card over, and she looks up, almost surprised. "The Wheel of Fortune," she says. "This card represents fate. Serendipity. A connection that appears by chance but is meant to be." Her gaze flicks between us, holding each of us. "I see love in your future. A powerful love, one that neither of you can see coming."

I let out a very unclassy snort.

The psychic narrows her eyes at me, a slight frown pulling at her painted lips. "The cards do *not* lie," she warns.

"Oh, I'm sure you're right. But people do—in fact, this isn't even our first date. Or any date."

The woman taps the cards emphatically. "The Wheel of Fortune. The Lovers," she says in a grim tone. "These cards do not appear together by accident. There's a bond here, whether or not you admit it."

Rafael leans in. "Yeah, Freckles. Maybe you're just in denial."

"Or maybe this whole thing is just as random as shuffling a deck of cards," I say pointedly.

The psychic collects her cards and straightens, eyeing me one more time. "You may doubt me now, but the cards have a way of revealing the truth."

"Duly noted," I say as we all stand.

I wait for Rafael to pay, then follow him as he walks out the door, but the psychic's voice calls, "You. Skeptic woman."

I glance back at her, the door handle gripped in my fist. "Yes?"

"A dark heart."

"Excuse me?"

"Gray with a dark heart," she says as she closes the cash register. "You'll understand when the time comes." She smirks. "You'll believe me then."

I blink, watching her for a couple of seconds as my mind spins. When she notices, she gestures at me to leave, and almost automatically, I close the door.

"Everything okay?"

Did she say . . . gray with a dark heart? Like—like *Rafael* Gray?

"Freckles?"

"Huh?"

Rafael walks closer, chin tilted down as he tries to look into my eyes. Shit, I'm basically panting.

"Uh, sorry. I . . ."

It's just a coincidence, Scarlett. That's how psychics—fancy word for imposters—make their living. By taking one generic detail, like the striking color of Rafael's eyes, and making it into a sinister warning.

"She said 'Gray with a dark heart.'"

"Son of a bitch, I thought she liked me." He looks back at the shop and then, with a chuckle, he continues, almost to himself, "Though I can't imagine she'll be the only person to warn you against me."

I blink, looking away for a moment. I know exactly what he means. Paige's parents never wanted her to be around him. No-good Rafael, reckless Rafael, who always gets in trouble.

"I'm sure she meant *red*," I say teasingly, trying to lighten the mood.

"Like our clothes?"

"More like from that big flag you're waving."

"Ah-ha," he fake-laughs. "I have half a mind to take my shoes back."

"Maybe after our next stop."

"Which is?"

"The ice cream shop around the corner." I take a step, then look back, where he stands still, watching me with a pleased expression. "You coming, Gray?"

A slow nod. "You bet, Freckles."

———

"I *knew* you were a mint chip girl," he says as he swirls his tongue around his cone. Truth be told, my ice cream order changes depending on my mood, so I'm not excluding the possibility that I've been conned into this flavor.

"Coffee and vanilla," I say as I glance at his cone. "What does that say about you?"

"I don't know. That I have excellent taste, while you're eating toothpaste?"

A laugh escapes as he shifts forward, leaning his elbows on the table. His eyes linger, warm and intent, as if he's cataloging the sound and the way it lights up my face. The intensity of it sends a flutter through my chest, and I quickly glance down at my cone, pretending to focus on a drip.

Over the years, my mystery-loving brain has contemplated several theories about Rafael Gray's sudden disappearance, ranging from the absurd to the unsettling. Like how he might have joined a secret society—one of those underground cults you read about in true-crime stories. Or how he was maybe recruited for some elite spy program, gone on to save the world.

Then there's the one theory I never liked to dwell on, but it's the one that feels most plausible. The night he disappeared, his father was attacked. Maybe *he* did it.

It had been a scandal. John Gray whisked away in an ambulance in the dead of the night, my dad responding to the scene, telling us that the assailant had left and Rafael was nowhere to be found, and then he never returned.

John Gray eventually gave a description of the culprit, who he said wasn't Rafael. But I always thought . . . *Maybe he lied. Maybe he was protecting his son.*

I push the thought away, wishing I could offer him my condolences, but I'd have to admit I know him, and it'd open the floor to a lot of questions I'm not ready for. Like who am I, have we met before, am I still the pathetic little girl who crushed hard on him? No, thank you.

But I will say, he's really not that bad. I'm almost reminded of why I liked him so much back in the day. His aura of mystery, his charming smile, his witty sense of humor.

He flashes me a look that could melt the rest of my ice cream. "Change your mind about me yet?"

My cheeks heat, and I look away, trying to muster up some sort of answer that doesn't betray how close he is to the truth. "Hm? No."

He raises an eyebrow. "No?"

"I don't think so."

"Do I at least get to see your face?"

When I shake my head again, he fishes into his pocket. "Well, I still have about . . . fifty dollars' worth of swoon to change your mind."

"Good luck with that." The streets are now empty, and I doubt there's even a single thing open this late. There's no way he'll find somewhere to spend it all tonight, not unless he wants to drive to Springfield or Providence.

"Pretty sure the motel up the interstate has a forty-nine ninety-nine package. Room, entrance to the strip club, *and* breakfast buffet."

I glare at him, but it's half-hearted.

"Ahh, there it is," he says, pointing a finger at me as if it's a grand discovery. "You want to be mad at me, but you can't. You know what that means, don't you?"

"That I'm tired?"

"Nope." He leans back, watching me with a cocky grin. "It means you *like* me, Freckles."

Like him? No, I don't *like* him.

The only boy I *ever* liked is Rafael, and with how long it took me to *un*-like him, I'm not about to start again.

I shrug. "You keep telling yourself that."

"I will. It makes me feel real good." I roll my eyes, and he snickers, the sound soft and warm like caramel, blending with the light breeze and the smells of sweet waffle cones drifting from the ice cream shop.

"I *don't* like you." Feeling his gaze on me, I add, "Because I don't like anyone."

"Anyone?"

"Ever," I admit, crossing my legs. Why am I even saying this to him? "If you're looking for a reason not to date me, that's probably it."

I shoot him a quick look, and his expression is calm, not as surprised as I expected.

"You must have had a boyfriend or two at some point."

"Just one. But it's not for me. I can't fall in love. Sometimes I think I might just . . . be incapable of it."

He snaps his fingers. "Maybe you're a psychopath."

"Do I look like a psychopath?"

"Well, you keep saying you don't like me."

I let out a soft, amused breath, focusing on my cone.

"Could you be a lesbian?" he asks. "Because that thing you keep saying about how you don't like me would make sense, then."

"Oh God," I whine, laughter bubbling up again.

"Okay, look," he says, shifting to a more serious tone as he adjusts his mask. "We met at a singles event that you stayed at for exactly seven minutes before you plotted an escape. So . . . are you incapable of falling in love or just unwilling?"

I shut my eyes for a moment, considering. I guess I'm not holding my breath waiting to meet the right guy. I don't really put myself out there, either, because I'm terrible at flirting and dating.

"I'm not romantic. Grand love gestures make me cringe, and I'm the person who forgets anniversaries, buys practical gifts, and thinks date night sounds exhausting."

"Not every love story needs to be a Nicholas Sparks book," he counters. "You choose what your love life should look like."

"Really? Even if I enjoy sleeping alone and only cuddle with my cat?"

"Sure." He shrugs. "The right person will respect your boundaries. And maybe you'll find out along the way how you like cuddling with them almost as much as you like to cuddle your cat."

"Or maybe I'm just too . . . broken for love. Too damaged."

He waves me off. "Every single person out there is irreparably damaged by their experiences. Enriched by them, too. That's what makes life interesting."

I tilt my head. "So . . . I am weird, but it's not my fault?"

"So everyone is weird, and it doesn't matter."

His words settle into some raw place that feels soothed, understood. "Everyone is weird, and it doesn't matter," I repeat.

Judging by his smug expression, he's aware he just won a million points.

My gaze wanders down to his shirt, hugging his chest and flat stomach, then to his long, muscular legs, wrapped in fitted dark red pants, and I can't ignore the pull of another thought entirely.

Love might not be in the cards for me, but now that I think about it, his motel idea doesn't sound so bad.

"What?" He looks down at his suit. "Did I get ice cream on my shirt?"

"Huh? No." I shift my gaze to the ground, warmth rising up my neck. "I guess it's your turn, isn't it? Any idea how we're going to spend that money?"

"I'm actually not sure." He bites his plump lip, looking around, and then his gaze settles back on me. "But I'm open to suggestions."

Should I? I shouldn't. It's crazy—I can't offer to sleep with him. Although he wouldn't have spent tonight with me if he wasn't interested, right?

"Well," I say, nervously pointing behind me. "There's a parking lot around the corner. I'm pretty sure we can spare two dollars to park your car there for a while."

There. I said it. So what if he says no?

His chest rises slowly with a long inhale. "And what exactly would we do there?"

"We could, uh, listen to some music. Or chat—we could chat, too."

"Uh-huh." A warm thread of tension crackles in the inches of space between us. "You said you're not good at that."

"Right. So maybe we could do something else," I manage, chewing on my lip. I'm pretty sure every book I've ever read taught me not to enter a stranger's car in the dead of night, but I'm channeling my inner Paige for once. *Forget about murders. Focus on horizontal gymnastics.* "Less talking and more *acting*."

"Ah." The tip of his tongue swipes over his upper lip. "Best way I'd ever spend two dollars in my life."

I grimace. "That makes me sound like a cheap prostitute."

"Heard it the moment I said it," he says, running a hand through his hair. The smile slips from his face, replaced by something softer, almost wistful. "I'd love to. Truly. But . . . I think I should go."

My heart skips a beat, my insides tangling together in a knot.

"Oh." *Okay, I think I'm ready to drop dead.* Did I misread all his signals? His looks, his closeness, his flirting—seriously, how is this happening?

"It's not like that." He shifts the mask over his nose, and for a moment I think he'll lift it, but he doesn't, and just tucks his hand back into his pocket. "If it's okay with you, I'd rather not rush it. I think I'll enjoy getting to know you little by little."

I trap the butterflies in my stomach, shove them into a bottle, and lodge it somewhere deep inside me, never to be found again. Getting to know me little by little? He didn't hear a word I said about my inability to catch feelings, did he? And besides, how long is he planning to stay in town? I'd assumed he'd leave again after his father's funeral.

"Are you sure you wouldn't enjoy sex more?"

Laughter booms out of him. "Sex is great. But I have a feeling that this . . ." He points at me, then at himself. "This will be better."

"I'm not *dating* you," I breathe out.

"I'll see you around, Freckles," he says, standing up.

Goddamn it.

"You don't even have my number!" I call after him as he walks away. "And I have your *shoes*!"

"You said it yourself." He turns to me. "Five thousand people in this town. I'm sure I'll see you again."

I watch him walk away, shoeless, for a moment, then walk in the opposite direction, toward The Oak's parking lot, the same tingle spreading through my skin and deep beneath.

I can't believe Rafael Gray just rejected me.

Again.

5

the friendly counsel

[trope]

a well-meaning friend or relative who doles out unsolicited but oddly
insightful advice that leads the main character to an epiphany

Across the table at The Oak, filled with the aroma of freshly
brewed coffee and the warmth of sunlight streaming through
large windows, Paige practically vibrates with excitement, her bright
brown eyes wide as she stares at me. We do this every Saturday—
though I sense today's coffee fix will come with a side of romantic
nonsense.

"Hold on a second," she says in a hushed squeal.

Here we go.

"You asked out your lifelong crush," she starts.

Quickly, I interject, "I didn't ask him out. It was a ploy to leave
the party."

"He showered you with money."

"Free money, technically," I correct her.

"Then he said no to sex because he . . . wants to take things slow?"

I open my mouth to argue, but that part is pretty accurate.

"Scarlett." She takes my hand over the table and squeezes. "Do you understand what's happening?"

We just went through what's happening, but I don't think that's what she means.

"You're *living* in a romance book."

"See, this is why I debated telling you," I say, pulling my hand back and glancing around. The soft clinking of mugs and the murmur of other conversations offer some cover, but Paige's voice still carries.

Quentin, behind the bar, waves, and I wave back. The last thing I need is my ex hearing about this.

"Are you kidding? The bet, the secret identity, the nickname— and his shoes? His *shoes*, Scarlett." She's nearly bouncing in her seat, her waves bobbing with the motion. "He's a classic book boyfriend."

"How come when I say that a crime book is coming to life, I'm crazy, but when you compare my life to a romance book—"

"Because one is about love and the other is about murder."

"Hmm." I sip my cappuccino, savoring the rich foam on my lips. "I wouldn't get all worked up if I were you."

"Why the hell not?"

"Because, Paige!"

She shakes her head like she doesn't get it.

With a groan, I slump back in the chair. I'm tired of repeating the same thing over and over again. "I don't fall in love. Especially not with Rafael Gray."

She waves me off. "You've been in love with Rafael Gray for half of your life."

"That was before—" I clamp my lips shut, but she knows. Before my parents died. Before my grandparents dumped me, before Quentin and I broke up, before my brother vanished from my life. Before a *lot* of things happened. "He's never been interested, Paige. And now I'm supposed to believe he's head over heels for me?"

She blinks. "Five years ago. He *maybe* wasn't into you five *years* ago."

"He also said that thing about how he's *trouble*." When she drops her forehead to the table, I insist, "Seriously, who says that? It's crazy."

"No. Fighting so hard against something that's clearly meant to be—*that's* crazy."

"I don't believe in destiny."

"So how do you explain him being at the only party you've been at in years?"

"Easy," I say, then take a sip of cappuccino. "Small-town life."

"And what the psychic said?"

Oh, for Chrissake. "She's a *psychic*." When her brown eyes pin me in place as if my rebuttal is somehow not valid, I offer, "She also said Gray has a black heart."

With an eye roll, she blows on her coffee. "Just tell me last night wasn't the most fun you've ever had with a man, and I'll let this go."

I pause. I can't do that, can I?

Last night was effortless. Like hanging out with a friend, but with a spark of unprecedented excitement. He knew exactly when to fill the silence and when to let me marinate in my thoughts. He didn't press too hard, didn't try to impress me with over-the-top antics or charm. Instead, he just *was*. And somehow that was enough. More than enough.

"You *do* like him!" Paige practically shouts as she kicks her feet under the table.

"Shh." The smile grows despite my attempts to contain it. "I . . ."

"I knew it! I just knew it!"

"Seriously—shh!" I hiss, casting a glance around. I catch Quentin's eyes again. "I'm not saying I like him, Paige. He's just . . ."

The guy who got into fights, but only with bullies. The guy who always carried food around for the stray dog that used to hang around outside school, who actually bothered talking to the weird janitor everyone avoided. Yes, he liked to break the rules, but there was so much more to him, and there still is.

"Different," I mumble. He's unlike anyone else I've ever met.

"I'll take it." She leans forward, her expression triumphant. "Rafael Gray. Who would have thought, after all this time?"

Not me. That was a closed chapter in my mind. In fact, it's been years since I thought about him last. Well, maybe months. Or weeks.

"Who knows, maybe this'll inspire your upcoming romance adventure."

'Cause there's nothing more romantic than a guy rejecting you *twice*. "Don't even remind me of that. Celeste will be expecting a script soon."

She barely acknowledges me. "When are you seeing him?"

"I don't know." I run my finger along the rim of my coffee cup, tracing the foam left behind. "I guess our paths are bound to cross—you know, since we're neighbors."

"Secret identity remains an *unparalleled* trope," she says, pulling her curls back. "Nothing like a little mystery to start off an epic love story."

Love, romance. Only the thought gives me shivers.

I can see it play out like a carousel in my mind. Rafael and me hanging out more and more, spending the night together, getting acquainted with each other's presence. And then something goes wrong, and suddenly I'm left there wondering at which stop Rafael got off and why my train is crashing at full speed against a brick wall. The mere idea sets my heart pounding with dread.

"This is why I don't like romance," I grumble, sinking back into my seat.

Paige takes a big bite of her donut. "Because you care about something?"

"*No*," I say, narrowing my eyes at her. "Because it takes over your brain and turns you into a mush of silliness. 'When will I meet him?' 'What should I say?'" I mock, rolling my eyes. "Gross."

"What's gross?" a familiar voice says as someone plops down next to me.

I turn to see Theo, his usual friendly expression in place. "Hey, stranger. What are you doing here?"

"On my way to pick Vanessa up. We're playing football." He leans forward and snatches Paige's donut, taking an obnoxiously large bite.

Paige immediately starts smacking his shoulder in protest. "Hey! Go play sports with my girlfriend and leave my donut alone!"

"I need my energy," he says, turning his attention back to me, Paige still grumbling about her donut. "So? What's gross?"

"Dating," I answer, hiding a frown behind my cup.

His brows knit together behind the frames of his glasses. "You're dating someone?"

"No!" I blurt out, far too loudly. "No, of course not."

"Rafael Gray is back," Paige interjects.

"Gray, huh?" I keep my gaze on my cup as Theo's eyes search my face. "You too?"

Yep. Me too. I was one of hundreds of girls who were head over heels for Rafael Gray. I wonder if now that he's back in town, women will start falling at his feet again.

"She had a crush on him by the time she was nine. And she never quite shook it off until she was eighteen."

Twenty, actually.

"Wait." Theo's head bobs from me to the bar. "I thought . . . Didn't you date Quentin? They're cousins, right?"

"I did, yes," I say, eyeing him behind the counter. "It's not like I ever really thought Rafael would give me the time of day," I explain. "You know the type of girls he used to date." Older, stunning, edgy. A far cry from the younger bookworm next door. "Quentin was the first guy who asked me out, and I was seventeen, and . . ." I slowly close my eyes. "I don't know."

"No, I get it," Theo says. "Teenager shit."

"Tell him about The Incident," Paige teases.

Shoulders dropping, I glare at her.

He gasps, straightening on the chair. "What incident?"

"*The* Incident," she coos.

Goddamn it. If I don't say it, she will, and she has a flair for the dramatic. "It's not that bad," I try, but it doesn't sound convincing. "Remember on Paige's eighteenth birthday, when a bunch of us got drunk for the first time?"

"Peach schnapps," Paige says with a grimace as Theo mock-shivers.

"Everyone was talking about their *boyfriends*, how they were so happy, so in love . . ." I wave a hand around. "And it dawned on me that I was just dating Quentin because he'd asked, while I was actually still very much into his cousin. So in my drunkenness, I might have"—I shrug—"told Rafael how I felt about him."

"*Oof.* You drunk-dialed?"

Paige snickers. "She drunk-penned, actually."

"I wrote him a rambling love letter," I explain, "and put it in his mailbox."

Theo hisses through his teeth. "Noooo," he drawls. "What did he say?"

My awkward smile falters. "Uh, he moved away, actually." I try to swallow through the sudden tightness in my throat. "I mean, I know it wasn't because of my letter, but . . ." But it felt like it. Irrationally, it still does.

One month later, my parents were gone, too. I was left withdrawing my enrollment from the university and searching for a job. Quentin and I broke up, my brother moved out, and I learned words like *escrow* and *estate*.

"Anyway, that's it," I say, attempting a casual shrug, though I feel like a frayed thread. "That's the entire story."

"I bet you Rafael never even got the letter," Paige says, her mouth full of donut. Noticing my skeptical look, she insists, "In romance books, the love interest always misses the letter."

"So now that he's back, you want to pick things up where you left off?" Theo asks.

"They went on a date yesterday."

"It wasn't a *date*," I scold.

"She offered to hook up and he said he wants to take things slow."

"Paige!"

Theo turns back to me. "Damn. *Gray*? I'm pretty sure the guy came up with one-night stands."

"Right. So I shouldn't." I fidget with the empty cup in front of me, then look up at him. "Right?"

Theo inhales, the scent of roasted coffee beans filling the air, then slowly exhales. "Well, you know I'll kick his ass if he messes up." He scratches the back of his head, gaze drifting to the bustling café around us. "But Scarlett . . ." His gaze holds mine. "You don't have to listen to me or Paige. You'll know what feels right. All you need to do is trust your gut."

———————————

Trust your gut, Scarlett, I tell myself as I sit in the worn leather chair, my fingers drumming an anxious rhythm on the armrest. Chief Donovan's office is a cluttered space, walls adorned with commendations and faded photographs of stern-faced officers.

I used to come to the police station all the time to bring Dad lunch, but I haven't stepped foot in here since my parents passed. It's smaller than I remembered. Cluttered, dusty, dead. Dad always talked of how with the nearly inexistent crime rate in Willowbrook, he barely even felt like a police officer. Mom always "praised the Lord" for it.

The silence is deafening, broken only by the occasional rustle of papers or the gentle hum of an ancient desktop computer. Through the grimy window, I can see the entire police force of Willowbrook—all four of them—hunched over their desks. Officer Jenkins, a portly man with a receding hairline, is wolfing down a jelly donut next to Trevor, while Wes, who was my dad's partner, pores over what looks like a stack of parking tickets. Vanessa, with her blond hair tucked under a cap, is smiling at her phone, probably texting Paige.

My eyes dart to the clock on the wall. It's 3:47 p.m. I've been waiting for a while, but I'm not leaving. I'm trusting my gut, just like Theo said.

I breathe out deeply, hoping to quell the butterflies in my stomach. This theory of mine is wild, I know. But the pieces fit together too perfectly to ignore. The flowers on Catherine Blake's body, the writing on the wall, the strangulation—I can't get any of it out of my mind, so I won't.

Seriously, where is this guy?

The door creaks open, and Chief Donovan shuffles in, his weathered face a map of wrinkles and worry lines. He settles into his squeaky chair with a groan.

"Scarlett, how are ya?" he says, his voice gravelly from years of cigarettes. "We haven't seen you in a while. How can I help you, sweetheart?"

"I appreciate you seeing me, Chief. I'm sure you're, um, busy, but I have some information about the Catherine Blake case that I think you need to hear."

His eyebrows shoot up. "What could you possibly know about it?"

I lean forward, bracing for what's coming. "When I read about the crime on the *Whistle*, I recognized the MO."

"The MO, huh?" he asks. His skeptical tone is already bugging me.

"Yes. There's this book—really popular—that came out just a couple of weeks ago. *The Thornwood Butcher.*" I wait for him to take a note, but he doesn't. "In the story, the victim is a historian who's kidnapped while she's out with her dog. Her throat is slit, her eyes removed. And her mouth is stuffed with flowers. The killer even leaves a bloody message on the wall."

He keeps staring at me, smoothening his thick white mustache. "Okay. So . . . you're suggesting that the author acted out his murder fantasy?"

What? "N-no," I mumble. "I'm suggesting that someone copy-catted the murder from the book."

"Hmm." He looks through the window, as if wishing one of his colleagues would come rescue him. "Well, sweetheart. I appreciate your visit. We'll be looking into this. Say hi to your brother when you see him, will ya?"

He stands, but I stay put, my shoulders rolling back. They won't look into it—hell, he didn't even write the title down. "I don't think you mean that, actually."

"Of course I do! Ethan is a good kid—"

"I'm talking about the book."

He sits down again. "Look, sweet—"

"*Scarlett*," I interject.

"Scarlett," he repeats after a moment. "Blake's eyes weren't re-moved."

"But she had abrasions around her eyes, did she not?"

"Yes," he concedes.

"So what if the killer tried to remove her eyes but couldn't?"

He looks at his watch, then back at me. "Why not?"

"Maybe it was their first try. Maybe they got spooked. Blake's daughter called her mom, right? Maybe the phone call—"

"What about the flowers, then? They weren't in the victim's mouth."

I exhale, thinking it through. "Rigor mortis."

"Excuse me?"

"If the killer was inexperienced, they might not have accounted for the rigor mortis. When the body stiffened, the flowers could have fallen out." I watch his blotchy face turn a sickly yellow. "Where were the flowers?"

"I can't tell you that, swee— Scarlett."

I've read countless articles about this—the flowers were *on* the victim. "Down on her chest?" I suggest.

His mouth opens, then closes.

"Look, I'm telling you, it's just too similar. Someone who read this book committed the murder."

He leans back in his chair. "Scarlett, where were you Thursday night?"

Oh, come on. "Really? *I'm* your suspect? I'm solving the case *for* you." When his expression doesn't waver, I roll my eyes. "I was home with my cat."

"Will your cat corroborate your story?"

Realizing he's just pulling my leg, I sigh and look away.

"Listen here, Scarlett. I've been doing this job for thirty years, and I've seen it all. You know what happens every time we get a weird case? Every amateur sleuth and conspiracy theorist crawls out of the woodwork."

I start to protest, but he holds up a hand.

"Last time, we had a fella from two counties over who swore up and down that it was the work of alien abductors. Said the pruning shears we found were actually a sophisticated extraterrestrial weapon. And let's not forget the conspiracy nuts who thought it was all tied to some government cover-up."

I feel my face flush with frustration. "Chief, you know me. I'm not some crackpot—"

"We're dealing with an actual victim here, a real family torn apart," he interrupts. "I can't go chasing after every wild theory that comes through that door."

"But this isn't just some random coincidence. The details are too specific, too exact. You *have* to look into it."

He sighs, rubbing his temples. "All right, Scarlett. We'll be in touch."

I notice him glancing at the TV on one side of the room. I must be keeping him from some important show, I guess. This feels like a waste of my time, anyway. He decided the moment he saw me that a *sweetheart* like me couldn't possibly help. Hell, I don't even think he really thinks I *could* have committed this murder.

I stand, then walk to the door. Before stepping out, I turn around again. Donovan is reaching for the remote, Catherine Blake already a distant memory.

"The past never dies," I say.

The remote falls from his hand and onto the desk with a dull thud.

"That's what was written on the wall, wasn't it? With the victim's blood?" He says nothing, so I press on. "That information wasn't released to the public. So it's one of two options, Chief Donovan. Either I'm your killer . . ." I step closer, then take a copy of *The Thornwood Butcher* out of my bag. "Or you and your people have some reading to do."

6

the right person, the wrong time

[trope]

when two people are perfect for each other but cursed by
the universe's terrible timing; marked by missed opportunities,
bittersweet glances, and life-altering events that keep them apart

A s I pull up to my house, my stomach clenches. Rafael is in his
front yard, crouched down and tinkering with something. His
black leather jacket shifts as he moves, uncovering more of the tattoos snaking up both arms, half-covered by his sleeves.

It's weird to see him there after so long. Actually, I can't remember him ever hanging around his house much even when he was here.

Time to come clean, I guess. Will he figure it out the moment he
sees me? When I say the first word? Or will he need to be spoon-fed
the information? And if that's the case, then what will it say about
him? About last night?

God, I hate this.

I grab my things and slip out of the car. I see him straightening out of the corner of my eye and immediately decide I *can't* do it. What if he doesn't think The Incident was just a goofy teenage faux pas? What if he's horrified to find out I'm *me* and I tried to sleep with him last night? What if he doesn't even *remember* about the letter?

Keeping my face angled down and hidden behind my hair, I hurry toward the door.

"Hey," he calls out, his voice light and friendly, though it feels like a thousand-pound weight on my shoulders. *Goddamn it.* "Hey, Scarlett?"

Ignoring him, I pick up the pace, practically bolting up the steps to my front door. My fingers fumble with the keys before I finally get it open, slip inside and shut it firmly behind me.

I press my back against the solid wood, holding my breath. I don't think he caught on, but it's just a matter of time. "Please let it go, please let it go," I whisper, eyes shut tight.

When there's a knock at the door, I nearly jump out of my skin. "Scarlett?"

Shit! What do I do now? I look around, grimacing. "Y-yes?"

"Hi, it's Rafael Gray, your neighbor."

"Yeah—hello."

I clamp a hand over my mouth, breathing hard. Okay, so he doesn't know it's *me*. Not yet, anyway. But if I don't end this conversation quickly, he'll probably put the pieces together. Or he won't. I don't know which one would be better at this point.

"I heard about your parents," he says, his voice muffled by the door. "I'm really sorry."

Surprised, I let my eyes drift to the picture of them on the entrance table—Mom in her wide-brimmed sun hat, Dad with his arm wrapped around her, both of them laughing at the camera. "Thank you."

"Your dad was always nice to me," he adds. "Your mom, too, but your dad was . . . I *really* liked him."

My lip stings as I pinch it with my teeth. Everyone liked my dad.

"I'm sorry about your dad, too," I say back.

"Thank you. Is it messed up that finding out about your dad's passing hit me harder? Talk about daddy issues, huh?"

I turn to the door, feeling the urge to open it. "I'm sorry."

"We've been through that part already."

"No, I mean . . . I'm sorry you and your dad weren't close."

There's a pause, then, "Open the door, Freckles."

My stomach plummets, the tightest knot forming in its pit.

He knows! He fucking *knows!*

"Yes, I *know*. I knew who you were the second I saw you at that party," he says, sounding amused. "Come on. Open the door. I promise I won't bite. Unless you ask me to, that is."

Oh God. Why didn't he say something?

"Okay," he says after a moment. "I'll leave. But I just ordered some Chinese food and have some extra. I'd love it if you could take it off my hands."

My stomach growls on cue, traitor that it is. Chinese food is my favorite, and the last meal I had was with him last night. "N-no, that's okay."

"I'll just leave a bag here," he insists. "All right? In case you change your mind. Or the raccoons can get to it tonight. Bye."

I press my ear to the door, listening as his footsteps retreat down the porch. A minute or two passes before my heartbeat settles, and I finally, cautiously, open the door.

"Got you." Rafael's hand catches the door as I try to pull it back, unabashed joy flickering in his gray eyes like he's savoring every second of my surprise. His rings tap lightly against the wood as he leans in. "You really are *something*, Scarlett Moore," he says as we stick to our positions, the door ajar and pressed between us.

I frown, scanning him. "Did you even bring Chinese?"

"Do you always have these sorts of trust issues?" The leather jacket looks older than him, the red lining showing where it's been worn down at the cuffs. He lifts a bag from Dragon Palace, giving me one of those arrogant smiles. "But you only get it if you let me in."

Reluctantly, I let go of the door, stepping back. He takes it as his cue to stroll in like he owns the place, shrugging off his jacket with practiced ease.

"There. Not that difficult, was it?" He shuts the door behind him; his jaw is rough with stubble and the scent of clean skin and woodsy cologne trails after him. "How'd you sleep?"

Seriously? He's going to act like this is normal? Like hanging out is something we just do? "Why are you here, Rafael?"

He hangs his jacket on the hook by the door, unfazed. He's wearing a worn charcoal tee, collar stretched, hem uneven. It looks *so* perfect on him. "Uh, because I'm hungry, and—"

"*Rafael.*"

"We had a good time last night, didn't we?"

I shrug, trying to keep my expression unreadable.

"Okay," he says, stifling a laugh. "Well, *I* had a *delightful* time. And I'd rather be anywhere other than my folks' place right now. So . . ." He points behind me. "Kitchen that way?"

I glance toward the hallway. "Yeah. But beware of the cat."

"Noted." He wiggles his brows before disappearing into the kitchen.

I follow, watching as he places the takeout on the counter and opens the containers. The familiar scent of sweet-and-sour chicken and garlic fried rice fills the air, and my stomach growls again, even louder this time.

He looks over his shoulder. "Easy there, T-Rex."

"Very funny."

"I try." He winks. "Plates?"

I point at the cabinet, and he walks over, then takes out two deep plates.

"You gonna help, or just admire the view?"

Cheeks flushing, I grab two glasses from the higher cabinet and get a bottle of water. "Don't flatter yourself."

I set it next to the food, the bite-size taste of daily routine making me feel all squirmy. Rafael Gray is at my house. He brought dinner over, as if eating together is something we just do. And now I'll be expected to make conversation with him *again*, which is surprisingly easy yet the hardest thing I've ever done at the same time.

"Do you still read while you eat?"

Taking a seat at the kitchen island, I watch him warily. "What?"

"You always read during lunch at school. You'd sit there with your book propped open, completely zoned out."

"Not *always*," I say, crossing my arms. "Just when the story was too good to put down. You know, *urgent* reading."

"Right, of course. Do you still do it?"

"Sometimes." It's a straight-up lie; I do it every single day.

"Would it bother you if I watch TV while you read?"

I blink, trying to process what he's saying. Is he suggesting we sit here eating dinner together but not actually interacting? Just existing side by side?

"Freckles?"

"N-no, that wouldn't bother me," I stammer.

"Cool." He reaches for the remote, switches on the TV, and takes a dumpling from the takeout container. He bites into it casually, leaning back as if he's done this a thousand times before. When he notices I'm still frozen on the spot, he tilts his head. "Where's your book, Scarlett?"

"Oh, uh . . ." I scramble to my feet, grab the paperback from the counter, and slide back into my seat. Pulling my hair up in a ponytail, I hesitate. "Are you sure? I mean, I can talk."

He chuckles and shifts his focus to the TV, the glint of one earring catching the light. "Just eat your dinner, Freckles."

"I thought you didn't do romance," Rafael teases.

I look up from the book in my lap, stifling yet another yawn. Dinner might have something to do with how sleepy I feel, but this crappy book is to blame for at least three of my last yawns. The story is bland, the plot dragging like a damp rag. "I don't."

"So why are you reading that?" He sets his chopsticks down next to the array of dishes scattered across the table. The food was incredible—garlic fried rice, wontons, sweet-and-sour chicken, and a spicy noodle dish that lingered pleasantly on my tongue. Rafael definitely overordered; leftovers are piled high in colorful bowls.

"Work. I'm a podcaster at—"

"Booked It, I know," he interrupts. Surprised, I watch his sharp cheekbones softened by the flickering shadows, his hypnotic eyes catching the warm glow from the lamp overhead. "Small town, Scarlett."

"Right. Anyway, my boss assigned me to *Passion & Pages*, our romance podcast. Which is great, because I'm finally full-time, but not so great, because . . ." I hold up the book, my eyes drifting to its overly flowery cover.

"Well, you're a bookworm, aren't you? Maybe you'll find answers to your love problems in books."

Maybe. So far, all I've found is repetitive dialogue and cringey lines that make me want to toss the book aside. "By the way, you remember Quentin and I—"

"Dated? Yeah, I remember."

"Okay." I guess it doesn't matter, right? The two of them weren't particularly close when Rafael left. Plus, it's been *years*, and Quentin's dated other people since our breakup. Still, the last thing I want is the whole town's attention on me. It took a long time for everyone to treat me seminormally after my parents died. I can only hope they won't care about my lukewarm love scandal with two cousins.

"Why?" Rafael lowers his chin, trying to catch my gaze. "Did you decide you'll give me a chance?"

"*No*," I rush out, the word slipping from my lips too quickly. "I mean . . . no."

"Well, I don't think he'd have the right to complain, anyway, seeing as he dumped you after your parents' funeral."

My chin jerks back as I once again wonder how he knows all of this. "*I* dumped *him*, actually."

"You did?" He seems genuinely surprised, then shrugs it off. "Either way."

Okay. So I guess *that's* not a problem.

I clean up the kitchen island, stacking plates. "And how long are you staying in town?"

He laughs softly, the sound rich and warm. "No hard plans, honestly." He meets my gaze. "I could be talked into sticking around."

"Don't you have a job to go back to?"

"Full-time, great salary. Would you like me to send you my last pay stub?"

I scoff and set the plates back down. "What, I was just making conversation."

"No," he muses. "You're trying to find a valid reason to set this thing between us to rest."

"I'm not—"

"You won't," he insists, his tone firm but light. "I've waited a long time to make sure you wouldn't."

I watch him, my lips parting in surprise. What does he mean, he's waited a long time?

"Anyway," he says, brushing the topic aside as if it were nothing, "I should go. Some family members I've never even met on my dad's side are coming to pay their respects tomorrow."

"Let me pack up your leftovers."

He holds a hand out, shaking his head. "Keep 'em." He points at me in warning. "Remember to eat them for lunch tomorrow."

"Okay." I feel a flutter of something in my chest. I swear I'm ten times more awkward when Rafael is around, but this man . . . *God*. Did he overorder on purpose? "Thank you."

I walk him to the door, the cool air from outside brushing against my skin as he steps onto the porch, leather jacket swung over one shoulder. I watch him wave and walk down the steps, my heart racing.

Why is he so different? Different from what I expected, from what I'm used to. Different from anyone I've ever met. The thought lingers, sweet and uncertain, until I can't hold it back. "Rafael?"

He turns to face me. "Yes?"

I feel a wave of regret hit me, but I can't stop myself. This is so stupid. *So, so, so* stupid. "Did you . . . did you get my letter?"

His expression shifts, and for a long moment, he just looks at me. When he finally nods, my heart stutters. "I did, yes."

Oh God, he did. Of course he did. I listened to Paige, and now I look like an idiot dredging up ancient history he wants to forget. Panic rises in my chest, and I spin on my heel. "Okay. Thanks. Bye," I blurt, heading straight to close the door.

"Scarlett, wait."

I exhale, forcing myself to stop and turn back around. "Yeah?"

"You were dating my cousin."

Shame washes over me like a wave, tightening in my chest, and my expression must betray my thoughts, because he shakes his head.

"No, no. I'm not saying this to make you feel bad. You were drunk, and . . . basically a kid." He smacks his pouty lips, as if recalling a distant memory. "But back then, I really couldn't . . . do anything."

I stare down at my shoes, trying to absorb what he's saying. It makes perfect sense, of course, but I spent half a decade believing he didn't care, that he just didn't think I was worth his time. Why did this not occur to me?

"Look, for most of my life, you were just the girl who lived next door. Three years younger, which at the time felt like a lot." He moves up the steps until he's standing on the last one, bringing his face close to mine. "I never really paid much attention to you. Until your sweet sixteen. Remember that?"

God, his nose ring is so sexy.

"You weren't there."

He glances over his shoulder. "Well, you had it in your backyard, which . . ." He gestures toward his old bedroom window, facing directly into my yard.

"Oh."

"I looked over and saw the party," he continues. He sounds almost nostalgic. "Everyone was having a great time. There were lights, music, food, those cute yellow decorations hanging everywhere."

Hence his guess of my favorite color. I can't believe he remembers all of this.

I shift on my feet. "I was reading a book."

"Uh-huh. All curled up, reading with this intense expression, like you were at a major turning point in the story. Completely lost in that world." His smile fades. "I was so jealous of you."

"*You?* Jealous of me?"

He nods, the vulnerability in his eyes quickly gone. "Anyway." He clears his throat. "You were lying on one of those loungers. Something must have happened in the book, because you jumped—like, full-body flinch—and your elbow smacked right into the arm of a woman walking past with a tray of drinks."

"Oh no."

"Oh yes." He's laughing now. "She dropped the whole thing. Someone nearby slipped in the mess, knocking into the table holding the cake—sent the whole thing flying."

"*What?*" I cover my face. "You're lying."

"Wish I was. The cake landed face down, your mom had frosting in her hair. It was beautiful. Tragic. But beautiful."

I groan into my hands. I vaguely remember Mom saying someone had dropped the cake, but I had no idea I was responsible.

"Nobody noticed the whole series of events, and you just kept reading, totally oblivious, while chaos exploded around you." He whistles, shaking his head. "It was just so . . . incredibly you. After that, I couldn't help but notice you every time you were around."

Is that so? Because he hid it *perfectly*.

"When I got the letter, I . . ." He shakes his head, his gaze dropping as he wrestles with the memory. "I just kept thinking, what if I'd come over during your sweet sixteen? What if I'd just come down the stairs and walked over to you and just . . ."

"Just?" I prompt.

"Just asked you what book you were reading." His eyes settle on mine, the same gray as a stormy sky that promises rain. "I really wanted to know."

"*Pride and Prejudice.*"

One corner of his lips quirks up. "Any good?"

"No, actually. It both created *and* cemented my hatred for romance."

With a light chuckle, he looks up at the evening sky, the first stars beginning to twinkle against the darkening canvas. "I would have kept you company, then. We could have just sat in silence, watching the party go by."

My stomach twists hard. When I dated Quentin, there was no sitting in silence and watching the party go by. He dragged me along to parties, meetups with his friends, football practice. This alternative sounds *much* nicer.

"You never even looked my way," I murmur. "Never talked to me, never said hi, never . . ."

"I was *nineteen*. You were *sixteen*." He presses his lips together. "And besides, I didn't know how to talk to you when you were so much better than me. Smart, sweet. I was the town's criminal-in-the-making, and you were a cop's daughter. A stellar student beloved by everyone. It was different with you, Scarlett." He inhales. "It still is."

I watch him, struggling to get a word out. I bet Paige would freak out, though. That she'd say something about how this always happens in romance books. How you eventually find out the love interest was pining after the main character all along.

"So that's why I didn't mention the letter."

"Okay." I take a steadying breath. "I get it."

"But I'm sorry I hurt you. You were really brave—braver than I was, for sure."

He's right. I *was* brave. While the other girls at school were busy daydreaming about him, I actually went for it. I tried. It went horribly, but I survived. "Sorry I said I was happy your spider died."

He huffs out a laugh, a glimmer of his usual mischief sparking back into his eyes. "Thank you. Hairy Houdini would have loved you."

"Can't say the feeling's mutual, but . . ."

"All right, all right."

He takes a small step back, watching me with the same glimmering interest as he has for the past twenty-four hours. The same look that sends my heart racing and my thoughts spiraling, as if he's studying every detail, every breath, and somehow finding each one fascinating. "Did you think about me at all?" he asks.

"Excuse me?"

"Over the years, I mean. Did you ever think about me?"

Only all the fucking time. "I guess."

"Good." He fits his hands into the pockets of his jeans. "I thought about you, too."

I feel queasy. Having dinner at my place felt completely natural, like falling into a routine that had been perfected over time. But the thing about routines is they can get swept away in an instant. A phone call, a car ride, and your universe is shattered forever. No more routines, no more love. No more nothing.

"Rafael, look . . ."

He grimaces. "Goddamn. There's no positive ending to that sentence."

"I told you I don't date," I say apologetically.

"Then let's not date," he says with a nonchalant shrug. "All I'm asking is that you keep doing your thing. And I'll just"—he waves a hand around—"exist around you. If you don't mind."

I blink, my tongue stuck to the roof of my mouth. What does one even say to that? Two days ago, I had no love life. And now there's this man who just wants to exist around me.

"You don't even know me," I point out.

"Don't I? I know you have a cat you'll always love more than me. And that your favorite ice cream flavor is mint chocolate chip. You forget to eat, and your favorite movie isn't *American Pie*."

"That hardly means—"

"I know you read during meals, and you miss your parents every day. That you pull your hair up every time you open a book, like you're preparing to go to battle, and that you spent your birthday with me, but you didn't want to celebrate it."

I watch him, mouth wide open. "How do you . . ."

"Because I *saw* you back then, and I've thought about you since."

This is so close to my recurring dream when I was a teenager that I nearly check for drool to make sure I'm awake.

"Look, I get that I hurt you. Really, I do." His shoulders roll back. "But if you're open to it, I'd really like . . . I'd like a second chance."

"Technically, you didn't get a first chance yet."

"Even better, then." He smirks. "Everyone deserves at least *one* chance, right?"

My phone rings, and with a quick apology, I take it out of my pocket. "Sorry, I . . ."

"No, hey. Take your call." He steps closer and kisses my cheek softly. "See you tomorrow, Scarlett."

The spot on my cheek tingles like his lips actually left a mark, and watching him walk away, I'm too dazed to answer the phone for a while. When I come to, I bring it to my ear and say, "Hello?"

"Scarlett? Hi. This is Chief Donovan."

Well, well, well. Chief Donovan. Something tells me he's read the book and I'm suddenly not such an idiot anymore. "Yes, hi, Chief. How can I help you?"

"I, uh . . . I have a few questions, if you don't mind."

Feeling even more smug, I say, "Of course not. What about?"

I wave when Rafael turns to look at me. His *See you tomorrow* echoes faintly in my mind. It's such a small promise, but it feels like much more.

Like the start of something.

"What, uh . . ." The chief's voice crackles into my ear. "What can you tell me about Rafael Gray?"

act II

[structure]

---

also known as the "emotional roller-coaster zone," where every
interaction drips with chemistry and every accidental touch sends
shock waves through the plot; expect long stares, heart-fluttering
moments, and inconvenient feelings that no one is ready to admit

7

the fake dating

[trope]

a rom-com-approved contractual arrangement in which two
people pretend to be a couple for reasons that are definitely
not feelings

"Look, all I'm saying is I don't buy the premise. Fake dating relies on the idea that being single is some kind of national emergency. 'Oh, no, my ex got engaged, so now I *have* to show him I'm totally over him by fake dating this guy I've hated since high school.' Because nothing says 'I'm doing fine without you' like staging an elaborate charade involving a man who bullied you during your formative years." I bite my nail. "And if it's not that, then it's 'My mom keeps setting me up with weirdos from her yoga class, so the best solution is to fake-date my *boss*.' It's like the entire world in these books is allergic to the concept of being single. *God forbid* you enjoy your own company for more than five minutes. No, no, according to these stories, you've gotta have a boyfriend on standby, just in case society tries to revoke your happiness card."

I pause just to breathe.

"Why can't the protagonist just tell her family, 'Actually, I'm perfectly happy with Netflix, a pizza, and not sharing my bed with a snorer'? Why does everyone act like being single is some sort of failure? Here's a wild idea—*maybe* it's okay to be alone sometimes. Maybe, just maybe, you don't need to invent a fake boyfriend to convince everyone else that you're happy. And maybe fake dating is just a convoluted way to say, 'I'm terrified of being alone.'"

Celeste blinks, then drops her glasses onto her desk. "Yes, Scarlett. So you said." She shows me the script. "For *six* pages. Is that really all you have to say about this book?"

"Well, I said *other* things," I mumble.

She narrows her eyes at me and, after clearing her throat, reads out, "'Every single page of this book feels like it was written for a rom-com algorithm. You've got the quirky heroine who's clumsy and adorable, the brooding love interest who's hiding a heart of gold beneath layers of emotional trauma, and a plot so predictable I could have outlined it in my sleep. The writing? Filled with so many clichés, it's practically a bingo card.'" She levels me with a glare. "This type of thing?"

"Yes." I shift uncomfortably in the chair. "What's the problem? It's not the first time I've criticized a book. You always say you want my honest opinion."

"Your *opinion*, yes. But this is slander, and it's not about the book. It's about the reader." She sets the paper down, her bob following the movement of her head shaking. "Maybe you were right and we just made a mistake."

"No, wait," I choke out. "I'll . . . I'll work on it. Maybe it was just the wrong book. Maybe I can rewrite it."

For the fifth time.

Celeste rubs her forehead. "All right. Think you can give me something by Friday? We need to air this next week."

"Yeah," I say, as if it doesn't mean I'll have to spend *several* nights up. "No problem at all."

"All right." She picks up a different paper. "Of course, the script for *Murders & Manuscripts'* next episode is immaculate. You made me want to read the book."

"I loved *The Widow's Veil.* The prose alone was astounding. And the way Anders Peterson makes your skin prickle—I swear, his words jump off the page and come alive."

She removes her glasses with a giggle. "This, Scarlett—your passion—is why you're my best podcaster. I need you to redirect some of it to romance." Picking up my script, she insists, "Because no one wants to listen to this."

Ouch. It's not like I spent most of my weekend working on this. "Okay. You got it." I stand when she looks back at the computer. "I'll work on a new draft."

I close the door of her office. Booked It is nearly empty this close to lunchtime, and Damien seems focused on writing, so I walk out of the building undisturbed.

The sun's shining and the parking lot is quiet, but as the door clicks shut behind me, an unsettling tingle crawls up my spine, the kind you get when someone's eyes are glued to your back. I peek over my shoulder, but nothing's weird.

Shielding my face from the bright light, I make my way toward my Toyota, but I get that prickling feeling again, like eyes burning holes in my back.

I whirl around, scanning the street. There are people going about their day, cars rolling lazily by. My heart hammers a little harder as I hurry toward the car, fumbling for my keys, the sense of being followed sticking to me like a shadow.

"Scarlett!"

I clutch my chest as I spot Vanessa in her uniform, then exhale in relief. She's hard to miss—tall, with broad shoulders that make the dark fabric of her patrol shirt look even sharper, blond hair pulled neatly into a tight braid. Her blue eyes scan the area as she walks closer.

"Geez, Vanessa, trying to give me a heart attack? What are you doing up here?"

"Just had a meeting." She points at the bank, on the ground floor of the Booked It building. "I'm on my way to work."

I catch my breath. "How's the apartment hunt going?"

Vanessa groans, and I can imagine her following Paige through a million different houses in her tailored off-duty clothes, a far cry from the tactical belt at her waist. "You know your best friend. She's got a list about this long." She spreads her hands so far apart I'm surprised she's still smiling, then snaps her fingers. "Oh, speaking of, we're canvassing your area today. We're checking if anyone saw or heard anything that could help with the Blake case."

Her radio crackles to life, and a voice summons Dispatch 105. She presses her radio. "Dispatch 105. Heading to the station now." She turns back to me. "Sorry. Duty calls."

"Hey, Vanessa," I call as she walks away.

She pauses. "Yeah?"

"I know you can't spill the beans on an ongoing case, but . . ." I trail off, trying to look as innocent as possible. "Do you have any suspects?"

She raises a blond eyebrow. "You mean like Rafael Gray? I know the chief called you Saturday night, Scarlett—I told him to, since I know you're neighbors."

I huff out a breath, glad I can drop the act. "Great. Then can you tell me what the hell you have on him? Because the chief had a lot of questions."

She pauses, rocking slightly on her heels. "Uh, nothing, really. You know he's had his trouble with the law."

"So?" I quip.

"So, previous perpetration of crime is the first predictor in propensity to—"

"Seriously? Once a criminal, always a criminal? He was just a kid."

"I know." She holds her hands up in defeat. "We're not arresting him or anything. Why are you getting so worked up? Are you close or something?"

My heart lurches, and I clear my throat, looking away. "I barely even know him." Technically not a lie, right? "I'm just . . . worried about the investigation. Did the chief tell you about my visit?"

"Yes." By her tone, I can imagine Donovan relating it like the latest crazy story from the dead cop's daughter who wants to play the hero. "And look, could it be a copycat murder based on that book? Sure. But even if you're right, it doesn't exactly lead us to the guy."

I bite my lip. She has a point. Knowing the killer is a bookworm doesn't narrow the suspect list. "Neither will focusing all your energies on Rafael Gray."

She hesitates for a moment. "Someone was seen fleeing by one of the victim's neighbors. Green cap with a visor, head down. Classic. Apparently wearing a gray T-shirt with some type of tree print on the front."

"Man? Woman?"

"Not sure. Tall and broad-shouldered, so probably a man. For now, we're digging into her life—exes, family drama. That's usually where the gold is."

"Got it," I say, leaning back. "Thanks for humoring me."

"You know I'm always happy to talk to you." Though I expect her to go, she stays put. When the moment of silence lasts just a beat too long, I point at the car.

"Well . . ."

"Yeah." She shakes her head, like she's brushing a thought away, and I wonder if she was preparing to tell me something. Before I can ask, she's already walking away. "Drive safe!"

"You too." I climb into my car, a thought buzzing at the back of my mind like an annoying fly.

Though my theory might not help them find the killer, if I'm right and this murderer is playing out a twisted homage to a book, one thing's certain.

There's going to be a sequel.

"Sherlock?" I call as the door shuts behind me. The house echoes faintly, the silence heavier than usual. He always greets me at the door, weaving between my legs, purring for attention. His absence can only mean one thing. "Son of a bitch, he's gone again."

Five years of minimal maintenance have turned my parents' place into a skeletal version of its former self. The paint is peeling, the tiles are cracked, and the distinct scent of age permeates the air. Somewhere there's got to be a hole just big enough for Sherlock to slip through, giving him the freedom to roam the neighborhood.

I'd bet anything he's with that labradoodle down the street. The Walkers have called me three times this month alone to come fetch him after finding him cuddled up with Georgina.

I set my bag down on the side table, the familiar weight of another Sherlock rescue already forming in my chest.

Before I can even kick off my shoes, a creak from somewhere deeper in the house freezes me in place. It doesn't sound like the usual groans of a tired old home. It's deliberate. Close. My heart pounds a little harder, my mind flashing unbidden to Catherine Blake's murderer.

"Hello?" I call hesitantly as I step forward, scanning the hallway. "Is anyone there?"

Silence. Then the bathroom door creaks open, and a voice—familiar yet unexpected—responds, "What's a Sherlock?"

My heart leaps into my throat before I can recognize my brother, and as Ethan steps into the light, it stops altogether.

"What the hell happened to your face?"

His features are barely recognizable under the purplish bruises blooming around his eyes. A gash splits his left eyebrow, still oozing slightly despite the bloodied towel pressed against it, and his bottom lip is swollen, a deep cut etched into the corner. Strands of dark blond hair hang limp and damp with sweat, plastered against his forehead.

He touches the side of his jaw gingerly, wincing. "No big deal," he mutters, as if he doesn't look like he just walked out of a bar brawl. His green eyes are bloodshot and dulled. "I hope you don't mind I let myself in." He holds up the bloodied towel sheepishly. "And used your towel to clean up."

"Of course not. Everything in here is yours, too." I suppress a grimace, noticing he picked a *white* towel. "I'll get you some ice."

I stalk toward the kitchen, my mind racing. The last time I saw Ethan was on his birthday, almost a year ago, and I know he's angry at me. He just won't say it.

It's my fault. It's been five years since our parents died, and I didn't fight to keep us close. Now I don't know a single thing about him, and the first time I see him in a year, he's bleeding on my couch.

Shoving the nagging sense of guilt deep down, I walk back and hand him the makeshift ice pack. "So? Did you lose a fight against King Kong?"

Ethan presses the bundle of ice to his bruised cheek. "Just ran into some trouble. But if I'd showed up at home like this, Grandma would have killed me."

I take a seat on the couch. "That definitely doesn't look like just 'some trouble,' Ethan."

He rolls his eyes and leans back, staring up at the ceiling like he's already over this conversation. "Seriously, what's a Sherlock?"

"A cat."

He gasps. "You have a cat?"

"Yeah. He's not here, though." I shrug. "Illicit love scandal with a labradoodle."

"Wow." Ethan shifts, pressing the ice pack against his split lip. "I've always wanted a pet—well, a dog, 'cause I'm normal."

"*Hey*," I warn cautiously. "Seriously, Ethan, what happened to your—"

"What's new with you? Besides the cat—you know, he'd eat you if you died."

"Well, I plan to stay alive for the time being." I know he's avoiding the topic of his face and whatever happened to it, but I try to think of something interesting to tell him about my mundane life. "Uh, I've got a new assignment at work. Romance. If the trial run goes well, I'll be making double what I do now."

He nods, seemingly impressed. "I've listened to your podcast a few times."

"Really?" I actually feel nervous. "What did you think?"

"That you're a nerd," he mocks. "I never read a book and had thirty minutes' worth of stuff to say about it."

"Aren't you charming?" I shoot back. But seeing him snicker makes my heart swell. I can't remember the last time I saw him happy.

"What about you?" I ask. "School okay?"

"It's fine. All my old friends are at Willowbrook High."

"I'm sure you've made new friends in Wethersfield."

He shrugs, a little too nonchalantly. "Not at school, but yeah. Jace. Grandma doesn't like him, though, so . . ." He shakes his head. "I don't see him a lot."

"Why doesn't she like him?" All I get in response is a grunt, so I ask, "What about love? Are you dating anyone?"

He frowns and looks away.

Bingo. "Do you go to school together?"

"I'm not dating anyone," he snaps, voice sharp and defensive.

Uh-huh, sure. "Really?"

"Yes, really." His frown deepens. "Are *you* dating someone?"

I stumble over my words, caught off guard. "Uh, I—no."

"Uh-huh." He raises an eyebrow. "Sure sounds convincing."

I feel my cheeks heat. "I'm not! I'd tell you."

He opens his mouth to rebut this, but a cacophony of bangs and angry shouting outside has us both turning our heads toward the door. What the hell?

"Wait here," I say as I stand and rush to the door, then look through the window. It's Vanessa, wearing her police uniform. But who is she fighting with?

"Shit," I squeal when she turns around and shoves a cuffed Rafael onto the hood of his car, his gray eyes bulging out as he absorbs the hit.

What the hell did he do now?

I come out in a flurry, both Vanessa and Rafael looking up. "Scarlett, please step back," she calls.

Ignoring her, I rush down the steps. "What is *happening*?"

"Everything is okay. If you could just enter the house and close the door—"

I walk closer. "No. Vanessa, what the hell?"

"Yeah, *Vanessa*, what the hell?" Rafael says, catching his breath. His white tank top clings to his chest, streaked with dirt from the hood of the car. The tattoos winding along his arms tense as he shifts, his hands cuffed behind him.

She glares at him. "I found this creep snooping in your backyard."

My eyes dart to Rafael, then back to her. "That's not— You know he's my neighbor."

"Well, he wasn't on *his* property." She puts more pressure on the cuffs, and Rafael groans. A curl of brown hair flops over his forehead, and he blows it away with an irritated puff of breath. "Were you? He was peeping into your place."

"I was not—"

"Shut up," she barks.

"You're arresting him for . . . being in my backyard?"

"He couldn't explain *why* he was there," she says. "Don't worry, okay? He's not under arrest. We'll just ask him a couple of questions down at the station."

She pats Rafael's shoulder and pulls him back up, but I take a step forward. "Wait, Vanessa." I can't let Rafael get arrested. This is ridiculous. "He's . . . he wasn't snooping. We're . . ." Oh God, I think I get fake dating now. "Seeing each other."

She straightens, lips parted. "He's your boyfriend? *This guy?*"

Rafael scoffs. "Gee, thanks."

Vanessa ignores him, eyes still set on mine.

"Yes, whatever. He's my . . . *boyfriend*. Can you uncuff him? Those must be painful."

"They are," Rafael says, though judging by the giddy smile on his face as he looks up at me, he's not in that much pain.

Vanessa pulls him back up. She looks upset, probably because I lied to her face earlier today. "Sorry, I guess. I just . . . I didn't know."

Rafael grins lazily. "I'm a recent addition. You know, a plot twist."

I shoot him a look, silently begging him to stop talking. "Sorry I didn't tell you. It's all really new."

The cuffs click open, and Rafael rubs his wrists. "Thanks, Vanessa. Real gentle touch you've got there."

"Don't push it," she warns, glowering at him before turning back to me. "And Scarlett, call me if you see anyone sketchy. Even if it's your boyfriend."

I wave. "Thanks, I will."

With a final suspicious glance at Rafael, she heads back to her car. As soon as she's out of earshot, I whirl around to face him. "Are you okay?"

He rubs his wrists again, a shit-eating grin on his face. "Your boyfriend, huh?"

Great. I think his brain disconnected after that.

"I had to say *something*," I say, crossing my arms.

He laughs, deep and amused. "Not that I'm complaining, but you could have said I was helping you with a window that was stuck, or that you'd heard a noise in the backyard and sent me to check, or that you couldn't find your keys, or—"

"Yes," I burst out, walking back to the house. "I *get* it."

But I *panicked*, that's it. And I guess I was still thinking about the stupid fake-dating book.

I only notice Rafael following once I step past the open door and Ethan's eyes move to him.

"I thought you didn't have a boyfriend."

He watched that entire performance, didn't he?

"Rafael, this is my brother, Ethan. Ethan, you might remember Rafael. He used to live next to us." I watch the two of them shake hands, and when all eyes are on me again, I add, "And he's *not* my boyfriend."

"Really?" Ethan glances over at Rafael, eyebrows raised. "He's looking at you like he's your boyfriend."

I follow Ethan's gaze to Rafael, who's standing there with a goofy smile, eyes bright, as though he's still riding the high of what I said. "Yeah, he does that sometimes."

Ethan gathers his things, and my stomach quickly clenches. "Wait—where are you going?"

"Home," he says, not meeting my eye.

"Already?" I sound a little too desperate, even to myself. "Why don't you stay for dinner? We can order from Mario's. You love their pizza."

"It's fine, really." He throws his bag over his shoulder and heads toward the door. "You're busy. With your *cat* and your *podcast* and your *boyfriend*."

"I'm never too busy for you," I say, his resentment digging a hole in my chest. When he ignores me, I follow him out. "At least let me drive you home." Our grandparents' place is a twenty-minute ride from here, and last I heard, Ethan didn't have a car.

"I'm on my bike."

I step out after him onto the porch, grasping for reasons to keep him here. "Well, I can fit it in the back of the car—"

He cuts me off. "It's fine."

I watch him unlock his bike from the fence, my chest tightening. I so want to be the cool sister. The one he can confide in, who respects his privacy and doesn't sweat the fact that someone hurt him. But I'm also an adult, and I can't ignore it.

"Ethan, we really need to talk about your face. Someone obviously attacked you—"

The moment he whips around, anger flashing across his face, I regret insisting.

"Let it *go*, Scarlett," he barks, his voice raw and bitter. He turns away from me and starts to pedal as he says, "Just like you did last time."

8

the bookstore

[trope]

a sacred location where the bookworm character gets gloriously
spoiled; it usually includes a "get whatever you want"—
no budget, no judgment, just pure, unfiltered indulgence
in bookish bliss

Nothing like buying a new book to hide from the fact that your
brother, who basically hates you, won't open up to you about
someone hurting him. Or at least that's what I say to myself as I
peruse the new arrivals at Providence's biggest bookstore.

"This one looks good," I say, before shoving another paperback
onto the pile in Rafael's arms. I grab a blue book, and as I read the
synopsis, he groans.

"Are they too heavy?"

He turns to the side, the tower of books covering most of his
face. "No, but I'll need to recant my answer to your question 'How

many books can you hold?' because it turns out 'As many as you want' might not be true."

"Sorry—give me some."

"No, no. I get it. Retail therapy with books." He steps back, holding the pile out of my range. "How about I leave these at the counter, then come back here for more?"

I watch him walk away. He followed me out of the house when Ethan left, even as I tried to tell him he didn't need to come along, and he doesn't seem to mind that we've spent two hours here.

"Reporting for duty," Rafael says as he approaches my side again, a contented smile still in place. Seriously? Even *my* feet are hurting.

"You can say so if you're bored."

His smile dampens. "Do I look bored?"

"No, but—"

"Good, because I'm not."

I chew on the inside of my cheek, searching his face for the smallest hint of a lie. But there's nothing—no flicker in his eyes, no twitch of his lips. I sigh inwardly and go back to reading the synopsis. Sounds like a historical whodunit, not my thing. I set it back on the shelf, then continue perusing the aisle.

"How often do you do this?"

"Not much. Just . . . whenever I'm upset."

"Every time? You picked, like, a million books."

"I get a special discount," I say defensively. "It's probably the best perk of the job."

"You must be single-handedly responsible for the deforestation on this side of the continent. Have you ever considered getting an ebook reader?"

"I like trophies."

"Like a serial killer?"

"Exactly like it." I turn a new book around and read through the blurb, but I can feel Rafael's eyes studying me. "Yes?"

"Your brother, um . . ."

I exhale, setting the book down. "Yeah."

"He looked like he got a good beating."

Which breaks my heart in ways I can't even explain. Almost as much as the fact that he won't tell me what happened.

"Do you want me to ask around? See what happened?"

"Thank you, but he lives in Wethersfield with my grandparents."

He shrugs. "I have a wide network."

"Really?" I watch him warily. "For work?"

He nods, picking up a book and reading the back.

He never really said *what* he does, did he? "Which is . . ."

"Exhausting but well paid." He opens the cover and flips through some pages. "Lots of traveling, too."

"*Really?*"

"I can't talk too much about it."

Oh, he's hoping to keep something private in this town? Mrs. Prattle will tell me all about his secret business by the end of the week. "Anyway, sorry about Vanessa. She's a good friend and my best friend's girlfriend and a little . . ."

He meets my gaze over the edge of the book. "Insane?"

"Intense," I correct. "What were you doing, anyway? In my backyard?"

"I thought . . ." He shakes his head as if doubting himself. "I'm probably wrong, but I thought I saw a cat."

"No, you're likely right. Sherlock always sneaks out to see his girlfriend."

We've reached the end of the aisle, so I give him another book and walk to the next one, my stomach immediately sinking when I notice the abundance of pink covers.

Romance.

I turn around and walk back to the crime section.

"What was that?"

"What?"

He points at my pursed lips, then turns back to the romance section. "What—*oh*. Romance books, of course. How's the podcast going?"

"Not great." I feel his gaze on the side of my face. "I delivered my first script about this stupid fake-dating book, and apparently, I didn't get the point. My boss might have called it slander."

He hisses through his teeth, then walks back. "So let's check out their selection."

"No, thank you."

He ignores me, standing in the romance aisle across from me. He picks up a book—a pink one—and reads the back. "This one seems nice. She's obsessed with weddings, but—"

"Nope," I snap.

"All right." He sets it back on the shelf, then picks up another. After his face scrunches, he discards that one, too.

Fighting a chuckle, I focus on the blurb of the book I'm holding.

"How about this one, then?"

I look up and see him holding a red book. On the cover, a woman with a detective trench coat and a slightly messy ponytail holds a magnifying glass. A man stands opposite her, holding a book in one hand and looking down at her.

The Love Alibi.

"What's it about?"

"A detective investigating a string of murders who falls in love with the suspect, a widower and bookseller who's withdrawn from the world."

I tilt my head, considering it. "I guess it beats wedding planning."

Rafael walks to my side of the bookshelf, then holds out the book. "Read a passage."

"Right here?" I ask, looking around at the semi-empty shop.

"Why not?"

"Because it's stupid."

"Come on, do it."

"Nope."

"Do it, or I'll start singing 'I Want It That Way.' Really loud."

Please. Not even Rafael Gray is that unhinged.

"*You are my fiiire,*" he starts, loud and off-key, startling the old woman sitting behind the cash register.

"Stop—fine!" I take the book and flip through the pages, stopping on chapter twenty-three. The scent of Rafael so close to me—cologne mixed with something warm and masculine—makes it hard to focus.

"Simone's heart raced as Luca reached for her hand, his fingers brushing hers with deliberate slowness," I read. "She looked up at him, her lips parting, but no words came. His thumb traced her knuckles, his touch featherlight but electric." I pause, feeling the weight of Rafael's presence at my back. Before I can continue, his deep voice fills the space between us.

" 'You're beautiful,' " he reads softly.

I peek over my shoulder at him, the heat of his breath so close to my ear making my pulse jump. "What are you doing?"

"Keep going," he urges, his hand gently resting on the book to keep it open.

"Seriously, I don't want to—"

"*The one*," he begins singing, immediately catching other people's attention, "*desiiire*—"

"Okay, okay." I hesitate, then focus back on the page. "Her breath caught in her throat as his hand traveled higher, settling against her cheek. She tilted her head, leaning into the warmth of his palm. 'Luca,' she whispered."

He doesn't miss a beat, his body brushing against mine. "'Tell me to stop,'" he reads in a low murmur. "'Tell me to go, and I'll do as you say.'"

I can barely see the page now, and my heart is pounding. My fingers grip the book tighter, my breath coming faster. I can't seem to tear my eyes away from the page, yet I'm hyperaware of every inch of space—or lack thereof—between us. "I'm pretty sure Luca didn't speak directly into Simone's ear like that," I protest.

"Creative interpretation." He taps the page. "Your turn."

I reluctantly comply. "Her voice trembled. 'I don't want you to stop.' His lips hovered just inches from hers, and time seemed to hold its breath as . . ." The words catch in my throat as I see where this is going.

"He kissed her, slow and deep, his hand slipping to her waist to pull her closer," Rafael continues for me.

Of course the random page I chose would be their first kiss.

At least, I hope that's all this is.

I skim the next section, and, noticing it includes words like "heated core" and "throbbing erection," I snap the book shut with a sharp *thwap*, nearly smacking his fingers, then hand it over. "Okay, that's enough."

He chuckles softly as I put some distance between us and pretend to be busy straightening the books on the shelf in front of me. "Not what I'm looking for," I say, proud that I sound almost normal now.

"No? I thought it had potential. A little mystery, a little romance, a lot of sexual tension."

Is he still talking about the book? Seriously, this is getting out of hand. I thought I'd frustrate him to death, not that we'd read smut together. "Nope. Not my thing."

"Kinda looked like your thing," he mutters under his breath, but when I glare, he sets the book down and raises both hands in surrender. "Please, continue your shopping."

I do, grabbing another three books to add to my stack. I stretch the whole process as long as I can, but there are no more bookshelves to explore, there is no more acceptable stalling, and he's still relaxed and upbeat, like he has nothing better to do than watch me shop for books.

"We can go," I concede.

One of his brows quirks in question. "You sure?" When I nod, he studies me, as if waiting for me to change my mind, then gestures toward the cashier. "All right," he says, walking ahead of me.

He pulls out his card, and I hurry to catch up. "What are you doing?"

"Buying a book," he says nonchalantly.

I narrow my eyes on him. "What book?"

"This one." He sets *The Love Alibi* on the counter.

I blink in surprise. When did he even grab it? And since when is book-buying part of the bad-boy package—and why is it working on me?

"N-no, you're not. What for? You'll never read it."

He tilts his head at me, amusement dancing in his eyes. "What are you, the book police?"

I'd like to retort, but no words come out. "Why do you want it?"

He just shrugs, that mischievous glint in his eyes growing stronger. "Maybe I want to see what happens next. Don't you?"

My cheeks flush instantly. I can still feel his breath near my ear as he read those lines. I quickly turn away, trying to hide my burning face. "Not unless the twist is that he turns out to be a serial killer."

The clerk joins us at the register, interrupting us. Once I've spent this month's grocery budget in books I won't get to read for weeks, Rafael effortlessly grabs the two large paper bags like they weigh nothing and heads for the exit.

Oddly flustered, I trail after him. He's making this seem so easy. Too easy. Like he was born to chauffeur me around and act like my personal shopper. Like doing things for me comes naturally.

Outside, he places the bags in the trunk of his car, then turns to me with that same bright, disarming charm. "Should I take you home, Freckles?"

"Sure, yes," I respond automatically, even though my mind is a mess of jumbled thoughts. I have a podcast episode to rewrite, yet I already know the man standing in front of me is all I'll be able to think about. The ease of being around him and the terrifying consequences of getting used to his presence.

I slide into the passenger seat, feeling the click of the seat belt as I buckle in. I wait for the engine to start, but Rafael leans back against the headrest.

"Everything okay?"

He exhales slowly. His hair's all messy curls, a few strands falling over his forehead. The silver hoop in his nose shines in the dashboard light. "Yeah. I had a great time. Did you?"

His words catch me off guard. A great time? *I* enjoyed myself, but I can't fathom how he could've had a *good* time, let alone a great one.

I nod, though it feels more like a reflex than a conscious response.

Turning his focus to the road, he sighs. Black ink curls into the shape of a snake winding around his left forearm, its head resting just above his wrist. He adjusts his grip on the wheel, the heavy silver ring on his middle finger glinting in the faint streetlights. "The funeral's tomorrow."

I blink, surprised he brought up the topic. So far, he's hardly mentioned his father, and I didn't want to pry. Will he want me to attend? I wasn't planning to—I didn't even like the man—but that was before . . . well, before Rafael came back. Before the last few days. "I know. How are you doing?"

After a moment of hesitation, he snickers. "I'm good. And awful. It'll be packed, won't it?"

The funeral of the owner of the only pub-bar-café-club in town? "Afraid so."

He tightens his grip on the steering wheel, his knuckles whitening. "I hate this. All of it. The thought of standing there, pretending I know what to say when people come up to me with that tragic look on their faces, telling me how sorry they are."

"Oh, that's easy. You say, 'Thank you for coming.' When they ask you how you're holding up, you say, 'One day at a time.' And to people who want to know what they can do for you, you ask them to light a candle in honor of your dad."

A long exhale, then he says, "I'm sorry I wasn't there for your parents' funeral."

It wasn't his fault, of course, but I wish he'd been there, too. It remains the worst day of my life, even worse than the day they died. It was at their funeral that it sank in that they were really gone.

"How was it?"

"The funeral? Uh . . . depressing. And long." I fidget with a lock of hair. "I kept shifting between being annoyed at what people said—like they didn't have the right to grieve because they hadn't lost as much as me—and wishing they'd keep talking about Mom and Dad, because it felt like it kept them alive a little longer."

I glance down at my hands, twisting them in my lap. "And after, I just felt . . . empty. Like I'd lost any sense of purpose. There wasn't the funeral to keep up appearances for anymore, and I was completely . . . alone."

Shit. Way to make it easier for him.

I quickly backtrack. "But it probably won't be the same for you." His gaze stays steady on me, and I catch the faintest glint of amusement in his expression. "Because I'll be there. If, um, you want me to. And I'll do what I can to help."

"*No,*" he says, his expression darkening in an instant. "I don't want you to go."

I swallow, looking away. "Oh. O-okay."

Great. Now I feel like an idiot for offering.

"Because I won't go either."

I turn to him again. He won't attend his dad's funeral? My mind stumbles over the thought. Rafael Gray skipping his saintly father's funeral would be the talk of the town for years. "Are you sure that's what you want?"

"You think it'd be terrible of me."

"No, I don't. All that crap about funerals helping with closure is just that—crap. You shouldn't go if you don't want to."

His fingers pause their drumming, and for the first time since we started this conversation, his shoulders seem to relax. He pauses, as if testing the thought out in his mind. "Can I ask you something?"

"Sure."

"Why were you alone?" he asks, turning his head just enough to look at me. His gray eyes are steady, almost too clear. "I mean, after the funeral. Your brother went to live with your grandparents, right? Why didn't you?"

"Uh . . ." I laugh, a humorless sound that echoes uncomfortably in the quiet car. "Depends who you ask. My brother thinks I abandoned him. According to my grandparents, I preferred my own space."

"Well, I'm asking you."

"I . . ." My throat tightens, and I clench my hands into fists in my lap, nails digging into my palms. "I never felt welcome with my grandparents."

He frowns, his brows pulling together as he waits for me to continue.

"I'm not actually related to them," I say eventually. "Drew adopted me when I was two, but they never really saw me as a granddaughter."

"I didn't know he wasn't your biological father."

"He might as well have been," I say, rubbing my hands together. "No one knew. It didn't matter to him, and it didn't matter to me."

"But it matters to your grandparents."

"Not that they'd ever admit it." I press my nails harder into my palms. "But they never liked my mom. And she was the one driving the car that . . ." My words falter, and I swallow hard, my throat thick. "It wasn't her fault, of course, but they only saw it as confirmation of what they already believed: My mom was a bad seed, and I was part of her."

"So when your mom and dad died, they sent you packing?"

"They kept insisting I *wanted* to be independent," I say with a bitter edge. "Craved to 'spread my wings' and 'head into the world on my own.' It became a little statement for me to parrot, and every time someone asked, I'd say that I'd *decided* to live in the house. That I *wanted* to drop out of college, take over my parents' mortgage, bounce through minimum-wage jobs."

"But you didn't."

"No. What I wanted was every bit of family I could catch."

His fingers brush mine as he moves his hand from the emergency brake. He cups my hand like he's holding something fragile, yet also like he's afraid I'll slip away if he doesn't hold tight enough. It's such a simple thing, but it drags all the restless, darting pieces of my thoughts into something still that makes me feel uncomfortably exposed. As if he's touching more than just my hand and has reached into that place I keep locked up tight.

"I'm so sorry."

"It's okay. I mean, I talk to them every few weeks, and my brother texts back sometimes, so . . ."

He squeezes harder. "Scarlett?" I meet his gaze. "That sucks, and I'm sorry."

I watch our hands, joined between us. I can't help myself—I trace the small tattoo inked across the back of his hand, a tiny black star just below the knuckle of his index finger. My thumb moves over it slowly, feeling the faint texture of the lines, trying to focus on that instead of how raw and seen I suddenly feel. "Yeah, it does suck. But at least I had Celeste."

"Celeste?"

"My boss." My lips twitch into a faint smile at the thought of her. "She was a good friend of my parents', and after their death, she took the one thing she knew could help me and turned it into jobs for us both." I shrug. "Books."

He huffs out a surprised breath. "You're kidding."

"Nope. She made me pick up a bunch of books, then told me to write out my thoughts like I was talking to a friend. Then she made me do it again and again. At first she'd badger me about it, and after a while, it started being fun."

His thumb rubs over my first knuckle, the soft contact making my stomach do somersaults. "And the rest is history."

"Right." Heat creeps up my chest. "She, uh, she used to work at the library when we were kids."

"Oh my God." His eyes bulge out. "She's Mrs. Morgan? Shit, she was terrifying. If you ever returned a book late, she'd add your picture to the wall of Library Delinquents. You know, she suspected I'd drawn a penis in a book, so she told me books had better memory than people and remembered who disrespected them. Scared the hell out of me, especially because I *totally* drew that penis."

I laugh, rolling my eyes. "She mellowed out. Mostly."

"Does she still smell like honey?"

"Oh, yes. It's her perfume—she always smells like summer."

I can't look away from our hands, still together, even knowing full well I should pull mine back. Hell, I should at least want to. "Anyway, that's my sad story."

"And that's not the version your brother heard," Rafael says, tilting his head slightly as if trying to read me better.

"No." A bitter taste rises in my throat. "And he never forgave me for it."

"So why don't you tell him the truth?"

Because the truth is worse than my lie. Knowing his grandparents all but kicked me out would leave him stranded in a house full of bitterness. "I guess I'd rather have him hating me than the people he depends on."

He exhales deeply. "That's a hell of a thing to carry alone."

"Some things are easier that way."

There's a pause, and then he shifts slightly, angling his body toward me. "Okay, it's probably not my place, but . . . don't you think he deserves the right to choose?"

"He's just a kid, Rafael."

"Wrong." His lips quirk upward, though his eyes remain serious. "As the president of that club for eighteen consecutive years, I know how to recognize a fellow member."

I frown, confused.

"He's not just a kid, Scarlett. He's a *miserable* kid." He leans back, starting the car with a soft rumble. "And something tells me the truth could help with that."

9

the small-town gossip

[trope]

a relentless information pipeline fueled by nosy neighbors, overzealous hairdressers, and the local diner waitress who knows everyone's coffee order *and* secrets; in rom-coms, it's the invisible network ensuring that every scandal, breakup, and steamy almost-kiss is public knowledge before the main characters have even processed it themselves

"So then after the bookstore we had dinner together, right? I swear he spent hours just listening to me talking about books. Asking questions, like he actually *cared*. We watched *The Silence of the Lambs*—yes, again—and there was a moment when he wished me good night. A proper *moment*." I grin at the memory of him hesitating, smiling somewhat shyly, then kissing my cheek before walking away. "He even said we'd watch *Hannibal* the next day. And guess what?" My reflection stares back at me in the mirror—

brown hair falling in soft waves around my shoulders, bangs slightly uneven from the last time I trimmed them myself. My fair skin looks even paler in the mirror light, freckles scattered across my cheeks and nose. "He was a no-show. No calls, no texts—I know, I know. We didn't even exchange numbers yet. I guess I'm just worried about him."

I pause, lowering the mascara and examining my reflection. "Did he really not go to the funeral yesterday? Is he okay?" I continue, grabbing a tube of lipstick. "Maybe he's just done with me."

"Rooo," Sherlock responds in his most judgmental tone.

"I'm not disappointed or anything." I glare at him through the mirror. "It's not like I didn't expect it."

"Rooo."

"Okay, so I guess I'm a *little* disappointed," I snap. And worried, mostly worried. I considered going to the funeral, just in case he showed up, but talked myself out of it when I remembered the way he seemed to absolutely *not* want me there. I knocked on his door twice, but nothing, and I haven't exactly been staring out the window, but I haven't seen him come or go at all.

I swipe the lipstick across my lips, the bold red instantly brightening my face, and when I see something moving outside, my eyes dart to the window, but it's just a bird.

Okay, so I guess I *have* been staring out the window.

Pathetic.

"Rooo."

Once again, I glare at Sherlock through the mirror. He probably just wants a cookie, but it feels a lot like he's judging me. "You could help, you know," I say, standing. "When I found out about your affair, I invited the Walkers over so you could spend time with Georgina."

My phone beeps, and I grab it from the bed. Theo's stuck in traffic out of town. I text back that we can record next week's episodes after lunch, then walk downstairs. Sherlock follows, both of us settling on the couch.

I really should work on my first episode of *Passion & Pages*, but the latest book I picked up smacked me in the face—literally, because I fell asleep trying to read it.

Maybe Celeste is right, and this is just a mistake. What the hell do I know about romance? Two days ago, a man held my hand for the first time in five years, and I still haven't recovered from it.

"Hey." I gently nudge Sherlock with my foot. "Wanna listen to the podcast? The episode aired last night."

He opens one eye.

I tap on the app and press play.

Welcome to Murders & Manuscripts, *the podcast where we delve into the darkest corners of crime fiction. I'm your host, Scarlett Moore, and today we're unraveling the chilling tale of* The Widow's Veil *by Anders Peterson, a story that blurs the line between love and madness.*

   Our victim is Elizabeth, a wealthy widow known for her philanthropy and grace, who is discovered in her grand, decaying manor. She's dressed in her wedding gown and seated at a long-forgotten dinner table set for two. The scene is haunting: Elizabeth's veil is torn, her face pale, and her hand severed. Can you guess the killer's weapon of choice?

I glance at Sherlock, whose focus is on licking his puffy black tail. "Spoiler alert: it's a *machete*."

Dozens of wilted roses and a collection of love letters surround her, each more desperate and delusional than the last. Now the Blackmoor police will have to find out who would stop at nothing to claim Elizabeth forever.

Sherlock's eyes are almost closed, and with a cluck of my tongue, I focus on my voice coming out of the speakerphone, but the noise of a car speeding, then someone shouting, has me pressing the pause button. I approach my door, spotting Mrs. Prattle outside, grumbling about something.

"Mrs. Brattle?" I call as I open the door. Her gaze meets mine from the sidewalk. "Is everything okay?"

"It's Lauren's damned kid!" she grouses. "One of these days, he'll run one of us over, you'll see."

I have no idea who Lauren's kid is, but Mrs. Prattle looks winded, so I walk closer, pointing back at my house. "Would you like to come in for a glass of water?"

"Oh, no, dear." She squints. "I think your cat just walked out the door."

I turn just in time to see Sherlock's tail as he hops off the side of the porch. "He always finds his way back home."

She gives me an unconvinced look.

I should go—I normally avoid the town's gossip queen like the plague, but . . . well, she still looks agitated. And I *guess* she might know something about Rafael that I don't.

Like where he is.

"So, um, anything new in town?"

Her eyes light up at the question. "It's been a scandalous week, Scarlett. Scandalous, I tell you!" She leans in conspiratorially. "You know the Walkers?"

I nod, wondering how I can redirect the conversation to Rafael. "Yep. Sherlock has a crush on their labradoodle."

"Well, rumor has it that Mr. Walker isn't actually the twins' father."

"No way. How did you hear about this?"

"Oh, I have my ways." She scans the rows of pristine houses and flower beds basking under the bright suburban sun as if they'll spill more tea about the town's latest drama. "And the Morgans— apparently, the man of the house officially moved out."

"Steve Morgan?" I ask, lips drifting open. "As in Celeste's hus- band?"

"Yes, dear. Didn't you hear? The two of them have been having screaming matches for months. The Barneses next door have called the police a couple of times."

I lean against the picket fence around my yard. I definitely con- sider Celeste a friend, but we don't exactly sit down to talk about our issues. Still . . . her husband moved out? I wish she'd said something. "Anything else?" I swear I need to take acting classes, because it feels as if it would be obvious from a mile away that I'm fishing for intel. "Like something about yesterday, or, uh—"

"*Ooh.* You want to know about John Gray's boy, don't you? About the funeral?"

Goddamn it. Busted within ten seconds.

"Oh, right. That was yesterday," I say casually.

"Rafael was a no-show." Her eyes sparkle. "Lupe, from down the road, swears she saw him take off early in the morning, and nobody's seen him since."

I frown, my mind racing. Take off? Like permanently? "Is she sure it was him?"

"With luggage and everything." Mrs. Prattle grips my shoulder. "Careful, Scarlett. You're a good kid. You don't want to be mixed up with men with bad intentions, and that man . . ." She taps her nose. "I can smell trouble from a mile away. Always could."

Shit, shit, shit.

I know there's no point in telling her to keep this to herself; gossip is fair game when Mrs. Prattle is involved. But I can't afford her telling the whole town about us. "It's not like that, Mrs. Brattle."

"Are you—what do you kids call it? Friends with benefits?"

I furiously shake my head. "Mrs. Brattle!"

"Oh, dear. I went through my fair share of men in my day." She pats my shoulder. "Had to stop eventually." With a knowing look, she continues, "Always fell in love with the bad ones."

"Well, nobody's falling in love. I promise."

"Protect this, right here," she says, tapping her finger on my chest before walking away. "See you later, Scarlett!"

"Bye, Mrs. Brattle," I murmur, the touch of her finger on my heart still echoing.

Celeste
How's that episode coming along? It's Friday!
Also, you left your laptop at the office!

I sigh as I come out of the car. I'm so utterly fucked. I've tried to rewrite this stupid episode four times, but I hated every version, and Paige, who's always the first person I send the scripts to, lied through her teeth when she gave me her positive feedback.

I grab my bag, slam the car door shut, and head for the entrance, throwing a look at Rafael's place. Celeste needs the episode, and unless inspiration strikes, I'll lose this opportunity. My boots click against the pavement, the sound almost drowned out by the persistent hum of my thoughts.

Then the blare of sirens snaps me out of my spiral, loud enough to rattle my nerves and bounce off the nearby houses. It starts with one, maybe two, and quickly builds into a chaotic symphony. I freeze on the sidewalk, bag slipping from my shoulder as I glance down the street. It sounds like it's not too far away. My pulse quickens, but curiosity gets the better of me.

I pivot and head toward the commotion, my heart pounding harder with each step.

The parallel street is crowded with neighbors and people clustered on the sidewalk, murmuring. I spot Vanessa near the caution tape, standing straight as an arrow, her blond hair pulled into the usual braid. I wave her over.

"Scarlett," she says, hands raised. "I don't have a lot of details yet."

"Can't blame me for trying, right?"

"Not you, no." She glances around before stepping closer, her tall frame blocking some of the gawkers behind her. "Look, it's another weird one. The victim is Mallory Young, and it happened last night. We're still piecing together the details, but . . ." She hesitates. "She was found seated at a table. And . . . she was dressed in a wedding gown."

A chill runs down my spine, and I feel my stomach twist. "A wedding gown?" The scene from *The Widow's Veil* floods my mind—the bride seated at the table, the haunting setup.

That's last night's episode.

No. No, no, *no*. This can't be happening, can it? Not again, not the night my podcast aired. Once was a coincidence, but two out of two? It means it's not just about the books—it's about *Murders & Manuscripts*. Someone's listening to *my* podcast and enacting the fictional murders *I* discuss. Me.

Her brows knit together. "I know what you're going to say, but—"

"*The Widow's Veil*." Vanessa isn't much of a reader, but she's a supportive friend, and Paige says she always listens to my podcast first thing every Friday. "The episode about it came out last night, Vanessa."

"I know."

"So . . . do you need any more proof? This isn't just someone who's recreating fictional murders. They're finding inspiration in my podcasts."

"Even if that were true, there's nothing—"

"There's *plenty* we can do!" I interrupt. "We can check the list of subscribers or . . . or . . . set up a trap for the killer on the podcast."

She sighs. "A trap like how?"

I scoff, not knowing exactly what to say. But we have to do *something*, right? This is obviously connected to the podcast, and I can't be responsible for another murder. For another victim. What if I'd discussed *Last Day on the Train* instead of *The Widow's Veil*? Would someone else have died instead of Mallory Young?

"Look, we already have enough people playing hero around here," Vanessa says, her voice clipped but not unkind. "Getting the chief to even *listen* to you will be difficult after what else happened."

I swallow my protest. "What else happened?"

Her expression falters, a grimace like she's said too much. Her blue eyes, wide-set and sharp even when worried, scan the street before she leans in. "Uh, nothing. Just Quentin—you know, from The Oak—he's a neighbor of Mallory's. Apparently, he had a run-in with the killer."

My breath catches. My ex Quentin? Rafael's cousin Quentin? No way. "What did he say?"

Vanessa hesitates, her eyes darting around again. "He stabbed the killer—well, in the arm."

"Quentin *stabbed*—" I slap a hand over my mouth.

"Shh!" Vanessa hisses. "Yes. And he's damn lucky the killer didn't react. Or that he didn't stab some poor innocent bystander in the chaos."

"Did Quentin confirm it's a man?" I cut in, my thoughts racing.

"Yes, but the point is—"

"And he didn't see the killer's face?"

"No, he didn't." She grips my shoulder firmly, forcing me to meet her eyes. "*The point is, Scarlett*, the chief won't accept any more interference. Quentin pulling a stunt like that has already set everyone on edge." Her hand lingers on my shoulder. "Let us handle this and stay out of it, seriously."

I slowly nod, but my thoughts are already spinning far beyond this conversation.

Stay out of it. *Right*.

Like that's even possible anymore.

10

the foreshadowing

[trope]

---

a sneaky literary maneuver in which minor details hint at
big, heart-throbbing, or painfully awkward events to come;
in rom-coms, often disguised as offhand remarks about never
dating coworkers, accidental hand touches, or a quirky side
character saying, "you two would make such a cute couple."
best enjoyed when you don't realize it's happening until
the *big reveal*

"So, what do you think?" I ask into the phone, pacing back
toward the couch. It's taken me a while to explain everything
to Celeste.

"I think you sound frantic, and I'd like you to calm—"

"We are way past calming down!" I screech. "Celeste, we *have* to
stop airing the episodes until this is over. We have to. That's the only
solution."

Silence. Then a disbelieving laugh. "Wait, what?"

"I'm serious." My heart hammers as I grip the back of the couch, fingers digging into the fabric. "I can't be responsible for someone else getting killed, okay? This is—"

"Scarlett," she cuts in. "Why don't you relax and take a breath?"

"I can't." My steps quicken as I cross the room and back again. "Just listen. Please. Think about the books, the crimes. Tell me you don't see it."

A pause. "I guess they're somewhat similar?"

"*Somewhat similar?*" I rub the heel of my hand against my temple. "Almost everything's the same! And the episodes aired on the same nights both times. How can you not see it?"

She sighs, and I can practically picture her leaning back in her chair. Maybe it's not that she doesn't see it but that she doesn't *want* to. "Scarlett, there are other podcasts out there covering these books. They're bestsellers, for crying out loud."

"But we're the only one in Willowbrook," I argue. "That can't be by chance."

"Okay. Let's say you're right. You know Booked It is struggling. If we stopped airing *Murders & Manuscripts*, I'd have to fire you and everyone else." She clears her throat. "And besides, shutting down the podcast might make this whole situation worse."

"What do you mean?" My steps falter, and I stop in the middle of the room, staring blankly at the floor.

"If the killer is using the podcast for their murders and we cut them off—" She hesitates. "We don't know how they'll react. They could go on a spree. Or even target . . . us. You, me, our families."

I swallow hard, the thought sending a chill through me. "So we just do nothing?"

"No." Her voice firms up. "I'm going to the police and telling them what's happening."

"But I tried, and they—"

"They'll listen to me, Scarlett."

Right. If anyone can make the police listen, it's her.

"I've got this."

I rub a sore spot on my shoulder. "Okay. Please, make sure they take it seriously."

"I will."

I breathe out, feeling like I've lost a hundred pounds off my shoulders already. Celeste being on my side is the closest thing to a parent watching over me that I have left, and I hadn't even realized how much I needed that today.

"Thank you," I say, before Mrs. Prattle's gossip comes back to me. Celeste should be able to count on me the same way I count on her, shouldn't she?

"And hey, Celeste, if you . . . if you ever want to talk about anything—not just work but everything else—you can. You know that, right?"

She sighs. "Oh, boy. What did you hear?"

"Nothing," I rush out, hoping it sounds convincing enough. "I just . . . I'm always depending on you. I want you to know you can count on me, too."

"That's sweet, Scarlett. Thank you."

"You're welcome." I bite my lip, giving her a moment to talk. When she says nothing, I venture, "So . . . everything good with you? Steve? The kids?"

"Everything's great, sweetie. Lara is still at UConn, Chris

graduates from high school next year. And Steve always asks about you."

I smile, though it's a sad little grin. I'll respect her right to privacy and won't call her out on her lie, but I wish she felt free to discuss all of this with me.

"I'll head to the police station now. Okay? I'll talk to you soon."

The line clicks off, and I let my phone fall onto the couch. For a moment, I just stand there, staring at nothing, my chest tight. Then, with a shaky breath, I turn and head for the bathroom.

A shower. That's what I need to get rid of this adrenaline. A long shower until it doesn't feel like I'm the reason these murders are happening. Like these people's blood is on my hands.

I strip off my clothes, each layer feeling heavier than the last as it falls to the floor. I step into the shower, and though the warm water hits me like a release, I feel as tense as ever, my muscles knotted tight. I press my palms against the cool tile and let the water fill my ears with a rushing sound that drowns out the churning in my mind.

I go over Celeste's words, trying to calm myself, trying to find some thread of logic to cling to. But the what-ifs swirl around me, thickening the air until it feels hard to breathe. What if the police don't believe her? What if this person—whoever they are—hurts someone else? Or comes after us?

The water turns from comforting warmth to a too-hot sting on my shoulders, but I can't bring myself to move. My stomach twists, every beat of my heart a pulse of panic.

Then I hear the doorbell.

"Fuck." I step out of the shower at record speed. "Coming!" I call, though I can't be sure they hear me, and once I have my usual yellow towel wrapped around me, I head down the stairs.

I nearly face-plant on the carpet before I open the door, peep-hole be damned, and freeze on the spot as my eyes land on Rafael's crookedly charming smile. My heart does an odd little flip.

Rafael's back. And he's at my door.

I smooth my wet hair, trying to mask the flurry of emotions swirling inside me. "You're here," I say. My gaze sweeps over him, taking in the loose white button-down shirt, sleeves bunched up enough to reveal his forearms, and the leather jacket swung over one shoulder. Sherlock is dangling from his arm, legs flailing as he tries to escape Rafael's hold. "Is that my cat?"

He steps forward, carefully placing Sherlock on the ground, who immediately trots over to me, tail flicking in irritation. "I found him snooping on my porch."

"Rooo," Sherlock protests, his eyes narrowing as if he's trying to defend his honor.

"Fun fact: he hates me," Rafael says with a lopsided grin. "But I *swear* he was making that noise before I got him," he adds, raising his hands in mock surrender.

My heart still races. "No, he's—that's how he meows." I glance at him again, struggling to believe he's standing at my door. "You're back."

He lifts a takeout bag. "And I got Chinese."

Of course he did. I watch him warily. "Did you get wontons?"

"What kind of barbarian shows up at a woman's house with Chinese food and no wontons?"

"Come in." I open the door wider, and his eyes flick down my body, taking in the sight of my towel. Though men have looked at me with desire before, the way his eyes instantly darken feels completely different. It feels . . . primal. Instinctual. Inevitable.

It shoots straight into my belly, warmth pooling at my core.

"How's it going?" I ask, but he doesn't seem to hear me, eyes still on the towel. "Rafael?" I call, fighting the instinct to clench my legs.

"Uh, wh-what?" he stammers, and I bite back a smirk. "Caught me looking, didn't you?"

My cheeks heat. "Uh-huh."

"Can you blame me?" He points up and down at me. "That is one *stunning* towel."

"Oh, yeah. Seventy percent cotton." I let him in, then follow him to the kitchen and lean against the counter as he unpacks the food. He names each dish as he uncovers it, and I can't help noticing the faint shadows under his eyes and the stiffness in his posture.

I wonder if he's okay—really okay. I know he skipped his dad's funeral, but where has he been? He looks tired. Maybe he needs to talk.

"Everything looks amazing," I say, breaking the silence as I take a seat.

"Yeah." He lets the kitchen towel flop onto the island, sitting down on the stool next to me. "It's also forty-eight hours late."

Meeting his apologetic gaze, I bite into a spring roll. So much has happened today that this seems almost silly to discuss. "We're diving in headfirst, huh?"

"I hear that's what people in mature relationships do. You know, communication and all that."

"Oh, I'm pretty sure people in mature relationships don't blow each other off."

When he frowns, I bump my shoulder against his.

"I didn't blow you off. In fact—" He digs into his back pocket and takes his phone out. "Can you just give me your number?"

I grab a wonton. "That depends. What happened?"

He sets the phone back down. "Nothing. I mean, just a work emergency. I would have texted you, but—"

"What emergency?"

He watches me as I chew, biting his lip.

"I thought mature relationships were based on communication."

He leans closer, gaze dipping to my lips. "So you admit we're in a relationship, huh?"

I fight a giggle. "That's some big talk from someone who doesn't even have my number."

He pushes the phone closer. "My boss sent me four hours away on an assignment. I hated every second, and I thought about you the whole time." He exhales. "Now, *please*, give me your number, Scarlett Moore."

"Hmm." When it looks like he can't take it anymore, I grab the phone. "Fine. But don't abuse it."

"Of course not. Just some good ol' sexting." He pops half a spring roll into his mouth and brings a hand to his chest. "Cross my heart."

Once I've tapped my number in, I give it back. I see his fingers moving on the screen, and after a moment, my phone lights up beside me.

I pick it up and read:

Rafael
What are you wearing under that stunning towel?

"Funny," I playfully scold.

His shoulder bumps against mine. "About as funny as keeping me on my toes all the time."

I shift on the stool, inching away from him. "Oh, I can stop immediately if you don't like it."

"No, I like it." He pulls me closer by my arm, then takes a forkful of noodles and shoves it into his mouth. "I'm just not sure I like how much *you* like it."

I watch him chew. The white shirt hangs open just enough to show a hint of his collarbone and the line of his throat when he swallows. His hair is as messy as ever, like he's been running a hand through it all night. It makes my stomach twist. "I *adore* it, actually."

He licks his lips, glistening with the noodles' oil. "There's some serious imbalance here. But you'll see, one day, really soon, you'll like me about half as much as I like you. And that day . . ." He huffs before he serves food onto my plate. "That day will be exactly like today, except I'll sleep better."

"Losing sleep over me, are you, Gray?"

"Hmm." He nods firmly. "Not nearly as good as dreaming about you, Freckles."

With a sense of contented giddiness coursing through me, I dig into my food. Very inconvenient, isn't it? How just having him around would make everything feel . . . less daunting. I've been so worried over the fact that he just vanished that I haven't let myself feel sad. Now it's hitting me all at once that I've truly missed him. That I barely know him, but having him in my life fills me with a new type of energy I refuse to renounce.

It's dangerous, and the hairs on my arms rise at the realization, but I can't help it, and maybe I don't want to, either. Maybe I want to like him half as much as he likes me.

"Heard about last night?" he asks, pointing his chopsticks at the window.

I immediately tense. There's no part of me that wants to discuss this murder stuff with Rafael. Celeste knows about the situation, and she'll go to the police, so there's nothing else I can do for now. If I told him my theory and he didn't believe me, that'd hurt more than I'd like to admit. "Yeah. Another murder."

"Second in a week. Are you worried? 'Cause I can hang around."

"I'm not. I mean, maybe a little." I pick at the noodles on my plate. "They're weird crimes, aren't they?"

"Definitely."

I fidget with the chopsticks, trying to act casual. "So what do you think is happening?"

"I'm not sure, but I think you're about to tell me."

I glance away. "No, I don't know."

"Really?"

He *so* knows I'm lying. "Really."

"All right." Looking past me, he stands, then walks to the kitchen counter where I abandoned my book earlier today. "Here. Part one of my extensive apology for my disappearance."

"My own book?" I bring it to my chest and bat my lashes. "Why, thank you."

"Dinner reading." He mock-zips his lips. "Pretend I'm not even here."

"What's part two of your extensive apology?"

He hums, as if trying to speak even though his lips are glued together. With a shrug, he resumes eating again.

"You're such an idiot," I whisper under my breath. I turn around and hand him the remote, and once he accepts it, I open up the book.

I'm completely lost in a sequence of enemies-to-lovers banter when Rafael breaks through my concentration. I look up, wondering if it's the first time he's tried to call my name, and he lets out an exaggerated sigh of relief.

"Gee, Freckles. I thought you'd gone into some sort of coma."

I grin. "Sorry. I dissociate from reality the way only a reader can."

He watches me, amused. "So, did they? Have sex?"

"Excuse me?"

"You said, 'They're going to have sex.'"

I look down at my book, then back up at him. Did I say that out loud? "Oh. Michael and Franklin got a room, but there's been a booking issue, and—"

"They have to sleep in the same bed."

I nod. "But Michael has a big presentation tomorrow, so—"

"Franklin said he'll take the floor?" He studies the cover. "I bet Michael answered that they're adults—they can share a bed without making it weird. Turns out they couldn't."

"Did you read this?"

With a chuckle, he shakes his head. "You seem invested. Are my eyes betraying me, or is Scarlett Moore enjoying a romance book?"

"I wouldn't alert the authorities just yet." It's certainly better than my first attempt but a far cry from entertaining. "I was exhausted from trying to rewrite the episode for *Love on the Second Floor*, so I'm giving this romance thing one last shot."

I drop the book onto the table.

"I actually might have something to help with that." He stands and walks to where he left his jacket. "I wasn't kidding when I said I missed you. And since I had no way of contacting you, I did the next best thing." Noticing my confused expression, he insists, "I read the book."

"*The Love Alibi*?" I ask, thinking of the romance he bought at the store. "Did you like it?"

"I did," he says. "Parts of it reminded me of you."

Oh my God, this is giving me a bookish boner. He lets me read while we eat together, he wants to talk about books, and now this?

"Really? Like what?"

He reaches into the pocket of his jacket, his movement careful, almost stiff, then takes out a mangled, wrinkled version of that perfect paperback I saw three days ago. "Why don't you find out yourself?"

I take the book, holding it between my hands like it might fall apart, my joy slightly dampened. "What did you do?" My heart squeezes for the bent pages and cracked spine. This is a murder. A literary murder, and not the good kind.

"I read it."

"With an axe?" I quip.

"Er . . ." He looks down at the book. "Did I read it wrong?"

"Yes," I say, nodding firmly. "You read it wrong."

His expression softens, his eyes boring into mine. He says nothing, but holy shit, the things he says with his silence. He keeps looking at me that way, doesn't he? With this intensity—like there's nothing else worth looking at. It makes my skin prickle, and not only with nerves.

Still, he *murdered* this book.

"You're not supposed to dog-ear the page." I grab my pristine paperback, then show him the bookmark perched between the pages. "See? And look at the spine." I flip the book around. "And don't put it in your pocket. Now it's all bent. You probably sat on it."

I try to flatten the pages, to bend it back to normal. With that goofy smile, you'd think I would have the word *adorable* tattooed on my forehead. But I'm not adorable, I'm horrified.

"Got it?"

"Got it, Freckles. Whatever you say."

I set the book back on my lap, grazing the front page. "So, you want me to read this?"

"Yes, if you want." His hand approaches mine on the cover, but just as I think he might interlace his fingers with mine, he opens the book instead. "I wrote some notes for you."

What?

I peer at the words scribbled over the edges and look up, mouth falling open. "You annotated it for me?"

"Yes. I figured since you love reading, which is an intrinsically lonely activity, maybe this would feel like doing it together." His face scrunches, as if he's doubting himself. "And hey, maybe it'll help with your podcast."

He annotated a book for me.

That is the sexiest, most romantic thing a man could ever do.

Forget about roses, gifts, trips. He wrote his most intimate thoughts for me to read. Thoughts about love, sex. He laid them all out and wants to share those bits of himself with me. It's the most precious gift I've ever received.

"Thank you," I say. "I mean, I don't condone writing in books, but . . ."

"But you'll do it for me?" he asks. "You'll annotate a book you want me to read?"

He can't possibly want that, can he? He *must* be saying what he thinks I want to hear. "You don't have to ask that."

"Scarlett, just assume that if I'm asking, it's because I want it." He holds up a fortune cookie. "Dessert?"

"Sure." I'm full of all the amazing food, but I take it, then nudge the other toward him.

We both unwrap and snap the cookies at the same time. I pull out the tiny slip of paper and read mine out loud: "Don't be trusting of the unexpected."

Shit.

Our eyes meet, a heavy silence where we both know exactly what's unspoken. "Damn. Even the cookie hates me."

I laugh, biting into the cookie. "What does yours say?"

He glances at his paper, and as I pop the rest of the cookie into my mouth, he reads out, "If you're lucky enough, the woman eating dinner with you won't notice her towel is slipping, and it'll just fall open."

I look down, realizing my towel has slipped much lower on my chest than I'm remotely comfortable with. Heat rushes to my face as I yank it back up, my cheeks blazing, while he munches on his cookie. That knowing grin? Hot.

I narrow my eyes in mock annoyance. "Do you ever stop flirting?"

He shakes his head, thoughtful. "Oh, I wouldn't call that flirting."

"What would you call it, then?"

He pauses as if considering. "Wishful thinking."

I try not to laugh. I fail. He does, too, and it's worrying how much I like the sound of it. Warm and deep, and like music to my ears, making every note reverberate through my body and sending shivers down my spine.

"You know what? I'll stop flirting as soon as it doesn't make you smile like that."

Goddamn it.

I force myself to exhale and push past the swirling mix of nerves and . . . something else bubbling under the surface. Standing, I grab a stack of plates to clear the table. We move around the kitchen in sync, quiet except for the clinking of dishes, in a silence that feels charged yet strangely comforting at the same time.

As he reaches for a higher shelf, his shirt shifts, revealing a flash of white gauze taped to his upper right arm. My brow furrows. "What happened there?"

He freezes, just for a second, before tugging his shirt back down in one swift motion. "It's nothing. Just a scratch."

I arch a brow. "A scratch my Sherlock might be responsible for?"

He chuckles, but it's thinner than usual, the humor not quite reaching his eyes. "Sherlock was a perfect cat. If you ignore the hissing. And the kicking."

I snort, shaking my head. Still, something about the way he brushes it off feels *weird*. But before I can press further, he's already turned his attention back to the sink, scrubbing at a plate with unnecessary vigor.

When I go back for the boxes of food, I see the fortune cookie note on his side of the table. Curiosity gets the better of me, and I pick it up, reading the small print: *The love of your life is right in front of your eyes.*

My stomach flips, and the noise of the kitchen fades into the background. When I glance back at him, his focus is on the sink, but there's something in the way his shoulders are set—tense, almost guarded. And just like that, the warmth twists into something harder.

Vanessa's words echo in my mind.

Quentin stabbed the killer in his arm.

I look back at Rafael, brows furrowing.

Just a coincidence, I'm sure.

11

the one-bed-only

[trope]

a diabolical plot device crafted by the romance gods to force
two characters into unbearably close proximity; defined by
awkward negotiations, sleepless nights (for one or both), and an
inevitable wake-up cuddle no one will admit to initiating. often
accompanied by an inexplicably small hotel budget or the phrase
"we're adults, we can handle this." guess what? they can't.

"Shit," Rafael mutters, glancing at the couch where he left his
jacket. He takes a hesitant step toward it, then stops in his
tracks. I sneak a peek at Sherlock sprawled out across it, his tail flicking lazily.

He lets out a slow breath and rubs the back of his neck. "Scarlett,
your cat is giving me *the look*."

I bite back a laugh. "Careful. Wouldn't want him to scratch your
pretty face, now, would we?"

"I just need my keys, Sherlock. Be reasonable," he pleads, but

Sherlock doesn't budge, and instead he stretches languidly, dragging his claws ever so lightly across the black leather of Rafael's jacket.

"You're going to have to bribe him."

"With what? My dignity?"

"You could try sweet-talking him. Maybe he'll find your charm irresistible."

He groans but kneels next to the couch anyway, leveling a serious look at the cat. "Sherlock, you're very cute. Truly, a vision of feline grace. Your fur is so . . . fluffy, and, uh, lustrous? But I really, *really* need my jacket, 'cause, you see, that's where my keys are."

Sherlock narrows his eyes and lets out a low warning chirp before flicking his tail harder against the cushion.

Rafael looks up at me, defeated. "Plan B?"

"Would you like a spare blanket?"

He sits back on his heels. "You know, I used to climb in."

"Climb in?"

"Yeah. Into my place. Through the bathroom window."

I turn, locating the tiny bathroom window in the house next door. Not the porch or even a low-level window—the one barely big enough to fit Sherlock on the upper floor.

He's not suggesting he do that now, is he?

I stand and reach for the jacket, but Sherlock immediately hisses, ears flat, and swipes at my hand with surprising speed. I jerk back, narrowly avoiding his claws as he growls and sprawls even more possessively over the leather like it's his new throne.

"Okay. Wow. Apparently it's his favorite jacket now."

Rafael presses his lips together, trying not to laugh.

"Give him a few minutes. He'll forget about it."

"Sure."

"Or you could . . . stay here," I suggest, walking away from the cat. I can feel myself blush instantly, but the thought of sleeping in this big house alone with a serial killer out there is not exactly *soothing*.

"You got an extra room, right?" He grins, eyes sweeping over me. "I firmly believe anyone over twenty-five shouldn't sleep on a couch."

My parents', not exactly accessible, and my brother's, but I'd never let anyone in there. It's Ethan's room—his bed, his desk. It's waiting for *him*.

"Uh, not really." Thoughts running back to the book, I grimace. I can practically hear Paige's singsong *You live in a romance book*. "But we could . . . share the bed." My heart picks up speed, but I keep my tone casual. "For sleeping only. Since, you know, we're taking things slow."

He doesn't say a word, watching me with the face of someone who just found the pot of gold at the end of a rainbow.

"It's just a bed."

"No, it's not that." He smiles widely. "This is the first time you acknowledge *we're* taking things slow. That we're *doing* something."

Oh. Well, we are. I'm not sure *what* we're doing, but something's definitely happening between us. "So will you stay?"

"I shouldn't. I don't want you to think this was a ploy to—"

"I guess I *am* a little on edge," I insist, looking out the window. "And I'd feel better if you stayed."

He tilts his head. "Well, since you're being so honest . . ." Teeth pinching his bottom lip, he holds his keys up.

"*Seriously?*" I squeak.

"I didn't think you'd admit you were worried." He laughs, stepping closer. "Can I stay over?"

I scowl. "You can have the couch."

"I don't think so. But I promise no cuddling of any kind will take place—not human-on-human cuddling, anyway. I'm a sound sleeper, and I don't mind the light on, so you can read as late as you like." He snaps his fingers. "We'll use Sherlock as a wall. Huh? What do you think?"

This guy, I swear.

How annoying that I'd like the scent of his aftershave on my pillow.

"There's some of my dad's clothes in the laundry," I say, walking past him. "I've been planning to donate them, so I was washing them. You'll find something that fits."

"Sure you don't mind?"

"All yours."

"All right. I'll see you upstairs in a minute."

I turn and head up the stairs, quickly followed by Sherlock, who, leather jacket long forgotten, watches me like he's waiting for an explanation.

"Don't give me that look." I sigh, collapsing onto the bed beside him.

Suddenly, spending the night together feels like the most intimate, nerve-racking thing in the world, and my mind spins with everything I haven't considered. What if I roll over and accidentally brush against him? What if my hair ends up all over his face? What if I snore?

Oh God, what if *he* snores? Do I even know how to sleep next to someone else? I'm used to stretching out with Sherlock curled somewhere around my feet, his snooty little huffs the only sound I ever need to worry about.

Just thinking about lying there in the dark, trying to settle down and relax with Rafael right next to me—*relax* being the key word here—it's almost laughable.

Besides, do I want him to see me in my regular mismatched pajamas? The ones I don't care about getting cat hair on, the ones that are just a soft oversize T-shirt with that faded print of a cartoon llama and sweats with a hole at the hem?

Should I take out the sexy ones Paige got me for my birthday a few years back?

I open the drawer, debating. I think there's still a tag on them, and putting them on would probably send the wrong message, wouldn't it? That this isn't "just sleep," at least not to me.

I settle on my regular pajamas as if I'm gearing up for a battle of wills—with myself. This is fine. It's just a bed. I tug at my faded llama T-shirt, eyeing the poor cartoon creature as though it's offering me courage. Right. The llama stays.

There's a knock at the door, and before I can talk myself out of it, I call, "Come in."

Rafael steps inside. I recognize the gray T-shirt from the pile, and it's slightly loose on him, the sleeves hugging his upper arms while the rest drapes down over his shoulders. He's traded his jeans for a pair of black athletic shorts that hang low on his hips, revealing the sharp cut of his thick thighs. Ink curls up his leg and disappears under the fabric: a skeletal hand holding a bouquet of roses on one leg, a minimalist hummingbird mid-flight on the other leg, and a band of barbed wire wrapping around just above his knee among *many* other tattoos. He looks like some model from a magazine shoot titled "The Bad-Boy Pajamas."

His gaze moves down to my shirt and the little llama, and to my relief, he seems more charmed than judgmental.

"You have thigh tattoos," I mumble, dazed.

"Uh-huh." He lifts his shorts, showing me more ink. On one thigh, there's a matchbook, a single flame rising from the torn edge. On the other, there's a half-finished chessboard disappearing into negative space, and near the hem, barely visible, there's a tally of five slashes inked onto the inside of his thigh. "Chest too," he says, voice low and smug. Then, with a cocky tilt of his mouth, "Like 'em?"

Oh, I *like* them. His body looks like a canvas painted with his favorite art. And those thick, muscular thighs . . . Jesus. Maybe I should have worn my sexy pajamas.

"The broccoli T-shirt," I blurt out.

"Huh?"

I point at the T-shirt he's wearing, hoping I'm not as flushed as I feel. "My dad, he . . . he used to wear that when I was a kid. My mom had one, too, and they'd put them on every time Ethan refused to eat his veggies, and they'd do this stupid broccoli dance." I shake my head at the memory of my mom and dad wiggling their arms in the weirdest performance. "We ended up eating our vegetables just to make them stop."

He pinches the big head of broccoli on the front of his T-shirt. "Should I—"

"No, you don't need to change."

"I was going to ask if I should dance, actually."

"Rooo," Sherlock interjects from the bed, his little growl effectively cutting through our conversation. He sits upright, watching Rafael with narrowed, accusing eyes.

"Oh, hey, Sherlock." Rafael extends his hand toward him cautiously, palm open. "Guess we've got to win each other over, huh?"

Sherlock edges forward, sniffing Rafael's hand with all the suspicion of a tiny security guard. He finally deigns to tap his hand with a dismissive paw, and when the nails make Rafael flinch, I warn, "Sherlock, claws in, or you're getting the boot."

"It's okay," Rafael says, chuckling as he rubs his hand. "I understand."

I arch a brow. "Yeah? You're territorial, too?"

He tilts his head, giving me a slow once-over that sends a shiver through me right down to my mismatched pajama bottoms. "Oh, you bet."

Heat creeps into my cheeks, and I quickly gesture to the bed, trying to brush his comment off. "So, um, which side do you usually sleep on?"

"Your bed, your rules," he replies with an easy shrug.

"I sleep in the middle."

He huffs out a deep, low chuckle. "Me too. Maybe I'll meet you there."

Always. So. Smooth.

I climb onto the right side of the bed, trying to keep my movements casual, though every nerve feels like it's conspiring against me. I turn the light off, and then the mattress dips as Rafael settles on the left side, shifting just enough to remind me he's right there—so close that his warmth radiates through the sheets.

Here we are. Not too weird, right?

I take a slow breath, staring up at the dark ceiling as I press my hands against my sides, willing my body to behave. But my skin is too aware of the space between us, of the way I can hear his slow, steady breathing, which only seems to amplify my own.

I shift slightly, feigning comfort, but my heartbeat picks up, and I squeeze my eyes shut, trying to force myself into relaxation. *Just sleep.*

"Was this your parents' bedroom?"

I flinch, twisting to look in his direction. "Uh, no. This has always been mine. My parents' room is now the guest bedroom. Or will be—there are only boxes in there." I turn on my back. "It'd be weird to sleep in their bedroom, wouldn't it?"

"I don't think so. I just keep picturing your dad giving me the stink eye."

"For sleeping here?"

"For missing out on so much. And not being there for you when he and your mom passed."

That's ridiculous. It's not like my dad ever entrusted him to me or anything. We've never been friends. "You know, Paige says I can't hold a grudge."

"Is that true?"

"It is. I get it from Dad." I exhale. "So I highly doubt that he'd ever have been able to stay mad at you. Or anyone."

"Hmm." Though I can't tell for sure, it sounds like he's smiling. "Who was your first kiss with?"

I inhale sharply, then exhale. Is that what he meant when he said he missed out? "Uh, Jacob Gallagher."

"Was it any good?"

"Not really. His mouth tasted like hot dog, and he lodged his tongue in my throat. It was kind of gross."

He laughs, the cover moving with him.

"And you?"

"Lily Goodwin. She asked me if I'd ever kissed anyone, because she wanted me to show her how to, and I lied. It was great—for me, at least. She'd probably describe it similarly to how you just did."

Lily Goodwin? I groan. "Damn it. I get my haircuts at her salon."

"And?" He snickers. "You can't possibly be jealous, can you?"

"*No*," I say defensively. But I'll definitely think about it every time I see her now.

"Yikes. I think I just cost her a client."

"You're seriously underestimating the loyalty of a woman to her hairdresser."

There's a beat of silence. Then, "What about prom?"

"Prom." He'd left just a few months before. "My parents had just died, so . . . I didn't go."

"Birthdays? Any memorable ones?"

"All of them, I guess. My mom used to make pancakes with ridiculous toppings—said it made the day 'taste adventurous.' After breakfast, a treasure hunt around the house. Pizza for dinner. It was a whole thing."

"Is that why you don't enjoy celebrating now?"

The familiar prickle hits the backs of my eyes. "It's hard to want a birthday when the people who made it magical aren't around anymore." I shove the thought away and breathe out. "Your turn. How was graduation?"

"Auditorium was packed, the choir sang off-key, and I couldn't keep that cap on for the life of me."

"I bet your dad was proud."

"I guess." He folds an arm behind his head. "He never said."

Never? Teachers had bets on whether he'd even graduate. After everything, how could his dad have said nothing? "Well, I was. I remember thinking you'd do incredible things."

He shifts a little closer, just enough for his pillow to brush mine. I face him, hands resting between us. His fingers graze mine, tracing slow circles and making my skin tingle.

He says softly, "The only incredible thing I want to do is be good."

"Good?"

He pauses. "We're just a blip in history, right? Here, then gone. I'd be happy if my life was unremarkable, except for the good I left behind."

"That's all you want?"

"Yep." His smile softens. "Well, that and you."

A flutter spins in my stomach. "I . . ." I steady myself. "I want a lot from life."

"Let's hear it."

"I want kids. To travel. Maybe a summer house in the woods. And a home library—with a ladder that rolls."

"Like in *Beauty and the Beast*?"

"Yes." I focus on the blanket. "A whole wall of books and a ladder to swing from."

"Can I be the Beast?"

I raise an eyebrow. "Only if you provide the library. And the castle."

He chuckles, fingers slipping fully between mine. "Guess I'd better get to work."

Sherlock stirs at our feet. "Rooo," he protests, casting us a withering look from his blanket nest.

"Shit. Did your cat just tell us to shut up?"

"Afraid so." I press a finger to my lips, stifling a laugh.

Rafael looks solemnly at him. "Sorry, Sherlock. We'll keep it down."

"Rooo . . ." The cat sighs and tucks his head back under the blanket.

Rafael gives my hand a small squeeze, and the thrill curls deeper. After a pause, he asks, "First concert?"

I look up at the ceiling, smiling as the memory rushes in. "Okay," I say, launching into the story.

———————

I haven't closed an eye all night, which is both not Rafael's fault and one hundred percent because of him. How could I sleep when there was this entire book he annotated for me? So when Sherlock admonished us for the second time and we decided to go to sleep, I waited for his breathing to become deep and even, then grabbed the book and read the whole thing.

I set *The Love Alibi* on my chest, looking over at him.

Turns out, the key to my heart is book annotations, because the son of a bitch has won me over. I mean, how could he not have?

I open the book to a random page and read: "See how he can't help but notice all the minor details about her, even the ones she doesn't think matter? I keep cataloging all the little things you do— like the way your eyes light up when you read a book you enjoy. It's my favorite thing to watch."

Biting my lip, I turn the page. I almost feel the need to annotate his annotations. Write little thoughts about his little thoughts, because they're a window into his soul. He wrote: "You do this, too. You fidget with your sleeves. Is it because I make you nervous, Freckles?"

Always so flirty.

"Hold the fuck up. Is this a thing? If men who cook are sexy, how about men who always pay for takeout?"

I bite my lip and flip again: "Nah. Unless the plot twist here is that he's from another planet, there's no way his junk can be compared to a soda can."

And then the bit about the main character seeing his love interest and feeling this sense of peace he's never experienced before. This longing and deep sense of satisfaction at the same time. He highlighted the whole thing and wrote, "Couldn't have said it better."

I could read every single annotation a million times over.

Sherlock, at my feet, begins stirring. I check the time on my phone, then meet his gaze. "Don't," I whisper, but he steps forward regardless. "Sherlock, do *not*."

"Rooo."

Fuck! I set the book on the floor as he steps even closer, knowing that no matter how much of a deep sleeper Rafael is, Sherlock *will* wake him up.

"Rooo!"

Rafael moves, still half asleep, and I close my eyes, settling against the pillow.

"Roooooo!"

I feel Rafael move again, and this time, he clears his throat. "Shh. Just five more minutes."

"Rooo."

"Come on, Sherlock. Let her sleep."

"Rooo!"

"Shh. Goddamn it. Where's your food?"

I smile into the pillow, then turn to the side, eyes half closed as if he just woke me up, too. "I can go," I murmur.

"No, no. Stay in bed." His hand brushes my hair away from my face. "Come on, Sherlock."

"Kitchen cabinet," I call out as I feel the mattress dip beneath me. The familiar patter of Sherlock's paws on the wooden floor follows, and then Rafael's muffled voice from the kitchen. I can't catch the words, but the tone sounds like they're having a full conversation. It's *so* cute.

Damn cat. I almost got caught because of him.

Moments later, I hear footsteps returning. Rafael climbs back into bed, his body shifting the mattress as he settles in behind me. "Does he always get hungry at five a.m.?"

"Afraid so."

"Hmm." He's so close to me, I can feel his breath on the back of my neck. "Did you like the book?"

My eyes bulge out. "Wh-what?"

His deep chuckle vibrates against my ear. "The sleepy voice was convincing. Unnecessary, but a great job."

I scrunch my nose, cringing. What the hell did I do that for? It's not like he cares that I've been awake all night reading. "I have no idea what you're talking about."

He laughs again, pulling me back against him. His body is warm on mine, the weight of his arm draped over my waist and his chest pressing lightly into my back, rising and falling with each breath. His legs tangle with mine, and the scratch of his stubble grazes the back of my head as he shifts slightly. "Is this okay?"

"Hmm?"

"I know I said no cuddling, but . . . I think we can both agree I'm not a great rule follower."

"It's fine," I whisper. More than fine, actually. It feels like every look my way, every word he says, is a cuddle, and this is just the natural evolution of that. It feels incredibly *right*.

"Get some sleep now."

I scoot back a little, testing the feeling of his body against mine, and my breath catches as I notice the unmistakable hardness pressing against my ass.

Holy shit. He's *hard*. And thick—extraordinarily so.

A tingling warmth spreads through me, and I can't help but mentally measure it against a soda can. Shooing the thought away, I try to stay still, not wanting to draw attention to it, but almost involuntarily, I shift my hips slightly.

His sharp intake of breath tells me he's noticed. His fingers flex against my stomach, but he says nothing. There's no way I'm falling asleep after this, though, and I lie still, slowly realizing that we're entangled, squeezed together intimately. And now his erection is pressed against me.

I shift my hips again, more deliberately this time.

A low groan escapes his throat, barely audible but enough to make goose bumps take over my body. "What are you doing?"

I swallow hard, my heart racing. "Nothing. Just getting comfortable." But I'm not. I'm testing the waters, seeing how far I can push this before one of us breaks.

His hand slides lower, fingers dipping just beneath the waistband of my shorts. "Still okay?" His voice vibrates against my neck, his lips brushing my skin.

I nod, unable to form words as his fingertips trace lazy circles on my hip. My eyes flutter closed, and I arch back against him again, craving more contact.

"Scarlett," he huffs. "You're making it very difficult to be a gentleman right now."

I turn my head slightly, glimpsing his face in the dim morning light. His eyes are dark, intense, fixed on me. "Maybe I don't want you to be a gentleman."

For a moment, we're both perfectly still, suspended in the tension. Then, with agonizing slowness, his hand slides farther down, fingertips tracing lightly over the delicate skin of my inner thigh.

"Rooo!"

We both flinch as Sherlock lands between our legs, like an unwelcome referee in our private game.

"Shit, hey, I just fed you!" Rafael complains as Sherlock swats his foot, his little tail flicking in indignation.

"Sherlock, stop," I scold, but it comes out breathy as laughter bubbles up. I scramble to my knees and shoo him away, then turn back to Rafael, who's cowering on his side of the bed, catching his breath.

"He wasn't *this* feisty when I served him breakfast."

I force myself to stop giggling. "He just wants a cookie."

"A cookie?"

"Dessert," I explain. "Very much like his owner, he believes every meal should end with dessert."

He watches the cat warily as he finally sets his feet on the floor. "All right, then. Let's go get you dessert, Sherlock."

12

the seemingly irrelevant details

[trope]

tiny, random bits of information dropped into a story that seem
so minor you'd forget them faster than an awful movie—until they
become crucial to the entire story's resolution

WILLOWBROOK ROCKED
BY SECOND CHILLING MURDER IN A WEEK

Mallory Young, 32, was found dead seated at a dinner table in
a grotesque tableau. Elements from the crime scene suggest the
woman might have had a stalker, whose identity remains unclear.

"This is bullshit," I murmur, scrolling through the article from
the *Willowbrook Whistle* on my phone. Mallory Young didn't
have a stalker. This crime wasn't about her at all. My podcast is at the
center, and Mallory just happened to be the target.

"Earth calling Scarlett!"

I flinch, turning to Paige, who sits at the table with our order. "Is everything okay? You look like you haven't slept."

"I haven't," I say distractedly as Vanessa joins us. The two of them insisted I meet them here at The Oak for lunch, but I honestly have no time for this. A second murder that follows the script of my episodes wipes any doubt away. Someone's listening to my podcast and using it to commit their crimes. Though since we're here . . . "What did Quentin say the killer looked like?"

Paige drops her head back, and Vanessa hesitates as she pulls her blond braid over one shoulder.

"Same old. Big guy, dark jacket, green cap."

"What about Celeste? Did the chief say anything about their meeting?"

Vanessa's brow scrunches. "What meeting?"

"She went to the station yesterday."

She shakes her head. "Nothing. But to be fair, we were pretty busy. You know, because of the victim whose hand was severed with a *machete*."

There's tightness around her eyes and the faint lines of exhaustion on her forehead. I can't even imagine what it's like to deal with something so gruesome, to see the worst humanity has to offer and still keep going.

Loud laughter bursts from the bar, drawing all our eyes. A cluster of customers is gathered around Quentin, who is gesturing wildly with his hands from behind the counter as his voice carries over the clinking of glasses.

"And I said, 'Not today, buddy!'" he declares, miming a stab with his invisible weapon. The group erupts into another round of laughter and cheers.

Paige snorts. "Will he ever tire of telling that story?"

"Nope. And each time, he adds a little more flair," Vanessa says. "What's he up to now? Three stabs and a headlock?"

"Four stabs and a roundhouse kick," I correct without missing a beat.

"Okay, no more murder talk, please?" Paige asks, hands joined in mock prayer.

"Fine, fine."

"Great! Tell me about Rafael. I can't believe you didn't text me the *second* he showed up."

I take a sip of water. "We spent every moment together until I left this morning."

She swats me away, then stops, eyes narrowing. "You mean last night?"

After a moment of hesitation, I say, "Yes, but—"

Paige screeches loudly enough to give me—and probably every single patron in here—a jump scare. "Oh my *God*, tell me you fucked his brains out."

"Jesus, Paige—"

"How was it? I mean, I know his dick is massive, but—"

"Paige!"

"Just tell me!"

I throw a sheepish glance around me. Quentin isn't around anymore, thankfully, but I don't want one of the waiters to tell him about this. I don't care what Rafael says, I still think it's weird. "We didn't have sex. Wait—what do you mean you know his . . . How do you know that?"

When she shrugs, I have my answer. Someone who saw it must have told her. Probably more than *one* someone, too, knowing Rafael.

"Anyway. He slept over because . . . I guess I was a little scared about being in the house alone after what happened to Mallory."

Vanessa's shoulders dip. "Oh, Scarlett. You should have called me. I'm a cop. I can protect you."

"*Hello?*" Paige waves an obnoxious hand in front of her face. "You were protecting *me*, remember? And besides, she doesn't need you. She has a hunky bad boy sleeping in her bed."

She chuckles even before finishing the sentence, and I can't help but join in. He really is a hunky bad boy.

"*God*, Paige," Vanessa says as she stands, her chair scraping against the floor. "Can you ever not be *on*? Give people a break?" With silence falling around us like cold snow, she steps back. "My shift's about to start. I'll see you later. Bye, Scarlett."

"Y-yeah. Bye, Vanessa."

Hurt flashes across Paige's face as she watches her walk away. Once the door closes, my eyes are on her. "What the hell was that?"

She shrugs, fidgeting with a lock of auburn hair. "Uh, nothing. We're wound up a little tight. You know, house hunting."

Right. I can imagine that'd be stressful, especially with someone like Paige, who never settles for anything less than what she wants. "Still, she shouldn't say stuff like that." I take her hand on the table. "You're never too much, you hear me?"

"Oh, I *am* sometimes."

"No, you're not. You're the exact right amount of yourself, and if someone doesn't see that, then *they* are not enough."

She squeezes my hand. "Thank you. Now, please, tell me about your night. I could use a chance to live vicariously through you."

I throw myself into a vivid description of last night's events, starting with the annotated book and going all the way to this morning, when he woke me up with soft cuddles to my back at eight a.m., then made me breakfast while I was in the shower.

"Scarlett, I'm *so* happy for you." Her eyes shimmer as if she's holding back tears. "And proud—that, too."

"I even"—I shrug, picking apart a napkin discarded on the table—"wrote an episode this morning."

"For *Passion & Pages*?"

When I nod, Paige squeals. "See? I told you! All you needed was someone to make you experience romance. Longing. Love."

"Whoa," I say, my mind instantly spinning. Can someone be allergic to a concept? "I wouldn't go that far. But I will admit I sat down at my desk this morning, and it just . . . flowed. It's like . . . like seeing romance through his eyes made me understand it better. There was this bit," I say, fiddling with the edge of my sleeve, "where the heroine is too afraid to tell the hero she loves him because she thinks she's not enough for him. She convinces herself that leaving is the right thing to do, because she's protecting him, right? But then he shows up at the train station, and he doesn't convince her to stay. He just tells her he'll be waiting if she ever comes back."

Paige's eyes soften, and she clasps her hands together dramatically. "The 'run to the airport.' A classic."

"Or a cliché. Anyway, I didn't get it at first. Why would anyone wait for someone who's walking away? But Rafael wrote something about how love is about understanding someone's fears and giving them the space to grow. And for the first time, it just . . . clicked."

"Is that how he makes you feel?" Paige asks.

"Sometimes," I admit. "And other times, like last night, he pushes me out of my comfort zone—always just enough to make me feel brave, not overwhelmed."

Paige sighs dramatically, like she's stepped right out of a Jane Austen novel. "Scarlett Moore, you're turning into a romantic. Next thing you know, you'll be crying at wedding vows."

I roll my eyes, but a small, genuine smile tugs at my lips. "Let's wait for Celeste's feedback before you plan my initiation ceremony."

"She's going to love it," Paige says, holding her hand up to ask for the check. "Because you did."

I push open the door of The Oak as Paige waves goodbye, then rushes away for the event she's planning this weekend. The midday sun beating down on the pavement is almost blinding after the dim interior. Just as I reach the sidewalk, a familiar voice calls out, "Scarlett!"

I turn to see Quentin leaning against the side of the building, a cigarette dangling from his fingers. His buzz-cut hair sticks up a little at the crown, and his gaze is just as dazed as I remember, brown eyes squinting a bit in the sun.

"Hey," I say, stopping but not stepping closer. Since our breakup, we've politely waved at each other, even asked "How's it going?" a couple of times, but nothing more than that. This town's too small to avoid your exes, but we've kept our distance.

So what's up now?

"How've you been?" he asks, before stubbing the cigarette out against the wall and tossing it into the trash.

I hesitate. "Busy. You know, work, life . . ."

"Still with that podcast of yours?"

"Yeah," I say. "Still there."

He rocks back on his heels. There's a weird tension in the air, which makes me regret not ever discussing our breakup. But he must know why it happened. He saw me back then; there was no space in me for a boyfriend.

"Well, that's cool," he says finally. "You're good at it."

"Thanks." I glance toward the street, ready to escape the awkwardness. "I should—"

"Scarlett, wait," he says quickly, stopping me mid-step.

I turn back, brows raised. "What's up?"

He hesitates, rubbing the back of his neck in that nervous way he always did when he was trying to figure out how to say something.

"Is it true?" he asks, gaze stuck to the ground. "Are you . . . are you seeing Rafael?"

Heat rushes to my face. "I, uh . . ."

"It's just . . ." He looks away, then back at me, his expression unusually serious. "I didn't think he was your type."

I laugh, though it's strained. "How so?"

"I don't know. He's just . . . not like you."

"Like me?" I ask. "What does that mean?"

"Look, I'm not trying to start anything. I just wanted to know if it's true."

I shift uncomfortably. "Rafael and I are . . . spending time together," I say finally.

He nods slowly, like he's turning the concept over in his mind. "Well, be careful."

"Okay," I say, though it comes out more like a question. "I heard about what happened with the killer."

His jaw tightens, and he looks away, exhaling through his nose. "Uh-huh. Not exactly how I planned to spend my night."

"Are you okay?"

"Yeah. I was just walking home from The Oak, late as usual. I saw this guy coming out of Mallory's place. Big dude wearing a green cap. Something about him screamed sketchy, so I hung back to see what he was up to."

"Oh God. And?"

"When I yelled out, he bolted down the alley. I don't know what got into me, but I took off after him, and I caught up a few blocks over," he continues. "He turned around, and I saw he had a pocketknife. I didn't think—I just reacted. We struggled until he dropped it, and I took it myself. Before I knew it, I'd jabbed him in the arm."

I blink at him, stunned. Quentin was never particularly brave.

"I wasn't just going to let him get away without trying to stop him."

"Well, I'm glad you're okay."

"Guess I got lucky." His shoulders relax slightly. "But if you ask me, this guy won't stop. Whoever he is, he's got a plan, and he's not afraid to follow through."

On that, we agree.

Someone walks out of The Oak and calls his name, so I step back. "Well, uh . . ."

"I'll see you around."

"Definitely."

I turn and walk away, and once I reach my car, I slide into the driver's seat, his story replaying in my mind.

I fasten my seat belt and start the engine, but a thought nags at me, persistent and unsettling.

Why would someone who had just murdered a woman in cold blood with a machete attack a potential witness . . . with a *pocketknife*?

13

the almost kiss

[trope]

---

a time-honored rom-com ritual where two characters lean in,
hearts pounding, lips dangerously close—only to be interrupted
by a phone call or an oblivious best friend; carefully designed
to keep audiences screaming

S omeone's in my house.

I freeze with the key inches away from the lock, and my pulse
thunders in my ears, louder than the muffled chatter seeping through
the door. I don't need to be a detective to recognize the low, rumbling tones of two men talking—one voice sharp, almost mocking,
the other deep and even.

Rafael.

Why is Rafael inside my house?

My key scrapes the lock as I turn it, the metallic click cutting
through the silence that falls inside.

The first person I see is Rafael. He's slouched against the foot of the couch, long legs bent, arms resting loosely on his knees. The dim light from the window cuts across the black mesh of his sweater over the lean lines of his torso, and a couple of silver chains shift against the fabric as he turns. Then I notice my brother sitting next to him.

"Ethan?"

His dark blond hair sticks up in uneven tufts, and he looks pale under the bruising around his eye—a purplish smear that still hasn't fully healed. He waves but doesn't take his eyes off the TV, gripping his controller tightly.

Rafael gets to his feet in one fluid push, the oversize sweater slouching off one shoulder slightly before he tugs it back up. "Hey. Welcome home."

I'm so confused.

"Thank you. What"—my eyes move to the game console sitting on my TV bench—"is happening?"

"I used my key," Ethan says simply.

Rafael heads to the kitchen, gesturing for me to follow with a tilt of his ringed fingers. After a moment of hesitation, I do, finding him filling a cup with coffee.

"I promised I'd check on him." He adds two spoonfuls of sugar, then walks to the fridge and grabs the milk. "I did. Then I figured you'd be happy to see him, so I asked if he wanted to play something on my old console." He adds just a touch of milk, then turns around and holds the cup out.

I take it, the warmth seeping into the palms of my hands. "Are you, uh"—what was that line he annotated for me?—"anticipating my needs even before I express them?"

He snickers. "I take it you liked my annotations?"

"Very much. And I wrote an episode for *Passion & Pages*, too."

"You did?" He looks around, as if he's searching for actual paper. "Well, can I read it?"

"No," I blurt out. "I mean, maybe. Once Celeste approves it."

"Which she will."

I smile, grateful for his blind confidence. "Anyway, I need to thank you. For luring Ethan here, but also the book. I know it must have taken you a long time, and it was a really sweet thought."

With his back leaning against the table, he smiles in that same charming, cocky way that always kicks the breath out of my chest. "As I said, I missed you. And I had plenty of free time."

"Weren't you working?"

"Yes. I get a lot of downtime, though."

Downtime, huh? Every time he talks about his job, I feel more uneasy. There must be a reason he's being so evasive about it. "Is it something illegal?"

He tilts his head in a silent question.

"Your job, I mean. You're not a . . . drug lord or a . . . human trafficker. Right?"

He seems to fight a chuckle before he says, "No, I'm not a drug lord. Or a human trafficker."

I feel relieved, though it doesn't last as I realize drugs and trafficking aren't the only occupations I wouldn't get behind. Before I can press any further, a knock at the kitchen door has us turning around.

"Hey," Ethan says, popping his head in. "I can just leave, you know?"

My back immediately stiffens. "What—*no*—why?"

He shrugs. "If the problem is that I'm here."

"Of course that's not the problem. I mean, there's *no* problem."

Except that Rafael is evasive. "I just had a couple of things to discuss with Rafael."

Focusing on him, Ethan points back at the living room. "Are you coming back? I can't remember how to switch weapons."

"L-one. I'll be right there." When Ethan heads back, Rafael squeezes my arm, hand lingering a beat too long. "I'll get out of your hair before dinner so the two of you can talk."

"Maybe you should stay." I throw a glance at the sliver of light coming through the door. "He seems to like you much more than he likes me."

"That's not true."

"Isn't it?" I grimace. "Please stay, okay? It'll help make things less tense. Pizza's on me."

"Well, in that case." He walks out of the kitchen, and I hear the two of them talking about games as I take out my phone.

I have a text from Celeste, and once I read the ominous "Did you do this?" I rush to open the link that follows. It's *Murders & Manuscripts'* subreddit, and it looks like someone just opened a new thread.

> *Did you guys notice?*
>   *I live in Wethersfield, next to Willowbrook, where the show is recorded. I swear I'm not crazy, but . . . Read these news pieces and tell me they're not exactly the plot of the last two books Scarlett discussed. And they happened on the same nights the episodes aired???? What!! Someone please tell me I'm not seeing things.*

I gasp, my heart immediately shooting into a frenzy. There are hundreds of comments already, people talking about how it can't be a coincidence.

It's out there.

And I know Celeste is pissed, but I for one can't help the immediate sense of relief washing over me.

I'm not crazy. I was right.

Celeste
The police won't be happy about this!!

"Well, maybe they should have listened the first time," I mutter. I write back, swearing that I didn't do it, then open the food-delivery app and order two family-size pizzas. Pepperoni was Ethan's favorite back in the day. I hope it still is.

I listen to Rafael and Ethan laughing about whatever Ethan did last in the game. I can't keep hiding out in here, but why do I have this sinking feeling that whatever I do or say will end up with Ethan being more alienated than ever?

I bite my lip and drink a sip of coffee.

I have to join them. *Come on, Scarlett.*

I enter the living room, and Rafael's eyes meet mine. He grins— a strength-infusing expression—like he's telling me I've got this.

"What are you guys playing?" I grab a cushion and settle next to Ethan on the floor.

Rafael hesitates, as if giving my brother space to answer. When he doesn't, Rafael says, "*GTA.* Have you ever played?"

"Uh . . ." I check the screen. "I don't think so."

Ethan scoffs, then hands Rafael the controller with a glare. "I'm gonna grab a smoke."

A smoke? He *smokes?*

"Oh, and we played *GTA* all the time when we were kids," he says, his green eyes glaring at me before he opens the door, then slams it behind him.

My shoulders slump, and heat creeps up my face. Maybe I shouldn't have asked Rafael to stay for this. It's embarrassing enough without an audience.

Did we really play this game? I can't remember it. How can I not remember it?

"Come here." Rafael tugs at my cushion, pulling me closer, then adjusts me between his thighs. Holding the controller in front of me, he shows me the buttons to the right. "This is to run. Jump. Fight."

I cock a brow. "I'm not much of a fighter."

"Okay. Then how about this?" He presses a few buttons until the character in the game hijacks a car. "This is the accelerator. Brakes. Control the direction with this one."

I pout. What's the point? It took less than a minute for Ethan to get pissed off at me.

"You know," Rafael says, chin brushing my shoulder, "if you learn how to play, maybe you can invite him over when I'm not around, too." When I twist around to look at him, he winks. "Huh? Try it out."

"Fine." I grab the controller, then speed up and stop, testing it out. I try again, crashing against the car in front of me until its tail-light shatters. "Shit—sorry."

"Insurance will cover that. Just keep going."

I try again, nervously driving around the other car and entering traffic. "Where am I supposed to go?"

"Wherever you want."

I turn right but end up in a congested intersection. Settling behind a bus, I exhale. "All right. It's not too bad."

"What are you doing?"

"Hmm?"

"Keep going."

I point at the TV. "The light's red."

"You're playing *Grand Theft Auto*, Scarlett."

"The theft has occurred already, *Rafael*. No need to cause another accident."

He grumbles something, and when I look to the side for a second, I find him watching me. "What's that look for?"

"Nothing."

"Really?" I click my tongue. "You stare at me a little too much for *nothing*, Rafael."

"You're right." He tucks some hair behind my ear. "Everything."

"Everything?" I echo, dazed.

"Yes. Everything."

I bite my lip, my gaze drifting from the cool gray of his eyes to the clean line of his nose with that distracting silver hoop, then settling on his mouth. This is dangerous, what I'm feeling—letting it grow when I'm not sure he's being completely honest with me. But every moment with him, every glance, every touch, pulls me further in.

His lips are so close that it feels like they're calling to mine. His breath hitches slightly, and the lightness in his stare dims just enough for me to know. This is it. He's finally going to kiss me.

My heart beats faster as I move in a little more, waiting for him to close the distance, but the door opens, my brother watching us with barely contained disdain. "What's happening?"

We quickly pull apart. "Your sister is embarrassing herself. I don't think she should be allowed to play again."

Ethan snorts. "The pizzas are here."

"Oh. I got it." Rafael stands and walks to the door. I'd argue, because I promised I'd pay, but Ethan comes to sit next to me, and when I hand him the controller, he throws a tight smile my way.

No way I'm leaving now.

"Wanna go rob a bank?"

I'm the cool sister. The cool sister he can play video games with. "Sure."

He turns to the screen. "Cool. Let's rob a bank."

I turn to the screen. *Cool.* He said "Cool."

The soft glow of the TV flickers across the walls, an old sitcom rerun playing quietly in the background and laugh tracks filling the silence. There's a half-empty pizza box on the coffee table and cushions scattered across the carpet. The faint scent of pepperoni mingles with the sharp tang of cola.

I glance at Rafael, sprawled on the couch with his eyes closed, his breathing even. He's been so good, keeping the atmosphere light during dinner, getting my brother to talk about video games, sports, and Formula 1, and somehow involving me in the conversation.

"Why did you say you weren't together?" Ethan asks.

I glance back at him. He's perched on the armchair, one socked foot tucked beneath him, a slice of pizza halfway to his mouth.

"Uh, we weren't when you asked." My gaze flicks back to Rafael's sleeping form.

"But you are now?"

"No, I . . ." I hesitate. "It's complicated, I guess."

"Did you DTR yet?"

"What does that mean?"

"Wow, you really are a hundred years old."

"*Hey.*"

"Define the relationship. Like whether you're in a situationship or dating exclusively or—"

Dating *exclusively*? "Is there another type of dating?"

Ethan laughs, a sharp burst of sound that seems too loud for the quiet room. "So how's it complicated? Either you're boyfriend and girlfriend or you're not."

I glance at Rafael again. His chest rises and falls steadily, his lashes unmoving. "I guess. But I've had . . . difficulties letting people in. Since Mom and Dad."

Ethan chews slowly, his gaze fixed on the TV but clearly not watching. "Oh."

"Did you?" When he just shrugs, I focus on the TV, too. "It's just, after everything, it's been really difficult to get attached."

Ethan finally turns to look at me.

"But Rafael . . ." I glance at him again, sleeping on the couch. "I don't know how he does it—he has this way of sneaking past every wall I've built. Like he sees them, acknowledges them, and then just goes around them. He doesn't push. Doesn't demand. Doesn't come in with bulldozers and demolish them. But somehow, piece by piece, he's tearing them down." I let out a soft laugh, shaking my head. "It's terrifying, honestly. And amazing."

Quiet joy lights up his expression. "Sounds like he's good for you."

"Yeah. Maybe."

There's a beat of silence, then, "People kind of expect you to get over it after a while, don't they?" he says tentatively. "Grief? You get a pass for a few weeks, or months, but then you have to move on. Even if you don't know how to."

I draw my knees to my chest, hugging them tightly. The familiar ache of loss spreads through me, settling like an old, unwelcome friend. "People like teachers? Friends?"

He gestures with his pizza slice. "Everyone."

"Well, for what it's worth, I don't think we'll ever get over it. I guess we've learned to live without them, but some part of us will always be mourning."

His eyes drop to the floor, his head nodding almost imperceptibly.

We've never really talked about this, have we? About Mom and Dad. For a while after their deaths, I didn't speak about them at all. But having this elephant in the room that everyone always tried to tiptoe around was almost worse. At some point, I realized I hadn't talked about them in so long it almost felt as if I was trying to write them out of my life.

"You know," I say, my voice softer, "for the longest time, I couldn't sleep with my phone on. I did at first, but I kept jumping at every notification. I was sure something had happened to you or Paige."

Ethan rubs his face, his shoulders slumping. "I have troubles with . . . cars."

"Really?"

"Yeah." He glances at me briefly before looking away again. "I get anxious. My therapist gave me these exercises—exposure therapy, she calls it. But I still have trouble even sitting in a parked car." He laughs, a hollow sound. "I can take the bus, though. It's weird."

"It's not weird at all. I didn't drive my car for almost two years after they died." His eyebrows lift in surprise. "When I did, I only went up to twenty miles an hour. Got cursed out *loads* of times."

He sits back, chewing on the inside of his cheek. After a moment, he asks, "Are you ever mad at them? Mom and Dad?"

The air freezes between us. I gape at him, unable to respond.

Grabbing another slice of pizza, he grumbles, "Forget about it."

"No, I . . . I get it, Ethan. But they did nothing wrong."

"I know that. I'm not *stupid*," he snaps. "But if it wasn't for their death, everything would be different." His voice rises. "They ruined my life, Scarlett. They died, then you were gone, and I had to move with Grandma and Grandpa, change schools, change friends."

Behind him, Rafael's eyes flicker open.

"I'm not gone. I'm right here," I say. Sherlock jumps off the couch and rushes up the stairs as he feels the rise of tension. "I know we've been apart for the last five years, but—"

"Oh, give me a *fucking* break!" He stands, his finger jabbing toward me like a deadly weapon. "You let them take me. Why didn't you come? If I had to move, why didn't you follow me? I was a kid, for fuck's sake. I needed my sister."

I open my mouth, but no words come out.

What can I say? I can't tell him Grandma and Grandpa didn't want me there. Throwing them under the bus won't fix the relationship between Ethan and me, and he's lost enough already.

"Now they're shipping me off to Virginia. Because *they* want nothing to do with me, and *you* don't want to deal with me. So quit acting like you give a fuck." He swipes at his cheeks angrily. "You're worse than them."

Rafael stands and clears his throat, his hand gripping Ethan's shoulder in a silent warning.

"V-Virginia?" I stammer, rising to my feet.

Without a word, my brother wrenches himself free, a fire burning in his gaze as he storms toward the door.

"What are you talking about?" My vision blurs with tears. "Virginia? Wait, Ethan—"

Rafael's hand finds my arm, holding me back as my brother yanks the door open and walks out.

I want to follow him, to tell him how much I care about him. That I've missed him, and I'm sorry I couldn't do more for him, and I'll do anything to make amends, but the door has slammed shut, and Ethan is gone.

The silence that follows is deafening.

I break free of Rafael's hold and run outside, but Ethan's already biking away.

I blink rapidly, tears streaking my face as my breath comes in ragged gasps. I walk back in and sink down onto the couch, cradling my head in my hands.

Rafael sits beside me, his hand resting on my back.

"No!" I shout, pulling away. "Why did you stop me? You had no right to do that. He feels abandoned, and the least I could do was follow him. But you held me back! Why did you hold me back?"

"Scarlett, breathe—"

"Why did you do that?" I insist, my voice turning even more hysterical.

He watches me, lips parted. "Because I didn't like how angry he was. It . . . it scared me."

I sniffle, my anger deflating as I watch *something* flash through his eyes. Scared? Why was he scared?

"I'm sorry," he says.

I grab a tissue, weakly shaking my head. He was just trying to protect me, as misplaced as his worry was. "It's okay."

"In that case, I'm not actually sorry."

I roll my eyes. I'm not at the stage of joking about this yet. "What . . . what was he talking about? Virginia? I don't understand."

A deep sigh. "I don't know, but we'll find out."

"I need to— I have to . . ." My voice cracks, and I look around helplessly.

His hand rests on my knee and squeezes. "Water?"

"No." I know Ethan's not the same eleven-year-old who was taken away from me, but the thought of him riding his bike alone, at night, when he's that upset . . . I *need* to do something.

"Want to drive around and see if we find him?" Rafael asks.

"Would you really?" I ask, sniffling.

"You call him, I drive," he says with an encouraging smile. "Let's go."

14

the problem

[trope]

the unavoidable complication that stands between the
protagonists and their happily ever after; often manifests as
a sudden breakup, an ex showing up at the worst possible
moment, or an unexpected plot twist

"Okay, Grandma. Sorry to wake you," I say before she hangs up,
as Rafael parks outside The Oak. We drove to Wethersfield
and back, went around in circles for a while, but Ethan was nowhere
to be found. He won't answer his phone, so I had to call our grandparents.

They were *not* pleased.

I follow Rafael inside and ignore the worried look in his eyes. I
need a drink. A strong one that'll put the buzzing in my brain to rest.

"I'll have a whiskey, please," I say once we approach the counter,
trying to sound sure of myself.

Sitting on the stool, I meet the bartender's eyes and realize I'm talking to Quentin, because *of course* I am. Not that I shouldn't have expected it. He started working at The Oak the moment he graduated from high school, and I strongly suspect he's been here every day since.

"Neat? On the rocks?" he asks, his eyes darting to Rafael before they settle on me again.

My mind races, as though the choice actually matters. I read somewhere that whiskey neat is a "serious" choice, didn't I? "Uh . . . neat."

Quentin turns to his cousin again, who's kept silent by my side, observing me. Rafael's gaze lingers a beat too long before he finally turns to Quentin. "Hey. Have any coffee?"

Quentin looks back. "Yeah. Sugar? Milk?"

"Yes, please."

I thought he took his coffee black, but I'm too rattled to inquire. I came here for a whiskey, to take the edge off after that encounter with my brother, and I ended up in the most awkward ex-slash-family gathering I can think of.

I need *less* tension, not more, because I'm *this* close to getting into my car, driving all the way to Wethersfield, and knocking on my grandparents' door with a million questions I'm not sure I want answered tonight.

But they *will* be answered tomorrow.

Quentin turns away to prepare our drinks. The awkwardness lingers, and I think I can take a guess at why.

I glance sideways at Rafael, my mouth dry. "You're sure Quentin doesn't care about us hanging out?"

"Yeah, we talked about it." He shrugs, looking unbothered. "He said he's okay with it."

They *talked* about it?

"How did that conversation go?"

"He came over to the house before the funeral. I asked him if he'd be okay with me asking you out. He said he didn't care." He drums his fingers against the table. "That he was seeing someone."

I raise an eyebrow. "Who?"

He laughs, a soft, teasing sound. "Jealous?"

"Not really. Who is it?"

Rafael shrugs. "He wouldn't say. I just hope she's old enough to drink."

We fall into silence as Quentin sets our drinks down on the counter, then walks away without a word. My whiskey is a rich amber, deceptively smooth-looking, but even from here I can smell the sharp tang of alcohol cutting through the heavier notes of caramel and oak. It stings my eyes, which I guess is promising.

"So, whiskey, huh?" Rafael breaks into my thoughts, looking at me with mild amusement.

"It's the strongest drink I could think of."

"Okay," he says, his tone so casual it almost unnerves me. "Shall we grab a table?"

"Yep." I need to sit down. I've never had whiskey, but I assume I'll be knocked out pretty quickly.

We settle into the closest booth, the surface of my drink rippling faintly under the dim light. I didn't know that *neat* meant undiluted. *It's just whiskey*, I tell myself. *People drink this all the time.*

"Want to order something else?" Rafael's knee presses against mine under the table.

I shake my head, mustering up a defiant look before I lift the glass to my lips. The scent is intense, smoky, and bold, and the moment I take a sip, a burning heat rushes over my tongue, down my throat, and straight to my chest. For a second, I just sit there, feeling it spread through me like wildfire. Then I shiver so hard my spine hurts. "Ugh. Oh my God. It's . . . *disgusting*."

One corner of his lips lifts as he stirs his coffee, the warm, comforting smell wafting around me. I should have gotten one, too. I *love* coffee. Why did I have to go with whiskey?

With one movement, he slides my glass toward himself and puts his cup in front of me.

Wait a second. Is this why he took his coffee with milk and sugar? Because he knew I'd hate whiskey?

"Did your dad tell you about the night I left?"

Any thought of beverages goes out the window as I meet his gaze. I know I have to play it cool, pretend that he hasn't just suddenly acknowledged the elephant in the room that I had figured he'd want to ignore at all costs. "The, uh, the night you left?"

Well done, Scarlett.

"No, he . . . he never said much."

He brings the glass to his lips and takes a small sip—*not* followed by shivers. "You know I did my share of dumb shit when I was younger."

"Dumb shit like driving without a license?" I tease.

"Yeah, well." He rubs his jaw. "My date really wanted to see some crappy indie band two towns away, and I'm nothing if not a gentleman."

I glare. "Go on."

"Right." He traces the edge of his glass with one finger. "I spent most of my life being pissed off because everyone thought my dad was such a good guy when he really wasn't. Angry at him for not being a better father, at everyone else for expecting the worst of me. Furious with myself for delivering every single time."

What he said about wanting to be good comes back to me, and my heart squeezes. Is that what he meant? That he wants to go against everyone's expectations of him being *trouble*?

"Rafael . . ."

"Let me finish." He rubs his jaw for a long moment. "It always felt like an endless loop. My dad couldn't be better, which meant that I didn't know better, which made everyone think I was . . . bad."

He holds my stare.

"Until I realized I found comfort in that. In knowing I could control the narrative, even though I was the villain in it. You know what was really hard? Not falling into the same pattern once I left Willowbrook."

It sounds like he's trying to make a point, but unsure of what it is, I ask, "Why are you telling me this, Gray?"

"Because maybe that's the reason you won't tell your brother why you didn't move in with your grandparents. Because as long as he doesn't know that, you're the evil guy, and you get to keep a . . . barrier between the two of you?"

Of course not. I don't want him to hate his grandparents. That's it. "I text him all the time, Rafael. I call. I *try*. You saw me begging for him to stay tonight, didn't you?"

He holds a hand on mine. "I did. But I also saw him reaching out to his sister and hitting a wall." Smiling softly, he insists, "You're terrified of losing him, so you keep him at a safe distance. Because as long as he blames you, he won't want to be in your life."

I slide my hand away from his, looking down at a spot on the table.

"Fear is irrational, Scarlett."

It makes sense, of course. Everything he said. But it's not what

I'm doing. I love Ethan more than anyone else in the entire world—creating distance between us wouldn't make losing him hurt any less.

"I'm *not* pushing him away."

Rafael's gaze lingers, his head tilting slightly, as though he's weighing my words. "Okay, then. My bad."

"I'm *not*," I insist.

"I believe you."

"I'm going to my grandparents' tomorrow and demanding an explanation. I definitely won't let them send him to Virginia, and I won't stand by and watch them make him miserable." I realize I've raised my voice, but I insist, "I love Ethan. I'd *never* do anything to hurt him."

"Scarlett, hey." He gently grips my forearm, leaning forward. "I'm sorry. I know you do, okay? Forget everything I said."

I exhale, trying to get my heart to settle, but before I can, Rafael's gaze moves beside me, and I look up to see Vanessa and Theo standing next to our table. They exchange glances, then turn their attention back to us with furrowed brows.

Shit. Did they hear me?

"H-hey, guys."

"Is everything okay?" Theo asks, giving Rafael an icy glare.

"Yeah." I tuck my hands into my lap. "What's, um, what's up?"

"We came to get a beer. Paige is in the restroom."

"Oh." The entire gang. I knew it was just a matter of time before they met up with Rafael, but I hoped it'd be at a better moment. "Well, this is Rafael," I say, gesturing in his direction. "You've met Vanessa."

"Gentle-touch Vanessa, sure." Rafael grins. "Off duty tonight?"

Vanessa crosses her arms over her pale gold blouse, neatly tucked into high-waisted black trousers. "Don't worry, I've got my handcuffs on me."

"And this is Theo," I rush out. "Sound technician at the podcast."

"Yeah, we met back in the day," Theo mumbles, pushing his glasses up the bridge of his nose.

"Sure, sure. You're Will's little brother." Rafael scoots to the side. "Would you like to join us?"

Vanessa shrugs. "Yeah—"

"Actually . . ." Theo gestures with his beer toward the entrance door. "Can I talk to you, Scarlett? Outside?"

Stomach immediately knotting, I throw a glance at Rafael, who winks. I can almost see it in his eyes: *He's going to warn you about me.* "Yeah. Let's go."

I stand and follow Theo out of the pub, the humid air turning my skin sticky. A streetlamp farther down the block illuminates the quiet street, and I glimpse a couple pressed close, the flicker of movement and the faint sound of muffled giggles giving away their very obvious make-out session.

Turning his back on me, Theo inhales but doesn't say a word.

"Theo?"

"Yeah. Yes." He faces me, hesitating for a long moment. "Look, I know this isn't my place. And I know you didn't ask, but Scarlett—"

This *is* about Rafael, isn't it? Already on edge, I cross my arms. "Just tell me what you need to."

"This guy . . . I don't trust him."

Goddamn it. I hate it when Rafael is right.

"When you came in, that was nothing, okay? We were talking about a bit of a sensitive subject."

"Wasn't he gone recently? Paige said he was out of town."

"Well, he's back."

"Since when?"

What does that matter? Theo and I have been friends for—hell, for as long as I can remember. Can't he just trust me?

"When did he come back, Scarlett?" he insists.

"Friday," I say, my anxiety spiking when he nods, as if that's exactly the answer he expected. It feels remarkably similar to answering the phone call from the police when my parents died. Even before they told me what happened, I knew something bad was coming next.

"Here's the thing," Theo says, one arm folded behind his head as he awkwardly rubs his neck.

"No." I stop him. I don't want to hear *the thing*. I want to go back in and know that Rafael is the place where I can hide from what happened tonight with Ethan. If Theo's right, and there's a *thing*, well, I plan to ignore it. "Give him a chance, that's all I ask."

I walk back toward the pub entrance, but Theo rushes after me. "He's *always* been a player. And now that he's around you, I can't help but think that—"

"That what?" I ask, whipping around to face him.

"That he's . . . using you."

Using me for *what*? "Look, I appreciate your concern. I really do. But Rafael has been nothing but supportive and patient. Trust me, I didn't give him a lot to stick around for."

"So why was he peeking into your window?"

"He was not—" I scoff, frustrated. I can't believe Vanessa told him about that. "It was just a misunderstanding."

"And you don't find his timing a little peculiar?" He shifts uncomfortably, and my heartbeat immediately spikes again.

"What do you mean?"

"He first showed up at the Single Mingle."

My fingers tingle, cold seeping through my bones. "And?"

"And what happened before that?"

My mouth opens, then closes, shock preventing me from forming words for a full minute. My birthday. The radio host talking about Catherine Blake, then the *Willowbrook Whistle* article. "You can't be serious."

"Then he vanished. And what happened the night before he reappeared?"

Mallory was killed.

"You think he's a *murderer*?" I whisper-scream. "Theo, *please*."

"Just think about it for a second."

I turn on my heels, ready to return to the pub. Fuck Theo.

He comes to stand in front of me. "Scarlett, wait."

"Why? Why would he do it?"

He looks around as if he'll find his answer. "I don't know. Sometimes there's no reason."

Wrong. "There's always a reason—at the very least, a catalyst. A big event in someone's life that leads them to lose control. A divorce, a job loss, financial troubles—"

"A death in the family."

My mouth closes.

"That's a catalyst, right? His father's death could have pushed him over the edge."

I stare at him, bile rising up my throat and leaving an acidic taste in my mouth. "That hardly proves anything."

"You don't know where he was Thursday night, do you?"

"I don't know where *you* were, and that doesn't make you a killer!" I burst out. "Why would he move back into town and kill two women he hardly even knows? How would they—"

"I don't know, Scarlett," Theo says, his brow furrowing. "I have no idea. But I don't trust him, and I don't like him."

"That does *not* make him a murderer."

There's a movement in the corner of my eye, so I look back at the couple making out in the parking lot. I squint. Is that . . . *Celeste*?

"It's not nothing! It's—"

"I'm leaving," I interrupt, walking around him and darting inside the pub. I veer for the bathroom and enter the first stall, then take a moment to calm down. Was that really Celeste I saw making out in the parking lot? What the hell is happening to the people in this town?

Theo has always been protective of me, but this is way over the line. Can nobody separate a rebellious teenager from the man he is today?

I step out of the bathroom, running a hand through my hair and trying to shake off the weird tension I'm carrying. As I look up, I see Theo sitting next to Rafael and facing Paige and Vanessa on the other side of the table. The moment Rafael notices me, he stands and makes his way toward me, his glass in his hand.

"Hey," he says, stopping a few feet away and studying my face. "Everything okay?"

"Yeah," I reply, forcing a lightness into my voice that I don't feel. "All good."

Without thinking, I reach for the drink in his hand, fingers wrapping around the glass. I tip it back before he can stop me and down the whiskey in one quick, burning gulp. The warmth floods my chest, and I close my eyes for a second, savoring the strange mix of comfort and fire.

"Whoa, hey." Rafael reaches out, a hand steadying me by the

waist as I lower the empty glass, my lips tingling. "Did you forget what it tastes like?"

"I told you." I set the glass back in his hand as the whiskey hits me. "Drinking often boils down to motivation."

He chuckles softly, but his hand doesn't leave my waist. "Boy, you're going to regret that," he murmurs. "Want to tell me what happened with your friend?"

"Not really." I glance behind him, where Theo, Paige, and Vanessa are chatting at the table. "I'm sorry about them, though."

Between Vanessa nearly arresting him and the obvious argument I had with Theo, I'm not sure he's getting the welcome party he deserves.

"Nothing to be sorry about. I'm used to it."

I watch his easy, honest smile and reciprocate. It might be the whiskey loosening me up already, but I decide right here and now that Rafael would never do what Theo accused him of. He's a good person.

With a playful glint in his eyes, he leans closer and asks, "But I've got to ask. Is that all they are? *Friends?*"

Oh my God, *of course* he thinks there's something between Theo and me. "*Yes*. Nothing's ever happened between us."

He glances back at the group. "Guess I just got a weird vibe."

"Theo's . . . a little worried," I say. "That's all."

"I get it." He tilts his head. "But I wasn't talking about Theo."

15

the caretaking

[trope]

---

a romantically charged act of nurturing, often occurring when
one character is rendered temporarily helpless by illness, injury,
or their own lack of common sense; the caretaking usually
culminates in a heartfelt confession or a poorly timed sneeze
that ruins the mood but wins hearts anyway

"*Dale a tu . . . something something, Macarena,*" I sing, swaying my
hips and bringing my hand to rest dramatically on one side.
I cast a quick look at Rafael, who's trailing a few steps behind me.
Shadows dance over his sharp features, softening them just enough
to remind me of how utterly unfair it is that someone can look this
good and take this long to kiss me.

"Wait," I say, stumbling slightly but catching myself. "Why aren't
you dancing the Macarena?"

Tone dripping with amusement, he says, "That would be because
I'm not drunk."

"I'm not drunk, either," I insist, wobbling just slightly as I toss my hair back.

"Is that so?"

"Yes—" My protest is cut short as my foot catches on an uneven patch of sidewalk. The world tilts, and before I can do much about it, I land ass-first in a low bush. Twigs poke at my back, and the leaves crumple noisily under me.

"You were saying?" Rafael asks as he extends a hand toward me.

"Okay, so maybe I'm drunk," I admit, grabbing hold of his hand. He pulls me up with ease, and we stand close, his steady hands brushing stray leaves from my dress.

"We're almost home. Can you make it?"

I glance around at the quiet street, with the distant hum of the occasional car and the soft rustle of wind in the trees wrapping around us. Actually, we're only halfway there, and though it's an objectively short walk, it feels like an eternity.

"I'm tired, and my heels hurt," I grumble, shifting my weight from one foot to the other.

He points down. "You're not wearing heels."

"Oh." I stare at the worn sneakers I laced up earlier in the night. "Then I'm just tired."

"All right." He steps closer, and his hand presses lightly against my back. "Arms around my neck."

I gasp. "Are you going to pick me up?"

"Yes, Freckles. Now, arms."

I comply, and his other hand slides under my knees. He lifts me like I weigh nothing at all until I'm snug against his chest, my head resting on his shoulder.

"Okay?" he asks, his breath warm against my temple.

I nod, settling in as he walks. His steps are measured and steady, and with his cologne—warm and woodsy—and his steady heartbeat, it's the most comforting combination.

And God, is he pretty up close. He was always pretty, even back in high school when most boys were gross and awkward. With that lazy smirk that got him out of detentions, the way he'd lean back in his chair like he owned the room, boots propped on the desk. The rumpled uniform shirt he never bothered to button properly, and the chain around his neck he wasn't supposed to wear. He wasn't the sweet, safe kind of handsome—he was the kind that made you want to break rules. But now? His jawline is sharper, his brows fuller, his lips . . . his *lips*. He's more than just pretty—he's perfect.

The corners of his mouth curl up. "Hi."

"I don't care what everyone says. You are *so* pretty."

He hums. "Did someone say I'm not pretty? 'Cause they're lying."

"No." I fidget with the collar of his sweater, relaxed and warm in his arms. "It's just . . . it makes no sense. People should know you're good. Nobody this pretty is bad—ever."

"Makes sense to me."

Of course it does. Rafael is too pretty, on the inside and the outside, to be anything but good. Anyone who doesn't see it is just . . . stupid.

"Theo thinks you're the murderer," I say. Something tells me I shouldn't say this to him, but I guess whiskey makes me honest.

"He does, huh?" He chuckles. "Well, if I were, I'd probably kill him for saying that."

I trace the black lines at the base of his neck. "The chief of police might think so too."

That gets his attention, because he looks down at me, his face inches away from mine. "Do *you*, Scarlett?"

"*No*," I spit out, as if the thought alone is insulting.

"That's all that matters."

I bask in the joy of being so relevant to this man, but I know he's not saying the whole truth. It bothers him that everyone thinks ill of him. "You know," I say, still staring at his mouth, "I like this."

"Hate to break it to you, but everyone loves drinking until they're hungover."

"No, not drinking." I wave a lazy finger between us. "This."

His hand, holding the spot behind my knee, tightens slightly. The motion is so subtle that I shouldn't notice, but I do, and it makes my stomach flip.

"I like it, too. Very much."

"What you said about pushing people away—maybe I do that. Maybe I've done it with you, because I'm scared."

"I know," he says simply, looking ahead. "You're afraid I'll disappoint you."

I fidget with the top button of his shirt. "No. I mean, yes, but no. Everyone eventually disappoints you. People change, sometimes without meaning to."

He keeps walking as he waits for my next slurred words.

"I'm not afraid you'll disappoint me. You're sweet, Rafael. You're caring, thoughtful, charming."

He slows to a stop under a tree, its sprawling branches casting dappled shadows on the ground. "Really? Keep going."

"If you think you need to prove something to me, you're wrong. I already know who you are. I've known it for as long as I've known you."

His smile is so soft I want to reach out and touch his lips.

"So you've changed your mind about love?"

"I don't know." Heat rushes to my cheeks. "Maybe the issue isn't that I'm not destined for romance. Maybe I was just meant for you."

"Ah." He nods, pleased. "The drunk confession. Really, a staple of the genre."

I scoff. "What? I'm not saying this 'cause I'm drunk."

"Really? You *genuinely* believe you were just waiting for me?"

I think about it for a long moment. "Yes, Rafael Gray. I was waiting for you. And you took your sweet time to come back."

Head shaking, he grins. "I got here as quickly as I could, Freckles."

We watch each other, and in the pause that follows, I think this would really be the perfect moment for him to kiss me. But he must disagree, because after staring at my lips for a while, he says, "You know, I told your dad that night . . ." He clears his throat. "I told him I liked his daughter and one day I'd come back for her."

He *what?* "Wh-what did he say?"

"That I should be the best version of myself when I did."

My mouth lifts, even as my chest aches. I know if Dad was here, he'd give us his blessing—not that we'd need it. But this feels like the closest thing to him approving.

"Is that what you were doing all this time away?" I tease.

"Yes, actually. It turns out it takes a while to become someone worthy of being yours."

Stomach, meet butterflies.

"See?" he whispers, as if sharing a secret. "You're doing just fine with this romance thing."

I huff out a chuckle, but it's short-lived. "People can just be taken away from you, Rafael." I exhale. "*That's* what I'm scared of. That love always ends with heartbreak. Just like life always ends with death."

"Maybe." We've reached the front of my house, so I wiggle, expecting him to set me down. Instead, he keeps a firm hold on me. "Yet you can't help but live, Scarlett. Can you?"

the subplot

[trope]

---

the secondary characters who are up to their own shenanigans and have their own plot points; often more entertaining than the main storyline, the subplot is like the side dish you didn't order but end up liking more than the entrée

"Oh my fucking God," I grouch as my eyes open. The light streaming in from the window is worrisome, to say the least—it's midmorning sun, which means I must be late for work. However, seeing as someone's playing Whac-A-Mole with my brain, I can't bring myself to care. "What have I done?"

I open one eye, then the other, memories of last night coming back in flashes. Theo talking about Rafael, then Rafael and me walking home. How he forced me to drink what felt like seven liters of water before letting me fall asleep and then was perfectly happy to have my body thrown over his. Finally, I realize it's Sunday. I'm off work.

Wait, where is Sherlock?

I straighten, immediately relieved when I see him curled at my feet. Rafael must have fed him again. I pick up my phone and find a text.

Rafael
Good morning, Freckles. I'm not sure how much you remember, so I figured I'd give you a summary of last night. Yes, we cuddled—you insisted, I swear— and that's all that happened. If you feel a sting in your gorgeous behind, that's because you fell into a bush. No thorns, I checked. As for the sting in your pride, you have the Macarena to blame. It was adorable. Sherlock has been fed, dessert included. Find breakfast in the kitchen and aspirin on the bedside table. I wish I could have stayed, but I had to go back to my drug empire. Call me later?

I blink a few times, rereading Rafael's text with growing giddiness. His message is the perfect antidote for the pounding in my head and the soreness from what I vaguely remember as a very embarrassing tumble.

"Adorable, huh?" I murmur, running my fingers through my messy hair as Sherlock stretches luxuriously at my feet. "At least one of us has their life together."

I climb out of bed, popping the aspirin into my mouth and downing it with the glass of water beside it. I grab my phone again to respond, but before I can, a notification catches my eye: "Inbox (217 unread messages)."

I frown, tapping the icon. My inbox rarely fills up this fast; I get maybe three or four emails a week from listeners of the podcast. My stomach twists as I see the subject lines filling the screen like a tidal wave.

Did you see the Reddit post???

Murderers like the podcast?!

You HAVE to address this in the next episode!

Is it true? Is there a connection to the books you talked about?

Scarlett, please respond!!

"What the hell . . ." I trail off, scrolling through the increasingly frantic messages. Some are from listeners asking if I've seen the post, others are full of speculation about recent murders, and some are disturbingly accusatory:

This is your fault. You inspired a psycho.

What are you hiding?!

Are you working with the killer?

My fingers tremble as I open the podcast app, my heart still racing. I tap on the podcast, expecting to see the usual stats—modest numbers, enough to keep it alive, but nothing earth-shattering.

But when the analytics load, my jaw drops.

The latest episode: *432,897 listens.*

The one before that: *389,452 listens.*

Even episodes from months ago—ones that barely broke ten thousand before—are suddenly soaring. I swipe through the stats, my jaw unhinging farther with every passing second. Comments are flooding in, too, faster than I can scroll.

"Holy crap." I stare at the numbers like they might vanish if I blink too hard. For a fleeting moment, my chest swells with pride. The podcast has blown up. After years of late nights, endless editing, and pouring my heart into this project, it's finally happening. People are listening. They care.

But the rush of euphoria is short-lived.

The spike isn't because I'm good at what I do. It's because someone out there—somewhere—is using my words, my passion, as inspiration for unspeakable acts.

My stomach churns as the thrill curdles into guilt, thick and heavy. I swipe to the comments, desperate for something, *anything*, that might make this feel less awful.

Scarlett, your podcast is incredible. Do you think the killer listens to it?

You're so insightful. Do you have a theory about the murderer?

I found your podcast after hearing about the murders. Obsessed already!

Obsessed.

The numbers don't feel like success.

They feel like a noose tightening around my neck.

I walk up the long, winding path to the front door, every step feeling like I'm inching closer to the end of a plank, teetering on the brink of falling into dark, unsafe waters. I haven't seen Grandma and Grandpa since Ethan's birthday dinner last year, when we kept things light and surface level. There won't be any of that today.

I am going to *demand* to know what's happening with Ethan—what's this Virginia thing he's brought up?—and my grandmother doesn't deal well with demands.

At least a bucket of coffee and several gallons of water later, I'm fully recovered from my hangover.

With an invigorating breath, I raise my hand to knock on the heavy wooden doors, ready to throw myself to the sharks. A moment later, my grandparents' maid opens the door.

"Scarlett? Mr. and Mrs. Moore didn't say they were expecting company."

"They're not. I, uh, I was wondering if I could talk to them."

She blinks, then opens the door wider to let me in. My grandparents aren't exactly the kind of people you pop in on unannounced, so she must be unsure about the protocol.

"I'll let Mrs. Moore know you're here," she says as she accompanies me to the sitting room. The furniture is upholstered in cream-colored fabric that seems more suited to a museum than to actual human use. Ornate gold-framed mirrors hang on the walls, reflecting an endless cycle of mahogany and marble, like some never-ending luxury loop.

I sink into a wingback chair that's as stiff as my nerves, perching uncomfortably on the edge. My gaze drifts to the clock in the corner, and I am half tempted to rearrange a pillow just to see what happens, but then the distant sound of heels clicking against marble reminds me where I am—and who I'm waiting for.

My grandmother enters the room in a tailored lavender suit that complements her silver hair, pinned back in a neat chignon. "Scarlett, dear." When I stand, she leans in for a perfunctory kiss on the cheek. "We didn't expect you."

"Yes, I know. Sorry, Grandma."

"Oh, nonsense." She sits primly on the couch, smoothing her already-perfect skirt. "You're always welcome."

Oh, she's proper mad.

"Thank you." I rub my hands together, the heat from my palms doing little to warm the icy knot of nerves in my stomach. "Is Grandpa going to join us?"

"He's at work, unfortunately." Her eyes narrow, the slightest twitch betraying her annoyance. "If you'd let us know, I could have had you over when he was available."

"That's okay," I say quickly, ignoring the veiled jab. "I just wanted to talk about Ethan."

She crosses her legs, her pearls catching the light. "Well, go ahead."

"I'm not sure if he told you, but he's come over to my place a couple of times." I adjust my position on the stiff couch. Her expression doesn't change—not a flicker—so I push forward. "And I couldn't help but notice that he's . . . struggling."

"Struggling," she echoes.

"Yes, uh, to make friends." I hesitate. "And you must have noticed his face. The bruises?"

She doesn't even blink. My pulse quickens, the tension in my chest tightening like a vise, until she finally says, "He's been spending time with this . . . friend. Jace something," her voice dripping with disapproval. "And to be honest with you, it's been nothing but trouble since then. He gets into fights, and the other day, I caught him smoking. *Smoking!*" She shakes her head, her lips twisting into a disdainful pout.

Relief washes over me that at least on this, we seem to agree. "Did you talk about it?"

"There's no talking to your brother," she snaps, waving a manicured hand dismissively. "It's all 'Mind your business' and 'I'm busy now.'" She sighs dramatically. "I went to see his teachers, then Dr. Waven, and he said—"

"Dr. Waven?"

"His therapist."

I rub my forehead, trying to process what she said. "Uh, Grandma . . . that's a huge invasion of his privacy. You can't do that."

"I wouldn't have had to if he talked to me."

"So, what message are you sending him? That he shouldn't trust his teachers? His therapist? That he has no right to privacy?"

Her lips press into a tight line, her irritation radiating off her in waves. "Well, thank God I did it, because Dr. Waven said—"

"I don't want to know," I say firmly, raising a hand to cut her off. "It's none of my business."

She exhales sharply, her nostrils flaring. "Of course." Standing abruptly, she gestures toward the hallway with a flick of her hand. "Well, it was lovely seeing you. I'll say hello to your grandfather for you."

I stay seated, my hands clasped tightly in my lap, digging my nails into my palms. After a beat, she sinks back into her seat.

"Is there something else?" she asks.

"He mentioned Virginia."

She pauses—long enough for me to know she didn't plan to share that particular piece of information with me. "Uh-huh. What about it?"

"You tell me. Are you shipping him off to another state?"

"Oh, don't be dramatic, Scarlett." The maid enters the room with a tray. Once she sets it on the coffee table, my grandma points at the teapot. "Tea?"

"Why do you want to send him to Virginia?"

She fills the first cup. "It's just a quick flight away."

A flight I can't afford. "*Why?*"

"Your grandfather and I have enrolled him in a boarding school that only a handful of lucky young men have access to. He'll get a sublime education and the experience of a lifetime."

That's it? She's sending him to some fancy school? He still has two years of high school left—is that how long he'll be gone? And she planned to keep it a secret from me?

"Then maybe you should let someone else seize this opportunity," I say, my frustration boiling over. "Someone who actually wants it, because Ethan doesn't."

"The choice is ours to make, and it's been made." She sets a tea bag into the first cup, then looks up. "I didn't hear an answer the first time. Would you like some tea?"

I'd like to strangle her, actually, but I force myself to stay calm. Hostility won't get me anywhere. Rationality might. "Grandma, I think . . . Ethan feels unwanted. He's angry about Mom and Dad's deaths, and he feels like I gave him up. If you send him away at the first sign of trouble—"

"Are you saying I'm abandoning my grandchild?"

"I'm saying that's how *he* sees it. He's filled with anger, and this won't help. I promise it won't."

Her gaze sharpens. "Ethan isn't fitting in, Scarlett. The way your mother raised him—" I watch her grimace. "And his actions reflect on us, too."

"So you're sending him away because you're . . . embarrassed."

"I'm sending him to a prestigious school where he'll have a new opportunity to fit in with kids his age. Without the influence of that . . . *delinquent*."

Right. So it's either my mom's fault or Jace's. "Someone's *bullying* him, and your solution is to send him away? To let bad people get away with unacceptable behavior?"

She brings the mug to her lips and takes a slow sip. "Can I know where all this sudden interest came from? You haven't been a part of Ethan's life for years, and now you decide you should have a say in his upbringing?"

Angry tears well up in my eyes, blurring the room's perfect edges. I understand Ethan saying this, but her? *She's* the reason I wasn't in his life. "You can't be serious."

"I am."

Guilt strangles me, closing my throat up. My eyes burn, but I refuse to let the tears fall, even with the same nagging voice that feels like a splinter lodged inside my brain.

I should have tried harder. Texted one more time. Called more. I gave up. This is all my fault.

She stands, brushing imaginary lint off her skirt. "Scarlett, I'm expected somewhere. So unless there's anything else . . ."

I rise slowly, then shake my head. I'm more mad at myself than at her, because I actually thought I could convince her to change her mind. That there was something I could say to make her listen.

She turns and strides toward the entryway, her heels clicking loudly on the polished floor. I follow in silence, my throat tight.

She opens the door, her voice sickeningly sweet. "We'll plan something soon, all right?"

I take a step outside, then pause, glancing back. My gaze moves upward, catching a shadow on the staircase. Ethan is flat against the wall, his eyes red-rimmed. He looks like he's about to cry, or maybe like he just stopped.

The disappointment I feel ignites into a fiery inferno of anger as I glare at my grandmother. "This doesn't end here," I say, and then I shift my gaze to Ethan. "And *that's* a promise."

17

the betrayal

[trope]

the gut-wrenching moment when trust shatters like a cheap
wineglass; often delivered by a lover, the betrayal flips alliances,
exposes secrets, and occasionally ends with someone bleeding
out on the floor

My knuckles tap against the frosted glass of Celeste's office door,
and her voice calls, "Come in," distracted and clipped.

I push the door open and step inside. She's hunched over her
desk, her sharp black bob glossy under the office light, the pale blue
glow of her computer screen reflected in the lenses of her black-
framed glasses. Her red-stained lips are parted slightly, like she's just
seen a ghost lurking in the pixels.

"Hey." I close the door. "Everything okay?"

Her gaze is still glued to the screen, her posture rigidly perfect
despite the tension in her shoulders. "Did you see these numbers?"

she asks, finally looking at me. "It's . . . crazy. We've never had this many listeners. Not even close."

My stomach churns, a mix of excitement and dread. After my visit to my grandmother yesterday, I completely forgot about this. "It's because of that Reddit post," I say, making my way in and flopping down on the chair. "The one about the murders. It went viral."

Her expression darkens, her brow creasing. "Scarlett . . ." She pauses, choosing her words with surgical precision the way she always does. "Don't take this the wrong way, because the podcast deserves recognition. But . . ." She gestures at the screen, her hand hovering uncertainly. "God, this isn't how I wanted it to happen."

I feel it, too, that strange, sour edge to our sudden success. "People are asking if we're going to address the murders in the next episode," I venture. "Do you think we should?"

"Absolutely not," she says in a firm voice. "We're a fiction podcast, Scarlett. That's what we do—fiction. We're not the news."

Frustration prickles at the edges of my thoughts. Part of me hoped she'd see this as an opportunity, a chance to do something meaningful for Willowbrook. But I can see the fear in her eyes, her desperate need to keep our little podcasting world separate from the horrors of reality.

"You're right," I agree. "Fiction it is."

Her shoulders relax visibly. "Speaking of fiction," she says, her tone brightening slightly, "I have some feedback on your first *Passion & Pages* episode."

I lean in, curiosity sparked. Celeste pulls a sheet of paper from her desk drawer and slides it toward me. There isn't a single mark or note on it.

"Really?" My eyebrows shoot up.

"Perfect, Scarlett," she says, her eyes twinkling. "Your analysis was spot-on. I mean, I might actually pick up the book. It's clear you really connected with the story."

Warmth spreads through my chest.

"The way you described the tension between Luca and Simone," Celeste continues, "it felt like the romance was jumping right off the page."

"Thanks." I hadn't even realized I was so nervous about this. "I really enjoyed it."

She glances at her screen. "Oh, and before I forget, I've booked you to record with Theo on Wednesday. Think you'll be ready?"

"Yeah, I'll be ready."

"Good," she says. When I stay put, she asks, "Anything else?"

"Uh, yeah, actually." I dry the sweat off my hands on my thighs. "I went to see my grandparents yesterday. My brother said something that . . . Anyway, it turns out they want to send him to Virginia. And I was thinking of maybe reaching out to Steve to see if he has any advice."

Her brows furrow tightly. "Are you at the stage of involving lawyers?"

"No." I clear my throat. "I just want to be ready if that time comes. But if it makes anyone uncomfortable—I mean, I know he's your husband, and . . ." *And you're lying about your separation.*

"Why should anyone be uncomfortable?" She grabs her cell phone and starts typing. "I'll tell him to clear his schedule for you."

She's raising her phone to her ear before I can get a word in, so I watch her telling Steve about the situation. Maybe Mrs. Prattle got it wrong—it wouldn't be the first time. But then again, I'm pretty sure I saw Celeste in The Oak's parking lot with someone who looks nothing like Steve.

Nah. It couldn't have been her. This woman making out in a parking lot? I glance at her—sleek black hair tucked neatly behind her ears, spotless crisp white blouse, nails perfectly manicured. She looks like she just stepped out of a boardroom, not a late-night scandal.

"Friday?"

She's talking to me, so I nod.

"Okay. Yes, eleven a.m. All right, I'll see you later. Bye." She hangs up, then claps. "All done. He'll help with whatever you need—and don't even think about paying any fee."

"Celeste . . ."

"Come on. Get out." She shoos me away. "We have work to do."

Reluctantly, I step out of her office, the door clicking shut behind me as I throw a last thank-you her way. I walk through the corridors of Booked It, my thoughts churning. *Steve will help*, I tell myself. Even though it feels like I have no control. Like Ethan is being taken away from me all over again.

I pause by my desk, my fingers brushing the edge of my computer monitor. Feeling observed, I look up and meet Theo's gaze. The air between us feels heavy, loaded with words left unsaid and accusations. My chest tightens at the memory of Saturday night.

I'm not ready to face him. Not now, not after he accused Rafael of being a *serial killer*. Without a word, I grab my bag and sling it over my shoulder.

"You heading out?" he asks as I step past him.

I avoid his gaze. "Yeah, just need some air."

He hesitates, and I think he might say something. Apologize, maybe. But nothing comes. Instead, I sense his eyes on me as I walk toward the door.

"Scarlett!" Mrs. Prattle cheers from the deserted office of the *Willow-brook Whistle*. I close the door behind me as she stands and quickly walks closer. "How are you, dear? I hear you had quite a lot of fun Saturday night, didn't you?"

I hesitate. "Uh, I—yes." I swear, I'll never get used to this part of living in a small town. "Did someone see me dance the Macarena?"

"They sure did, honey," she says as she finally reaches my side. With a snap of her fingers, she turns to the coffee machine. "Oh, let me get you a coffee."

"No, I'm fine, I—" She's already filling a cup, so I let it go. "I hope I'm not bothering you."

"Please! They only want me here to watch the place, and Tuesday's a slow day." She holds the cup out for me. "Nowadays, the kids do all their work on their *computers*."

I accept the cup. Only hearing the way she says "computers" like they're offensive makes me feel better.

"What brings you here?" she asks, gesturing at the cluttered office.

"Uh, I actually . . . I was wondering if you had any material about Catherine Blake and Mallory Young that hasn't been published."

With a curious tilt of her head, she walks to the closest desk. "What a terrible ordeal, isn't it? The police say it's someone local, but what do they know? Chief Donovan can't even play a hand of poker, and that young cop they hired, Trevor? He smokes *grass*." She moves a pile of folders and papers. "It's gotta be someone from out of town, right? Who would kill a woman as sweet as Mallory?"

She looks like she expects me to weigh in, so I nod. I wish I could tell her the police are wrong, but they have a point. It makes sense that the killer would choose to hunt on familiar ground, which would make them a local.

"I just hope the police know what they're doing," she says as she grabs a large box, then sets it on the desk. "She was going to be married in March, you know."

"Mallory?"

"Had just sent the invitations out." When she cups her mouth with a shaky hand, I reach into my bag for tissues. With a sniffle, she refuses them. "Oh, don't worry about me, darling. You'll find some pictures here—my nephew took them."

"Thank you."

"Is this something for your . . . radio show?"

"Uh, no." I grab the first stack of pictures, looking through shots outside Catherine's house. "I'm just . . . curious, I guess."

Her brows knit together, but she quickly wipes the dubious expression off her face. "Always said you take after your father. Well, I'll be outside—wouldn't want to miss the after-Pilates gossip."

I smile in a silent thank-you before she walks away, then sit on the closest chair and begin going through the pictures. I'm not sure what I expect to find. It's not like the killer posed for a picture in front of the police. But maybe I'll notice some similarities. Something that connects the two victims. Something that'll tell me how the killer chose them.

Honestly, I just want to find *something*.

As I flip through the pictures, a flash of purple catches my eye through the window. It's Paige, in her favorite oversize hoodie, talking to Mrs. Prattle and waving cigarette smoke away. Her auburn curls are pulled into a haphazard high ponytail, a few damp tendrils stuck to her temple from what must have been an aggressive Pilates session.

Mrs. Prattle must have told her I'm in here, because Paige turns her head and meets my gaze with a puzzled expression.

Just great.

She pushes the door open and leans in. "Tell me you're not obsessing over local murders, I beg of you."

I set the photos down. "It's not my fault this time."

"Isn't it?" She walks in, closing the door behind her with a pointed hip-bump, and struts over. Seeing the stack of pictures of Catherine's funeral, she sighs. "Oh, boy."

"No—seriously. I just needed to run away from Theo, and I didn't feel like being at home."

"Run away from Theo?"

I guess he didn't tell her. "Saturday night, he said . . ." I scoff. The thought, although baseless and absurd, makes me uncomfortable. "He said Rafael might be the murderer."

With a half-hearted chuckle, she drops onto the chair next to me. "Wait, what?"

"I know, it's crazy."

Eyes drifting over the desk, she gasps. "You don't believe him, right?"

"I *just* said it's crazy."

"Right. It *is*." She points at the pictures. "So what are you doing, exactly?"

I don't know. Maybe I want to discover who the killer is so I can prove Theo wrong. Maybe my trust issues are deep enough that even his baseless accusations are making me pause. Maybe it's because I want to trust Rafael, but he *is* keeping a few secrets.

"Okay, Scarlett," Paige says, rolling her chair closer. She takes both my hands in hers, squeezing hard enough to make my fingers tingle, and her green eyes lock on mine, deadly serious. "Do you want *me* to become a serial killer? Because I will kill you, then Theo."

"Technically, that's not 'serial'—"

"Jesus, Scarlett. Theo has always been protective of you. You know that."

"Yes, I know, but—"

"So don't let what he's saying affect you. Promise?" When I nod, she pats my hand and stands up, then tucks the chair back against the desk. "Vanessa is waiting for me for brunch." Throwing a disdainful look at the pictures, she sighs. "Please find something a little cheerier to obsess over?"

I mumble "Bye" when she waves, watching her walk out of the *Whistle*. It's not like I believed Theo before, but knowing she also thinks he's being unreasonable makes me feel better.

I go back to the pictures, and with one stack out of the way, I sink farther into the chair and look up at the ceiling. Catherine and Mallory both lived in houses—there are few apartment complexes in Willowbrook anyway. They were both women, and they both . . . had white mailboxes, I guess. Everything else about them is different.

According to social media, their ages, occupations, friends— nothing was similar about them. They dressed differently, they lived in different areas, and I wouldn't be surprised to find out they never even exchanged more than a couple of words.

"What am I even doing?" I ask as I grab a stack of photos. The picture on top was taken at Catherine's funeral, and I can spot her family next to the casket, their expressions filled with the type of sorrow that only comes from unexpected grief.

I set the stack of photos down, sending a bunch of them sliding over the desk. This is pointless.

"Find anything interesting?"

I turn to Mrs. Prattle entering the office, then shake my head as she walks to the computer. She says something about the times we live in, and I figure it's my cue to leave. I probably won't find anything here.

I group all the pictures together, and one slips under the box. Before I can put it back on the stack, I notice that the angle caught someone withdrawn from the crowd, standing next to a tree that shadows their face.

But I know who that is.

Those wide shoulders, the curls over his forehead, the tattoos peeking out of the collar of his shirt. It's Rafael.

My heart gallops in my chest until I find the stack of photos from Mallory's funeral. I flip through them, lungs burning with every breath, until I find a shot of the mourners . . . and Rafael is in the background.

He was there. At both funerals. He's only been back in town less than two weeks—how could he possibly have known both victims well enough to go to their funerals? And why wouldn't he have said anything?

Unless . . . unless he *is* their killer.

Unless he's interested not in me but in my podcast.

Unless I'm living not in a romance but in a very twisted thriller.

"Scarlett, dear. Is everything okay?"

When Mrs. Prattle cups my shoulder, I flinch, looking back but not really seeing. My brain is a mosh pit of tangled thoughts, and fear is choking me, shutting down my airway.

"You need a glass of water. And to stop looking at those sad pictures."

I watch Mrs. Prattle saunter over to the coffee machine, then take a bottle of water from the cabinet. Quickly, I grab a stack of pictures and shove them into my bag, not even sure they're the right ones. "It's—it's okay, Mrs. Brattle. Thank you." I set the remaining pictures back in the box, then grab my bag. "I need to go. I'll, uh, see you later."

"Are you sure?" she asks, but I'm out the door before I realize I'm not in a condition to drive, and I don't know where to go.

Home is where Rafael is.

And Rafael might be a serial killer.

18

the sole caregiver

[trope]

the overburdened, fiercely responsible hero(ine) who has been
carrying the weight of the world on their own tired shoulders for
far too long; prone to emotional walls and martyr tendencies,
the sole caregiver has no time for romance—until someone
determined enough breaks through their defenses and reminds
them they're allowed to want something for themself

The recording room at the Booked It office is colder than usual, the
hum of the air conditioner filling the Wednesday silence. Perched
on the chair, I sit drumming my fingers against the table.

I've been here for over an hour, staring blankly at the screen of
my laptop, the pictures tucked away in my bag.

I keep pulling them out to study them, hoping I'll see something
new if I check just one more time. But Rafael's still there, and I still
can't make sense of it.

I tap on the mic in front of me, the empty chair across the table impossible to ignore. Celeste said Theo would meet me to record the episode for *Passion & Pages* at two, but that was twenty minutes ago. After Saturday night's fight, what if he doesn't show up?

The cursor blinks on my screen, and I tap my fingers on my paperback copy of *The Darkened Stacks*. It's not the best book I've ever read—predictable in parts, rushed in others—but it's perfect for one reason: a murder in the local library.

And Willowbrook only has one library.

If only Theo agrees to let me rerecord tomorrow's episode of *Murders & Manuscripts* last minute instead of the episode for *Passion & Pages*, the killer will be exactly where I want them, and this time, I'll be there, too. I'll be ready.

In the meantime, I've convinced myself that Rafael isn't behind this, that there must be another explanation. But doubt keeps gnawing at me. What if I'm wrong? What if it *is* him? The way he dodges questions about his job, how cagey he is about his past and his father—it's hard to ignore. Quentin stabbed the killer's arm, and Rafael's arm was bandaged. And Theo is right, he resurfaced exactly when the killer struck for the first time, then vanished again right before the second murder.

Throat thickening, I try to banish the thought. No. It's not him. It *can't* be him.

The door creaks open, and my heart skips. Theo is there, standing in the doorway, looking hesitant. His black-framed glasses catch the light before he steps inside, closing the door softly behind him.

"Hey," I say, wiping my arm over the table to clean up the crumbs left by my Pop-Tart.

He walks over and slides into the seat. His broad shoulders

hunch slightly as he leans forward, trying to make himself smaller in the too-narrow chair. "Sorry I'm late. Traffic from New Haven was a bitch."

"No worries." Neither of us speaks, and I can't quite bring myself to meet his eyes again. "Fair warning," I say, tapping my laptop. "It might take me a while to get it right."

"That's okay. It's your first episode."

"Yeah. I know."

We sit in the silence that follows, the hum of the air conditioner suddenly louder than ever. He shifts in his seat, dropping his worn canvas bag onto the floor with a dull thud. A hotel key card slips out and skitters across the linoleum, coming to rest against the leg of the table. He snatches it up quickly, tucking it back inside without a word, but the tips of his ears go red.

Recognizing the orange logo, I ask, "Are you staying at the Wildflower Inn?"

"Hmm? N-no."

"Oh, I thought that was—"

"Give me just a second to set up and we can start."

"Okay." I can't tell if he's upset or hiding something. Why would he have a room at Willowbrook's only hotel? Is he having issues with his apartment?

My phone buzzes on the table.

Rafael
Drunk-cuddling, then leaving me on read for days? And here I thought we had something special.

I set the phone on silent and put it down, trying to hide my flustered expression.

Fuck this. I need Theo's help, so whether or not he's upset, I'll have to just come out and say it.

"I want to apologize about Saturday night," I blurt out.

"Apologize?" He shakes his head, the chair creaking softly under his movement. "Scarlett, I was way out of line."

"No, you weren't." My fingers nervously trace the edge of my coffee cup. "You're one of my best friends, and you were concerned. I should have listened to you."

"Well—what do you mean? Did something happen?"

"No," I blurt, perhaps a bit too quickly. Nothing happened, and nothing *will* happen, because Rafael isn't behind these murders. "I just . . . I could use your help."

"Whatever you need," he rushes out.

Exactly what I hoped he'd say.

"Instead of the *Passion & Pages* episode, I want to rerecord tomorrow's *Murders & Manuscripts*."

His eyebrows shoot up in surprise. "Why, is there something wrong with the original?"

"No, nothing's wrong. I decided to rewrite the script, highlight another book instead."

"Oh?" He glances at my laptop, fingers hovering over the keyboard. "Is it written already?"

"Yes." Though it's probably shit, since I wrote it in two hours. "The problem is, Celeste hasn't exactly approved. Because I didn't tell her."

"What?" He swivels slightly, the wheels of his chair whispering on the carpeted floor. "Why not?"

Because I know exactly what she'll say. Not enough money to rerecord, not enough time—and besides, she'll want to know *why*.

"Look, I know it's a lot to ask," I say, hands flat against the table. "But I can't afford her saying no. It's really important that I rerecord the episode."

"But—"

"You can't ask me why."

Theo's mouth closes, his jaw tightening. I must be freaking him out. Hell, *I'm* freaking *myself* out. But right now, I need him to trust me.

"I promise I'll take all the responsibility. And I'll buy you lunch. Or dinner. Or . . . something."

His lips form a tight line. He knows Celeste too well to believe me. "I really wish you would tell me what's going on. Can you promise me it's nothing crazy or dangerous?"

"I can." *Probably.* I'll take precautions, of course.

"Okay." He pushes his glasses up the bridge of his nose. "I guess . . . I guess we can do it."

Relief washes over me, so strong I'd like to squeeze him. "Thank you. Seriously." I stand and grab a headphone set from a nearby hook, the leather padding soft and worn from use. "Let's get to work, then. We'll be here a while."

He sets up the computers, and I move on to the recording station.

Step one of the plan completed. The easiest step, honestly. Step two? Catch a killer. If Rafael isn't the murderer, everything will be fine. Tomorrow it'll all be over. But if he is, I'll stop him.

I'll catch him in the act, back him into a corner.

And then I'll put an end to Rafael Gray.

A quarter past nine on Thursday.

Tonight's the night.

I've been dodging Rafael like a storm cloud. Calls, texts—even when he came over and knocked on the door, begging me to just let him know what went wrong and how he can fix it.

I let my heart take the hit, but I didn't open the door. And now I'm ready for the truth. I'm ready to catch the killer, to find out if Rafael has been playing me since the beginning. And if he's not guilty, then I'll figure out how to make it up to him.

"One step at the time," I remind myself as I put on my shoes and grab my pink Taser. The drive to the library takes five minutes, and the episode won't be aired for another half hour, but I'm not taking any chances. I want to be there before the killer. I want them to find me there and know they've fucked up.

I open the door, jumping back as my brain processes that someone is standing there. "Jesus!" I squeal, clutching a hand to my chest, then immediately letting it drop when I notice it's my brother. "You scared the shit out of me." I catch my breath. "Is everything okay?"

He stands stiffly on the porch, dark blond hair sticking to his forehead like he's been sweating on the bike ride here and a few fading bruises still yellowing along his cheekbone. "Y-yeah. Yes," he stammers, glancing at his feet. "I was just about to knock."

My heart is still racing. I glance past him, scanning the street for any sign of Rafael. The coast is clear, but I really wish Ethan and I could just go inside. I wouldn't know what to tell Rafael if he came over.

And what is Ethan doing here tonight? I'd never send him away, but his presence at my door could derail the plan considerably.

"Actually . . ." Ethan pulls me back. He's always been thin, but tonight he seems smaller somehow, shrinking into himself like he wants to disappear. "I've been here for twenty minutes, trying to find the courage to knock."

The courage to knock? Why would he need to psych himself up for that?

The usual open injury pumps guilt into my bloodstream, but I keep my expression light. "Well, part one is done now, huh?"

He huffs a weak laugh, his gaze flicking to mine briefly before dropping back to the porch floor. "Yeah. I guess."

My fault. My fault. My fault.

I glance at my car, parked at the end of the street, but the gravity in his voice—the way he's holding himself like he might break apart—roots me to the spot.

"Come in," I say gently, stepping aside to give him room. He doesn't move, rocking on his heels. His sneakers squeak slightly on the worn wood. "What's wrong? Whatever it is—"

"What's the truth, Scarlett?"

My stomach tightens as I think of Rafael. The podcast. The murders. "Excuse me?"

"Why don't you live with us? Why didn't you come to stay at Grandma and Grandpa's place with me?" His voice cracks just a little, betraying the sixteen-year-old under all that forced composure. "It's their fault, isn't it? They didn't want you to move in."

I inhale deeply, looking into his green eyes, too sharp and too knowing, just like Mom's. "You have to understand, Grandma and

Grandpa love you very much. They might not show it in the right way, but they do."

He shoves his hands deeper into his pockets. "But they don't love *you*? Why?"

"Well," I start, choosing my words carefully, "they never really liked Mom. You know that."

"So they didn't take you in because you're her daughter? I'm her *son*."

"But you're also Dad's son."

"And you're his daughter. He adopted you. He loved you like—"

I grip his forearm, squeezing lightly. "I know."

"You were just two years older than I am now, and they refused to give you a place to stay. It's . . . it's so fucked-up, Scarlett."

Anger radiates off him, a fire that fills the small space between us. I step closer, cautiously reaching out to squeeze his shoulder. "Come in. We'll talk about it over hot cocoa."

"I'm not a *child*." He shrugs my hand off and starts pacing, his footsteps heavy on the creaking porch. "This is . . . It's just so typical of them. That's who they are, you know? Selfish *bigots* who only care about appearances. And it only took me ages to figure it out because . . ." He stops, turning to face me, his eyes blazing. "Why didn't you tell me? I blamed you for everything, Scarlett."

I swallow hard. "I didn't *want* you to blame them. It was already difficult for you, Ethan. With Mom and Dad being gone, then losing me—it's not like there was anything I could do. I thought if you didn't resent them, things would be easier for you."

He rubs his face with both hands, a sharp exhale from his lips. "How can I love them when they don't love my sister?" He looks at me—really looks at me—desperate for an answer I don't have. I still don't understand how two adults with the means to support their son's adopted child would choose not to. I still don't get why blood matters so much to them when it bore no relevance to Dad.

I shake my head. "I'm sorry, Ethan. I only did what I thought was best for you. I planned to tell you eventually, but I thought it could wait. Until you were older. Until you could choose for yourself."

"It's not your fault," he says, leaning against the wall. His shoulders slump, and he huffs out an insincere laugh. "I spent five years blaming you. I'm not doing it anymore."

I playfully nudge him. "Well, that's refreshing, isn't it?"

He smiles, but it fades quickly, his expression turning solemn again. "Scarlett, I can't live there anymore." His voice is low, almost pleading. "I just . . . I *hate* them. They want to change me into the grandson they wish I was—maybe into Dad. But I'm nothing like him. I'm not a model student, I don't like their friends, and I don't want to go to boarding school in Virginia."

"I know. I'll do something about it." I have no idea *what* to do, but I mean it. I'll figure something out. I have to.

"They think I'm damaged. That there's something wrong with me." Tears slip out, though he seems to fight to keep them in. "I can't feel like that anymore. I just can't."

"You're not . . ." I pull him to me, holding him in a tight hug. Good God, he's taller than me now. Taller than Dad was, too. "You're not damaged or wrong. You're yourself, and I love you. I wouldn't change a single thing about you."

He slightly pulls back, his gaze locking on mine. "I want to live here. With you."

He . . . *what*? The world seems to tilt, and I stare at him, speechless. In the quiet, the faint chirping of crickets feels deafening. He watches me, waiting, and all I can think is I can't deny this to him, no matter what it takes. I'm just not sure he realizes what he's asking me to do.

His eyes fill with resolve. "Scarlett, I want you to be my legal guardian."

19

the timeline collision

[trope]

the pivotal moment in a rom-com when the present finally collides with that dramatic flash-forward we glimpsed at the beginning; cue the exact showdown and awkward confession, now unfolding with every bit of chaotic energy and dramatic flair we were promised

---

Hunting down a serial killer is *not* as glamorous as they say. For one thing, my teeth have been chattering throughout the drive to the library, so now my jaw hurts. And once I finally got here and found the door had been forced open, I hid behind the shelves, squeezing my little pink Taser. I accumulated so much tension in my shoulders that I can actually *feel* the muscles cramping.

I tiptoe between the towering bookshelves, clutching the Taser like it's a medieval sword. I really hope my heart doesn't betray me by bursting out of my body entirely.

A faint rustling sound catches my attention, and I freeze mid-step. The noise comes again—somewhere in the far corner of the library. I inch forward, weaving through the shelves, my breaths shallow and my steps quieter. My palms are clammy around the Taser's handle, and my breath feels obnoxiously loud in the silence.

Then I see him. He's there, at the end of the aisle, all dark and brooding, with that stupid, soft, infuriatingly perfect hair.

It's him. Rafael.

I can't believe it's Rafael.

Eyes closing, I try to push every single feeling down, the disappointment screaming so loud in my head it might just kill me, then peek out from behind the shelf. He's still there, silently waiting like he has nowhere else to be. Meanwhile, I'm pretty sure I'm about to faint.

God, it's really him.

I move forward, inching closer and closer until I'm right behind him. My heart's hammering, and I can almost feel the electricity of the Taser pulsing in my hand. One more step, and I'll have him.

My hand is poised to strike, but just as I'm about to make my move, he turns around with startling speed. His speckled gray eyes lock onto mine, and I see the recognition flicker in them. His hand moves in a blur, pulling a gun from his jacket and pointing it directly at my forehead.

Rafael has a fucking gun. And it's not pink, either.

"Really?" I mutter, blinking at him. "You *had* to bring a gun?"

He arches an eyebrow, a half smirk that would be incredibly attractive if I wasn't so busy internally screaming. He's dressed in all black, the usual leather jacket worn and creased at the elbows, and under it, a fitted black turtleneck that clings to his broad frame.

"Were you planning on . . . *stunning* me with that?" He gestures to the Taser in my hand like I've just brought a rubber duck to a knife fight.

I glare at him, desperately trying to retain some level of dignity while simultaneously trying not to wet my pants. "I promise it won't feel as pink as it looks."

His eyes sparkle as he chuckles. *Chuckles.* Like this is all some grand joke. "You know, I had you pegged as smarter than this," he says, his chin jerking down. "You lead me here and show up with that? What did you figure would happen next, exactly?"

Goddamn it, he knows this is a trap. Just as well, because, though it worked, based on the gun pointed at me, it clearly didn't *work.* "You're here, aren't you?"

He pulls at the collar of his turtleneck, tattoo ink curling up his neck like smoke. "Yes, I'm here. And you're coming with me now." He jerks his gun to the right, his eyes flicking behind me. "After you, Freckles."

There's no point in running. I'm fucked.

I turn around, a sharp pain settling over my chest. Like a stomachache, but where my heart is.

A chest ache.

Maybe *this* is what heartbreak feels like.

I walk, aware that his gun is still pointed at the back of my head. That the man I started to feel something for wants to kill me, and probably will. Because, of course, I can't take him with a stupid pink Taser. And I didn't tell anyone where I am—all Ethan knows is that I'll be out for a while, and if he needs something, he should call Paige. But he'll never recover from this, will he? From losing someone else?

"How could you do this?" My voice echoes faintly off the library walls and through the stale air.

Rafael doesn't say a word behind me.

"I defended you," I continue, the words ripping out of me like shards of glass. "Even with everything pointing at you—even when common sense and *evidence* told me otherwise—I *still* defended you. I *believed* you."

When he says nothing, I face him, and he glances around. I'm done. I'm not going anywhere, not until he explains. If I'm dying, I want to know *why*.

A horrifying thought punches through my chest like a wrecking ball. "Did you . . . did you do all of this for me? The podcast, the murders?"

Still no answer.

"*Say something!*" I yell, the Taser sparking faintly as my hand jerks.

Finally, he speaks, his voice calm but weighted with something dark. "Why are you here, Scarlett?"

The question throws me, and I look at the gun in his hand like I'm first noticing it now, my stomach twisting into knots. It's still pointed at me. A motherfucking *gun*.

"Why are you here?" he asks again, softer this time, but his gaze darts to the shadows around us like he's expecting company.

I straighten, my grip tightening on the Taser. "I *led* you here. I picked this book, this place—to force you into the library and catch you."

His shoulders drop, and to my surprise, he steps back, his expression thoughtful. "Of course you did."

What?

"Tell me about Reddit," he says, his tone oddly casual, as if we're discussing grocery lists instead of murder.

"Reddit?" I snap.

"The post. It was you, right? You wanted people to notice the pattern. You wanted more people to listen to the podcast."

"*No.* How could you even think—" My breathing turns shallow, and my grip on the Taser loosens for just a second. "Do you actually believe I *wanted* this?"

"Don't you? Your podcast was struggling," he says, his tone infuriatingly calm. "Your job's on the line."

"You've *killed* people!" I scream. "This isn't about a podcast or a job. This is *murder.*"

He exhales slowly, tilting his head. "The flowers, then. Can you explain those?"

"The . . . what?"

"The flowers you ordered two weeks ago. You signed for them."

I stagger back a step, my brow furrowing. "What are you *talking* about? You used my podcast, Rafael," I insist, tears stinging my eyes. I don't know why he's stalling—talking about Reddit and flowers—and I honestly don't care. "You've tainted my work and made me feel responsible for these murders. You lied to me about everything." I take a shaky breath. "Whatever reason you had . . . it's over. You're done. I'm going to the police." My heart pounds so hard it hurts. "Unless you're ready to kill me, too."

Slowly, he lowers the gun, the tension in the room snapping like a taut string. He sets it into the back of his pants and calls out, "Is this enough?"

"What?" My head whips around, and before I can process his words, officers emerge from the shadows of the library, their guns drawn but not aimed. Wes and Chief Donovan.

My heart stops. The police. They're *here.*

Thank God they're here.

"It's h-him," I stammer. "He's the murderer. He . . ." My words trail off as I realize Rafael just talked to them, didn't he? *Before* they revealed themselves. He knew they were here.

What the hell is going on?

"Y-you're a cop? You're a . . ."

"I'm not," Rafael says, his gaze soft but unbearably heavy. "Are you okay?"

He reaches for my hand, but I yank it away like his touch burns. If he's not the murderer, but he's not the police, either, then . . . "Who *are* you?"

"I'm a private investigator," he says in a worried voice. "Scarlett, you need to come with me."

"No." I back away, shaking my head. "I'm not going anywhere with you."

"Scarlett, please." For a second, he looks like he's in pain. Like he knows he just ruined everything. "You're safe now, okay?"

"N-no." I cross my arms, trying to get my body to stop shaking. It must be the adrenaline drop. "Y-you pointed a gun at m-me."

"I know." His hand falls to his side. "I'll explain everything, I promise."

Promise? Sure, I'm relieved he's not a murderer, but he still lied about *everything*. Just how many promises has he made and broken already? "I think I'm tired of your promises, actually."

Chief Donovan steps closer. "Better listen to your boyfriend, sweetheart. You need to straighten out a few details, and things aren't looking good for you."

"Seriously, Chief? *I'm* your suspect?"

"You knew details about the crimes that weren't disclosed to the public."

I breathe out slowly, letting the implication sink in. "So . . . this whole time, you've been focused on me? Please tell me you have other suspects."

His eyes dart to Rafael, who raises both hands in frustration. Un-*fucking*-believable.

"And now they might finally start focusing on *actual* suspects," Rafael says, his voice sharp enough to cut. Then, softer, to me, "But we still need to talk."

"Why?" I croak. I can barely stand to look at him right now.

He reaches forward, as if he's going to tuck my hair behind my ear. Noticing the way my gaze darts to his fingers, his fist clenches and settles back at his side. "Because someone's trying to frame you for these murders."

————————

So this is why Rafael never let me into his place—because the walls of his living room are smothered with photos, papers, and notes scribbled in a chaotic network of suspicion. Celeste, Vanessa, Theo. There's a shot of Mrs. Prattle watering her garden, one of Paige laughing.

And he's done this in the space of weeks?

It's so eerie, so invasive, that it feels like my skin is crawling.

I don't even realize I'm holding my breath until Rafael sets a steaming mug in front of me, startling me into a sharp inhale. The scent of coffee mingles with that of his cologne—a warm, woodsy scent that used to make me feel safe. Now it's just another reminder of how deeply he's infiltrated my life.

"Here. This'll help," he says carefully, like he's afraid I might shatter if he speaks too loudly.

My hands tighten around the mug, and I fix my eyes on the chipped edge of the table without thanking him.

"How are you feeling?"

I finally look up with a glare. "Like someone I trusted just pointed a gun at me."

His face tightens, the faintest flicker of regret crossing his features. He drags a chair next to mine and sits so close our knees almost touch, and I instinctively roll my chair back an inch, the scrape of the wooden legs loud in the suffocating silence.

"Scarlett, the police have protocols," he pleads. "A suspect holding a weapon is a threat. If I hadn't kept my gun on you, they would've stormed in, and I needed time to get you to admit you had nothing to do with these murders."

I still can't wrap my head around the fact that *I* was their main suspect. "Why didn't they question me? Why didn't Vanessa tell me anything?"

He exhales. "The chief kept her out of the loop, since you two are close. He was investigating you, but didn't want to question you until they had further proof—look, don't get me started on this. Dealing with these *cops* makes me miss the city."

"How long have you been working on this case?"

His mouth opens, then closes. It's as good as a confession.

Everything since the Single Mingle has been a lie.

Knuckles turning white around the mug, I say, "Just tell me why you brought me here."

"Okay." He wipes away beads of sweat glistening on his forehead, then pulls a paper from the pile in front of him. My stomach twists when he slides it across the table. It's a receipt for an online flower purchase made in my name.

"What's this about? I didn't buy flowers."

"You also signed for the delivery." He hands me another paper, this one showing a scrawled signature that looks remarkably like mine. "These flowers were used in the first murder."

He holds up a picture but hesitates as he studies me.

"Let me see."

"You don't have to, if you—"

"Yes, I do," I insist.

He hesitates again before laying the photo on the table. I glance at it. Catherine's naked body is rigid over the chair, her wrists tied together behind her back. Her skin is unnaturally yellow, and the red petals contrast even more against it. I turn my face away, my stomach churning.

Rafael quickly snatches the photo back, but I raise a trembling hand. "It's fine. I can do it."

He sets it down again, watching me closely. It's horrifying, enraging. Someone did this to her—and is doing this to me, twisting my life into their macabre little masterpiece.

"There's more," Rafael says, scrolling through a tablet, then showing me a screenshot of the post on Reddit. "Look at this."

Reading-fictional-murders? "That's not my account," I say.

"It was posted from your laptop."

"That's impossible," I say, shaking my head. "I always have my laptop with me."

Rafael's nod is stiff. "I know. Look, I'm working on it, okay? I don't want you to worry. I promise I'll find out who's behind it."

A bitter laugh bubbles in my throat. Again with that word—*promise.* Does he seriously think it means anything now?

"I don't get it," I say. "You showed up exactly when these murders began. And your dad just *happens* to—" My lips seal shut. His dad had a stroke—I read the obituary on the *Whistle*. Could it have been foul play?

"Poison." He brushes an imaginary speck of dust from the soft-looking turtleneck. "The police had no reason to suspect foul play. An old man dying of stroke alone in his home? Pretty normal. But they found a letter of apology addressed to me."

"*The Lonely Man*," I whisper, reminded of the book I discussed on the podcast just before Mr. Gray's death. "Wait, but the press didn't say anything. The police didn't—"

"Chief Donovan didn't believe me at first. After Catherine Blake's murder, when you visited the chief, they went back to look at the case."

He gestures at a piece of paper. I take it and read:

Upon reevaluation, toxicology screening detected trace amounts of digitalis (commonly found in foxglove). The concentration in the bloodstream suggests intentional ingestion. No prescribed medication or medical condition accounted for this.

"You okay?" he asks, his hand reaching for me but dropping before he can actually touch me.

Am I *okay*? My mouth is filling with saliva quicker than I can swallow it, and cold sweat is accumulating over my lips. "I think I'll go home now."

"I'll walk you."

I study him for a long moment, seething at how damn good he looks right now. Angry that I can't even enjoy it. Furious that some traitorous part of me still wants him to stay the night. And enraged that he did this to me.

I shake my head. "It's okay," I say coldly, slinging my bag over my shoulder. "I don't need you to."

"Scarlett . . ."

"What happens if the actual murderer shows up at the library tonight?" I ask, walking past him.

"Uh, there are a couple of officers stationed outside, but . . ." He glances at his watch. "I doubt anyone will show up."

Why, though? How could the killer have known that tonight's episode was just a ruse to catch them? Maybe they noticed the police. Goddamn it. How is the killer always one step ahead?

"Let me walk you home," Rafael insists as he comes to my side.

With a glare, I rush to the entrance, then out the door. The air outside is cool against my flushed cheeks, but the ache in my chest doesn't ease. Not even a little.

"Scarlett, wait." His voice chases me down, sharper than the night air nipping at my skin.

My steps quicken, but so do his.

"I know you're disappointed." He's by my side now, his breath fogging in the cold. "But I knew you weren't guilty, Scarlett, and I had to prove it. That's why I'm here, why I came to Willowbrook— not for that asshole who was my dad. You have to understand. Some- times the police don't care about the truth. They just want a neat story, a suspect who fits their narrative. And I knew it was just a matter of time before they connected the murders to the podcast. To you."

And how did *he* know to look into my podcast after he'd been gone for five years? Actually, forget about it. That's *not* the point.

"Not me, though," he presses. "I *knew* you had nothing to do with this, and I've proven it. I'll catch the real killer, and—"

I whirl around, my boots crunching against the gravel. "*That's not the problem!*" I shout, my voice sharp in the otherwise silent neighborhood. "You told me, didn't you? Since the beginning, you said you were here for the wrong reasons. You blamed it on Dave, Lucas, some stupid *bet*—but you told me. And you warned me you were *trouble*."

"That was . . ." Rafael's shoulders slump, his face pale under the glow of the streetlamp. His hair hangs over his eyes, but not enough to hide his pained expression. "I couldn't tell you," he says quietly. "I didn't want things between us to move forward until I did."

"Uh-uh!" I raise a finger, a grimace twisting my lips. "You don't get to talk. You don't get to explain, or justify, or make this all better. You get to live with it. With the fact that you lied. That there will be nothing else. Not even a hello if we pass each other on the street. No Chinese food, no Macarena, no sleeping over. *Nothing*." My voice shakes, but I force it out anyway. "That these are my last words to you."

The silence is deafening. His gaze drops to the ground, his lips tightening into a grim line. It makes a dull ache settle in my chest— seeing him like this, knowing I'm responsible for his suffering.

But he deserves worse.

"You know, if *this* is the best version of yourself, then I'm sure my dad would agree with me when I say . . . I wish you hadn't come back at all."

He blinks, eyes watering, and immediately, I hate myself for saying that. Yes, I feel betrayed, but no one deserves the kind of hurt I see in his expression.

Before I can fold and apologize, I walk away with purposeful steps. My place is only a few feet away, but the distance feels endless. By the time I walk up onto the porch, my hands are trembling so badly I nearly drop the keys, especially as the tears come hot and fast, blurring my vision.

I slam the door shut, the sound reverberating like the finality of everything I just said, and as I let the first sob out, the realization settles over me: this isn't the only door closing.

No. I'm closing every door.

And this time, it's for good.

the groveling

[trope]

---

the sacred rite of passage in which one character—usually
after a spectacular display of idiocy—embarks on a dramatic,
heartfelt apology tour to win back the other; characterized by
impassioned declarations and grand gestures

"How are you feeling?"

I shove another book into the cart, pretending Paige's question doesn't sting. I spent most of last night awake, replaying every single moment of the last two weeks between Rafael and me, so I'm tired. And heartbroken, though I'll never admit it. Then today I woke up to Celeste shouting at me, telling me how disappointed she was that I'd gone behind her back and rerecorded the episode. I tried to explain that if the police wouldn't do anything, then we had to, but . . . well, let's just say it's a miracle Theo and I still have our jobs.

And even with this shitstorm raining on me, I had to keep up appearances for Ethan, who hasn't changed his mind about moving in since last night. Had to make breakfast and make conversation like half of my world hadn't imploded.

"I'm seeing Celeste's husband today. He squeezed me in, and hopefully he'll help me understand the next step to get custody of my brother."

"That's good. Great. And how do you feel about . . . *him*?"

Him. I know it's not Ethan or Steve. "I'm fine."

Her long fingers tap her chin. "Really?"

Of course I'm not fine. Rafael lied about *everything*. And the worst part? I knew something was off, but I ignored every single sign. Theo told me to trust my gut. Why didn't I? And why, out of all the people in the world, did I give that lying sack of shit a chance?

"At least now I know. And it's only been a couple of weeks, so . . ." I trail off. I'll be okay. I have to be, because there are more important things for me to think about, like Ethan.

"Sorry I didn't answer last night," she says. "I didn't see your call until this morning."

I lazily look over the books in front of me. "Where were you?"

I couldn't stand being alone last night, and when I got back home, Ethan was sleeping. So I walked to her place, which was empty, then to Vanessa's. Paige wasn't there, either, and when Vanessa invited me in anyway, I realized my best friend was the only person I wanted to talk to.

Paige turns around, looking through the shelves. "Uh, just at Vanessa's."

Wait, what? Why is she lying?

My brows knit together, but I don't think she notices as she picks up a book and begins reading the back, green eyes skillfully avoiding mine. "You know, this kind of thing happens all the time in romance."

"What does?"

"The big betrayal, where it turns out the love interest was initially pursuing the main character because of some ulterior motive."

I arch a brow. "Like what?"

She tilts her head thoughtfully. "Like maybe they've been sent by their Mafia boss? Or the king."

I stare at her across the aisle. "The king?"

"Yeah. If the love interest is a prince or something."

When I make no movement, she plucks a book off the shelf. "Look," she says, turning it in her hands and reading aloud. "'When Tristan Montgomery was asked by his father to uncover every secret of Saddlehorn Ranch, he knew Patty was the key to everything. What he didn't plan for was falling in love with his sunshiny neighbor.'" Paige holds the book up, her brows raised as if she just proved a point. "See? Happens all the time."

And? What is she trying to say?

I walk over, pick up another book, and skim the back cover. "'Can serial killers fall in love? Finding out the love of my life is my stalker wasn't on my bingo card. But I forgot about the bodies in his backyard the second his hands were on me.'" I hold it up triumphantly. "This is also romance. Should I date a stalker next?"

Paige sighs as I stride back to my aisle, though I notice her slipping the serial killer book into her own stack. "No, of course not. But you chose one of the black covers on purpose."

"Romance is not a credible resource for actual relationship issues, is my point."

"Ha! So you *are* in a relationship with Rafael?" she asks, her curls bouncing with the bob of her head.

God, she's starting to sound like him.

"I *was* in a . . . *situationship*," I correct. "It's definitely over now."

The bell above the door jingles, and, registering my admonishing look, Paige falls into silence. The last thing I need is the whole town talking about my non-breakup.

But then I sense someone stepping beside me, and when Paige gasps, dread coils in my stomach. I look up from my book, meeting the gray eyes I've come to adore in the past few weeks. They're not playful like before but soft. Apologetic.

"Hey," he says, his voice hesitant.

He's so handsome, some voice echoes in my mind. Truthfully, he looks disheveled, like he hasn't gotten any sleep. He's wearing the same clothes as last night too.

"Goddamn it." I glare at Paige, but her wide eyes tell me she had no part in this.

"She didn't tell me anything." His voice softens further. "I know you. I know where you go when you're upset."

"I'm not upset," I counter sharply.

His gaze flickers to the pile of books I'm clutching like a lifeline. "Uh-huh."

"And I have nothing to say to you." I grab a random book and pretend to read the back.

"Let me say my piece, Scarlett, please. And if you want nothing to do with me after, I'll respect that," he insists. "I know you needed a great deal of trust to let me in, and I've betrayed it. I just want you to understand—"

"What?" I snap, rounding on him. "That though it all started as a ploy to steal my ranch's secrets, you couldn't help but fall for my sunshiny demeanor?"

His brow furrows. "What? N-no—"

"Let it go, Rafael. You have a killer to catch, and sorry to disappoint, but I'm not them."

I turn back to the shelf, silently praying that he'll let go. That he'll leave the bookstore, leave me. Maybe leave Willowbrook altogether.

"This was never about the case, Scarlett." He almost sounds sad enough to make me pause. *Almost.* "My feelings for you aren't a side effect. They're the illness and the cure. They were here long before any of this, and they'll be here after."

Tears blur my vision, hot and uninvited, sliding down my cheeks as I try to hold on to the rage, try to make it make sense. But I can't. The beauty of his words, the ache in his voice, they get under my skin. They rip through those same walls he always manages to climb over.

"Scarlett, I told you. I fell for you when we were nothing more than kids. I've only *done* something about it now."

And how am I supposed to believe anything he says? "Bullshit."

"No, it's not bullshit. How do you think I even connected the murders to your podcast?" When I glance up at him, he sighs. "Because I connected my father's murder to your episode about *The Lonely Man*. Because I've been listening to *Murders & Manuscripts* since the first episode."

He's been listening to my podcast? For five years?

"I don't believe you," I say, the realization bitter on my tongue. I don't believe a word he says, and there's nothing I can do about it. "Please, just *leave*."

He looks at me like I've slapped him, eyes shining with hurt. "You're really going to do this?" His voice drops, hoarse. "You're really going to pretend we don't mean anything?"

I don't answer. I can't.

His chest heaves once, twice. "Jesus, Scarlett," he breathes, almost pleading. "Don't—" But then he cuts himself off, biting down on whatever else he was about to say. He turns on his heel, and the bell over the door gives an accusing jingle as it slams shut behind him, the sound ringing in my ears long after he's gone.

There.

It's done.

I meet Paige's stare, my mind still in a haze. "What?"

"Will you just toss me aside, too, when I do something wrong? Hurt me before I hurt you more?"

For a second, I stare into her stormy eyes, unsure of what to say. "Seriously, Paige? What he did is hardly just 'something wrong.' "

She crosses her arms, leaning slightly forward. "Yeah, well . . ."

"He lied about *everything*," I add, my tone dropping.

"Oh, Scarlett, come on. He lied about his *job*. He couldn't tell you."

"I can't believe you're defending him." I grab my stack of books and shove them onto the nearest shelf. Is she really so in love with romance that she'd turn a blind eye to something like this? "You know what? I'm done with shopping. Let's go home."

"Scarlett . . ."

But I'm already out the door.

I knock on the door to Steve's office, and once he invites me in, I enter and close the door behind me. The smell of pastrami and mustard lingers in the air, mixing with the faint scent of coffee and paper. "Thank you so much for seeing me, Steve."

He waves me off, salt-and-pepper hair and a friendly smile softening the otherwise angular lines of his face. "It sounded urgent, and your mom was one of the good ones. Whatever I can do to help."

He balls up a napkin and aims for the trash can, but he misses, and the napkin bounces onto the floor, settling in the messy corner of his cluttered office.

"Thank you." I sit down in the worn chair across from his desk, which squeaks under my weight. "My brother showed up at my door last night, and . . ." I trail off. And a lot of other stuff has happened since—so much, in fact, that I almost forgot the appointment I set with Steve, Willowbrook's favorite lawyer. "You've read the files, right? Please give me good news."

He straightens, wiping his hands before pulling a folder from the top of a precarious stack. His brow furrows as he flips through it, his reading glasses slipping down his nose. "Well, let's see," he says, pen poised above a notepad. "It sounds like we'll have to get creative." Noticing my expression, he explains, "You already know that under the terms of the will, your parents gave your grandparents custody of Ethan. Under normal circumstances, I'd bring this to a judge, say that the situation has obviously changed."

Right. *Everything's* changed.

He pauses. "I would tell you that we should go after them for custody or get Ethan emancipated. Paperwork, hearings, and, depending on how cooperative your grandparents are, possibly mediation or even a full trial."

God, I feel queasy.

"But you're *not* telling me this?"

"No. Because it'd take months, if not years."

Months, years. *We don't have that.* "So . . . so what's the solution?"

His eyes narrow slightly. "An emergency hearing. Much quicker but much more difficult to win, because we'll need to prove beyond a doubt that your brother is in immediate danger."

"Danger?" I hesitate, my throat tightening. I don't think Virginia can be considered "dangerous."

"Danger. So . . ." He clears his throat and watches me attentively. "Besides his reluctance, do we have anything concrete that proves this move is *not* the best choice for him?"

I bite my lip, mind reeling. "His mental health," I say, thinking of his struggles at school. "Taking him away from everything he knows—from me—is only going to make things worse."

Steve's pen taps against the desk, a steady rhythm that mirrors the pounding in my chest. "Great. How do we prove that, though?"

I relate most of what Ethan told me, and Steve listens, his expression measured. "I won't sugarcoat it, it's not going to be easy, and we want no surprises, so if there's *anything* I need to know, this is the moment to bring it up."

I shake my head, thankful for once that I have the most boring life ever.

"Good. Then we need to build the strongest case we can, and fast."

"Got it," I say with a decisive nod. "I'll do whatever it takes."

Steve offers me a small, encouraging smile. "We're going to war, Scarlett," he says. "Be prepared."

The room feels heavier, the faint shadows cast by the desk lamp creeping across the walls. I inhale deeply, letting it all settle over me.

"I will be."

21

the whodunit

[trope]

a tantalizing puzzle wrapped in deception, where everyone's
a suspect and trust is a dangerous game; expect red herrings,
dramatic gasps, and at least one overly confident detective
jumping to the wrong conclusion

"What the hell," I mumble as I drive along my street and notice the police cars lined up. "Good God, not again."

My heartbeat thunders in my chest the second I catch sight of the police tape sealing off Mrs. Prattle's house.

"No, no, no," I say under my breath, pulling to the side of the road hastily. I'm out of the car before I can think it through. Wes and Vanessa are talking to a neighbor, their expressions grim, and they don't notice me slipping past them, stepping under the taped-off area until I'm inside the house.

The metallic tang of blood hits me like a brick wall, making my stomach churn, but I force myself to keep moving, wobbling un-steadily down the narrow corridor into the small living room.

Until the pools of red soaking into the couch and carpet blur my vision, making my knees buckle.

"No," I say, my hand finding the wall as I fight to stay upright. My breath is shallow and rapid, my pulse roaring in my ears. *Mrs. Prattle.* What the hell happened here? Last night's episode was set in the library. This . . . this doesn't fit. What's going on?

"Scarlett?"

The voice sounds distant, muffled, like I'm underwater. I try to focus, but everything feels disjointed, surreal. Oh God, I can't breathe.

"Scarlett?" The voice comes into focus this time, and so does Rafael's face. Gray, worried eyes. A straight nose that once nuzzled the back of my neck. Soft, full lips that he used to press kisses to my cheeks. "Are you okay?"

Someone says something in the background, but I can't make out what. Rafael does, though, because he turns and says, "I know she's not supposed to be here." Then he faces me again, his hand gripping my shoulder. I should hate his touch, I know I should, but it grounds me just enough to feel the floor beneath my feet.

"Can you walk?"

"Penelope?" I manage as I point at the traces of blood. My throat feels raw, like I've swallowed glass. I don't think I've ever called Mrs. Prattle by her first name before, but it slips out now.

"She's safe at her son's place. This was Mrs. Brattle's next-door neighbor," Rafael says grimly. "His wife said he used the spare keys last night when they saw something across the street at Mrs. Brattle's house. He must have surprised the killer."

It takes me a second to process, then my chest heaves as relief washes over me. It's *not* Mrs. Prattle. But it lasts only a second before it's swallowed by guilt.

"Rob," I say. "Oh my God, Rob."

Rafael nods solemnly.

Rob Wilkins. One of Ethan's old teachers, and the man who mowed my lawn without fail every month and never asked for anything in return. The man who's now . . . I don't even want to think about it.

"B-but I don't get it," I stammer.

"We don't, either," Rafael says, holding me up. "Do you have any idea why the killer would stray from the pattern? Is there something in the last book about . . . axes or logs or—"

"Logs?" I interrupt.

"Yes. They were placed around the body like a . . ."

"Like a pyre," I finish for him, my voice hollow.

His brows furrow. "But that wasn't part of the book, was it?"

I can't answer. My legs feel like they're moving on their own as I push past him and step into the kitchen.

Rob's body lies sprawled on the cold tiled floor. His arms are pinned at awkward angles, and a pool of dark, viscous blood spreads beneath him. Around him, logs of wood are arranged in a grotesque pattern. His shirt is torn, the pale flesh of his chest marred by deep gashes, slashes so clean they almost look surgical.

His eyes are wide open, staring blankly at the ceiling, frozen in an expression of terror that makes bile rise in my throat.

"Rafael," I call weakly, and in an instant, he's at my side. His hand steadies me.

"You're okay," Rafael says soothingly. He's next to me, his hand stroking my hair and tucking it away from my face. Leaning against him, I walk outside.

I'm supposed to be furious with him. Hell, I *am*. But I can't afford pride right now. My heart is hammering, my ribs straining against each inhale as I crouch over the grass.

He's quickly kneeling beside me, his forehead creased with worry, but he doesn't look nauseated—or bothered at all.

"Not your first corpse, I take it?"

He solemnly shakes his head. "I've seen plenty."

"Plenty," I repeat, struggling to imagine a reality where this is a regular Friday.

I've lived my life fascinated by the morbid. Murders, serial killers, mysteries. It sure as hell feels different when it's not within the pages of a book.

"Why do you do it? This job?"

He exhales, adjusting his jeans over his hips. "I wanted to be a cop, actually."

"Really? A cop?"

"Yeah. Like your dad."

I say nothing, brows arching.

"The academy probably wouldn't have been good for me, though. I work best alone."

"Rafael," I say, accepting the water bottle Wes hands me, then waiting for him to walk away. "You need to work this case with *me*. I want to help you catch the Lit Killer."

His brow furrows, the soft lines of concern hardening into something sharper. "The what now?"

"The Lit Killer."

He presses his lips tight as if to contain a chuckle.

"What? Lit, like literature. I just figured . . . Stop laughing! It makes sense!"

I continue before he has a chance to say no. "This is my town. My podcast. And they went for Mrs. Pr—Brattle." My words tumble out in a rush. "That woman is . . . She's *Mrs. Prattle*! She bakes cookies for the neighborhood kids and lends out books from her personal collection like she's running her own damn library. And Rob is such a great guy. He didn't deserve—"

"I know," he says with a grimace. "But you're too close, Scarlett. You can't be objective."

"What if I have information that will reduce the pool of suspects to only a handful?"

His lips flatten into a thin line, his resolve cracking. "Fine," he relents. "You can help—but only if you promise not to put yourself in danger." He points a finger at me, his tone deadly serious. "Promise."

"I promise."

He gestures for me to speak, so I lean closer. "Last night's episode—the library—was a setup for the murderer." He nods, his sharp eyes narrowing. "Which I only came up with on Wednesday. But the original episode was *this* one." I point back at the house, shivering as the memory of the bloodstained kitchen flashes in my mind. "It never aired."

His expression darkens, the realization sinking in. "Wait. That means the killer . . ."

"They've either read my scripts or listened to the podcast *before* it's aired." My eyes dart toward the familiar faces of neighbors lingering behind the police tape. A chill runs down my spine as I scan the crowd, suspicion gnawing at me. "It must be someone from Booked It."

One of my colleagues.

"I looked into everyone at Booked It," Rafael says, cutting through my spiraling thoughts. "Every single person has an alibi—except . . ."

Don't say it.

"Theo."

"It's not Theo!" I blurt out.

His lips twist, but I insist. "It's not him. He edited the library episode. He knew it changed."

"And if he's the killer, he knew it was a trap."

"It's *not* Theo."

He exhales sharply. "Would you have reacted differently if I told you that Celeste didn't have an alibi?"

"It's not Celeste, either!"

"Scarlett—"

"It's not!" I snap. "She's in full denial, Rafael. She went to the police, and trust me, she was *pissed* when people connected the murders to Booked It."

He looks away, his hand raking through his hair. "I know it's not Celeste. She was visiting her kid at UConn in Groton during two of the murders. But your colleagues aren't the only people who have access to the episode before it airs. Whoever this killer is, it must be someone close to you. Too close for you to be objective."

I stare at him, searching his face for answers, my thoughts buzzing as one name after another flits through my mind. Until . . .

"Paige." My voice is barely audible. "She's the first person I send the scripts to every week."

His expression tightens. "Your brother has had access to your laptop, too."

"My *brother*?" I squeak, horrified. Remembering the curious crowd watching from behind the tape, I blush and lower my voice. "You can't seriously think Ethan is involved."

He shakes his head. "I don't. But I can't rule it out, either. Do you understand? You actually *can't* help with this investigation, because I can't ask you to suspect your best friend—or your family."

I exhale, ready to protest some more.

"Come on. I'll walk you home."

"You don't need to."

"Did that come out as a question? Because it wasn't."

We fall into a comfortable pace past the small crowd, an awkward silence lingering between us. I just know he's about to bring up the situation between us, and frankly, I'm not in the mood for it. "Ethan . . . he's staying at my place."

"He is?"

"Yeah. We talked, and I saw a lawyer. He thinks we might have grounds for an emergency hearing. To fight for custody."

He bumps his shoulder against mine. "*What?* That's amazing."

I guess Rafael was right. He'd said I should tell Ethan the truth about our grandparents. "I just hope I know what I'm doing."

"You don't." When I whine, he laughs. "You don't! But that's okay. You'll figure it out together. All Ethan wants is a chance to do that."

I guess he's right. I guess that's all I want, too.

He opens the small gate that leads into my front yard, and I'm about to thank him when I notice a box on my porch. Weird. The postman knows not to leave stuff unattended outside, with the way Sherlock likes to destroy cardboard.

"Did you buy something?" Rafael is in front of me before I can take a step.

"No." I follow, my heartbeat spiking at the tension radiating from him. What does he think is in there? "Rafael?" I call, catching up to him just as he crouches by the box. His hand, poised to lift the first flap, hesitates when he turns to me.

"Scarlett, step back."

He thinks there's something bad in there. Something dangerous or traumatizing, like a severed hand or some other type of creepy message.

Before Rafael can stop me, I step up and pull the first flap open.

The smell hits me first—cloying and metallic. It's dark inside, but the red, sticky substance is unmistakable. And the black fur.

"Don't." Rafael's hand wraps around my arm, yanking me back. His body is solid behind me like an unyielding wall, and the cold leather of his jacket presses against the bare skin of my arms, sending an electric jolt through me. My breath hitches, ragged and shallow, catching on the rising tide of panic that claws at my throat.

Sherlock has been gone all night, hasn't he?

I've been so caught up with everything that I didn't realize he hadn't slept in my bed.

"Sherlock?" My eyes are unseeing as Rafael breathes hard in my ear. "Is that Sherlock?"

"Roooo."

Both our heads snap to the side. Perched on the railing, Sherlock sits, his usual disgruntled expression in place, tail sinuously twitching behind him.

"Oh, you stupid cat," Rafael grumbles, the tension draining from his body as he leans against me. I can't tell if I'm holding him up or if he's holding me up, or if we've somehow become the perfect mess of relief propping each other up.

He lets me go slowly, hands dropping to his sides with a reluctant drag against my arms. I take an unsteady step forward, sucking in a shaky breath, then I turn to look at him.

He's watching me, eyes dark, chest rising and falling like he's run a marathon. He lifts a hand, hesitating for just a heartbeat before the back of his finger grazes my cheek—light as a sigh. "You okay, Freckles?"

"I thought . . ." My voice wavers. "I really, really thought . . ."

"I know."

It looks like he's about to say something—something I'm *not* ready to hear, so I pick Sherlock up and give him a smooch.

Rafael opens the other flap of the box. "It's a plush toy," he announces. "And blood—animal, I hope."

Letting Sherlock down, I cross my arms. "So it's a message."

"And the message is 'Stay the fuck out of this,'" he says, holding up the decapitated black plush cat.

Even with Sherlock safe at my feet, the sight of it makes me queasy. I don't care what Rafael thinks, my brother would never do this. Paige, Theo—they know how much I love this cat.

But whoever *did* do this?

They've messed with the wrong cat lady.

22

the cringeworthy chaos

[trope]

maybe not a classic trope but a personal favorite of this author;
it's that deliciously embarrassing moment that has everyone
laughing . . . and low-key wishing they could disappear

"Who are you seeing?" I ask Ethan as he shoves a water bottle into the side pocket of his backpack.

"Jace," he says, the word clipped. Noticing the tilt of my head, he stops to look at me. "Can you please meet him before you judge him?"

"I'm not judging him," I lie, crossing my arms.

"You're judging him," he says flatly.

"I'm just—"

"You know," Ethan interrupts, "Grandma used to call Mom a troublemaker, too."

I hand him his cap with an eye roll. He's right. Grandma always has something to say about people, and it's rarely positive. "I'd feel better if I met him."

"And I'd feel better if you trusted me," he says, slinging the blue backpack over his shoulder. When I give him an insistent look, he groans. "We'll see."

He takes a step, then turns around and gives me and my towel a once-over. "Unless you want me to stay?" he says half-heartedly. "If you don't have any plans or—"

If it wasn't for the pity laced in his voice, I'd be touched. "I have plans," I lie. "I'm going out."

"Date?"

"Sure." Actually, since privacy will take a new form now that Ethan is staying here, I have some *vibrating* plans for tonight. But I'm afraid he'll ask about Rafael, and I'm not ready to talk about it. "And you talked to Grandma about staying here?"

"Yes." He pulls his dark blond hair to all sides as he checks his reflection in the mirror. "I told her that since she's shipping me off to Virginia, I want to spend time with you. She bought it."

"Good. Good." I fidget with the hem of my towel.

He exhales, the sound heavy with finality. "I'm going."

"Wait. Let me give you a set of keys." I dart toward the bedroom and open the bedside drawer, a mess of receipts, loose coins, and random junk. The doorbell rings as I grab the spare keys, and my head jerks up.

"Hey, man."

Oh, fuck. That voice . . .

"Hi. Come in," Ethan says casually.

"Thanks. Is your sister here?"

No, no, no. My legs feel like lead as I inch toward the hallway.

"She's just getting ready," Ethan answers.

I bolt from the bedroom just in time to see Rafael step into the living room in a dark purple crewneck over a crisp white dress shirt, which would almost look preppy if it wasn't for the black tattoos along his fingers and up his wrists.

Ethan points at the menu he's holding. "Are you guys ordering Chinese again? I thought you were going out."

Too fucking late.

Rafael's eyes meet mine. His expression shifts from mild confusion to something sharper, his gaze flicking over the towel wrapped around me and back to my face. His lips curve into a thin, tight smile. "We're going out?"

"Uh, no." My voice is too loud, too quick, as I shove the keys into Ethan's hand. Seriously, did Rafael have to show up *now*?

"What?" Ethan's brows draw together, his head turning to me, then to Rafael, then back again. "Who's taking you on a date, then?"

Goddamn it. My laugh comes out awkward, forced. I wave vaguely toward the door. "You were leaving, weren't you?"

"But—"

"Be back by midnight, please."

Ethan mutters something under his breath and, with one last glance at me and Rafael, heads out, closing the door behind him.

Silence falls over the room, heavy and oppressive, until Rafael clears his throat. "You're going out with someone else? I thought we'd cleared the air."

"We did, yes. I just—"

"Who is it? *Theo*?"

I pause. Why does he make it sound like the most ridiculous thing he's ever heard? "Theo is an *amazing* guy, okay? And you don't know him, or our relationship."

"You're right. I don't. So why don't you tell me about it?"

"Because I don't owe you any explanation. We're going to work the case together, and that's *it*."

"Yeah, you're *not* working the case."

I watch the anger playing on his face, and my jaw clenches. "Because I'm going out with someone? Are you *that* petty?"

"Because you're not trained," he bites out. "And I need to catch this killer, not babysit you."

Babysit me? My hands clench at the edges of the towel. He wouldn't even know what the hell happened with the latest murder if it wasn't for me.

"You can hate me for the rest of your life, Scarlett, but I will never put you in danger. *Ever*. If that means you go on a date with someone else, then have the best fucking night."

"Oh, I will!"

He looks like he's about to argue but stops himself. Instead, he reaches into his back pocket, the hem of his shirt shifting, and pulls out a small box. He sets it on the coffee table with a frown, his rings clacking lightly against the wood. "I got you this. It's a tracking device."

I blink. "What?"

"For Sherlock." He steps away. "There's a camera on it, too. I figured you could use it to see how he's getting out of the house and track him when he sneaks out."

A mix of anger and warmth spreads through my chest. I haven't let Sherlock out of my sight since yesterday, but knowing I can't keep watching him that closely forever has left me anxious and worried. And Rafael just knew.

God, it pisses me off.

"You don't get to do this," I say, rushing to the door just as he opens it. My heart is pounding in my chest, stress hunching my shoulders. "I'm not the bad guy here, and you don't get to act like I dumped you."

"But that's what happened, isn't it?" he says, spinning around to face me on the porch.

"No. You *lied*—"

"Fuck that, Scarlett. You're *scared*," he interrupts, his voice rising just enough to cut me off. His eyes burn into mine, and I feel exposed, laid bare. "Just admit it. You're terrified of the way you feel, and you're taking the easy way out."

"How *dare* you!"

He looks away, jaw set. "Yeah, you know what? Now that I think about it, you and Theo would make a great couple."

"Yes, we would."

He clicks his tongue. "Too bad you have feelings for me."

"Yeah, it's too—" I clamp my mouth shut as he mock-gasps.

"Gotcha," he says before he turns around and walks away.

"You arrogant *jackass*—" I shout, stepping forward, but something jerks me back sharply, and I stumble, my back slamming against the door with a thud.

What the hell just happened?

He turns back, confused at first, but when his eyes drop to my waist, his lips curve into a slow, smug smile.

Oh no.

I follow his gaze and realize what's happened. My towel—the one barely clinging to my body—is caught in the door. The shut, locked door.

Are you *fucking* kidding me?

Heat crawls up my neck as I frantically try to yank the towel free, but it doesn't budge. Worse, the motion makes the towel shift precariously lower. I force myself to meet Rafael's gaze, though the grin tugging at his lips makes me want to crawl into a hole.

"Well, then," I say, attempting nonchalance. "Bye."

"*Bye?*" he mocks, his voice dripping with amusement. "You sure you want me to go?"

I lift my chin, willing myself to act like nothing is wrong. "Yeah. I'm sure."

"All right." He studies me for a beat and then, with a shrug, turns to leave. "If you say so."

I bite my lip, conflicted. I don't *want* to ask him for help, but I'm stuck. Literally stuck. "Wait!" The word bursts out of me before I can stop it. "I need—I need help."

He pauses, slowly turning back to face me, a delighted sparkle in his eyes. "Really?" he says with pretend surprise. "With what?"

"You know with what."

"Hmm." He tilts his head. "I don't, actually."

I glare, seething. "My towel is stuck in the door. Which is still better than being a small . . . petty . . . *bitter* man."

"Is it, though?" he says, chuckling. He walks toward me but veers off toward the side of the house.

"What are you doing?" I call after him, twisting to see where he's going.

"I'm going to climb through the bathroom window and open the door from the inside," he says, as if it's the most reasonable plan in the world.

"No, wait!" I blurt, my voice cracking. My stomach drops as I picture the scene awaiting him: my pink vibrator sitting on the vanity, bold and unavoidable. "You can't go in."

He stops, turning back with a confused expression. "Why not?"

"Uh . . ." My brain scrambles for an excuse. "The house is a mess. Really, you'll trip over something."

His brow arches, his interest clearly piqued. "Scarlett, if you don't tell me the truth, I can't help you."

"There's nothing to say." I swallow hard as he steps onto the porch, closing the distance between us and sending my heart into a frenzy. "Just, uh, pull the towel free," I say, trying to sound confident.

He leans in, his arm sliding behind me, his body only inches from mine. His scent—maddeningly cozy and warm—sends a spark racing through me. "The only way you're getting free without me entering your house," he says, his breath tickling the skin of my cheek, "is by dropping the towel. Which I'm more than okay with."

My face flames at the suggestion, and I shift uncomfortably. His proximity, the heat radiating off him, the stupidly hot nose ring—it's too much.

"Stop flirting with me," I snap, though my voice is weaker than I'd like.

He shakes his head, a teasing spark in his eyes. "Tell me why I can't go inside."

I hesitate, my pride warring with my desperation. Finally, I crack. "I was going to . . . you know, use my vibrator in the shower, and it's on the vanity."

For a moment, he looks genuinely taken aback. Then his grin returns, bigger and brighter than before. "Before a date?"

"Well, it's not like I'm going to sleep—"

I grimace the second the words leave my mouth, but it's too late; his laugh, rich and low, rumbles between us. "With Theo? Right. Why would you ever?"

"That's not what I meant," I huff. "Leave Theo out of this, please."

Another car drives by, and I tug the towel up higher, trying to preserve the last shred of my dignity. "Can you help me now?"

"Sure," Rafael says, far too smug. Instead of walking away, he steps closer, his chest only inches away from the hand I'm using to hold the towel. "As soon as you admit it."

"Admit what?"

"That I'm the only man in your life."

My eyes flick to his lips, then away. He leans in, my knuckles brushing against his sweater. "That I'm the only man you want to kiss. The only man you want to fuck."

My throat constricts, my heart pounding painfully against my ribs. I force myself to meet his gaze, but it's like trying to stare down a storm. "That's not all that matters, Rafael."

Expression softening, he tucks a lock of hair behind my ear. "Then admit that your heart doesn't beat for anyone else the way it beats for me."

For a split second, I know it's true. No one has ever made me feel like this, like I'm standing on the edge of a cliff, one breath away from falling, yet also like I've finally found my footing. "Please, just . . . open the door."

I think I see it. See the fight in him die, see him decide he's over this. Over apologizing and opening his heart to me. With a sad, crooked smile, he says, "Whatever you want, Freckles," and stalks around the house without another word.

I wait a few unbearable seconds, wondering if what I feel is relief or regret. Then the door opens behind me, and I stumble back into freedom. "All set," he says, stepping out. "Enjoy your date."

23

the push and pull

[trope]

the exhausting but oh-so-satisfying romantic dynamic where
two characters play hard to get, only to fall into each other's
orbit at the most inconvenient times; expect long stares,
dramatic exits, and circular conversations about feelings
that they both want and resist

"Where would you hide a vibrator?" I ask into the phone,
lifting one of the couch cushions and letting it flop back
into place.

"Excuse me?" Paige asks. "What's going on?"

Pinching the bridge of my nose, I glance at the dust collecting
on the floor, another reminder of the chaos that is my life. "Rafael
came over. We argued. My towel got stuck in the door, and my vibrator was on the bathroom vanity. He set me free and now the
vibrator's gone."

She laughs, the sound so high-pitched I move the phone away. "Are you sure you checked everywhere?"

"Nothing on the couch, the bookshelf, the side table, the rocking chair, the TV set." I groan, rubbing my forehead. "It's just gone."

Paige pauses, then surprises me with a burst of laughter. "I'd say he took it."

Took it? "What . . . Who does that? Who steals someone's only source of pleasure?" My cheeks burn as indignation flares. "A sociopath. A menace—that's who."

"Or . . ." Paige cuts in, her tone teasing. "Someone who's trying to replace it."

I hear the knock at my door and already know who it is before I even open it. My heart does this annoying little flip, but I remind myself I'm still mad. Enraged, actually. "He's at the door. I'll call you later."

"Tell him he can keep the vibrator if he gives you his d—"

I end the call and yank the door open, ready to tell Rafael off, but the words die in my throat when I see him standing there, all brown curls and soft eyes.

"I couldn't help but notice your date was . . . canceled?" Ten points for not calling me out on lying about having a date like a pathetic teenager. Twenty points when he lifts a takeout bag, the familiar logo of the Chinese restaurant catching my eye. My stomach growls on cue, betraying me. All I have in the fridge is half a lemon and a bottle of ketchup, which makes holding on to my anger even more difficult. Fifty points when he raises his other hand, revealing a folder.

I squint at the name scribbled on top: "The Lit Killer." I chuckle, head shaking. "I thought you said my nickname was stupid."

"I never said stupid."

"Not in so many words."

Rafael shrugs, that damn smirk tugging at the corners of his lips. I hate how attractive he looks when he does that, the way his gray eyes crinkle slightly, flecks of gold and brown catching the light. I want to trace every one of his tattoos. Find out how many more are hiding under his shirt, maybe farther down. I'm so ecstatic that he's here, that he's not done . . . that I can't feel any of the fury I'm supposed to.

He didn't give up.

The anger is still there, simmering beneath the surface, but it doesn't stand a chance.

I grab the file from his hands and make my way to the table, flipping it open to scan the contents. My eyes catch on phrases like "crime scene" and "book-inspired murders," but I'm acutely aware of Rafael watching me with that quiet intensity of his. He doesn't say a word as he sets the takeout bag down on the table, the familiar scent of Chinese food filling the room.

The crinkle of the bag and the soft thud of containers being placed on the table break the silence. I glance up from the folder, catching him peeling back the lids, releasing even more of that delicious aroma.

I like the familiarity of this routine.

He fills my plate with a little of everything, and I keep the folder open as I make room for the plate. As he begins eating, I stand, grab the remote, and hand it over. I still feel his gaze on me as I walk back to my seat, but I focus on my material.

Once he lands on an old sitcom, we eat. He watches TV; I read. I've missed this—missed him—and that's much more terrifying than anything in the folder in front of me.

I look back down at the pages, but the words blur. I'm not angry anymore. I'm scared. Was I ever angry at him? Or is he right, and I just jumped at the chance to break things off?

"Anything catch your eye?"

I flinch. "Uh, I . . . actually, I've been thinking about your father's murder."

"Uh-huh." Rafael lifts his gaze off the screen. "What about it?"

"Well, in *The Lonely Man*, Rourke was poisoned. There was a letter seemingly written by him to his son."

"Just like with my father's murder."

"But in the book, there was so much more. Ink under the victim's fingernails, like he'd tried to claw something off a page. A faint chemical burn on his lips and ash in his lungs, suggesting he tried to burn something before he died." I pause. "And the ink? It was this specific shade of red the son always used when forging his father's signature. How ingenious is that? Symbolically, it's—"

Noticing the hint of a smile playing on his lips, I swallow my words.

"It doesn't matter. The point is, why stop at the poison and the letter to the son? The next murders they recreated were much more detailed."

"Maybe the killer was testing their plan out. Or they were interrupted." He clears his voice. "Maybe the first one was meant to be a secret."

"Or maybe they had the opposite problem." I keep reading. "The police ruled it accidental."

He leans forward, intrigued, but I see the slight wince when his arms cross over the table. "While it's obvious the killer craves attention. Recognition."

Exactly. I close the folder. "Was it you?"

"Hmm?"

"Quentin ran into someone he thought was the killer, stabbed him." I point at his arm. "I assume that was you."

He pulls the sleeve up, revealing the bandage. "You might make a fine detective after all."

I hiss through my teeth—that's a pretty big bandage. Did he have to get stitches? "I can't believe your cousin stabbed you."

"You and me both."

"It's kind of hilarious. You thought he was the killer, he thought you were."

"Yeah, hysterical," he says flatly. "Six stitches." Eyes rolling, he continues. "And I never thought he was the killer. Nobody *that* stupid can be a serial killer."

A laugh bubbles out. "Then why did you attack him?"

"Attack him? Is that what he's saying?" He scoffs. "*Idiot.* I bet in his story, I'm seven feet tall and had a shotgun, but somehow he managed to overpower me, huh?"

"Well, there might have been some talk about roundhouse kicks. The two of you fighting for your knife—"

"Yeah, that was not my knife. Trust me, if I'd thought for a second he was the killer, he'd have been looking at the barrel of my gun." He bites into a dumpling. "I was monitoring calls to the police, went to check out the house, and *Quentin* nearly pissed himself when he saw me in the building. Scaredy-cat had this tiny-ass pocketknife, and as he *fell*," he says, pausing for effect, "he accidentally slashed my arm."

This time I can't help it: I burst into a heartfelt laugh. I knew Quentin was full of it, that there was something about his story that didn't ring true, but I couldn't have dreamed of something so good.

"Moron," he says, still shaking his head.

With one last chuckle, I reach for the next paper in the pile. It details a series of large payments made to the Booked It account over the past few months—thousands of dollars, transferred at intervals.

"Rafael," I say over the sound of the sitcom.

He glances over. "What?"

I hold up the papers. "These payments to the podcast account. What are they?"

He pauses, setting his plate down and wiping his mouth with a napkin. "Donations."

"Donations? Who's donating that kind of money to podcasts about books?"

"I don't know. I've been trying to track it, but every lead I've followed has hit a dead end. Whoever's making these transfers knows how to avoid being tracked."

"So it must be connected to the murders."

"I don't know for sure," he says. "But that's my guess, yes."

My heart races as I go through the papers again. If someone is using my podcast to plan these murders and then sending us money afterward, what does that mean? Some sort of twisted reward system? A thank-you for the inspiration?

God, this is so fucked-up.

"Did you check that last police report?"

I rush to the last page and quickly read. "Wait . . . the killer came back to the scene?"

"Just today. And they *must* have known the police would still be there." He shakes his head. "I've no idea why they'd do that. They smacked Wes in the back of the head and snuck in—he's fine, don't worry. The police don't think they took anything either. When they left, they were so rattled, they knocked down one of the garden gnomes—it's just . . . weird."

I pluck the crime scene photos from the pile and, trying to ignore Ron's lifeless body, focus on everything else captured by the camera. It all seems to belong—the faded floral armchair draped with a knitted afghan, the cracked teacup balanced on a stack of gardening magazines, an old-fashioned radio—except . . . "Is that a hotel key?"

"Hmm?"

"Right there," I say, pointing as I hold the picture closer.

He leans forward. "It looks like a credit card."

"No, look, see the orange flower? That's the Wildflower Inn logo."

He scratches his jaw mindlessly. "Why would Mrs. Brattle have a room in a local hotel?"

"She wouldn't. And I bet if you ask the police to find this, they won't."

Rafael takes out his phone and begins tapping. Pulling the picture back, I let my next thought slowly trickle in. Theo. Theo had a card key to the Wildflower Inn with him only a couple of days ago. And he was *so* cagey about it too.

No. Theo, one of my best friends, is *not* the killer. He's just not.

I go through more papers, finding my name everywhere. Information about my family, my love life, friends.

"Psycho," I whisper, just loudly enough for him to hear.

He nudges me with his elbow. "Did you say something?"

I playfully glare at him. "I want my vibrator back, *psycho*."

With a snort, he resumes eating.

24

the letter

[trope]

---

a heartfelt, ink-stained declaration of love that arrives just in time for maximum emotional impact; always read with trembling hands, a lump in the throat, and a montage-worthy imaginary soundtrack in the background

I dig my heels into the ground, resisting Paige's insistent nudges. "Seriously, I don't want to do this."

The glow of The Oak's neon sign flickers against the pavement, throwing erratic shadows on the cracked concrete as the faint buzz of conversation and occasional bursts of laughter leak out from the pub. It seems pretty full for a Sunday night.

Her eyes widen like those of a crazy person's. "I think I have enough dirt on you to make you *crawl* into that pub, so don't make me." She exhales, crossing her arms over her orange dress. "You and Rafael need to get over this already. And it's your turn to show him you care."

I turn to Vanessa for help. She leans casually against the brick wall of The Oak, one foot propped up as if she has all the time in the world. Her police radio crackles faintly at her hip, but she doesn't seem to notice.

"Come on, Paige. If she's not ready—" Vanessa starts, but Paige cuts her off with a sharp wave of her hand.

"She *likes* him, Vanessa."

"But he lied to me!" I blurt, though it doesn't sound convincing at all. "I can't just pretend that didn't happen, right? *Right?*"

Paige circles around to stand in front of me. She grabs both my arms, her grip stronger than it needs to be. "That's not the real problem."

"It is! It—"

"Tell me the truth, Scarlett."

"I'm . . ." My eyes dart toward the pub door as if it might explode at any second. "He's tried to apologize so many times, and I kept pushing him away, and—"

"And you're scared he won't ask again."

Vanessa snorts softly. "He definitely should learn the meaning of the word 'no.' "

She raises her hands in defeat when I glare at her.

Paige lowers her voice. "Just go in, have a beer. Say hi. And if he's a jerk, I'll pour my drink over his head, okay?"

That earns her a reluctant chuckle, though it dies quickly as I glance at the door again. I take a hesitant step forward. "Fine. But if this goes horribly wrong, I'm blaming you."

"Deal." Paige grabs my arm and practically drags me toward the door. Vanessa follows at a safe distance, saying something about needing a drink herself.

As we step inside, the pub's warmth envelops us like a scratchy wool blanket. The scent of fried food and stale beer hits me first, followed by the hum of overlapping voices and the occasional clink of glasses.

And then I see him.

Rafael, effortlessly casual, one hand wrapped around a beer, the other tucked into his pocket. He laughs, low and easy, as he leans slightly toward a brunette. Her curls cascade down her bare shoulders, catching the light.

He's flirting with her.

Rafael is flirting with some woman.

"Oh, for fuck's sake," Paige says, her voice low but sharp enough to pierce through the din of the pub.

I step back in reflex, colliding with someone behind me. The next thing I know, a cascade of glasses falls to the floor, the crash of shattering glass and sloshing drinks cutting through the pub like a gunshot. Every pair of eyes is on me in a second, including Rafael's and those of the woman next to him, who I realize is Tanya, the previous host of *Passion & Pages*.

The smile slips from Rafael's face. His lips part, and though I can't hear him over the ringing in my ears, I see it clearly—my name.

My heart lurches as he takes a step toward me, his beer forgotten on the bar.

I can't do this.

I spin around, nearly knocking into Paige, who barely has time to grab my arm.

"Scarlett, wait—"

But I'm gone. I shove through the pub door and break into a run, the sound of my ragged breaths and pounding heart drowning out everything else.

I knew it. I knew I was right about him, and I knew that letting him past my walls—my safe, comfortable walls—would only allow him to break my heart.

Behind me, I hear the door creak open, then Rafael's voice, faint but unmistakable. "Scarlett!"

I don't stop. I can't.

"Scarlett, wait!" He catches up, a hand hovering close—so close—but not actually touching me, as if he's afraid I might combust on impact. "It's not what you think, I *swear*."

"Isn't it?"

"No." He keeps up with me as I walk. "It's just work. A previous employee could still have access to the podcast and all the motive to want to destroy it."

Just work.

"Really?" I laugh, though it's humorless. "So you weren't flirting?"

His mouth opens, then closes.

He said it was *just work*.

"Just how many times have you done this? Slithered your way into a woman's life, flirted, made her think she was special—all of it, only because of a case you're working?"

"Never." When I glare at him, he sighs. "Okay, flirting? I do it all the time. Sometimes it's easier than the alternative. But you and me—it has nothing to do with the case. Nothing, and you *know* it."

I ignore him and keep walking, but he doesn't let up.

"And besides, you're seeing other people, aren't you? You don't want me."

"No," I burst out, my voice sounding squeaky. "I don't."

"Well, this is a small town. We're going to keep running into each other while I'm here, so—"

"And when *are* you leaving again?" I whip around, pinning him with a glare.

His face tightens, like I've just lobbed something heavy at him, and there's this fleeting, bitter satisfaction. Why should I be the only one who suffers? The one who's been made a fool of, the one who gets to be left behind? He should know exactly the pain I experience seeing him every day, second only to the pain I can already taste that I'll feel once he's gone.

We stare at each other, our hurt crashing together in one big, painful wave. Until his expression softens. "Scarlett, I . . ."

"You *lied* to me," I say, my chin quivering hard.

"I omitted some things—"

"You just won't admit it, will you? You *lied*."

His shoulders drop. "Okay. Yes, I lied. But Freckles, I couldn't tell you—"

"Don't call me that." I start to walk again, but he moves to stand in my way. "You shouldn't have pursued me. Until you were sure—until you could be honest, you just shouldn't have . . ." Let me think he was different. Made me believe, for once, in something I'd told myself never to count on.

"I thought I'd catch the killer in no time. I thought I'd get to tell you, and we'd laugh about it." He edges closer, his gaze piercing. "Scarlett, I'd already pushed you away once. I couldn't do it again." He leans closer. "But I didn't so much as kiss you. I knew that until I could tell you the truth, I couldn't touch you."

A bitter laugh bubbles past my lips. "You set limits for yourself so you wouldn't feel guilty. You drew the line at kissing or sex because you *knew* what you were doing was wrong." The prickling sense of betrayal makes my chest ache. "Only it turns out our lines are different, Rafael."

He rubs a hand over his face.

"While you draw yours at kissing or . . . whatever—"

"Scarlett . . ." He groans.

"—*I* draw mine at sneaking into my life. At sharing Chinese in my kitchen. At sleeping in my bed and playing video games and making me feel important and . . . and *safe*!" My voice is rising, tears welling up as I realize people are looking. *Perfect*. "Just forget about it, okay? I'm leaving."

"You're right. I fucked up," he says as I open the car door and set one foot in.

"Agreed," I shout back.

He leans forward, holding the door open. "No, Scarlett, I fucked up when I said you wouldn't find any reason to push me away. When I told you I wouldn't disappoint you. Because you were *looking* for a reason not to be with me, and it was just a matter of time before you found it."

"Yeah, okay." I flip around, facing him. "But no matter how many times I looked over my shoulder, *you're* the one who jabbed a knife there—actually, you pointed a *gun* at me."

He doesn't say a word, and with a final exhale, he lets the door go. Can I be both happy this conversation is done and devastated? Because I definitely feel both.

"Dear Rafael Gray, I love you," he says.

I turn to him, hand poised to close the car door, and see him unfolding a piece of paper, the logo of Paige's dad's dentist office on the bottom. Is that . . .

Oh my God.

"I know it might sound crazy because we've barely ever spoken to each other," he reads. "But I've been in love with you since the fourth grade, when Duncan Powell tried to exclude Harry Cooper from your game, and you told him that bullies are like sandpaper, scratching you and scratching you until you're polished and smooth and they're nothing but useless trash."

I swallow, the memory fresh in my mind as if it was yesterday.

"Since that day, I've loved you, and I know I always will."

"Will you stop reading that?" I snap. "It's just drunk rambling from a seventeen-year-old."

He ignores me, trudging through. "You might think I'm just a kid. That my hormones and peach schnapps are making me write this ill-advised letter, and that I can't possibly love someone I never even kissed. But you'd be wrong."

Good God, I remember the stupid letter.

"I see love every day. I see it in my parents, in my mother's eyes when she looks at my brother, and in my best friend, who loves love. I know exactly what it feels and looks like."

"Enough," I insist, my voice shaking precariously.

"And what I feel for you is even stronger than that. It's so strong that if I never saw you again, if after reading this letter you didn't love me back, I'd still love you. I'd still carry you with me wherever I go, whatever I do. Because love stories always end with a happily ever after, and not a minute before that. And I know for a fact that we'll get ours."

I press my lips tight, willing myself to breathe.

"I love you, Rafael Gray," he continues. "I love you until happily ever after and beyond."

I stare at the piece of paper in front of his face until he lowers it.

"PS. Sorry if this letter smells like peach schnapps barf."

A chuckle bursts through my lips, the need to laugh momentarily stronger than the anger, and Rafael laughs, too, folding the paper, then putting it back into his wallet.

With a sniffle, I ask, "You kept it all this time?"

"Yes." Wallet back in his pocket, he looks down at me. "You want to know why?"

I nod, chin still wobbling.

"Because when I read that letter, I thought, I want to love this girl." He tilts his head. "And peach schnapps? Gross. But mostly the love thing." He moves closer. "I knew if I let myself fall in love with you, I wouldn't have been able to help it. That it would have been easy, the easiest thing I would have ever done. And that I would have never stopped, because love stories don't end. Not before the happily ever after."

My heart's nearly bursting.

"Scarlett, if I never saw you again after today, if you never gave me another chance, I'd still carry you with me wherever I went. Forever."

Why does he have to be so good at this?

I hold my hand out, and he takes it, his head tilting forward as if half of his body just relaxed.

"Can I get a ride?" he asks, thumb rubbing the top of my hand. "I haven't been able to sleep properly, and I'd just like to go to bed knowing you'll text back in the morning." He crouches down next to me, soft eyes looking longingly at me. "Can we do that?"

I watch him, expecting the same big warning to flash before my eyes, conflicting with the need to just let him in again. But there's no warning. No resistance.

I miss him in my bed.

"I'm not texting back in the morning," I say as I stand. At his worried expression, I toss him the keys. "You can just talk to me from the other side of the bed."

He exhales in relief. "You got it, Freckles."

25

the interruption

[trope]

a perfectly timed plot device sent by the universe to ruin a pivotal romantic moment; defined by ringing phones, intrusive exes, crying babies, or a well-meaning friend bursting in with snacks.

We enter the house, dark and silent, the faint hum of the refrigerator the only sound. Ethan is still out, which makes sense since it's only ten thirty. That gives us about one and a half hours before he's back. Ninety whole minutes of just us.

I glance at Rafael as he shrugs off his jacket, the muscles in his forearms flexing slightly. The mustard-yellow fitted T-shirt beneath clings to his frame, the bold, horizontal stripe and GOOD TIMES, BAD DECISIONS lettering stretching faintly over his chest as he moves. His eyes catch mine, and his lips curve into a small, knowing smile that sends a shiver racing down my spine. He glances around. "Ethan?"

"Out," I reply, my voice a touch too breathy.

"Oh." His gaze sharpens for a beat, the implication sparking there. "Too bad. I was hoping to play some *GTA*."

Sure he was.

He steps closer, his movements deliberate. "When will he be back?"

"Midnight."

He checks his phone, the glow illuminating the sharp planes of his face. He lets out a low whistle. "Plenty of time, then."

My heart is pounding against my rib cage. The scent of his cologne fills my lungs, mingling with the faint tang of beer on his breath. My thoughts keep circling back to last week: his hands gripping my hips, the hard press of his body against mine.

His fingers brush over my forearm, light and teasing, leaving a trail of fire in their wake. His chest is almost against mine. "Should we read? Watch something?"

"No," I say, making the corner of his mouth twitch.

He leans in, so close I can see the gold flecks in his gray eyes. "Then what should we do?"

Oh, I know what we *shouldn't* do. We *shouldn't* kiss. We *shouldn't* let our hands wander. We *shouldn't* give in to the electricity crackling between us. It's a bad, *bad* idea.

Apparently, I like bad ideas now.

"Each other?"

He laughs, the joyful noise quickly turning into a quiet smile. He tucks a piece of hair behind my ear. "I'm sorry I hurt you. But if it's all right with you, I'd really like a second chance."

"Technically, *third* chance."

"Third time's a charm, right?"

I lean into him, lips hovering inches from his, his warm and heavy breath fanning over me. There are no more secrets now, no more reasons to hold back.

I think we're about to kiss.

The noise of a key rattling in the door has us both turning to the right. I take a step back as Ethan comes in, one hand on the side of his face.

"Ethan?" I gasp.

An angry purple bruise is blossoming across his cheekbone, and blood trickles from a scratch on his cheek.

"Please," he mumbles, swaying slightly on his feet. "Don't make a big deal, okay?"

I grab his good arm to steady him, my mind reeling. "What the hell happened?"

Ethan's one good eye darts nervously over my shoulder, landing on Rafael, who walks closer and puts a hand to the small of my back. "Get the first aid kit," he says. "I've got him."

I move, dazed. Someone hurt Ethan, and it isn't the first time, but it's the last, because I'm not settling for half answers tonight. I want the truth.

I walk into the bathroom, then rush back into the living room with the first aid kit. Rafael has helped my brother settle on the couch, and he's dabbing his face with a washcloth. "How bad is it?" I ask as I drop onto the couch next to Ethan. "Should we go to the hospital?"

"I'm fine."

"Nuh-uh." I open the first aid kit and take out the disinfectant. "I wasn't asking you, I was asking Rafael. The only thing you can tell me is the truth, and nothing else."

"There's nothing to tell," Ethan says. He winces when Rafael dabs his bottom lip. "Everything is fine."

I meet Rafael's amused gaze, then scoff. This kid is going to drive me insane.

"Get some ice, Freckles."

I blush, throwing a pointed glare at Rafael. *Not in front of my brother*, it says, but I doubt he even notices. After my expedition to the kitchen, I come back with ice in a cloth. Ethan holds it over his eye, and Rafael steps back. Now that he's cleaned off the blood, it feels like I can breathe again. He's hurt, but he's going to be fine.

"Okay. Come out with it, Ethan. I want to know what happened and who did this. Right now."

Ethan rolls his one good eye, then winces. "I don't want to talk about it, Scarlett."

"Well, you will anyway."

Ethan looks away, as if that's going to magically change my mind. "I said forget about it."

Shoulders hunching, I try as hard as I can not to cry. How am I supposed to make this work? How can I hope to convince a judge he's better-off staying with me than with my grandparents when I can't even get him to open up?

As he handles a piece of gauze, Rafael shoots a look my way. "I get it. He doesn't feel like opening up to his *sister* and some guy she's dating. He's not wrong."

Ethan bobs his head up and down in firm agreement. Whose side is Rafael on? And why did he say "sister" like that?

"You know who would know about it, though?" He snaps his fingers. "His friends."

Ethan shifts on the couch, throat working hard.

Oh, so *that's* what Rafael is doing. Of course, no teenager wants their sister to meddle in their life publicly.

"Right." I pretend to be deep in thought. "Jace—that's his best friend. My grandma must have his number."

"Jace, huh?" Rafael's eyes focus on mine as if Ethan isn't even in the room. "Not that common. I bet if I run his name through the system, I'll find only one Jace who lives in the area and is about, what, sixteen? Seventeen?"

System? What system?

I shrug. "Let's just do that, then."

"You can't!" Ethan stands, sweat accumulating on his forehead. "Seriously, man? I thought we were friends."

"We *are* friends," Rafael says. "And friends tell each other the truth."

"It was just a stupid fight, okay? No big deal. I'm not lying."

"Friends," Rafael insists as he grips his shoulder, "stand up for each other. We're friends, Ethan. Would you let this go if you were in my place? If your sister was?"

When Ethan looks back at me, I say, "Tell us who did this. And I promise, Ethan, today's the last time they lay hands on you. I'll make sure of it."

"You'll make it worse," he pleads, his voice breaking.

It feels like my heart is ripping open. Someone's terrorizing him into silence, and I don't know what to say to make him feel safe. To make him trust me.

"Okay. Forget about it," Rafael says as he slumps back on the couch. "Wanna play some *GTA*?"

"S-sure."

Ethan watches me warily as Rafael stands and turns on the console. He must think it's weird we'd just let it go, and so do I, but I assume this is all part of Rafael's plan.

"You know, I was bullied, too, when I was your age."

Ethan wipes his face with the sleeve of his shirt. "Yeah, right. I know about you—bad boy Rafael Gray. Nobody would have ever *dared* bully you."

Rafael makes his way over with the controllers. "No, nobody at school would bully me. At home, however . . ."

I watch Rafael sit next to Ethan, trying to gauge whether he's being honest or just making up a whole thing for my brother's benefit.

"What does that mean?" Ethan asks.

Rafael crosses his arms, focusing on a spot on the floor. "My dad was a bully. He smacked me around, but that honestly hurt less than the stuff he said. That was . . ." He swallows. "Hard to take."

I take a seat on the armrest of the couch, not daring to make a noise.

"Stuff like what?"

Rafael's gaze darts to me, and I don't really know what to do with myself. I think he's being honest, and if Ethan wasn't here, I'd hug him. Sit on his lap or touch him some other way, hoping that the skin-on-skin contact could provide him some sort of comfort. But Ethan's here, so I offer a light smile.

"Lots of things. How I was a constant disappointment. Stupid. A waste of space. How I'd never do anything with myself, and my mom leaving us was all my fault."

I'm pretty sure my lips twist in disgust. What kind of parent would say things like that to their own son?

Ethan scoffs. "What an asshole."

"Yeah."

Yeah. A real asshole.

Ethan shakes his head. "But it's nothing like that. Nobody's saying anything to me."

Rafael's eyes are on me again, as if weighing something. Then he leans forward, elbows on his thighs, and says, "You were pretty young when I left. Do you remember what happened?"

Ethan shakes his head.

"Well, that night my father was having one of his fits of rage. Hitting me, insulting me. I knew if I just let him use me as his punching bag, everything would be fine. He'd eventually stop, and life would move on."

"Why was he hitting you?"

Rafael hesitates, eyes stuck to the floor. "He . . ."

"Rafael," I finally interject. "You don't have to—"

"It's okay." He looks up at me, almost apologetically. "He found a letter that was meant for me."

It takes a moment for the words to sink in. For the meaning to really permeate every piece of my being.

A letter. *My* letter.

"A letter from whom?" Ethan asks.

"From a girl who said she loved me." He presses his lips tight. "He made me read it aloud, then he got really . . . *really* mad. She was a minor, and he assumed I was doing something I shouldn't have been doing."

My voice shakes. "But you weren't."

"It's not supposed to make sense, Scarlett. Abuse never does," he says. I catch the undertone of reassurance, but it does little to soothe me. "My father was a horrible man, that's all."

"What happened then?" Ethan asks.

"He always hit me somewhere nobody could see, but that night, he couldn't contain himself. He kept . . ." He pauses, then clears his throat. "He kept asking if I was a . . ." He shakes his head.

I was *seventeen*! Three years younger than him—*three*.

"When he made me read the letter, he saw it made me happy. And name-calling was one of his favorite tricks. Abusers always know exactly what to say to take your insecurities and turn them into the most twisted version of the truth."

I blink, feeling my eyes sting with unshed tears. I was right. He left because of me. Because of my letter. I always thought I was being egotistical to think so, but it's true.

Rafael grips Ethan's shoulder. "So that night, I reacted. For the first time, I didn't just let him beat me and insult me. I beat him back, and I almost killed him. I was filled with so much anger, I think I *wanted* him to die."

Ethan sniffles. "That's why you left?"

"Uh-huh. Your dad, he came over. He called an ambulance, told me everything would be okay. I think he saw my injuries and figured out what was going on."

My mind reels, the pieces of his story colliding with everything I thought I knew. Why wasn't Rafael arrested? Why didn't my dad bring him in?

My shoulders sag. "He let you go."

"Yeah. He saw me sneak out, and he told me I didn't need to leave, that we'd fix it. But I couldn't take the thought of being here when morning came and everyone found out."

Ethan looks away, and I exchange a glance with Rafael. Something he said has struck a chord.

"Ethan, I was too stupid to accept your dad's help. If I had . . ." His eyes meet mine. "I missed lots of stuff. Wasted a lot of time."

Focusing on Ethan again, he gives his shoulder a squeeze. "Don't be like me. Ask for help."

Ethan sniffles again, his lip shaking, then bursts into sobs, dropping the washcloth and ice on the couch. He turns his back to us, and when Rafael stills, holding my gaze, I know he's telling me to be strong for Ethan right now. To give him a second to let him come around.

"The skate park," Ethan whines.

I straighten, rushing to his side. "That's where they are?"

"Hunter Sullivan and his friends."

I pull him into my arms, where he continues gasping and crying. I meet Rafael's gaze over Ethan's shoulder, his eyes sparking with something dangerous as he cracks his knuckles.

"I hope you're ready for a new side of me, Freckles."

I follow Rafael through the dark skate park, Ethan walking beside me. "What's the plan?" I ask as we step up a small hill and a group of kids Ethan's age come into view.

"We're playing it by ear," he calls without turning our way. He walks hurriedly, aggressively. Enough to make us scramble to keep up, and to scare me to death.

"He's a minor," I remind him before we're in earshot, as the group turns our way. There are six kids, two girls and four boys. Even without knowing who Hunter Sullivan is, I am *sure* it's the tall blond kid standing in front of the others, like the boss of their own little gang.

"Look who's back," the kid mocks as he turns to his friends. "Did you bring your mom and dad with you? Oh, right, you can't. They're d—"

Rafael grabs the basketball out of one kid's hands, then throws it straight into Hunter's face. When the ball falls down with a dull thump, I can't believe our luck that he's not bleeding.

"*You asshole!*" Hunter screams, bringing a hand to his nose.

Rafael stands too close to him for comfort, looking down at the stupid kid like he's lunch. "Hey, Hunter," he says in a voice that's inharmoniously chirpy. "I figured we should talk."

"Who the fuck are you?" Hunter asks, stepping backward as his friends move away. I steal a glance at Ethan, who's watching the scene out of the corner of his eye, head tilted down.

"I'm Ethan's friend. Remember him?"

Hunter tries to push Rafael back but ends up having to take a step back himself. "Oh, okay. Are you his *boyfriend*?"

Ethan flinches next to me, but I keep my eyes on Rafael. On the walk over, I made him swear he wouldn't do anything illegal, as it could cost me the custody case, but he looks beside himself.

"Ohh, I see. I'm supposed to feel insulted by you calling me gay."

Hunter shrugs, his lips twisting in a sneer. "Only if you are."

Rafael steps forward, and I don't see exactly what he's doing, but the two of them struggle. When he moves away from Hunter, he's holding a phone. "Passcode?"

"Fuck you," Hunter says as he tries to reach for the phone. When Rafael grasps his wrist, he grunts, powerless as Rafael drags his finger over the bottom of the screen.

"Here we go. Easy-peasy." He steps closer to me and Ethan, a wicked smile on his lips. "Let's see what delights await us. Ethan, where would you start with this?"

Ethan startles. "Uh . . . his texts?"

"Yeah, texts are good. But you know what's better?"

"His photos," I say as I glare at Hunter, standing there pathetically as he fidgets with the pocket of his jeans. Bet he's nervous now.

"Jackpot." He smacks the back of his hand against the phone. "Dick pic, dick pic, dick pic." He turns to Hunter. "Is this *your* peanut?"

"Of course it's—" He breaks into nervous laughter as his friends sputter and chuckle.

"Damn." Rafael brings the phone closer to his eyes, as if he's struggling to see anything. "You shouldn't be *too* worried. I'm sure there's another growth spurt in your future."

I barely stifle a chuckle when Ethan breaks into quiet laughter.

Rafael, noticing, shows him the phone. "I'm not lying, am I?" Before Ethan can answer, he turns to Hunter. "All right, Hunter. I want you and your peanut out of my face, so let's wrap this up." He holds the phone out, but just as the kid goes to grab it, Rafael drops it, then stomps on it. "Shit, Peanut. Sorry. So clumsy."

"You fucking *sissy!*"

Rafael grabs his shirt, pushing him back until he's holding him against a tree.

"Rafael!" I squeal, cringing as I cup my mouth.

He winks at me. "Everything's under control, Freckles." As he focuses back on Hunter, his voice drops. "You should read a book, Peanut. Learn better words."

Hunter struggles, but Rafael keeps him there.

"Look, I'm sorry your life is shit. That your dad likes the bottle and screams at the TV that *fairies* are ruining the country. And I'm sorry you struggle to understand why you feel all tingly in the locker room and not when you're with one of those ladies." He jerks his head toward the girls. "But work it out in therapy, Peanut. Learn to love yourself, fuck men if that's what you like, and most important, leave Ethan alone."

"Let me go!" Hunter has teared up, which makes me feel bad for him. Maybe he really is gay, and he hates himself so much he has to take it out on someone else.

"Not until you understand, Peanut."

"I understand!"

Rafael immediately steps back, holding his hands up. "That's all I needed to know."

Hunter observes him carefully, and I would, too, in his place. Rafael is purposefully acting like a lunatic, and I wouldn't want to be on the receiving end of his erratic behavior.

When Rafael steps closer, Hunter flinches. It makes Rafael chuckle, but he leans closer still and whispers something in his ear. I can't hear what, but I swear it's what will send us all to prison, because Hunter's face goes white. No—green. Ripe-pear green.

After patting his shoulder, Rafael turns to Hunter's friends and points at them one by one. Without saying a word, he winks at me and begins walking.

Ethan and I follow right behind, my heart beating wildly in the silence of the skate park. I can't believe he did this. If this kid presses charges, God, we're all fucked.

"Ethan, come here," Rafael says as we approach the parking lot. "What's Peanut's ride?"

Ethan laughs excitedly. "Seriously? The BMW." He points at a car in the far corner of the parking lot, and Rafael gives him his car keys.

"Walk back to my place. Grab the bat in the trunk of my car."

"No—no! Ethan, don't you go anywhere." Eyes bulging, I grip Rafael's arm. "Have you lost your mind?"

He pinches my chin, pouting slightly. "There's nobody around. No witnesses."

"That's not the point!"

"You said we couldn't get caught doing something illegal."

I clench my fists at my sides. "I meant we shouldn't *do* anything illegal."

Rafael frowns. "Well, that's not what you said."

"*Rafael.*"

He glances back at the car and I could swear his eyes stick to the plate, but he moves away before I can say anything, and we all make our way out of the parking lot.

As soon as we leave the park, a strange calm settles over us. Adrenaline is still running high, but none of us says a word until Ethan bursts into laughter, and through his gasps, I can make out the word "peanut."

I chuckle, and Rafael turns to me, his eyes oddly soft, like he enjoys the sound. I hope he knows how grateful I am for this. Ill-advised as it was, he helped my brother. There's nothing as attractive as a selfless man who fiercely protects others.

Actually . . . there's no one as attractive as Rafael.

we shouldn't, but we will anyway

[trope]

the irresistible gravitational pull between two characters who know better but absolutely refuse to do better; typically fueled by questionable decisions, forbidden circumstances, and a complete lack of self-control, this trope features stolen kisses, whispered "this is a bad idea" declarations, and enough sexual tension to power Willowbrook for a week

The bed creaks softly as Rafael sits on the edge, and I climb in beside him, pulling the blankets over my legs. The room is dim, lit only by the glow of the streetlamp outside filtering through the blinds.

"Good to be back?" I ask as he settles next to me. The old wooden headboard creaks faintly as he shifts, the quilt rumpling under us.

"Oh, yeah." He smiles widely, and it lights up his entire face. He's wearing a plain black T-shirt that clings to the lines of his shoulders and chest, his arm tattoos perfectly on display and immensely distracting. "Feels like coming home."

I'd roll my eyes if he didn't look so completely sincere. And you know what? He's right. He looks so at ease here, broad frame relaxed against my too-small bed, hair mussed from the shower. It *does* feel like he belongs here.

The warmth of that thought is immediate, but it's accompanied by a tight pang of guilt. Everything he said tonight comes rushing back in a painful flood—his past, the abuse, the reason for his sudden disappearance.

"It's not your fault, Scarlett."

I let out a puff of air, shaking my head. Rationally, I know he's right. But emotionally? That's another story. "It was my letter. My stupid, drunken letter."

"*You* didn't hit me. It's not your letter that was wrong—it was his reaction. In fact, he hit me plenty before your letter, and if I hadn't left, he would've hit me after it, too."

The blanket shifts as he leans closer, his knee brushing mine under the covers, warm and reassuring despite the subject. But the logic of his words does little to loosen the crushing grip of guilt on my chest. It was my drunken mistake. My feelings that got him into trouble.

"Scarlett." His fingers tangle with mine, the metal of one of his rings cool against my skin. "I blamed myself for my father's actions for so fucking long. Don't do that to yourself." He lifts my hand to his lips and presses a gentle kiss to the top. "Please."

The pressure builds behind my eyes. To distract myself, I reach up and run my fingers through his hair, pushing the strands back from his face. "You're overdue for a trim, huh?"

"You don't like my hair?"

"I love it, but it must be uncomfortable. It always falls over your eyes."

He hesitates, then reluctantly gathers his hair and pulls it back, revealing a long, jagged scar etched into the skin above his temple.

My breath catches.

That's why he wears his hair like that? To hide a scar?

My fingers inch closer, trembling slightly as I trace the rough skin like a road map through the years of torment he's endured. "Is it from that night?"

His eyes flicker closed, his lips parting as if he's savoring the feel of my touch. "Yeah. He hit me in the head with something. I didn't even see what, because he was on top of me just moments after."

I trace his scar again, as if my touch could erase it. "I hate that he hurt you. He was supposed to love you, to protect you."

He turns his head, his nose brushing against my wrist, and inhales deeply. "I'm okay now, Freckles. I'm so . . . *so* okay."

The heat of his breath is against my skin, warm and uneven. My hand trembles as it slips down from his scar, the faint rasp of his stubble brushing my fingertips.

His gaze drops to my lips, and the way his chest rises and falls matches the pulse thrumming in my veins. "We don't have to," he says, voice hoarse, like he's fighting to hold himself back.

"I know," I reassure him.

"We have all the time in the world for kissing and . . . everything else. I just want *this* right now," he says, his finger dangling between us. "It's enough—*more* than enough, actually."

"Rafael?"

"Yes?"

"This is the part in the romance book where the hero shuts up and kisses me."

He leans closer, the space between us dissolving until his lips brush mine in the barest, most excruciating tease. The blanket bunches around his waist, his hand resting heavy and possessive over my knee. Then his fingers come up, curling around my wrist, and his lips part against mine. He takes the lead, achingly slow, like he's savoring every second, every tiny movement, every piece of me.

It's not tentative—we've waited too long for that—but it's not an expert kiss, either, because we've never done it before. It's certainly better than I could have ever pictured, and I spent a lot of time in this very room doing that.

Maybe it's what a gentle kiss from a wild soul feels like.

When we finally break apart, his forehead rests against mine. "You undo me, Scarlett," he says, so softly I almost miss it.

"Really?" I rub my thumb on his nape. "Sometimes it feels like you hold me together."

His lips crash into mine again, and this time, his hand slides to my back, pulling me closer as if the space between us is unbearable.

This kiss is different.

Maybe it's what a wild kiss from a gentle soul feels like.

I press into him, my hands fisting in his shirt, desperate to close the invisible gap, to feel more of him. His teeth graze my bottom lip, and I let out a soft gasp that he swallows with another fierce, all-consuming kiss.

"Someone has a thing for sad boys, huh?" he says, an inch away from my lips.

"Oh, yeah," I tease back.

"Then I should mention," he says seductively as he maneuvers himself on top of me, "that my prom date left with someone else."

I chuckle, the laughter quickly dissipating as he bites my earlobe, then softly kisses the spot beneath.

"And the anniversary of Hairy Houdini's death is coming up."

"Hmm." He presses soft kisses along the curve of my neck, each one leaving a trail of warmth. "That's downright depressing."

"Wait until I tell you about my nana's last words," he murmurs, smiling against the skin of my chest.

I laugh, holding on to his hair as he presses wet kisses right above the hem of my shirt. "Rafael," I breathe, my voice catching as his lips trail lower. My fingers tighten in his hair, torn between pulling him closer and pushing him away. "Wait."

He pauses immediately, lifting his head to meet my gaze. His eyes are dark, pupils dilated, but there's concern there, too. "Everything okay?"

I try to catch my breath. "Yeah, I just . . . my brother's in the next room. We have to keep it PG-13."

Rafael's eyes sparkle with mischief as he leans in close, his breath hot on my ear. "I think I can work with that."

My hands slide down his back, touching the muscles shifting beneath his shirt as he moves. He keeps his weight on his forearms, hovering above me, but I can feel the heat radiating from his body.

"I'm so glad you're not a serial killer," I breathe. Though, to be honest, knowing how having his body inches away from mine feels, I'm not sure that would have stopped me anyway.

"Right back at you."

His hand cups my face, thumb stroking my cheek as he kisses along my jaw. I tilt my head, giving him better access to my neck. The scruff along his jaw scrapes softly against my skin, sending little sparks of sensation down my neck. When his teeth graze a sensitive spot, I gasp, my fingers digging into his shoulders.

"Shh." He chuckles softly, the sound vibrating through his chest where it brushes mine. "How about PG-14?" he asks, his voice low and husky.

I nod, not trusting myself to speak. My heart is racing, every nerve ending on fire where he touches me. I want more, so much more, but I'm also acutely aware of my stupidly thin walls.

I pull him flush against me until his erection presses on my waist, and I can't help but roll my hips forward, craving friction, my lips pressed together to smother any noise.

The muscles in his arms jump under my palms as he braces himself, holding back, with a groan. "Hear me out," he says as he thrusts against me, his hard erection rubbing between my legs. "I won't make a noise. I won't let you make a noise, either."

"As if."

We really, *really* can't. Ethan just moved in, and he shouldn't be welcomed by his sister's moans echoing through the house. And there's just no way Rafael would keep me silent.

But even with the clear protests coming from my mind, my body has a will of its own, and I grind back against him, and he against me, again and again, until we find a rhythm that has us both panting. A slow dance of our bodies pressed close. Every movement is deliberate, restrained, as we try to maintain our silence, until it feels so good it's hard not to voice my enthusiasm. Rafael's lips find mine again, swallowing any sounds that threaten to escape as his hands roam my body, greedy and rough.

"Fuck, Scarlett," he breathes before burying his face in the crook of my neck and muffling a groan.

Our hips rock together, the pressure building low in my belly and his fingers digging into my hip as our movements become more urgent, more frantic.

The bed creaks softly beneath us, and we freeze, listening for any sign that we've been heard. I can feel his heart hammering against my chest in perfect, frantic sync with my own. When silence persists, we resume our dance, slower this time.

His breath comes in short, controlled pants against my neck, and when I turn my head and gently tug on his earlobe, he shudders. A low, helpless sound catches in his throat, half groan, half whimper. He must be close, because his hips stutter in their rhythm, and I'm not far behind, the coiling tension in my core winding tighter with each roll of our bodies.

"Freckles," he breathes, so quietly I barely hear it. His voice is strained, desperate. "Fuck, you feel so good."

I kiss him, our mouths sliding together, wet and warm, teeth knocking in our urgency. My fingers tangle in his hair, holding him close as we move together, chasing our release.

I'm a wet mess as his cock rubs my clit back and forth, again and again, in the most perfect of spots. The pressure builds and builds until, finally, it crests. My body goes rigid, waves of pleasure washing over me as I whimper. I bite down on his shoulder to keep from crying out, my teeth sinking into the hard muscle there. I feel him tense above me, a strangled noise breaking in his throat as his own climax hits moments after mine.

"Scarlett, God . . ." he moans into my mouth, the vibrations prolonging my pleasure as I clench around nothing.

We lie there, both of us trembling and panting. Heartbeats clashing.

"Well," he says, "I think we might have pushed past PG-14 there."

I giggle, smoothing his hair back. "Just a bit."

He lifts his head to look at me, his eyes soft and full of warmth.

A strand of hair falls across his forehead, and I reach up to brush it away.

He has the prettiest, softest hair.

"Are you okay?"

"I'm . . . *happy*, actually."

"Yeah? Wait until I get you out of your clothes." He kisses my lips and settles next to me. "I've waited half a decade for the chance to make you *happy*." He looks down. "But I'm afraid I just disgraced your dad's pants in the process."

"I *really* wish you hadn't said that."

He laughs, pulling me closer. "You sure you're okay? Not just with . . . this, or us. You know, everything that happened with your brother and Peanut?"

I settle into his arms, tracing the shape of his tattoos. A snake, a mask, a rose. My head rests comfortably on his chest. "You think tonight was enough? That he'll leave Ethan alone?"

"Oh, yes. Trust me, Hunter is done bullying people," he says before he leans in, brushing soft kisses along the side of my face.

I guess. He really looked terrified.

"What did you tell him?"

"Hmm?"

"Right before we left. You said something into his ear. Based on his reaction . . . a death threat?"

He pulls back just enough for our eyes to meet, a hollow laugh slipping from his lips. "Oh. I told him that if he has a crush on Ethan, he should just ask him out."

My lips part. "You think this is an extreme case of pulling someone's ponytail on the playground?"

"Maybe." His hand moves to my waist, as if he can't help but touch me. "If it's not, the implication made him uncomfortable enough that he'll never want anything to do with Ethan again."

I let out a small laugh, though it's more nerves than humor. He could be right. I wouldn't put any of this past a sixteen-year-old. Hormones make you stupid.

"Rafael?"

"Yes?" His nose presses against my temple, my heart stuttering at the softness of his voice.

I bite my lip, hesitating before looking up. His eyes are on mine, watching carefully, waiting for me to unravel whatever's running through my mind.

"Do you think . . ." My voice falters, but I press on, my fingers brushing against the collar of his T-shirt. "Do you think Ethan's gay?"

His gaze is steady as he slowly nods. "Yes, I do, Detective."

27

the breakthrough

[trope]

the exhilarating moment when the protagonists uncover the crucial piece of evidence; expect a mix of gasps, dramatic reveals, and the classic "I've suspected you all along!" moment, culminating in the satisfaction of finally piecing together the mystery

"I just don't get why he didn't tell me," I whine, the smell of coffee mingling with the sound of sizzling eggs. Rafael leans against the counter while I whisk a bowl of pancake batter. "He knows Paige is bi. He's met Vanessa. He *has* to know I'm as LGBTQIA+ friendly as it gets. So does he not trust me?"

"It's not about you, Freckles," he says, lazily stirring a pot of oatmeal. We've been having the same conversation since last night, but I can't stop thinking about it. Or convince myself that it's not my fault. I should have created a safe space for him, made sure he'd feel comfortable talking to me about this.

"Then what is it?"

"I told you. He's sixteen. He's probably still figuring it out."

"But why?" I insist, pouring a ladleful of batter into the pan and watching it spread. "He could figure it out with me. Why do it all alone?"

"Because he's scared people will judge him." He expects my next question and says, "Yes, even you."

"But—"

"Scarlett." He sets the spoon down with a soft clink. "His sexuality doesn't matter to you or me, but this is a small community. Your grandparents' world is even smaller. Ethan knows these things *do* matter, unfortunately."

I glance over my shoulder at the hallway, making sure he's nowhere around. The pancake bubbles, so I flip it, lost in thought. "I just hate that he has to deal with this. That he even has to *consider* what other people think."

He watches me closely with that intense gaze. "That I get. You have the right to be mad at the world for making him feel this way."

I set the spatula down, the same thoughts buzzing through my mind in an endless loop. "How do you think the other kids found out?"

"They probably saw him kiss his boyfriend," he says matter-of-factly.

I spin around. "His *what*?"

He arches a brow. "Come on. Really?"

"Wait—Jace?" I gasp. "Oh my God, Jace is his boyfriend. Of course!"

"Uh-huh."

I run the timeline through my head. Ethan's cryptic complaints about our grandparents—how they want him to be something he's not, how they hate his new friend. "Our grandparents know. They know Ethan is gay, and they didn't say a word."

Rafael nods solemnly. "And my guess is they don't approve. Which is why their solution to Ethan not fitting in is to send him away. They probably know at some point he'll come out, and they don't want him around for that."

"Those *animals*," I hiss, slamming the spatula onto the counter. "What have they been saying to him? Oh, I'll straighten them out *immediately*. I'll—"

I start to stomp toward the front door, but Rafael grabs my arm and spins me back around. "Or," he says, calm as ever, "you take a more tactical approach." He reaches for my phone on the counter and hands it to me. "Book a meeting with your attorney. I bet he'd love this information. Don't you?"

His words sink in slowly. He's right; Steve could really use some ammunition to file that motion. But this is a small town. If I tell Steve, and Steve brings it up to the judge, Ethan will be outed. One way or another, it'll become common knowledge.

"I can't," I say, shoulders sagging. "It's not my secret to tell."

Rafael, brows tightening, tugs at my arm. "Come here." He pulls me toward him until my forehead rests against his chest. "Everything's going to be okay."

"God, I hope so." I sink further into him. My mom used to say worrying was like spinning on the spot: lots of work and it got you nowhere. Right now, I feel like one of those colorful wind spinners Paige's front yard is plagued with.

"Ugh, gross. Can you not before breakfast?" Ethan asks as he enters the kitchen. When we both turn, he points at the table. "You're making me not want to eat."

"It's a *hug*," I say, letting go of a snickering Rafael.

"It's the *way* you're hugging."

With an eye roll, I serve breakfast. I know it's stupid, but I can't help throwing curious looks at my brother as I set the first pancake on his plate. Like now that I know he's gay, I'll see something that'll explain why he doesn't feel free to come out to me.

"What?" Ethan asks, his eyes narrowed.

"Hmm?"

"Why are you looking at me like that?"

"I—" Flushing red, I turn to the stove. "Nothing. I . . . Nothing."

"Are you taking the bus to school?" Rafael interjects, sitting at the table with a cup of coffee.

"Yeah." I can still feel Ethan's eyes on the back of my head, but I refuse to acknowledge him. "And apparently, so will Hunter. *Someone* trashed his car last night. Spray-painted 'Proud and fabulous' on the hood."

I whip around, immediately meeting Rafael's gaze.

"Yes, Freckles?"

"You did *not*."

Ethan laughs, the first bite of pancake shoved in his mouth. "Too fucking cool."

"Hey—language!" I tap the back of Ethan's head with the spatula, then point it at Rafael. "Seriously? Tell me it wasn't you."

He sips coffee. "Uh, I'd rather not. You don't like being lied to."

Oh, unbelievable. How did he even do it? I had no idea he'd left the bed at any point. "You know, if you're going to be around my brother, you'll need to lead by example." I point at Ethan. "What does this teach him?"

Rafael's lips purse, as if he's considering my words, even though

Ethan's shaking his head and chuckling under his breath. "Okay, yes. You have a point." He sets the mug down. "Ethan, damage to property is *not* a great way to solve your problems," Rafael says, his tone serious. Then he crosses his arms and leans back. "Unless the property belongs to Hunter, and he absolutely deserves it. Then it's . . . an educational experience."

Ethan chokes on his pancake, half laughing, half gasping. "You're my hero."

I glare at both of them, spatula still pointed like I'm about to execute them, then I turn to the stove. "My boyfriend, everyone."

They both stop eating, stop moving, and my body stiffens, muscles tightening as ridges of tension form along my shoulders and back. My fists clench so tightly that my knuckles turn white around the spatula.

Did I just call him my boyfriend? Out loud? *To his face?*

Rafael must have noticed, too, because the silence continues until Ethan says, "Did you just accidentally DTR?"

I don't have the heart to turn around and check Rafael's expression, so I just nod stiffly.

"Oh. Errr . . . well. I'm late for school."

His chair scrapes against the floor, and I barely hold myself back from asking him to stay. Rafael will say things now—lots of things. Goddamn it, me and my big mouth.

I hear Rafael's chair being moved, then his steps. Sliding an arm around my waist, he comes to stand behind me. His breath is hot against my ear as he murmurs, "Flip it before it burns."

"Huh?" Oh, the pancake. I flip it around as his fingers pull up my shirt an inch and rub over my hip.

He kisses the side of my head. "Come to eat?"

"You can start. I'll just—"

"I'll eat when my *girlfriend* sits at the table and not one minute before that."

Eyes wide, I turn to him. For a second, I really fooled myself into believing he'd let it go, but of course he won't. He's Rafael. "I'm not—we're not . . ."

His eyes soften. "Would it be so bad?"

"No," I rush out. "Of course not. But it's not just me I have to think of. You see how Ethan looks up to you. If things between us didn't work out—"

His nose brushes against mine. "What if they did?"

If they did . . . I wouldn't have to deal with any of this alone. I'd have him to count on, for better or worse. My bed would never be empty, and I'd get to see his arrogant smile every day. See the twinkle in his eyes every time he teased me. We'd fix up the house, maybe. At some point, get another cat. I'd like to have a kid one day, and based on the power imbalance I just experienced with Rafael and Ethan, I'd want it to be a girl. We'd travel, grow old together, live a simple, normal life.

What's better than normal?

He gently tucks my hair behind my ear. "Yeah," he says, as if he's read every single one of my thoughts. "It'd be just like that."

But what if it isn't? the same sneaky voice insists. What if Ethan is here for only a few weeks before we lose the custody case? What if Rafael gets sick and dies? What if he stops wanting to be here?

"Okay, how does this sound?" he begins. "I forget you said anything, and we eat breakfast. Then I make you late for work—just ten minutes, enough to make out with you on the couch." His gaze lasciviously drips down my body. "And then I make you a little more late." Looking back up into my eyes, he adds, "No labels whatsoever."

I nod, relief and self-deprecation holding me on a weird edge. "For now."

"Yes, for now."

"Okay." I accept the kiss he offers as he leans forward. "I'm sorry."

"Sorry?" His lips twist as if the word has no meaning. "I've waited half a decade to be with you, Scarlett. Frankly, whether you call me your boyfriend or anything else doesn't really matter to me, as long as I'm the one you call."

Lips parted, I watch him sit back down, as if he hasn't just said the most swoon-worthy thing I've ever heard. As if he didn't just commit to me again.

I'm still starstruck when Ethan knocks on the doorframe. "All good?"

"Yep," Rafael says, watching me.

"Cool. I'm going."

He waves and walks away, and then I hear the door closing. Finally, setting the last pancake on the stack, I join Rafael at the table. He cuts into his pancakes, and my gaze drifts to the window. Ethan didn't look worried about going to school, and I guess Hunter won't be a problem anymore. He won't, right?

"He'll be okay, Scarlett." He squeezes my hand over the table. "Come on, eat."

He's right. There's nothing I can do right now anyway. But if Hunter messes with him again, I swear I'll stomp on his head. He'll *wish* it was still the good old times when Rafael was trashing his car. "Can I ask you something?"

"Of course."

"Have you ever been with a man?"

He swallows. "Once."

"Really?" My voice pitches up in surprise.

He chuckles. "Why are you so shocked? Don't knock it till you've tried it."

"What happened?"

"Nothing too glamorous. I had a buddy who was gay. He took me out to this club with his friends, and I had a little too much to drink. This guy hit on me all night, so I followed him to the restroom."

"And?"

"And he kissed me. I remember little, except that he asked me to, uh, take things further, and I realized I was irreparably straight."

I snort out a laugh.

He leans closer and kisses my cheek. "What about you? Ever been with a woman?"

"I have, yes."

"Relationship or hookup?" he asks, biting into a strawberry.

"Hookups," I say, spreading jam over my pancake. "But a woman asked me out on an actual date once."

He arches a brow. "And?"

"I said no the same way I would have to any man . . . except you, I guess." I chuckle, thinking back. "Actually, it's funny. You know who it was?"

"Who?"

"Vanessa." When his smile fades, so does mine. "What's wrong?"

"*Vanessa* asked you out?"

"Yeah, like, two years ago. Why—"

"How did she end up with Paige?" he cuts in.

I hesitate, brow furrowing. "Uh . . . they met a few months later."

"But who asked who out?"

"Vanessa. Vanessa asked Paige out. Why?"

His jaw tightens as he sets his coffee down. "I knew I got a weird vibe from her."

A weird vibe? From Vanessa? "You don't think . . ."

"Could she be the one who sent those payments to Booked It?" he says, jumping to his feet.

"I . . . I don't know." My throat tightens as I think back to Vanessa sneaking up on me in the parking lot. She said she was on her way to the bank, on the first floor of the Booked It building. "I did run into her on the way to Horizon Trust once."

His face goes white. "Holy shit."

I stare at him, dumbfounded. I remember the feeling of someone watching me just before she appeared. How I figured I was just creeped out after Catherine's murder. "Is that where the donations came from?"

"It is." He walks out of the kitchen, his pancakes nearly untouched on the plate.

I follow, finding him at the entrance pulling his shoes on. "But why? I mean, she's not even a fan. She only listens to the show because we're friends. Why would she do something like that?"

His jaw ticks with annoyance, eyes set deeply into mine.

"Me? You think she's doing this for me?"

He rubs his jaw. "She happened to be there to handcuff me when I sneaked into your backyard. And with Paige having access to your episodes before they air, it's plausible that she would have access to them, too."

Well, that's hardly enough to accuse her. Although . . . she offered to come to my place when I admitted I was worried about the killer. She was horribly mean to Paige when she tried to redirect Vanessa's attention to herself. And every time I mentioned Rafael, she directed snark at him.

If he's right, and Vanessa's been playing Paige for over a year, what does that mean for my best friend? For us?

"Vanessa's at work." I join him, putting my shoes on. "Her shift on Mondays ends at five."

He hands me my bag. "Is my girl suggesting we break into a cop's apartment?"

Holy shit. I guess I am.

28

the confession

[trope]

the climactic moment when the villain finally spills the beans, often under duress, guilt, or the sheer weight of their own melodrama; usually accompanied by tears, maniacal laughter, or an overly detailed recounting of their evil plan. why don't they ever lawyer up?

"You're a bad influence, you know that?" I ask as we enter Vanessa's apartment. My heart hammers, the thought of being caught breaking into a police officer's home making me question my sanity. How did I even get here?

"I'm surprised *you* didn't know."

I follow Rafael into the open space, heading toward the kitchen while he steps into the living room. He explained the drill in the car before he pulled out a series of lockpicks at her apartment: look through documents, peek into drawers—search for anything unusual, basically.

I tug open the first drawer I find, expecting utensils, and am instead met with a chaotic assortment of mismatched takeout menus, crumpled receipts, and a lone rubber duck key chain. Shoving it shut, I move on to the cabinets, scanning rows of mismatched mugs and an alarming stockpile of protein bars. "Rafael," I say as I stop in front of the fridge.

"What?"

He walks over and stares at the piece of paper stuck to the fridge with a small magnet. It's the reminder of an appointment at Vanessa's bank. Horizon Trust.

"If there's one, there must be more. Let's keep looking."

Right. Hundreds of people in town must have an account at Horizon Trust, and this means nothing. But as I truly, fully consider that Vanessa might be the killer, I no longer wish to hide from it. Quite the opposite. If she's been playing Paige, I want to find out right now.

I walk to her bedroom, looking for her laptop. Once I locate it on her bedside table, I pull it open, but it's password-protected. "You don't happen to have any hacking skills, do you?" I ask Rafael as he comes to stand by the entrance.

"Afraid not. What are you looking for?"

"Paige would never give her access to the scripts without telling me. If she is reading them before they're recorded, she must have access to Paige's email."

"Try the usuals. Birthdays, one-two-three, first names."

I do so as he goes through the drawers of her dresser. "Nothing."

Setting the computer aside, I walk out into the corridor and toward her home office. I don't remember ever seeing the inside of this room, actually. Whenever we came over for a movie night or dinner—even the first time, when she showed us around her place—

this door was always closed. Work stuff, she said. With her being a cop . . . I didn't think it was weird she'd been secretive about it.

"Here," I say as Rafael walks behind me. "Whatever we're looking for is in this room."

"All right." He tries to open the door, but it's locked. He takes out the small set of lockpicks from his pocket, the metal tools glinting in his hand. Kneeling down, he inserts the tension wrench into the lock and works the pick, his fingers moving with precise ease. A faint sound as the first pin falls into place, then another, and another, until finally—*click*. He twists the wrench, and the door unlocks with a quiet snap. He stands up, tucking the tools away, and pushes the door open as if it had never been locked at all. "Holy . . . fucking . . ."

" . . . shit," I conclude.

The dim room is a shrine. To *me*. Every inch of the walls is covered in photos of me—at the coffee shop, walking down the street, laughing with Paige. Candid shots taken from a distance, like Vanessa had been lurking just out of sight, following my every move. Some pictures are blurry, hastily snapped, while others are crystal-clear close-ups of my face, my expressions frozen in time. Among them, there are photos of Rafael and me together, taken from outside my place, through the windows. Moments I thought were private, now pinned up like a twisted scrapbook.

But it's not just me. Theo, Celeste, Paige, Quentin—they're all here, too. Their faces captured in stolen moments, mixed in with newspaper clippings about the murders. The articles scream headlines about the bodies found, the police investigations, all cut out and arranged carefully beneath the photos. Red ink circles the names, underlines the dates. It's all so deliberate, so obsessive.

I can feel my skin crawling, the air too thick to breathe.

Rafael throws a glance at me over his shoulder. "Do you want to wait outside?"

"I'm fine," I say, my voice so weak it must be obvious I'm *not* fine.

He heads to the folders neatly placed on the side table against the wall and opens the first, the sound of pages being flipped drowned out by the white noise in my head as I notice several pictures she took when I was leaving the office. I *knew* I felt observed.

"Bank statements. Looks like we found who sent those donations."

Approaching the wall plastered with newspaper clippings, I read the large text she's printed and hung above. "Must save the podcast."

"And I guess we have a motive."

He holds up another folder. "Transcripts of your episodes." Turning around, he checks my expression. "How are you holding up?"

I'm not sure, really. Part of me feels violated. But most of it is . . . anger. How could she do this? How could she trick all of us and, most importantly, Paige? I'll have to tell her. I'll have to look my best friend in the entire world in the face and tell her that the last year of her life has been a lie. That romance has failed her once again. That her girlfriend is . . . *obsessed with me*. That she's a murderer. "I'm not scared."

"Didn't say you were." His arm brushes mine. "But if you wanted a hug or something—"

With no hesitation, I land against his chest, hiding my face in his T-shirt. I guess I *am* a little scared. Unsettled, maybe. How far has she gone? Has she broken into my house? I trusted her for a whole year, and now we know she's capable of murder.

His arms wrap around me, deliciously heavy, his hand stroking the spot below my shoulder. "I'm taking you home now. I'm putting on a nice movie for you, tucking you under a blanket, and then I'm taking care of this."

"No, I—"

"*I'm* taking care of this. And I'm looking after you. Always."

My heart stutters. *Always* is such a big promise. Such a long time. And look at this. Paige and Vanessa are looking for a place together—I know at some point, Vanessa promised her forever. Always. My parents weren't "forever," and my friendship with Vanessa ended up not being "always."

I *really* want Rafael to be always.

I pull back and open my eyes to find him looking at me, his gaze filled with the usual mix of tenderness and fierce protectiveness.

Then I notice something blinking in the corner of the ceiling.

A camera.

"Rafael?"

He turns, his shoulders dropping once he sees where I'm looking. "Goddamn it. I don't know what it says about me, but I want to hit that woman with my car."

"You have to take pictures of this, and—" I gasp. "Her laptop," I say, rushing out of the creepy lair. I enter the bedroom, then open the laptop and stare at the password field. With a wave of nausea rising up my throat, I type 0306, and after a second of buffering, I'm in.

"What was it?" Rafael asks. I hadn't even noticed he'd followed me, but he's watching over my shoulder, his hand stretched forward and holding out a USB stick.

"My birthday." If she saw us through the camera, she might be on her way here—or getting ready to run away. She might try to delete the contents of her laptop remotely.

"Look." I point at the screen, where Paige's inbox is open. "That's how she has early access to the episodes."

He makes an unimpressed noise. "You'd be surprised how often people fuck up their whole lives by sharing a password."

Making a mental note to change all my passwords as soon as possible, I insert the USB stick into the laptop. "We need to copy this," I say, my heart racing as I navigate through the folders, copying everything that looks even remotely suspicious—photos, emails from the bank, the episodes, hidden files I almost miss.

"Come on, come on . . ." I watch the progress bar slowly inch its way across the screen until Rafael leans over my shoulder.

"I want you out of here, Freckles. Let's go."

"One second." I take my phone and snap a picture of the inbox, just in case, then scroll through the emails on the hunt for incriminating messages. "This has to be enough," I say, pulling out the USB stick as soon as the files finish copying.

"Out, come on."

My phone rings, and seeing Paige's name flash on the screen, I answer. "Hello?"

Rafael takes my hand in his, then pulls me out of the room and through the corridor.

"Scarlett?"

The blood freezes in my veins as my feet stick to the floor. "Vanessa?"

Rafael whips around.

"Hey. I think we need to talk."

"Where's Paige?" I ask, my hand shaking around the phone. Rafael mouths "Speakerphone," so I tap on the button until her voice blasts in the entrance.

"I just drove her home. I knew you wouldn't answer if I called from my phone, so I took hers. An alarm gets triggered when the door to my home office is opened."

Home office? How about *creepy stalker lair*? "Okay, well, I'm here."

"Scarlett, I need you to know I'd never hurt anyone. Especially Paige, or you. I love you both, okay?"

I bet the families of the people she killed would disagree with that statement, but I know there's no point in trying to reason with her. "Okay."

"I'm *not* a bad person."

Rafael's eyes roll.

"I believe you, Vanessa. But you're wrong about something. Paige *will* be hurt by this—and I am, too. You lied about . . . so many things."

"I know." She sounds distraught, her voice shaking before there's the sound of a horn in the background. "But I tried to save the podcast. I knew if you only gave me a chance, we'd be happy together. I can be what you're looking for, Scarlett. I swear."

I look up at Rafael, hoping for a suggestion about what to say. All I find, however, is an annoyed tick of his jaw. Is he jealous? Seriously—right now?

"Vanessa, you're a . . . great person," I force out. "But I'm with someone else."

She sniffles, then sobs. "These guys—none of them deserve you," she spits out. "Quentin, that idiot, or Rafael. They don't love you, Scarlett."

I throw an awkward glance at Rafael, who's staring down at the phone. I really wish she hadn't said that—it's way too early to drop the L-bomb.

"Vanessa, you're dating my best friend, and she's in love with you. Nothing can ever happen between us. You understand that, right?"

There's a moment of silence, and then the sobbing starts quietly, a choked gasp on the other end of the line. But then it breaks free, raw and jagged, each sob heavier than the last. It's the sobbing of someone who's losing control, teetering on the edge, and no amount of words can pull her back from it.

I focus on Rafael, and he must have the same thought as I do, because he takes out his phone and mouths, "Where?"

"Where are you, Vanessa?" I ask.

"I love you," she wails. "I love you so much, and I thought . . . I don't get it. I've done everything I can. I ruined my whole life for you, and you—" The sobbing starts again, and, heart hammering, I rub my forehead. "You still don't love me. Why, Scarlett? *Why?*"

"Tell me where you are. I'll come to you, and we'll talk. We'll fix this, Vanessa."

Her voice is shrill as she shouts, "*There is nothing to fix!* It's over, Scarlett."

It sounds like the traffic noises in the background are growing louder, closer. Is it because she's driving? Or is she walking into the street?

"Everything is over," she says. Does she mean prison? Or . . .

"Vanessa, please—" The noise on the other end shifts, and I freeze. It's faint at first but unmistakable: a low, rhythmic clank in the background, like a metal heartbeat echoing through the line. The distinct clattering of the train-crossing bell.

My blood runs cold as I realize where she is.

The train tracks. There's only one place in town where you can hear that sound so clearly—the old crossing by the river. And the horn I heard earlier? The train must be close. Too close.

I hold a hand over the phone. "The train crossing," I say. "Go."

He shakes his head. "No chance I'm leaving you here. I'll call the police. Let them deal with her."

"The police?" I whisper-scream. We both know we won't convince the police to do a thing, and if we do, they'll get there too late. "Rafael. We can't let her die."

He hesitates, watching me, then the phone. I know he's worried about me, but I also know he's a much better person than people give him credit for. "Promise, no matter what happens next, you'll go home."

I hesitate, but seeing his expression, I know there's no point in arguing.

"Promise. You'll walk straight home, and you won't move until I'm back."

Oh God. He's being dramatic, isn't he? But I know he won't agree any other way, so I say, "Fine. Go."

He groans and then, after stealing a kiss, turns around and walks away, rushing down the stairs.

"Vanessa? Are you still there?"

"Yeah," she whines.

"You said you love me, right?"

"Yes."

"And you love Paige?"

"I really do, Scarlett. So much."

"Then please, don't hurt us any more than you already have. Step away from the tracks, and we'll talk." I hold the phone closer, as if that's going to help. "I know that you're not a bad person. That this whole thing just . . ." How do I justify a year of lies and stalking crowned with multiple murder? "That it just got away from you."

"It did," she insists.

"So we'll deal with it together. I'm your friend, Vanessa. I care about you, and Paige does, too."

For a long moment, there's nothing but silence.

Maybe it's a good sign. Maybe I've convinced her.

I wait, and it feels like my heart does, too, the beats slowing down as if they're waiting for her answer. Then there's the horn again. Louder. Closer.

"Goodbye, Scarlett."

the emotional fallout

[trope]

the inevitable, soul-crushing moment after the case is closed when the detective (or amateur sleuth, who really should be in therapy) stares into the middle distance, questioning their life choices; symptoms include insomnia, excessive whiskey consumption, and monologuing about the darkness of human nature

"Still no word from Rafael?" Paige asks, burrowing farther into the couch as her spoon scrapes against the bottom of the bowl she's holding.

Immediately, I set the phone down and meet her eyes, red-rimmed and puffy from hours of crying. The skin beneath is dark and smudged, and tear tracks still cling to her cheeks. "Sorry. I'm just . . ."

"You're worried, I get it." She wipes her nose with the back of her hand. "Does it make me a horrible person if I say I hope she jumped in front of the train?"

"No, because you don't mean it."

"Don't I?"

I shake my head. Of course she doesn't want Vanessa to be hurt or, worse, dead. She's just rightfully heartbroken. Traumatized, angry, confused. Hell, who wouldn't be? I've seen Paige pour out love for years, barely getting any back. And now, with Vanessa, it really felt like she'd found something good. Something that would withstand the test of time.

But she's a stalker. A liar, and a sick individual. A murderer, too . . . right?

Right, I tell myself, brushing the thought away.

"I just don't *get* it." She puts the bowl down, the little ice cream left now a sad brown liquid. "What was her plan? She knows how close we are—if anything, dating me would only close the door on anything romantic happening between the two of you."

I set my bowl down on the coffee table. "I don't think there's anything rational about what she did, Paige. She murdered people— actual people. For a podcast."

"For *you*."

I exhale, bringing my knees to my chest. "Yeah. She's just . . ."

"Crazy."

"Sick, probably," I correct. I cup her knee. "She needs help. And you need tons of ice cream, un-romantic movies, and nights out."

"Yeah." She attempts a smile, but it resembles a grimace more than anything else. "I knew we were going to break up, you know?" With a pout, she sinks back into the couch. "I mean, I didn't know all of *this*, but we've been at odds for a while now. Constant petty arguments . . . It was exhausting. Some nights I just avoided going home out of fear she might come over."

I think back to the scene I witnessed at The Oak last week. "I guess that explains last Thursday," I say. "You said you were at Vanessa's, but I went there, looking for you, and you weren't there."

A sniffle as she bends her legs to cradle her knees. "Yeah."

"So where did you go?"

"To my parents' house, at first. But they were getting worried, so Theo got me a room at the Wildflower Inn." She sniffles again. "It was sweet."

Oh. So *that's* why he had that key card. And maybe that's why the killer—*Vanessa*—had one, too. To stalk her girlfriend, of all people. "Why didn't you tell me, Paige?"

"Because." She pauses, her gaze distant as she loses herself in thought. "You're already so skeptical of love, and then you finally found Rafael. I didn't want to add fuel to the fire."

I grip her hand. "Paige, that's preposterous. I'm your *best friend*. You're supposed to tell me about your love life. About your problems."

"I know." She smooths over the throw blanket next to her. I swear she looks so sad, even her curls look flatter. "Funny, though, isn't it? I called you paranoid for thinking you were dating a murderer, and it turns out *I* was."

"Yeah," I mumble. I hand her the remote, and as she lazily flips through channels, I can't help but glance at the phone. Still no news from Rafael except for "Police at the scene. All good."

Someone really needs to teach that man how to text, because none of that tells me enough information about what happened. Is Vanessa okay? Is he? Did he give the police the USB stick? Did they believe him?

"Maybe you were right after all," Paige says, tucking the blanket under her chin. "Love is just a construct we cling to so we'll forget that we're ultimately alone in a flawed world."

"You don't believe that, Paige."

"Maybe I do."

No, she doesn't. Sometimes I think she likes the thought of being in a relationship more than the people she dates. That she wants me to be in love so we'll both experience this magic feeling she longs for so much.

"You know how you told me that the reason I never fell in love was that I kept everyone at arm's length so I wouldn't get hurt?"

"What do I know?" she mutters.

"No, I think you're right."

She frowns. "Well, now I'm conflicted. I'm mad at love, but I *love* being right."

"Love is terrifying, Paige. I don't know how you do it. How you get your heart broken, brush your knees off, and jump on that horse again and again. I mean, you give so much power to someone else. The power to break you, to destroy you. And then you trust that they'll take care of everything fragile you've given them. Hope they don't drop it or lose it along the way."

"Is that how you feel about Rafael?"

My lips pinch. "It's only been two weeks, Paige."

"That's not an answer."

"And we haven't even had sex."

"Also not an answer."

I puff out an exasperated breath, but before I can say anything, there's a knock at the door. We both jump up, but Paige remains in front of the couch while I sprint to the door and open it. I meet Rafael's eyes, then land against his chest hard enough to make him grunt.

"You okay?"

Me? Am *I* okay? God, I'll cry. "Are *you*?"

"I'm fine. Hey, Paige." His hand rubs softly against my back, and my fists are probably hurting the skin of his back where I'm clutching at him. "Let's go in. What do you think?"

I nod, though I can't fathom the thought of letting go of him now. I was so worried something had happened to him, but he's okay. He's all in one piece. *Mine*. My Rafael.

"Okay," he says, awkwardly turning around and walking without letting me go. I don't protest but let him drag me inside the house as I inhale the scent of his chest for a few more moments.

Once the door closes, I reluctantly loosen my arms, my hands still roaming over his body to make sure no part of him is hurt. "What happened? I've been worried out of my mind."

"I know, I . . ." Eyes shifting to Paige, he says, "Vanessa's in custody."

Paige sniffles, and I join her by the couch, rubbing her back. "So it's true?" she asks. "I mean, not that I didn't believe you, but—"

"It's true. They're charging her with multiple homicide, stalking, breaking and entering . . . among other things." He presses his lips tight. "I'm sorry."

Paige looks small and fragile, her eyes glassy with unshed tears. She stands on shaky legs, her fists balled tightly at her sides. "Okay. I'm going home."

"What? No, Paige. Please stay."

"This house is at full capacity already," she says, gathering her things. "And besides, no offense, but I really don't feel like being around a couple right now."

I watch Rafael, whose eyes dart to me, but he doesn't say a word.

"Are you sure?" I insist. "There's plenty of room, and we promise to keep the . . . romance to a minimum."

"I'm sure." She gives me a quick hug. "I'll call you in the morning, okay?"

"Yeah." I walk her to the door, then watch her step away, a heavy weight settling in my stomach.

I close the door slowly and lean against it. I should've done more, said something better. She's always been there for me, and now that she's the one who's in need, I feel perfectly useless.

"How's she doing?" Rafael's voice pulls me from my thoughts.

Turning around, I see him standing a few steps away, hands shoved into his leather jacket pockets, his brow creased with concern.

"I'm worried about her," I admit, crossing my arms. "But I'm also just . . . so relieved you're okay."

The space between us shrinks as his eyes search mine. "I'm fine, Freckles. I promise. Are you?"

I nod, though my chest feels tight. "Your texts are embarrassing. 'All good'?" I playfully smack his chest. "That's not even remotely helpful."

"Sorry. I had to say something quickly before they took my phone, because I . . . *kind of* got arrested."

"You *what*?"

"Well, I had to explain to Chief Donovan how I knew Vanessa was guilty, and . . . serial killer or not, breaking and entering is illegal."

Holy crap. Holy *fucking* crap! "And he arrested you?" I gasp. "Oh my God, will I be arrested next?"

"Yeah, 'cause I ratted you out to the cops," he says flatly. "Of course not, Scarlett. I told them I was alone, and Vanessa confirmed it. Guess it's the one upside of her being psychotically obsessed with you."

I exhale, but the relief is quick to vanish. "So . . . wait, what happens next? You won't go to prison, right? Will they take your PI license? Oh my God, Rafael, will you—"

He cups my face with both hands. "Released pending further in-vestigation. I won't lose my license unless I'm charged and convicted. Definitely not going to prison for criminal trespass." He kisses the tip of my nose. "It'll be okay. I have a buddy who's a lawyer, and he'll eat them for breakfast."

I lean into his touch, my eyes fluttering shut. "Are you sure? You're making it sound too easy."

"It is easy, because Willowbrook's police force is a joke." He smiles softly. "Relax, Freckles. We're okay."

I try, really. "Thank you for being okay."

"I couldn't leave you like that." His forehead dips to rest against mine. "What kind of happily ever after would that be?"

We stay still, close and quiet, our breaths mingling in the still-ness of the room, until his lips meet mine, gentle and easy. Once I reciprocate, the kiss becomes more intense, his grip on my waist tightening as he draws me closer.

I wrap my arms around his neck, standing on tiptoes to meet him, and his fingers slide under the hem of my shirt, grazing my skin, until a small noise escapes me. I press closer, my heart racing as his lips leave mine to trail along my jaw, down my neck.

"Ugh. *Gross.*"

The voice cuts through the haze like a bucket of cold water, and I jerk away from Rafael, spinning around to find Ethan standing in the hallway. His arms are crossed, his face twisted in mock disgust. "You're not about to have sex, are you?"

I gape at him, my cheeks burning. "No!" I burst out, just as Rafael says, "Yes." I whip my head back, and, noticing my expression, he corrects. "No?"

Ethan's eyes dart between us. "Well, I'm going to sleep, and I'd just like to warn you that if I hear a single noise, I will run away and leave barf in my wake."

He scoops up Sherlock and leaves the room. "You don't need to see that, either, Sherlock."

Ethan's footsteps fade up the stairs, and in a second, Rafael is back to nibbling on me. My skin tingles where his teeth pinch lightly, but I can't focus, my thoughts running to the horrors we witnessed today. To Paige, heartbroken, and to Vanessa.

"Where are you?" he asks, pulling back.

I awkwardly smile. "Sorry."

"You did nothing wrong." He rubs my shoulders. "Today was a lot, huh?"

"I just keep thinking about Vanessa. The conversation we had . . . and— I don't know."

"What is it?

"Something doesn't sit right with me."

"Something like what?"

I shake my head, not sure of it myself. "She said, 'I'd never hurt anyone.'"

"Oh, yeah. I thought about it, too."

"You did?" I widen my eyes. "Rafael, what if we got it wrong? What if she's not the killer?"

"Whoa." He exhales sharply. "Not so fast. Every single piece of evidence we have points at her."

"Not every single one." When his brows rise, I clarify. "Both witnesses described a man."

"Which was me. Not the murderer."

"Quentin saw you and, well, *stabbed* you," I concede. "But the first witness, in Catherine's case? That wasn't you, was it?"

"No." Rafael tilts his head back, his eyes fixed on the ceiling as if the answer might be written there. "So they're wrong. It wasn't a man. I mean, Vanessa is a big girl."

"But a T-shirt? I just don't see Vanessa gearing up for murder in a T-shirt."

"You're not seriously considering that Vanessa could be innocent, right? You *saw* that room."

"I did." But even in a state of psychosis, would a serial killer say they would never hurt anyone with such conviction? "What did she tell the police?"

He hesitates, and when I gasp, he raises a hand. "Hold up. Ask around in any prison: everyone's innocent."

"Yes, but—"

"She's confessing to things she can't deny and denying things she can't confess."

Maybe so, but something doesn't fit. Something about Vanessa, about all of this.

"So you admit we don't have indisputable proof of *everything,*" I say, folding my arms across my chest. "Like, okay, the killer tried to frame me," I point out. "If Vanessa loves me so much, then why would she do that?"

Rafael leans with his back against the wall and chews on his lip. "All right," he says slowly. "So, is the theory that there's a stalker who's obsessed with you and a serial killer who has it in for you?"

"No, of course not."

He presses his lips together tightly, the muscles in his jaw flexing. "Then what's the motive?"

"The podcast," I say, almost automatically.

He clicks his tongue. "I told you, I've checked all the men connected to Booked It. Followed them, looked into their past, their families, their whereabouts during the crimes. Nothing."

I tap my fingers against my arm. "What about the women? They have husbands, or brothers, or—"

"I've checked them, too," he interrupts. "None of these people were anywhere close to the crime scenes when the murders took place."

I exhale, my mind blank. We have no investors, no obsessive following, no one in town who would gain from our podcast blowing up because of these murders. The only people who would profit from this are the ones working for the podcast.

"Hey," Rafael says, his voice softer now. He takes my hand in his and smiles, a lopsided grin that somehow manages to be reassuring. "Sherlock Holmes says that once you eliminate the impossible, whatever's left, however improbable . . ."

"Must be the truth," I conclude, mirroring his expression despite the knot tightening in my chest. "You've read Arthur Conan Doyle?"

He inhales sharply, his head tilting left to right in a mock display of hesitation. "I, uh . . ." Breaking into a chuckle, he admits, "I've watched the movies."

I laugh, the sound light and fleeting, but it's enough to ease the tension, if only for a moment.

The doorbell rings, and, wondering if today will *ever* be over, I turn to the door and pull it open. My breath is kicked out of me as I see Grandma and Grandpa, their matching expressions of disdain enough to make my blood run cold.

"Scarlett," Grandma begins, her hair in its usual tight bun, her sharp eyes narrowed as she looks me over. "What on earth is this nonsense? Papers? An emergency custody hearing? Have you completely lost your mind?"

"Esther, please." Grandpa holds a hand up, his suspenders stretching over a neatly pressed shirt. "After everything we've done for you, this is how you repay us? Dragging us into court like common criminals?"

I guess Steve must have served them papers. "Hi, Grandma. Hi, Grandpa. Nice to see you, too. Oh, and this is not about you. It's about what's best for Ethan."

"*What's best for Ethan?*" Grandma scoffs, stepping closer. "And you think that's you? A mess of a girl who can't even keep her life together, let alone raise a teenager?"

My fist presses around the door handle. "You have no idea what I've been through in the last five years, or the person I've become," I say, voice sure. "And you don't get to stand here and act like you've done a good job with Ethan when you're stopping him from being *himself.*"

Grandpa's face darkens. "This is a responsibility you're not ready for, Scarlett. Tell your two-bit lawyer to backtrack on this, or you'll end up regretting it."

Rafael comes to my side, his hand tightening slightly against my back in a silent show of support. "Respectfully, Mr. and Mrs. Moore, you two could use a tolerance seminar," he says. "We'll see you in court." Then he pushes the door closed, nearly smacking it in their smug faces.

When he notices my stare, half shock and half reverence, he huffs out a breath. "It's not like we were getting an invitation for Christmas anyway."

30

the found family

[trope]

the ultimate potluck of personalities, where everyone's got their own baggage, but they somehow make it work; at its core, this trope proves that sometimes the family you choose is even more important than the one you're born into

I push open the glass door to Booked It, the heels of my boots clicking against the hardwood floor as I step inside. The familiar scent of coffee and printer ink greets me, but today it feels different. My stomach churns with nerves, the kind that make you wish you could turn around and call in sick.

It's Tuesday. Another episode of *Murders & Manuscripts* will be ready to air on Thursday, and this time, the only victim will be fictional. Right? So why can't I shake this ominous feeling?

Before I can even scan the room properly, there's a sudden shift in the atmosphere. Heads turn. Chairs squeak. And then . . . applause.

Loud, enthusiastic clapping fills the air, startling me so much I almost trip over my own feet. Everyone is looking at me, their faces lit up with joy. My pulse quickens. What the hell is going on?

"Scarlett, you absolute badass!" Sarah calls out, clapping so hard I fear she might injure herself.

"You're a legend, Scarlett," Damien chimes in. "Willowbrook owes you everything!"

I blink, heat creeping up my neck.

"Uh, thanks." I give an awkward wave, my cheeks burning, and I'm fairly certain my face matches the shade of the office's fire extinguisher. "What, um . . . what are you talking about?"

"You caught the Lit Killer. *That's* what we're talking about."

"What—who—"

She holds out a copy of the *Whistle*, and once I grab it, I see my picture plastered on the front page.

Son of a bitch.

The headline reads, "Local Hero Scarlett Moore Brings Justice to Willowbrook." Beneath it, there's a picture of me, and the article goes on to detail how I "single-handedly" uncovered Vanessa's web of lies and deceit, connecting her to the string of murders that had haunted the town for weeks.

Son of a bitch!

"What about Rafael?" I ask, looking up at Sarah as if she had any part in this. "Why don't they mention him?"

"Uhhh . . ."

"He—he did much more than me. He *saved* Vanessa. He figured out she was the killer, and—" I stop, realizing I'm causing a scene. Did the police not mention him at all?

He's the hero, and once again, he gets none of the credit?

This is bullshit.

"Sorry, I should . . ." I shuffle farther into the room, then knock on Celeste's door, and she invites me in. She's beaming from behind her desk. Her black bob is razor-sharp, not a strand out of place, and her small glasses sit perfectly on her nose, accentuated by a bold swipe of red lipstick. The moment she sees me, she jumps up, arms wide like she's about to hand me an Oscar.

"Scarlett!" she shouts, her voice so full of cheer it nearly bounces off the walls. "The woman of the hour! You're amazing. Incredible. The podcaster-slash-detective who solved not one, not two, not three, but *four* murders? Who does that?"

"Well, it was technically only *one* killer," I say as she wraps me in a hug. It's one of those overly enthusiastic, bone-jarring hugs, and I let my arms dangle awkwardly at my sides, like they're confused about how to participate.

When she finally lets go, I straighten my shirt. "And besides, it wasn't me. It was Rafael. I mean, solving mysteries is literally his job."

Celeste waves her hand, brushing off my words like they're a stray piece of lint. "Please. Rafael didn't turn this podcast into a *sensation. You* did! If you think our numbers were impressive last week, you'll be pleasantly surprised today. We're everywhere—headlines, social media, the freaking *news*. I even got an email from some guy wanting to turn your story into a movie. Can you believe that?"

I laugh weakly, more out of politeness than anything. "A movie. Wow, that's . . . something." I wonder if Rafael's character would make it past casting. "But, uh, speaking of the podcast . . . Theo sent me a text about the next episode of *Passion & Pages* being pulled? Was there an issue with the script?"

"The script was flawless, like everything else you do. But . . ." She waves her manicured hand. "I have some *monumental* news."

More monumental than a potential movie deal?

"We've attracted some *serious* attention," she announces, leaning forward with her hands on her desk. "Big names. Investors, sponsors, people with actual money. This is our moment, Scarlett, and I've decided to capitalize on it."

I blink, waiting for her to elaborate.

"I'm hiring someone for the romance podcast!" she says, as though she's handing me a golden ticket, sitting back down and lightly spinning in her chair.

"Oh." The word comes out flat. "Does . . . does that mean I'm back to part-time?"

Celeste laughs, loud and bright, like I've just told the funniest joke. "Oh, Scarlett, no. Absolutely not. You're the face of *Murders & Manuscripts*. Or, well, the voice. The podcaster who solved the murders—people can't get enough of you. Which is why I want to double the weekly episodes. Twice the content, twice the buzz. Full-time. All murder, all the time."

She leans back in her chair, looking thoroughly pleased with herself. "This is everything you've wanted, right? No more romance scripts, just crime fic. Isn't it amazing?"

I open my mouth to agree, but nothing comes out. She's right. This is everything I've wanted. Or . . . it was, wasn't it?

I think back to the romance books I used to dread, the over-the-top love stories that made me roll my eyes so hard they practically got stuck. Somewhere along the way, though, they stopped being a chore. I started looking forward to them, to reading the banter, the confessions, the ridiculously grand gestures.

I started to . . . like them.

And now? I'm supposed to be thrilled about this new chapter. I *should* be thrilled. But I've only gotten a taste of love, only read a handful of romance books, and I want more. I want the comfort of a predictable ending, the joy and ache of the slow burn, the way two people can hate each other on one page and fall apart in each other's arms on the next. I want the longing looks across crowded rooms. The hand brushing another just to feel it. The "I hate you" that really means "I'm terrified of how much I want you." The second chances and the big speeches in the rain.

Romance books showed me that no one is too damaged to be loved, no meet-cute too ridiculous to spark something real. They made me believe that the right person won't fix you, but they'll sit with you while you heal.

And because of them, love's a story I want to keep reading even if I know how it ends.

"Wow," I manage, shoving the thought away. "That's incredible news, Celeste. Really."

"Of course it is," she says, oblivious to the way my voice wavers. "This is just the beginning, Scarlett. We're going to take this podcast to heights you can't even imagine. You and me—we're *unstoppable*."

I try to match her energy, but it feels like I'm dragging my body through wet cement.

By the time I leave her office, the buzz of her excitement is a distant echo. The hallway feels cold and too quiet, but my thoughts are loud enough to make up for it.

Unstoppable, she said.

So why do I feel like I'm spinning in circles?

"What did the lawyer say?" Ethan asks as he fiddles with the edge of his sleeve. His dark blond hair flops over one eye, and there's a bruise still fading on his cheekbone.

I set the phone down on the counter and grab a stack of plates from the cabinet. My heart has been hammering throughout the call with Steve for the last forty minutes. "The judge set up an emergency hearing for Friday."

"*Friday?* I guess that's what they mean by emergency, huh?"

I can tell he's trying to be funny, but he's too tense for it. "It'll be fine, Ethan," I say with as much confidence as I can muster. Truthfully, he's not nearly as terrified as I am, but one of us needs to play the part of the steady rock, right? And *I'm* the adult here.

He leans against the counter. The scab near his eyebrow is almost gone, but he keeps touching it like it still itches. "You really think so?"

"Steve will prep us. He's already gathering evidence, getting people to write character statements, all the things we need. Everything will be okay."

"And if it's not?" He avoids my gaze. "What happens if we lose?"

I swallow hard, trying to push past the lump in my throat. I can't let him see how scared I am. Not now.

"Uh . . ." I start, my voice faltering for just a second. "Then we try again. We appeal. We don't give up."

His eyes search mine. "So you won't let them take me to Virginia?"

"Never," I say firmly, stepping closer to him. "Not to Virginia, not anywhere you don't want to go to."

"Okay," he says, and the single word carries a weight that nearly breaks my heart. "I just hate that it has to be this way."

I place a hand on his arm. "I know," I say, squeezing gently. "But you don't have to handle it alone. I'm here, okay?"

He rubs at the edge of his jaw like it aches, then shrugs. "Okay," he says, a hint of relief in his voice. "Is Rafael coming over for dinner?"

"I hope so, because he's providing the food," I say, reaching for the napkins.

"Awesome." Ethan drops into a chair and pulls his phone from his pocket, and on cue, the doorbell rings.

"I'll get it," I say, my heart skipping just a little as I head to the door.

Rafael stands there, a crooked smile on his face and a bag of food in his hand. Before I can say anything, he leans in and kisses me, sending a pleasant hum through my body. "Freckles."

"Gray." I step aside. "Come on in."

He kisses me again, and this time, his tongue intrudes into my mouth and meshes with mine.

Ethan clears his throat exaggeratedly. "I can *hear* you," he calls out.

Rafael chuckles under his breath, his arm brushing mine as we separate, but his hand lingers on my lower back for just a moment before he moves ahead.

Every time he's around, I feel safe, comfortable, and, at the same time, weak in the knees.

I enter the kitchen, where the table is half set and Rafael and Ethan have fallen into an easy rhythm, unpacking the containers of food as they chat. Sherlock, probably attracted by the smell of pasta sauce, saunters into the room and starts rubbing against Ethan's legs, purring loudly.

I can't help the warm swell in my chest. This little routine—this strange, mismatched family we're building—fills a space I hadn't realized had been so painfully empty. Since my parents died, I've been so focused on survival that I forgot what it felt like to simply exist in moments like this.

We settle down to eat, and, taking advantage of a pause in the conversation, Ethan says, "So . . . I wanted to talk about something."

Holy shit, is he about to come out?

I glance at Rafael, who meets my eyes with a knowing smile.

"Jace's parents are going to the beach tomorrow. In Blue Haven. And they invited me."

Oh. Jace. His *still*-secret boyfriend, unfortunately.

"We'd leave right after school and come back at night," Ethan continues, speaking quicker, "and Jace's mom invited me to spend the night tonight." He finally looks up, his expression sheepish. "Think I can go?"

Is he asking *me*? Right—I make these decisions now.

"Will Jace's parents be there?" I ask as I spear a piece of chicken with my fork.

"Yup."

I chew thoughtfully before speaking again. I'm not sure what the policy is about secret boyfriends and sleepovers. Do Jace's parents know they're dating? And how can I ask any of this while respecting my brother's privacy? "Can I have Jace's number?"

My brother tilts his head, suspicion flickering in his eyes.

"And his parents' numbers?"

He sighs, leaning back in his chair. "Are you going to call them?"

"Why? Are you hiding something?"

"*No*," he says pointedly. "I'm just afraid you'll embarrass me."

Rafael snorts into his drink, and when I glare at him, he looks away, shaking with suppressed laughter.

"Well, that's reassuring," I say dryly, before softening my tone. "Look, I'll just introduce myself and thank her for inviting you. After that, I promise I won't call unless I have a reason to believe you're stuck in a ditch or . . ." I pause dramatically. "Or you've been eaten by a shark."

"Deal."

I feel the knot of worry in my chest loosen slightly. It's a win-win, isn't it? Ethan gets to spend time with his boyfriend, and I get to spend an entire night and day with my . . . Rafael.

"I'll get ready to leave after dinner," my brother continues, his mood lightening as he eats with more enthusiasm.

"Sounds good," I reply, leaning back in my chair and catching Rafael's gaze. He gives me a small wink, and I know no matter what bad decisions Ethan might make tonight, I'll be the one making the most dangerous ones.

31

the grand gesture

[trope]

the rom-com holy grail; typically involves an elaborate,
borderline-ridiculous display of love designed to win someone
back—or just leave them speechless. success rate: high

"Seriously, what is going on?" I insist, stumbling forward as
Rafael's hands press over my eyes. I can see the light of the
streetlamp filtering through his fingers but not much else.

"You do know what a surprise is, don't you?"

"I don't *love* surprises."

"Well, at least this one won't last long." He stops, and after a
tentative step, so do I. "We're here."

We are? We've barely left the backyard. What exactly is this surprise?

His hands are gone, and I blink, watching his house. "Uh . . . I'm
confused."

"Your surprise is inside."

I turn to look at him over my shoulder. "Oh? We're going to your place?"

"We can spend the night, if you'd like." Wrapping his arms around me, he buries his nose in my hair and inhales. "I'm pretty sure the mattress was bought in the last decade."

"*Fancy*," I tease. "Will I get hotel treatment?"

His hold on me tightens. "You'll think you're at the Four Seasons."

I chuckle, leaning back when he nibbles at my jaw. I can't even bring myself to care that someone might see. Hell, I want everyone to know about us. I want to write it on the walls, hire one of those cheesy planes to fly a banner across the sky reading "Rafael Gray belongs to Scarlett Moore."

"Ready for your surprise?" he asks as he pulls me with him. We stumble into the front yard in a cloud of giggles, and, giddy with excitement, I follow him to the door and wait for him to open it.

We step in. Everything's dark and eerily quiet, but the faint scent of wood and fresh paint fills the air. My curiosity spikes.

"Rafael, what is happening?" I ask, hands up to make sure I don't walk into a piece of furniture.

"Patience," he teases, stepping away to fumble for a switch. A soft click echoes, and the room floods with warm light.

I freeze, my breath caught in my lungs.

Against the long wall of his living room stands a massive black bookshelf, the fresh paint glowing. My eyes trace the intricate details—the perfectly aligned shelves, the smooth curves of the wood, and the small brass accents at the corners. A rolling ladder is attached to the top rail, its polished wood gleaming under the light.

Most of it is filled with books, with a mix of dark and pastel covers, which makes me think he picked from among very different genres.

"I bought every single book I found. I don't think I'm allowed inside any bookstore within twenty miles. And I checked yours to make sure I didn't get you anything you already have, but I might have made a mistake here and there."

I breathe, still too stunned to speak. There's a saw against the blanket-covered couch, a paint bucket next to it.

Laughter bubbles out of me in pure exhilaration. "Oh my God, Gray." I step closer, running my fingers along the nearest stack of books. "You . . . you *made* this?"

He leans casually in the doorway. "I told you I would. I figured if you like it, Ethan and I could move it into your place this weekend. While I work on your . . . castle, was it?"

I spin to face him, still laughing. "I can't believe you actually *made* this."

"Can't you?" His grin widens. "I'm crazy about you, and I've been pretty open about it."

He has, hasn't he?

I'm speechless, standing there with the black masterpiece behind me and the man who built it in front of me.

Rafael pushes away from the doorway and crosses the room toward me. His hands find my face, his touch warm and sure, and before I can even catch my breath, his lips are on mine.

"Let me be clear." He kisses the corner of my mouth, his scruff scratching softly against my skin. "I intend to pursue you, Scarlett Moore. Privately, publicly, silently, and out loud. I plan to do it to your face and even when you're not around, behind your back." He smiles, like being this vulnerable just comes naturally to him. "Until our happily ever after, and beyond, I intend to give you a love worthy of a romance book."

I nearly melt, and every thought dissolves under the heat of the next kiss. I reach up, curling my fingers into his shirt, but then he breaks away just enough to smirk against my lips.

Without a word, his hands glide down to my hips, firm and commanding. Before I realize what's happening, he lifts me effortlessly, and a surprised laugh escapes me as he settles me on the rolling ladder.

"Rafael!" I gasp, clutching the sides for balance.

He leans in, his mouth grazing my ear as he murmurs, "You look good on it."

His mouth captures mine again, more intense this time, his hands bracketing my thighs as the ladder creaks softly beneath us.

"I love this ladder," I say against his lips, my nipples hardening as his chest brushes against me.

He withdraws just enough to watch me with hooded eyes. "Do you?"

With a gentle nudge, he lets the ladder roll to the left, and I shriek, clutching the rails tighter.

"*Rafael!*"

"Relax, I've got you." He lets it glide a little farther before pulling it back toward him, his hands sliding to grip my waist. His voice drops, low and rough. "I'll always get you."

My heart stutters. "Always?"

"Mm-hmm." His gaze roams over me, and then his mouth is on mine again, stealing whatever witty reply I might have had. "And now I get you *naked* for a whole night. In my bed. No interruptions." He lifts my chin, kissing my pulse point. "Legs around me, breathless whimpers, sticky with sweat."

"Someone's feeling confident."

"You're about to find out." With a swift motion, Rafael lifts me off the ladder, his strong arms cradling me against his chest. I wrap my legs around his waist, clinging to him as he carries me out of the living room and up the stairs. His lips never leave mine, stealing kisses with each step.

Once we reach the bedroom, I quickly slide back to the floor. Our hands move of their own accord, fumbling with buttons and zippers, the rush making it impossible to focus on anything but getting closer, removing every barrier between us. His hands slide under my shirt, fingers skimming up my back as he pulls it over my head.

As he removes my bra, too, I shiver, the cool air hitting my skin only to be replaced by the warmth of his gaze. His finger follows the curve of my chest, brushing my nipple and tracing down my stomach, his lips parted, like he can't believe what he's seeing.

"Your freckles," he whispers. "They're everywhere."

I swallow, fighting the instinct to cover up. "Too much?"

"I wonder if I could kiss them all." He leans forward, pressing a soft kiss to my shoulder. "Lick them all," he continues, tongue sliding down between my breasts.

Clinging to him when my knees turn wobbly, I tug at his shirt, needing to feel his skin against mine, and he quickly obliges, the fabric falling to the floor as we stumble toward the bed.

It's the first time I've seen him without a shirt on, and as the mattress dips under my weight, I hold him back, wanting to take it all in.

Tattoos scatter across his chest—black lines slipping down his ribs, a half-finished compass at the edge of his collarbone, script curling just under his heart. He's lean, not bulky, but there's definition in every plane, like he's someone who doesn't try to sculpt his body, just uses it. A little hair trails down from his sternum, and I blink when I catch the glint of silver—a barbell piercing through one nipple.

He winks when he notices that's what my gaze sticks to, like he knew I'd like that, then his body is pressing against mine. I can barely get used to it before his hot breath is on my collarbone, and he maps a path of kisses down to the swell of my breasts. It's hard to think, to breathe. His hands are everywhere—caressing, exploring, teasing.

He takes one nipple into his mouth and sucks hard on it while his left hand continues to tease the other. I arch my back, trying to get closer to him, and he doesn't disappoint as he switches to my other nipple and gives it the same treatment.

"Sensitive," I say in between gasps, my fingers tracing the muscles of his shoulders.

"Hmm—perfect."

His lips keep trailing down my body until they reach my thighs. After he glances at my expression, his fingers hook into the waistband of my panties, and he drags them down my legs.

Spreading my thighs wider apart, he watches intently. "I'm not going to make it, am I?"

"What?"

"I'm going to come the second I lick up this dripping pussy."

I blush, eyes fluttering closed. "Rafael, *please* . . ."

He leans forward, his breath hot against the sensitive skin of my inner thigh. I bite my lip, trying to breathe as he presses a kiss to the tender skin just above my knee.

"You're teasing me—" I say, my voice catching in my throat as his fingers brush against my clit before pulling away again.

There's a playful glint in his eyes, his lips curving into a wicked grin. "Can you blame me? You look so pretty like this, desperate for me."

A rush of heat licks up my body, and I can't hold back a whimper. "*Rafael*," I plead.

"Yes?" His lips hover just above where I want them, and his fingers continue brushing lightly over me, sending shivers of pleasure rippling through my body.

I press myself against his touch, desperate for more. "Don't make me beg."

"Why not? I think I like you begging," he says before his fingers slip inside me. His mouth follows suit, his tongue tracing slow, torturous circles around my clit.

"Oh—*oooh*." The sensation is overwhelming, a wave of pleasure crashing over me with such force that my fingers curl into the sheets. Every movement, every flick of his tongue, and every thrust of his fingers sends me spiraling higher and higher, until I'm lost in the sensation, the feel of him, the sound of his name on my lips, the intoxicating scent of sex.

"How long have you been dripping like this for me?" His tongue snakes out, and he licks me from my entrance to my clit. He repeats this motion again and again until I'm moaning loudly and tugging on his hair. He focuses on my clit, sucking it hard between his lips until my legs shake. "Since you asked me to fuck you in my car that first night?"

"M-much earlier than that."

He hums against me, my hips bucking involuntarily as I try to hold on to the last shreds of control. "Oh God, Gray," I moan, my voice breathless and shaky. It's like explosives are going off everywhere—my brain, my body, my mind. My world shatters in a burst of white-hot pleasure, my body trembling as I pull on his hair greedily, keeping him where I want him.

He doesn't stop until I'm writhing beneath him, and when my muscles finally relax, he pulls away, his hands soothing as they slide up my body.

He kisses his way back up, his lips brushing against my stomach, then my chest, before finally capturing my lips in a heated kiss. "You like the way you taste?" he says against my lips. "I don't want to go a single day without you coming on my tongue."

I pull him closer as I kiss him back with everything I have. "How about I come around your cock now?"

My hips shift restlessly beneath him, seeking friction, and his smirk fades as he grunts.

"Not yet," he says as his hand finds my wrists, pinning them gently above my head. He holds them with one hand, then leans to the right, probably fetching a condom.

He's on me a moment later, his lips coaxing mine apart and his tongue exploring my mouth with deliberate, languid strokes. It feels like heaven. Like the laziest, most decadent pleasure. Like he's pouring feelings straight from his chest to mine.

When I feel something cool and smooth glide across my stomach, my eyes open. He kisses me, keeping me from seeing what the hell that unfamiliar object is. It traces lazy patterns on my skin, sliding lower and lower until it reaches the sensitive area between my thighs.

My breath catches in anticipation as I think I recognize what it is, and a powerful vibration erupts against my already swollen clit, making me moan into his mouth. The vibrator slides slightly, slick with my arousal, creating an obscene wet sound that echoes in the room. It's overwhelming, bordering on too much after my recent orgasm.

My legs clamp down around Rafael instinctively, trying to close and shield me from the onslaught of sensation, but he keeps me spread open, his strong thighs preventing me from escaping until he finally withdraws enough to let me breathe.

"Rafael!" I cry out, raw and desperate. "Oh God, please!"

He doesn't let up, keeping the vibrator pressed firmly against my sensitive flesh. His eyes are dark as he watches me squirm, drinking in every gasp and moan.

"Please what, Freckles?" he murmurs. "Please stop? Or please continue?"

I can't form coherent words, my mind clouded by the intense pleasure coursing through me. My body jerks uncontrollably as I hover on the edge of another orgasm.

"I . . . I can't . . ." I gasp. It hurts and at the same time feels better than anything I've ever experienced, my eyes nearly crossing.

He leans down, his lips brushing against my ear. "You wanted your vibrator back, didn't you?"

My body lifts off the bed, every muscle taut as waves of pleasure crash over me. I cry out, an orgasm ripping through me until I'm breathless and sparks blind me.

Just when I think I'm about to faint, he switches off the vibrator and tosses it aside. He releases my wrists, and his lips find mine in a searing kiss.

Immediately, I wrap my arms around him, pulling him close as our bodies meld together.

"You're incredible," he says, his words muffled by the ringing in my ears. "So beautiful when you come undone for me."

I can't say a word, moans still ripping out of my mouth. I can feel him shifting, hear noises I can't decipher, then his chuckle, rumbling through his chest and into mine.

"Tell me you still want it, Scarlett."

I dig my fingers into his back. "Hmm."

"Ten for enthusiasm, but I need you to say it."

Forcing my eyes open, I meet his gaze. He's tense, his eyes darker than black, his hair messy after all my pulling. My finger traces the damp skin of his cheek, then his jaw. "Yes." I sound drunk, and I feel it, too. Weightless. Euphoric. "I would very much still like your c—"

He thrusts into me with a force I'm not prepared for, my mouth opening in a soundless scream as I adjust to the way he stretches me.

"Ooh . . . *fuck*." His jaw clenches, his eyes closing for a long moment as I clamp around him. "You're, hmm . . . so tight," he mumbles. "Tight and, shit, so wet, Scarlett."

He pulls back quickly, and his hips snap against mine, setting a relentless pace.

Holy crap, this man might just break me. Actually, I might just *ask him* to break me. Moan after moan, I cling to him desperately, my nails raking down his back as I try to hold on to him.

"*Scarlett*." He whimpers, face falling against my neck. The sound sends a thrill through me, and I tighten around him deliberately, savoring the way his breath hitches in response.

"Only for you," I gasp out.

"Fuck yeah." He hisses through his teeth. "Say it's *my* pussy."

"It's"—*thrust*—"your"—*thrust*—"pussy!" I cry out.

"Christ." His pace becomes more frantic as he sinks inside me deeper and harder. I feel the tension building in his shoulders, his balls slapping against my ass, his cock parting me again and again, hitting the spot that makes my eyes roll.

"I can't take this—I need to pull out," he says under his breath, and it sounds like he's telling himself more than me. His expression is strained, a mixture of focused concentration and unrestrained pleasure. His eyes, usually so controlled and steady, are now wild and dark, locked onto mine as my heart races even faster.

I'd *die* to feel him release inside me.

Can I ask? Should I?

"Take the condom off," I blurt out. "P-please?"

His rhythm falters as he meets my gaze. "Freckles, are you sure? We don't need to—"

"I . . . well, I haven't been tested in a while, but I'm good."

He hesitates. "I get tested regularly."

Gently, I push him back until his cock slips out, then remove the condom over his shaft. His eyes roll back, and the second my hand abandons him, he drives inside me hard. His movements become erratic as a low, primal rumble resonates through his chest.

"You want my load, Scarlett?" His face contorts in a grimace. "You want me to fill up this tight cunt?"

"Yes," I manage, another orgasm building fast deep in my belly. "Fill me up, Gray."

"Every single drop. *Fuck, fuck, fuck*—" His brows furrow, and his mouth opens in a silent scream as he finally reaches his climax. His body tenses, his muscles contracting as he drives into me hard with a shuddering push until he's buried inside me.

He moans, loud, and the sensation of him pulsing inside me is enough to trigger my release, another orgasm washing over me violently.

"Fuck." His body shivers, his grip on my hip tightening until it hurts as his movements become slower, more deliberate, and he rides out the waves of his orgasm. He leans forward, his breath hot and uneven against my skin and his forehead resting lightly against mine. "Fuck."

I chuckle as he slowly pulls out, cum gushing out of me and dripping down my ass, hot and dense. "You said that already."

"Trust me," he says, his words slurred, before he kisses me. "You're not ready to hear what I *want* to say."

"What's that?"

He meets my gaze, and even though he doesn't utter a word, my skin prickles all over, my heart in overdrive.

When I look away, he chuckles. "That's okay." He presses a kiss to the spot beneath my ear. "When I finally say it, you'll never want me to stop."

32

the filthy smut (yes, more)

[trope]

the not-so-guilty pleasure of romance novels; frequently hidden behind innocent-looking covers and read in public with an impressive poker face. often, these scenes should come with a "do not try this at home" disclaimer

I stir awake, my eyelids heavy with sleep, and immediately notice the mattress beneath me isn't the usual thin, lumpy one; this one is plush. And the sheets—they're smooth and cool against my skin, not the cheap, scratchy ones I have at home. There's a faint, clean scent lingering in the air, fresh linen with a hint of lavender.

I open my eyes, a sense of warmth spreading through me as I realize I'm in Rafael's bedroom. But his side of the bed is empty, the sheets rumpled. My heart skips a beat. Did he leave?

Just as I'm about to get up and look for him, the air carries the smell of breakfast to me. Bacon, maybe eggs. "Rafael?" I call out.

His voice comes from downstairs. "I'm making breakfast. Stay where you are!"

"Why? Are you hiding another woman?"

"Yes," he replies, his tone teasing. "That's exactly it."

I sink back into the pillows, grinning up at the ceiling. The cozy warmth of the blankets wraps around me, and everything feels so perfect I have to stop myself from squealing. The mattress cradles my body in all the right places—which my sensitive skin needs after last night—and I'm giddy with excitement at the thought of Rafael coming back.

My phone buzzes on the bedside table, and I glance at it, contemplating whether I should answer, then quickly realizing I lost the luxury of ignoring my phone the moment Ethan moved in. I grab it and scroll through the notifications, but everything can wait, and Paige hasn't answered my latest texts yet.

Quickly, I open the *Whistle*'s website. No news.

Rafael walks into the room, a pleasant distraction wearing nothing but a pair of low-waisted shorts, most of his tattoos on full display. His dark hair is wet from the shower and pulled back, and his muscles ripple slightly as he moves.

I bite my lip, memories flooding back—his hands on me, the way his hips felt pressed against mine.

My body aches in the best possible way.

"You Judas," I say as he sets a tray down in front of me and the smell of breakfast wafts up, making my mouth water. There's a plate of perfectly cooked bacon, golden scrambled eggs, and a stack of pancakes drizzled with syrup and topped with fresh berries. "I can't believe you showered without me."

"Well, I needed to so I could make you breakfast in bed." He holds a ringed finger up. "And I got you a shirt, too. Not one of mine, 'cause I figured it'd be too big. *But*—" He walks to the dark wooden dresser and opens up a drawer. "I see your one dead parent's broccoli shirt and raise you . . ."

"Oh my God!" I sit up, holding the blanket over my chest. It's *another* broccoli shirt, exactly like my dad's and mom's shirts. "How's that even . . ."

"I thought about it and figured it was one of three possibilities. One: someone at some point gave out these shirts for free. Two: a local up-and-coming broccoli stylist we've never heard of. Or three: a vegetable secret society."

"Ha! Number three is my favorite."

"Mine, too." He throws the shirt my way, and after catching it in the air, I pull it on. The mattress dips as he climbs back on.

"So, is it a thank-you breakfast for what I let you do to me last night?"

He chuckles, a low, rich sound. "Oh, absolutely. That's exactly how I wanted it to come across." He rests his weight on one elbow. "Thank you for the mind-melting orgasm, Scarlett. Enjoy bacon and eggs."

"Well," I say, taking a bite of pancake, the syrup sticky and sweet on my tongue, "you might want to start planning lunch in bed."

He pauses and gives me a curious look. "Lunch?"

I run my finger down his chest. "Yes. A thank-you lunch for what I'll let you do to me this morning."

His eyes darken just a little as he leans closer. "I think I can manage that."

"Good." I lift the tray and set it on the bedside table, right over my phone. When I turn back to him, he's licking his upper lip. I want to feel that tongue *everywhere*. "Because I'm really hungry."

The blanket falls off me as I climb over him. His eyes dart to my shirt, my nipples stiffening against the fabric, and once I rub myself over his crotch, I feel him hardening. Pleased, I lean down to kiss his soft, beautiful lips.

It's a drawn-out, lazy kiss. I do feel the urgency behind it, but it's subdued by the need to say something we can't possibly say with words.

When I lean back, my eyes trace over the contours of his face, memorizing every detail. The golden and brown flecks in his gray eyes, the softness in his gaze that contrasts with the strength of his jawline. His straight nose, with that flirty ring, and his lips slightly parted, as if waiting for mine to find them. Every feature, every line and curve, it's all him—and it's all perfect.

His presence fills a space I never knew was empty.

"I'm . . ."

His thumb rubs a small circle on my thigh. "You're . . ."

Falling in love with you.

I trace his shoulders with my fingers, then drag them across his chest, over the hair sprinkled on it.

I can't tell him. The last time I told him I loved him, he vanished for five years. "I'm . . . going to ride you now."

He cocks a brow at me. "All right. Thank you for the heads-up."

"You're welcome."

He grips my hair and gently but surely pulls my face to his. He kisses me, this time hazy, rushed, hungry.

I fumble with his sweatpants until his erection springs free between my legs.

"Ride me, Freckles," he says, pulling my hips up, then helping me back down, taking his cock inch by inch. "I'm not done with you yet."

I fall back onto the mattress, trying to catch my breath. My skin is damp, and my whole body tingles with the lingering heat of effort and pleasure. Rafael pulls me closer, dragging the blanket over us.

"I guess I owe you dinner in bed now."

"I guess you do," I pant back. I glance at the breakfast tray and the lunch tray still perched on the bedside tables. "But then again, we didn't eat breakfast *or* lunch. Plus, we need to leave this bed at some point today."

He chuckles, his lips pressing against the sweaty skin of my chest. "We *did* shower."

"Did we? I don't think you can call it showering when you come out dirtier."

With a distracted hum, his lips trail along my collarbone. It's like he can't get enough. We've been fucking the whole day, in every single way I know how to. Softly. Punishingly. Like crazed animals that function purely out of instinct. Everything hurts, but in the right way. The way one's body should hurt when it's been used and consumed.

When I let out a soft whine of displeasure, he inches away slightly. "I should start preparing for the hearing on Friday."

"No, you *are* prepared for the hearing. What you need is to keep your mind busy so you don't freak out about the hearing."

"Let me guess. That's where *you* come in."

"Oh, I come in and out, pretty much wherever you want, so long as I come *last*."

I giggle as he keeps teasing me with his lips and teeth, making it harder and harder to keep my legs pressed against him so that he won't slide all the way down.

I'd imagine one would be basically numb after this much sex, but my skin seems more responsive to him than when we started. The more of this we do, the more of him I crave.

"You know," I say in between pants. "I don't think I've ever gone this much time without reading."

"Hmm." He slides farther down, fingers grazing my legs as he kisses my inner thighs. "That's unacceptable." A flick of his tongue over my clit has me gasping, my whole body clenching. *God, I'm sensitive.* "Open the drawer there."

I look to the right as his mouth slides lower, his tongue flattening and licking me all over until my eyes roll back. "Hmm."

"Come on. Drawer."

I open it and immediately see the book inside. It has a blue cover, but it's romance, I'm sure. "Are you reading that?"

"Yes. And now you are." I gasp when Rafael's mouth wraps around my clit, his chuckle vibrating against my drenched skin. "Go on."

I'm not sure I get where he's going with this, but I open the book to the bookmarked page and read the first line. *Holy smokes.* "This is *spicy.*"

My body squirms at every slow movement of Rafael's tongue on my swollen clit, my hold on the book tightening.

"Read it to me, Freckles."

Reminded of his very similar request at the bookstore, my heart flutters. I clear my throat, trying to focus as his tongue continues its delicious torment. "They knew they couldn't surrender to their passion. Not with the curse looming over their heads. But they also couldn't stay away. 'We can't,' he groaned when she pulled him into her bed. 'You know we can't.'"

I feel Rafael's breath hot against my inner thighs as he pauses, listening intently.

"'Then show me,' she said, cupping his cheek. 'Let me watch you give yourself the pleasure I wish I could give you. Show me, and I'll do the same. I'll show you all I have.'"

"Ooh." Rising above me, he drawls, "Interesting. Keep going."

I swallow hard, my eyes flicking between the book and Rafael's intense gaze. His fingers move inside me slowly. I lick my lips and continue reading.

"He hesitated for only a moment before he leaned back and un-buttoned his pants, his hand moving to grasp his hard length. She watched, transfixed, as he began to stroke himself."

Rafael's fingers withdraw from me, and I whimper at the loss. But then I watch him mirroring the actions in the book. He sits back on his heels, lit by the soft glow of the bedside lamp. His chest rises with shallow breaths, lean muscles shifting under skin marked with all of his beautiful ink. One nipple glints with silver, and the subtle flare of his nose ring catches the light as he tilts his head, watching me watch him.

"Go on," he says, gripping his hard cock.

I struggle to focus on the words. "She . . . she couldn't tear her eyes away from the sight of him pleasuring himself. Her own hand drifted down her body, fingers circling her clit as she matched his pace."

I let out a shaky breath as Rafael gently grips one of my wrists and moves my hand between my legs. His eyes darken as he watches me touching myself, his hand sliding up and down and his chest rising and falling sharply.

"They moved in sync, eyes locked on each other as they brought themselves closer to the edge. She felt daring tonight—daring enough to spread her legs wider and watch his jaw drop. His desire was intoxicating, pushing her to test the limits."

"Hmm. Spread those legs real wide for me."

I do, the book wobbling in my hand as I stroke my clit. "Sh-she used two fingers to open herself for him, his guttural moans sending pleasure straight to her core."

"Fuck," he interjects when I open up my pussy for him, the cold air giving me shivers. "This better end with me destroying that pretty cunt."

His hand moves faster around his length.

"She could see the muscles in his abdomen tightening, knew he was close. She knew she shouldn't, but she thrust two fingers inside, whimpering at the fullness. But it wasn't enough."

A groan escapes Rafael's lips as I fuck my hand. I can't tear my eyes away from him, my fingers working furiously.

"Focus, Freckles."

Right, right.

" 'I need more,' she whined. She could have achieved an orgasm if she continued, she knew that. But her greed and lust demanded more. 'Just . . . just the tip,' she pleaded, her hips rocking restlessly. 'Give me the tip of your cock.' "

Rafael sprints from his position, quickly settling on top of me. "*Please*, tell me he said yes," he pleads, tip teasing my entrance.

I take a deep breath and continue reading, my voice trembling. "Slowly, agonizingly, he pushed the tip of his cock inside her, both of them groaning at the sensation."

"Thank God." He pushes, sliding in effortlessly with how drenched I am. He begins to move, shallow thrusts that make my breath catch in my throat but can't get me there. "Fuck, you're soaking me."

I keep reading over the wet noise of his small pushes, eager to get to the part where he fucks her brains out. "She wrapped her legs around him, urging him deeper. 'More,' she begged. 'Just a little more.'"

He responds to the words as if they were my own, sliding deeper inside me with a low groan. I struggle to keep my eyes on the page, legs wrapping around him.

"He knew he shouldn't, knew the consequences, but he was powerless against her pleas. Inch by torturous inch, he pushed farther inside her, reveling in her tight heat until she cried out in ecstasy. He bottomed out inside her, her nails raking down his back. *The curse be damned*, she thought. This was worth any price."

My words dissolve into a moan as Rafael fills me completely. The book slips from my grasp, falling forgotten to the side as I tilt my head back.

I gasp as he begins to move in earnest, his hips rolling against mine in a steady rhythm. "Oh my God, Rafa—"

"Don't you want to know what happens next?"

"I can't." I pant, my fingers digging into his shoulders. "I can't read any more."

He chuckles, his breath hot against my neck. "That's okay," he murmurs, nipping at my earlobe. "I'll show it to you."

His hips snap forward, driving into me with renewed intensity, and I arch my back, meeting his thrusts. "Harder," I gasp. "I need more."

He obliges, pounding into me with punishing force. The headboard slams against the wall with each push, the bed creaking beneath us. I cry out, overwhelmed by the exquisite mix of pleasure and pain.

"Fuck," Rafael growls, his hips grinding against me. "You like it when I fuck you like this, don't you? Hard and deep, stretching you open."

"Yes—it's so good—perfect." I gasp again, my words punctuated by sharp cries as he begins pounding into me. "I love it—love . . ." *Don't, Scarlett.* "Love your cock."

He lifts one of my legs over his shoulder, changing the angle and hitting even deeper.

"Show me how much you love it. Squeeze me inside you with your orgasm, and I'll give you every drop of mine."

Almost on command, my eyes cross, my pussy clenching around him hard enough to make him whimper.

He drives into me with a series of stuttering thrusts, sending us both spiraling into an intense climax. I cling to him, our bodies trembling against each other, and for several long moments, we remain entangled, panting and shaking.

Finally, he lifts his head from where it had fallen against my neck.

"Now, *that*," he says with a satisfied sigh, "is how you make reading interactive."

I let out a breathless laugh, running my fingers through his sweat-dampened hair. "I don't think regular reading will do it for me anymore."

"In that case . . ." He presses a soft kiss on my lips. "God bless filthy smut."

act III

(structure)

---

the grand finale of the rom-com; this act is where all
misunderstandings, awkward confessions, and missed
connections collide in a whirlwind of chaos, character arcs
are wrapped up with a bow, exes are confronted, and somehow,
against all odds, love prevails

33

the insurmountable obstacle

[trope]

the colossal hurdle that stands between the couple and their
happy ending; characters will spend a solid chunk of this
whispering, "there's no way this is going to work."
spoiler alert: it *always* works out, but not without
some serious emotional cartwheels.

The courtroom is colder than I expected, a cold that seeps into your
bones and makes you wish you'd brought a sweater. I clasp my
hands together over my long, black skirt to keep them from trembling and turn around, my eyes scanning the room. Ethan's sitting
right behind me in his Sunday best, and he gives me a hesitant smile
that quickly falters. My heart squeezes. This is all for him. I have to
remind myself of that.

At least it's Friday. The latest episode of *Murders & Manuscripts*
aired last night, and no one in Willowbrook died. Which must mean
Vanessa was behind all of it, just like Rafael said.

Next to Ethan, Rafael leans back in his seat, looking uncharacteristically tense. He's wearing a suit—a boring gray one that seems to smother him. When he sees me looking, he gives me a thumbs-up.

Steve is going through papers as he stands next to me, calm and collected like a lighthouse in the middle of a storm, and across the room, my grandparents sit stiffly, my grandmother's hands folded over her purse, my grandfather's back as straight as a surfboard. It's strange seeing them there, on the opposite side, like we're enemies, but I can't think about that right now.

Right now, we *are* enemies.

The door at the front of the room opens, and the bailiff steps in, his voice booming, "All rise for the Honorable Judge Harrison."

We stand, the room falling silent as Judge Harrison, a stern-looking redhead with sharp eyes, enters and takes her seat at the bench. She clears her throat, bringing the room to absolute silence.

"Good afternoon," she begins. "This court is now in session. We are here today to address an emergency custody matter concerning the minor Ethan Moore. The petitioner, Ms. Scarlett Moore, is seeking temporary modification of the existing custody arrangement. The respondents, Mr. and Mrs. Moore, are contesting this request."

My heart pounds as her words echo through the courtroom. This is it, the moment everything changes for Ethan and me.

The judge's sharp gaze flicks to me. "Ms. Moore, you're represented by Mr. Morgan, correct?"

"Yes, Your Honor," I reply in a shaky voice.

"And the respondents are represented by Mr. Jennings?"

"Yes, Your Honor," says the tall, silver-haired man seated beside my grandparents. His calm, confident demeanor sends a chill through me—he's clearly prepared to fight.

Judge Harrison reviews the file in front of her. After a moment, she sets it aside and looks up. "Very well. Mr. Morgan, you may proceed."

Steve rises, his confident presence beside me both comforting and daunting. "Your Honor, we are here today because Ethan Moore's grandparents, Mr. and Mrs. Moore, intend to send him to boarding school, against his express wishes. This decision will have profound and immediate consequences for his emotional well-being."

He steps forward, his voice strong but measured. "Ethan's facing significant challenges in his current school. He's struggling to fit in, and he's been the target of bullying. Rather than addressing these issues directly, his grandparents have chosen to remove him from the situation entirely and send him away. Their focus seems to be on avoiding conflict and protecting their own social standing rather than addressing what's best for Ethan."

Steve glances at me before continuing. "Ms. Moore has built a life where he can feel safe and supported. She has a stable job, owns a home, and is ready to provide the love and care Ethan needs to heal and thrive."

He steps back, nodding at me as he takes his seat.

I'm not sure what I expected, but that was good, right? I can't tell if the judge thinks so, too, but a quick glance at Ethan and Rafael shows they think it's promising.

"Your Honor," Mr. Jennings says as he rises, "my clients believe their decision to send Ethan away is in his best interest. The school they've chosen is a prestigious institution with a strong academic and social support system."

He paces slightly. "We dispute the claim that Mr. and Mrs. Moore are more concerned with their reputation than with Ethan's well-being. They've provided him with stability and security for the past five years—*not* Ms. Moore."

I dig my nails into my palms, biting back the words I want to shout. It wasn't my decision. They made it for me.

"I have here," the judge begins, her voice calm but firm, "transcripts from Ms. Moore's podcasts. Mr. Jennings, these were submitted as part of your evidence. Can you explain the relevance of this material?"

I stare at Steve, silently wondering the same, but he raises a hand as if he's not the least bit surprised.

"These transcripts highlight a concerning aspect of Ms. Moore's lifestyle. Her preoccupation with dark and violent themes raises serious questions about her ability to provide a nurturing and emotionally stable environment for a young and impressionable child."

What? I feel my stomach drop. I discuss crime fiction, for crying out loud. That doesn't make *me* dangerous.

Before the judge can respond, Steve stands. "Your Honor, there is absolutely *no* evidence to suggest that Ms. Moore's work has ever negatively impacted her relationship with Ethan."

The judge listens carefully, her expression giving away nothing. She sets the transcripts aside and picks up another document.

"Next, I have a copy of Ethan's recent school report and notes from more than one teacher expressing concerns about bullying, submitted by Mr. Morgan." She reads thoroughly, then lifts her head again. "And this is a copy of the *Willowbrook Whistle*. Why am I reading this, Counselor?"

Jennings says, "Because Ms. Moore, who claims her affinity for darker themes is fictional and limited to her job, has been credited with the events that led to the arrest of a serial killer. Apparently, she took over a local investigation."

"And?" I snap before I can stop myself.

"If you don't mind, Ms. Moore, I will ask the questions," the judge says. When I nod, cheeks heating, she turns to Jennings. "So, is your argument that Ms. Moore is an unfit guardian because of this?"

"Once again, Ms. Moore seems to be inexplicably attracted to danger and darkness. Her professional life, her love life, and even her interests seem to speak of someone who isn't suited for the role of caregiver."

I stand, my chair loudly scraping against the floor. "Are you serious right now?"

"Scarlett—" Steve begins, also standing.

"You've neglected to say I also host a podcast about romance. Does that make me a *prostitute*?" I bark.

"*Scarlett!*" Steve whisper-screams.

"And my love life?" I insist. "How's that in any way relevant to this?"

"Ms. Moore," the judge's voice thunders. "Sit down and let your lawyer speak for you. That's what you're paying him for." She exhales sharply. "Unless you'd like me to find you in contempt."

"No, Your Honor. Ms. Moore won't say another word," Steve answers in my place. He gestures at me to sit down, and I do, pressing my lips together.

This is *unbelievable*.

Jennings grabs a stack of papers and holds them out for the judge. "We have a supplemental document we'd like to submit into evidence."

"Objection," Steve rebuts. "We were not given any notice of additional evidence, and we haven't had the opportunity to review or respond to whatever this is."

"We received it late yesterday and moved as quickly as we could to review it."

The judge reads through the paper, then with a pointed look at me, she sighs. "I'll allow this to be entered into the record, but with caution," she says, her voice tight. "Given the late submission, opposing counsel will have the opportunity to respond before any ruling is made."

As Jennings hands Steve a paper, he says, "This is a record of one Mr. Rafael Gray's criminal history." I see Rafael face-palming out of the corner of my eye. "Mr. Gray is Ms. Moore's romantic partner, and his past behavior cannot be ignored. He's been in trouble with the law before—even suspected of his father's assault. Most recently, he's been arrested for breaking and entering by the local police."

Holy *shit*.

A hush falls over the courtroom as Steve's head snaps toward me. I can feel his gaze burning into the side of my face, but I can't bring myself to look at him.

Yes, I didn't mention Rafael—or his arrest—but *he's* not the one asking for custody. And besides, without him breaking and entering, we would have never caught the Lit Killer.

"His history shows a pattern of instability, and allowing Ethan to be exposed to such an individual raises significant concerns about his safety and the environment Ms. Moore is offering."

The judge's brows rise as she goes through the papers, and I can feel the shift in Steve. He's not as confident as before—he knows we're losing.

Eventually, she looks up and sets the papers down, utterly unimpressed. "I will need additional time to review the statements submitted by both parties," she says. "Given the seriousness of what's being requested here, the court does not take this lightly."

Her gaze settles on me.

"Ms. Moore, I trust you understand the significant life changes this motion would entail—both for you and for the child. If this request is granted, the court expects a full and sustained commitment to that responsibility." She narrows her eyes. "And compliance *will* be monitored until the child is of age or no longer under your care."

When I nod, the judge continues. "We will reconvene Monday at nine o'clock to continue this hearing. I'd very much like to hear Ethan's testimony. Until then, court is adjourned."

She bangs the gavel, and the tension in the room seems to snap like a taut wire. I exhale shakily, feeling the weight of what just happened pressing down on me.

I fucked up, didn't I? I really fucked up.

"Jesus, Scarlett." Steve turns to me, his tone hushed. "What the hell? Why didn't you tell me—"

"I didn't think it mattered, Steve. It's really . . . new, and—"

"*Really?* You didn't think you needed to share this with me?"

"I—I don't know. I thought you knew. I mean, everyone in town . . ." Rafael calls my name, but I keep my eyes on Steve. "Look, the only reason he was arrested is that he broke into the *serial killer's* apartment, which led to her arrest."

"You mean the ex-cop?"

Oh, God. "What did the judge mean?" I ask. Terms like "significant changes" and "monitored compliance" echo in my mind like a bad omen.

He hesitates. "Scarlett, you have to understand, emergency hearings are extremely hard to win even in cases where there's clear neglect, and this . . ." He scratches his temple. "Nothing but absolute perfection will do. What the judge meant is that she might grant your motion, but only if you cut ties with . . . with anything that might hurt Ethan's upbringing. That there will be regular checks to make sure you continue to maintain an appropriate environment."

"Nothing in my life will hurt Ethan."

Certainly not Rafael, if that's what he means.

"Look, I'm sorry. But you might need to decide what your priority is here. If it's your brother . . ." He glances behind him, where Rafael is waiting for me. "Or your boyfriend."

After a quick "Excuse me," he leaves to talk to Jennings. I still haven't processed his words as I turn to Rafael and notice Ethan's not there.

Rafael points his thumb over his shoulder. "He just bolted."

Bolted? I glance at the doors, watching Ethan pull them open and disappear behind them. My heart sinks as I push through the crowd, the sound of murmured conversations and shuffling papers blurring into the background.

"Ethan, wait!" I call after him as I walk out of the courtroom, but he doesn't stop. I catch up to him just as he's pushing through the courthouse doors and out onto the front steps.

He spins around to face me, his face flushed with anger and a crazed look in his eyes. "You promised me, Scarlett," he spits out. "You said you'd get custody. You said everything would be fine. But you had to go after a killer, and read those stupid books, and—and date Rafael!"

I flinch, feeling a sting deep in my chest. "Ethan, I didn't—"

"Stop, okay? Just stop giving me *hope*!" he shouts, cutting me off. "These weeks—I could finally breathe, Scarlett. I could see the light at the end of this never-ending tunnel. And now—what, am I supposed to just go back? To go to *Virginia* and never see you again?"

"No, of course not. Ethan, this is just . . . a hiccup. Okay? Steve will fix everything, and you'll get to talk to the court, too. It'll be fine, I promise."

"Stop promising things!" Passersby turn to us, but he doesn't seem to care. "You act like you can fix everything, but you can't! You couldn't do anything last time, and you can't help me now either."

"Ethan, please, just listen—"

"No! Why did we even do this? Why?" He shoves me back, and I stumble, nearly losing my balance.

Before I can react, Rafael is there, stepping between us, his face a mask of cold fury. "Do *not*," he growls, his voice low as his face nears my brother's, "raise a hand against your sister."

"Rafael, stop!" I grab his arm, pulling him back. "Everything's okay."

Ethan glares at him, his fists clenched, then he looks at me with an expression so hateful I barely recognize him. "I hate you," he says, and it's like a knife twisting in my heart. "I *knew* this was a mistake!"

Then he's gone, running down the courthouse steps and disappearing into the crowd.

the third-act conflict

[trope]

the moment when all hope is lost and our protagonists find
themselves in a sea of existential dread and overly dramatic
internal monologues; not beloved by readers, yet this story
needed it. yes, it did! because I said so!

Rafael's car slices through the quiet streets, the engine a low hum
beneath the tension that fills the space between us. The streetlights blur past the windows, but I barely notice them, my mind too
caught up in everything that's happened. I keep scanning the sidewalks, the parks, anywhere Ethan might have run to. He can't have
gone far without a car.

Rafael glances at me, his eyes full of concern. "How are you holding up?"

I exhale, trying to collect myself. How can I possibly feel? The
case isn't looking great, my brother hates me, and now he's run away.
"All of this, it's because . . ." I trail off.

"Because he's a dramatic teenager drunk on hormones?"

I tilt my head back against the headrest.

"Because of me," Rafael says.

"*No*, Rafael. This isn't on you." I glance out the window, watching the world blur by, the streets empty. "It's because of me. I went after a murderer. I didn't tell Steve a word about your existence. All me."

He grips the steering wheel a little tighter, his knuckles turning white. "Ethan is just scared. But he loves you, and he knows none of this is your fault."

His words fall flat, bouncing off the wall of guilt that's built up inside me. "But the way he looked at me, Rafael. He was so disappointed, so hurt. And he's right to be. I ruined everything."

I see a flicker of pain cross his face, but he doesn't look away from the road. "You ruined nothing. You'll win the case. It'll be fine."

I close my eyes, replaying the scene outside the courthouse in my mind, wanting to jump into my memories and change them. "You shouldn't have done that."

He glances at me. "Hm?"

"When you stepped between us. What you said to him. That was a mistake."

His jaw tightens. "He pushed you. I won't stand by and let anyone put their hands on you."

"I know, but—"

"*No one*, no matter their age or gender or relationship to you. *Ever.*"

Oh. His reaction when Ethan stormed out of my place comes back to me. How Rafael held me back, said my brother's anger had scared him. It's about his dad—of course it is. I don't know how I didn't realize it before, but after the abuse he suffered, he must be triggered by screaming matches and violent fights.

I reach for his arm, rubbing it soothingly with my thumb. This isn't how we'll deal with conflict moving forward, but we don't need to discuss it right now.

Steve's words come back to me, painful like a thorn lodged under a fingernail. *You need to decide what's your priority is here. If it's your brother . . . or your boyfriend.*

Maybe there is *no* going forward.

We drive in silence for a while longer, and I keep searching the sidewalks, hoping for any sign of him. We pass the park where we used to play when he was little, and I feel tears sting in my eyes. What if he's gone somewhere I can't find him? What if he doesn't show up at court on Monday?

Finally, Rafael pulls over near the skate park, killing the engine. "Let's check here."

We get out of the car, the evening air cool against my skin, and start walking. Darkness feels like it's closing in around us, but I push forward, scanning every shadow, every bench, every tree, hoping, praying that he's here.

Rafael stays close, but as we search the empty park, my heart sinks deeper.

Then the phone's sudden ring cuts through the stillness, jolting me out of my frantic thoughts. I fumble for it, my heart racing as I see Jace's name on the screen.

"Rafael," I croak. "It's Jace."

His eyes are steady on mine, silently urging me to answer.

I swipe to accept the call and press the phone to my ear. "Jace? Is he with you? Is Ethan okay?"

There's a pause on the other end, and I hear a measured breath before a low voice says, "He's here, yes. He showed up about fifteen minutes ago."

Relief washes over me, so overwhelming that my knees buckle. I reach out, gripping Rafael's arm for support as I let out a breath. "Thank God."

"He's okay," Jace says gently. "He's upset, though. I tried talking to him, but he doesn't want to say much right now. I told him you'd be worried sick if you didn't know he was safe, so I called."

"Thank you. Just tell him I love him, okay? That we'll figure this out, no matter what happens. Please, Jace, just make sure he knows that."

"I will."

"Sorry we couldn't meet under more pleasant circumstances."

After a quick goodbye, the call disconnects.

Rafael's arms wrap around me, and it's a balm to the raw edges of my soul. I cling to him, letting out a shuddering breath. For a moment, it feels like everything might be okay, like we might find a way through this storm together.

When he lets me go, I sit on a nearby bench, the air refreshing against my tear-streaked face. My body is heavy, the adrenaline of the day wearing off all at once as I glance up at Rafael, leaning against a tree with his gaze fixed on the distant horizon.

"We should head home," I say. I get up and walk, but as I glance back, I realize Rafael hasn't moved. He's still standing by the tree, looking away.

I step back to him, my heart fluttering wildly, as though it might burst. "Is everything okay?"

He turns to face me. "Yeah," he says quietly. "Everything's fine."

"Are you sure? You're not—"

"I'm fine," he interrupts gently. He takes my hand in his. "Let's go home."

"Rafael, wait . . ."

"You think I don't know what happens when we get home, Scarlett?" he asks. Though his gaze radiates anger, his voice is soft. "I'm not an idiot. I know these are the last moments, the last . . ." He buries his face in his open hands. "I wish I'd known this morning. I would have kissed you one more time. I would have kept you in bed longer, and hugged you for one more fucking minute, and . . ."

"Rafael, no. I'm not—"

"Yes, you are." He laughs, but it's devoid of humor. "Ethan needs you, and you need him. And I won't be the reason you don't get custody."

"So you're dumping me?" I ask. I can't feel the wind blowing around us, though the branches of the nearby trees wiggle enough for me to know I should; it's like I'm having an out-of-body experience. Like I've turned into a marionette, moved around by strings I don't control.

He scoffs. "N—" After closing his mouth, he mutters, "I can do it *for* you if you need me to."

"No. *No*, we're not breaking up." A sob rolls through my chest. "We're not even together yet. We're not breaking up." He stares at me, brows knitted together, as I panic. "We're *not*. Rafael, we're—"

"Okay, okay." He clears his voice, attempting a smile. "You're right. We're not."

He holds his hand out and, reluctantly taking it, I follow him to the car.

Are we breaking up? That's what Steve meant when he said I'd have to choose, right?

The drive home is silent, and as the streets blur by, I know that this can't be the end, because if it is, any chance at love dies with our sort-of relationship tonight, and I'm done.

We make it back to my place, the same unnatural quiet between us as we sit on the couch.

"I need you both," I mumble, voicing the thought that has been buzzing in my mind since the park.

I need Ethan. He's my brother, the only family I have left. And I need Rafael, too—breakfast in bed, annotated books, waking up to his face. The way my brother opens up when he's around, and every single meal he's let me read through.

I'd miss all of it so much, it feels like I can't possibly picture it right now. Like this is the kind of loss I'd only feel as it happened, as his presence became a memory instead of a routine. As I watched him come and go, knowing I no longer had the right to know where. As he moved on without me, and I without him.

It's a grief I can only imagine right now but that I'd feel every day.

"I know," he says, his hand squeezing mine. "But I don't think who *you* need is what'll tip the scale."

I still, letting his words sink in. The second my shoulders shake, he wraps his arms around me.

He's right. It's not about who *I* need the most but about who needs *me*. And that is, without a doubt, Ethan.

The second I start sobbing, he shifts closer, pulling me tighter into his chest like he can hold the pieces together if he just squeezes hard enough. My fingers clutch his shirt. I want to crawl into his chest and stay there, safe and selfish. I want it all to stop hurting.

I cry into the hollow of his throat as he cups the back of my head, fingers sifting through my hair with such care it only makes me cry harder.

"It's okay," he murmurs. "You're going to be okay."

No, I won't. I'll never be okay.

He tilts my face up, gently, reverently. His thumb wipes beneath my eye, then again, slower. His gaze drags over every tear before he kisses my cheek, just next to the corner of my mouth. Then a little higher, catching a tear with his lips like it's something sacred. And again, slower this time, lingering by my temple, his breath warm and trembling.

My hand finds his jaw, and I tilt forward just enough that our lips brush together.

When he responds, it's with a kind of aching restraint, like he's kissing someone he knows he might have to say goodbye to. Like he wants to memorize it. Every angle, every breath.

I sigh into his mouth, and his arms wrap around me fully, his hand cradling my jaw as the kiss deepens. We shift together until I'm straddling him, knees bracketing his hips, the warmth of his chest meeting mine.

"Rafael," I breathe out. He withdraws a little to meet my gaze, his eyes dark and wild. "*Please.*"

"Yes," he says as he kisses me again, slower this time, savoring. "Everything you want, Freckles."

We move together like we've done this a hundred times and never before—every touch familiar, every kiss brand-new. His hands tremble as they slide up my thighs, fingers curling into the bare skin just beneath the hem of my shirt.

I feel the shake in his breath, the restraint in his hands. I feel *everything*.

When I kiss him again, I taste salt. I don't know if it's his tears or mine, but I just hold on tighter, as if getting closer might stop time. Might give us another chance.

"This isn't fair," I whisper into his mouth. "None of this is fair."

His forehead presses to mine. "I know."

I shift my hips forward, and his breath stutters—his hands tightening around my thighs, thumbs dragging along my skin. I press myself closer, chest to chest, trying to brand the shape of him into my body. The tattoos on his chest. The soft give of his waist. The way his heartbeat slams against mine like a warning bell.

Every time I touch him, it feels like an apology. Every time he touches me, it feels like a goodbye.

I don't want this to be the last time. I don't want to forget any of it—the way he exhales when I slide my hands under his shirt, palms skimming over the warm lines of muscle. The way he lifts it over his head like it's the easiest surrender in the world. The way he cups the back of my neck like he owns me.

I want to remember the way he always breathes my name like he's saying it for the last time.

I kiss him deeper, slower, dragging my mouth across his jaw, down his throat, along the slope of his shoulder. I reach between us, fumble with the button of his jeans. He exhales like it's painful, helping me. Then his hands move to my waist, slipping beneath my panties, and when his palms find bare skin, he stills—just for a second, forehead dropping to my shoulder.

He whispers something against my skin, too quiet to catch. But his voice cracks halfway through, and it undoes me.

I guide him to me like someone reaching for a ledge while falling, and the room is silent except for the rustle of fabric, the stutter of breath, the soft slide of skin against skin. When he finally presses into me, we both go still. One breath. One heartbeat. One unbearable second when everything inside me splinters.

I bury my face in his neck. "Rafael."

He presses a kiss to my temple like he's sealing a promise. "Scarlett."

I love you.

I don't say it out loud, only in the way I move against him. In the way I meet him, over and over, fingers curling in his hair, his breath breaking against my mouth. In the way I fall apart with his name on my lips, my body arching into his, my whole soul wrapped around the gravity of him.

He holds me through it, one hand tangled in my hair, the other splayed at my lower back and we fall together, breathless and aching and broken open.

Even when the shaking stops and silence falls, we stay wrapped around each other.

There's a heaviness in the air now, a sadness that wasn't there before.

This is the end, isn't it?

Finally, he pulls back. A hollow ache settles in my chest as I stand and straighten my clothes, trying to compose myself.

When I look at him, I see the same grief I feel reflected in his eyes.

Immediately, he walks over and wraps his arms around me.

"It's okay, Freckles." I shake my head against his chest, but he soothingly shushes me. "Yes, it is. You can do for him what nobody did for me. You can help him, guide him, make sure he becomes the best version of himself."

He knows this isn't what I want, but I feel the need to tell him anyway. That I wish there was something else I could do, some way to keep him with me. "I'm sorry," I whisper. "You don't deserve any of this, and now—"

He grips the back of my neck with one hand, his mouth lowering to my ear. "I don't regret you for one *second*, Scarlett. Do you hear me? Not one."

My crying intensifies, my arms wrapped around his neck so hard I'm probably hurting him.

I'll never feel love again.

I know everyone says it, but I *know* it. In fact, I don't even want it. If the last five years have taught me anything, it's that it's Rafael or no one at all for me.

"Thank you," he says quietly, not looking at me. "For everything. For . . . you. And Ethan." His words are a knife to my heart, the way his voice shakes, the way he doesn't *truly* mean any of it. "You know where to find me, okay? If you need me."

"Okay." We both know I won't go to him for anything. That I can't, though I'll most definitely need him. "Thank you."

He leans over, pressing a gentle kiss to my forehead. When he pulls away, he walks away without looking back, like he knows that if he doesn't go now, he never will.

The door closes behind him, and once the weight of it all finally crashes down on me, I crumble.

This is it. We're done.

My brother's gone. Rafael's gone.

I am completely alone, again.

I bury my face in my hands. Tonight was the end. I'll never feel his touch again, or hear him say my name. We'll never share another moment like that.

It's the right thing to do. It *has* to be.

So why does it feel like the worst mistake?

35

the aftermath

[trope]

the chaotic whirlwind that follows a breakup, where our
protagonists navigate the emotional fallout like a pair of lost
puppies in a thunderstorm, and possibly with a new haircut

It's been five days since Rafael and I said our goodbyes. Five days of
silence, of waking up to an empty bed, of going through the motions, feeling nothing at all.

The trial was postponed to Friday, which is good, because Ethan
won't answer my calls—or anybody's, really. Jace tells me he's okay,
that he just needs time. How much time? No idea.

I sit curled up on the couch, the remnants of a cold cup of coffee
on the table beside me. The TV is on, but I'm not watching it—just
another noise to fill the quiet.

A soft thump draws my attention, and I turn to see Sherlock
padding down the stairs, his tail flicking lazily behind him. I purse
my lips, annoyed at his indifference after having been gone all night

and day. He hops onto the couch, his tiny weight settling against my side as he curls up, purring softly.

"You know this isn't a hotel, right?" I murmur, scratching behind his ears. "I haven't seen you since yesterday."

He blinks at me, his yellow eyes unbothered, as if to say, *I have my own life, thank you very much.*

When I touch his collar, I find myself holding the tracking device Rafael gave me. Reminded about the camera, I reach for my phone, saying, "I think it's finally time we find out where the hell you're escaping from."

I open the app, a small pang of pain hitting me at the thought of Rafael, who helped me set it up. The screen lights up, showing a dotted line that crosses the town. My brow furrows as I zoom in.

"What the hell, Sherlock?" I scold half-heartedly.

The map shows him wandering near Rafael's house earlier today before heading back to mine. A flicker of something—morbid curiosity, maybe—makes me tap the camera icon. It takes a second to load, the grainy image jiggling, but when the video clears, I see the familiar exterior of Rafael's house.

My chest tightens as I catch a brief glimpse of movement—Rafael, standing on his porch, talking to someone I can't see. His hands are stuffed into his pockets, his head tilted slightly as he listens. He looks . . . normal. Like nothing has happened. Like he's fine.

I slam the phone down onto the cushion beside me, the image burned into my mind.

I can't believe Sherlock recorded him. What else did he catch?

I unlock my phone again and continue playing the feed. I swipe back to earlier in the day, setting the speed to 2x. The shaky image bounces with each of Sherlock's steps, and I can only make out snippets of the neighborhood.

There seems to be nothing relevant, except yet another visit to Sherlock's dog lover, so I go even further back, catching more than one feline fight, several people trying to approach him, and a few familiar faces—until the camera shows the view through my kitchen window, looking out at Mrs. Prattle's house across the street. I can see Sherlock's reflection, perched on the windowsill, his tail curling as he observes the quiet neighborhood.

The camera shakes, as if something caught Sherlock's attention, and it picks up a figure moving across Mrs. Prattle's yard.

I pause the footage, staring at the screen. The figure is bent down, fiddling with something on the ground. When they stand and walk away, the camera catches it clearly: a broken gnome lying in the grass.

My heart pounds as I remember the police report. Vanessa knocked over the garden gnome when she went back to the crime scene.

The timestamp on the footage matches the report, twelve days ago.

The figure turns around just long enough for the grainy image to offer a hint of their identity. But it's not Vanessa. It's a man wearing a hoodie pulled low over his face. Even with the poor quality, I recognize the walk, the slight hunch in his shoulders, the way his right foot turns out slightly with every step.

Quentin.

I rewind the footage. Watching again, frame by frame, it's unmistakable. It's him, coming out of Mrs. Prattle's house, of a sealed crime scene.

Could we have it wrong? Could Vanessa *not* be the killer?

My phone rings, pulling me from my haze, and I glance at the screen and see Paige's name. A part of me wants to ignore it, to stay cocooned in this numbness, but I know she needs me more than she's letting on.

"Hey," I say as I pick up.

"Hi. It's good to hear your voice. How are you holding up?"

I swallow hard, trying to keep my voice steady. "I'm . . . managing. You?"

"You know. We're coping differently," she says with a laugh. By "coping differently," she means that I've isolated myself, as opposed to the way she's thrown herself into work, hobbies, and casual sex. "Have you heard from Ethan?"

The question twists the knife in my chest a little deeper. "No. He's still not answering my calls. I've left messages, sent texts . . . Nothing."

She sighs. "He'll come around. I'm sure he will."

"Yeah. I hope so," I say, though really, time's almost up. We're supposed to be back at court on Friday, and Steve was clear: after that shit show, if Ethan doesn't show up, I'm done. I'll lose the case.

There's another pause, this one longer, before Paige speaks again. "Have you gone out at all? I know you've been taking time off work, but everyone's worried about you. You've been holed up in that house for days."

That's because of *who* is right outside.

"I'm fine," I say quickly, too quickly.

"No, you're not. You're going to have to leave the house at some point, you know?"

"I've been busy," I lie. "But I'll be in court Friday, and back to work on Monday."

"Tell me you haven't been staring out that window for five days," she says in a sharp voice. "Tell me *convincingly*."

"I haven't." Another lie. I *have* been watching. I've been noting when he leaves the house, when he comes back. He's had people over, women, too, has been going out at night, living his life like nothing happened. Like *we* never happened.

Two days ago, I ordered food, and when I opened the door to collect it, Rafael was leaving his house. He didn't even glance in my direction, and I keep telling myself he didn't see me, but deep down, I know he did. He just didn't acknowledge me.

Paige sighs, like she knows I'm lying. "Scarlett, you know I understand heartache more than anyone, but a breakup doesn't stop the world from spinning."

I know she's right, but it feels like everything has stopped. Facing the courthouse again, seeing Ethan's hurt and anger, feels impossible. The weight of it all is suffocating, and the only thing I've been able to do is sit in this house and pretend the world outside doesn't exist.

"Look, I . . . I didn't want to tell you this, but I don't know what else to do."

My stomach drops. "What do you mean?"

"Rafael . . ." she says softly. "Rafael sold the house."

"What?"

"I figured he'd tell you eventually," she continues, her voice gentle. "But, um, he's leaving."

I can't breathe. My mind races, trying to make sense of her words. "He sold the house? When? Leaving where?"

"Just today. Scarlett, I'm telling you this because you should move on, too. *He's* doing it."

I clutch the couch cushion, trying to steady myself. This makes no sense. He never spoke about wanting to sell the house, and now he's done it in five days? "Why?" I ask, more to myself than to her. "He didn't even tell me," I insist. "And now he's just leaving?"

"Scarlett—"

"I have to go," I say, ending the call before she can respond.

The silence in the house feels suffocating now, and my pulse pounds in my ears. He's leaving. He's cutting ties, erasing me. The realization claws at my chest, leaving me raw and breathless.

My gaze shifts to the window, to his house next door. The thought of him packing up, walking out of my life forever, ignites something inside me.

No. Like hell I'll let him go without saying goodbye.

My knuckles tremble as I knock on Rafael's door. The wood feels solid, unyielding beneath my touch, so different from the way I feel inside—cracked open, bleeding, barely holding together. I hear footsteps on the other side, and when the door swings open, the sight of him nearly undoes me.

His dark hair is wet, falling just above his intense gray eyes, and he's wearing black sweatpants. They sit low on his hips, hanging loosely, and the matching worn T-shirt clings slightly to his broad shoulders and chest.

His face falls the moment he sees me. "Scarlett," he says, his voice breathy. "Is everything okay?"

"Were you going to tell me?" I blurt out.

"What?"

"You sold the house."

His lips part, and he looks down with a groan. "Fucking small-town bullshit," he mumbles. "It happened two hours ago. Seriously, *how*—"

I swallow the lump in my throat, my heart pounding against my ribs. "Were you going to tell me or not?"

"Yes, of course I was. Scarlett, this was always part of the plan, okay? I've been staying here because of . . . well, you, but this house was never supposed to be a permanent solution. This is the place I spent the first twenty-one years of my life hating."

He's right, of course. But I've got too much pent-up anger now. "Where are you going, then?"

He pauses, as if trying to find the right words. "Scarlett, me leaving town makes your life easier."

"Really? That's how much I meant to you?" I snap. The casual dismissal of what we had, what we were, has tears blurring my vision, and I swipe at them angrily. "Five days after our breakup, you're moving on?"

"Don't say that," he says, his voice rough. "Don't imply that anything I said wasn't the truth, that I'm not hurting. You have no fucking right to do that."

"But you have the right to ignore me?" I hate how vulnerable I sound, but I can't help it. "To have women come and go at all hours—"

"Prospective buyers."

"—and to go on with your life, and talk, and work, while I'm there mourning the love story of my life?"

His anger dissipates in an instant, his expression softening into something that breaks my heart all over again. His mouth opens, but no words come out, and I realize I've said something I can't take back. I can't believe I said it like that—that I called it a *love story* through tears and anger, lashing out like a wounded animal.

"I'm not over anything, Scarlett," he finally says. "I'm hurting. I'm breaking into pieces. I hate my life, and I hate this house, and I hate knowing you're there, because I can't come to you. It's driving me insane. I hate seeing you not leave the house because you're hurting, and not knowing exactly how much you're hurting, and not being able to do shit to make you feel better anyway."

I try to hold back the sobs, but it's no use. All I want to do is throw myself into his arms. He steps forward and wraps me in his embrace, pulling me against him.

I cling to him, burying my face in his chest, his warmth the only thing keeping me from collapsing entirely.

"I have to leave, Scarlett," he pleads. "I need you to be okay, to move on. And you can't do that if I'm here, if you're afraid of running into me every time you leave the house."

We stand there for what feels like forever, my tears soaking into his shirt, his hand stroking my hair as if he's trying to memorize the feel of it.

I can't let him go. I don't know how to.

Eventually, I calm down, my sobs turning into quiet, shuddering breaths. He leans back, and I see the tears on his cheeks matching mine. He wipes my cheek, his touch gentle, and I wish I could freeze this moment, hold on to him for just a little longer.

"How's Ethan? I heard the hearing was rescheduled."

I press my lips together in a tight line, feeling the weight of another worry pressing down on me. "I don't know if he'll show up. He won't talk to me. I'm *really* trying, but . . ."

Rafael's brow furrows. "He will, Scarlett. He knows how important this is. He'll be there."

I want to believe him, but doubt gnaws at me. "I miss you."

His eyes close briefly, as if my words are too much to bear. "I miss you more," he breathes. "But you should go. God forbid that jackal lawyer or one of his spies sees us together."

He's right, and even though it feels like the hardest thing I've ever done, I slowly, reluctantly pull away from him.

"Rafael," I say, rolling my eyes. "I saw something, and I know Vanessa is a good fit for these murders, but . . ."

"What did you see?" he asks, brows furrowed.

"Remember the camera you got me for Sherlock?"

He nods.

"Well, he was home the day after Rob's murder, and the camera caught Quentin tripping over the gnome in Mrs. Prattle's yard."

His chin jerks back. "Quentin?"

"Yeah. And I thought, maybe we just assumed it was the killer who did it, while it was actually Quentin who accidentally broke the gnome. But—"

"But why wouldn't Quentin have said something? Why would he have been at the crime scene?"

"Exactly."

He sighs, gaze lost in the distance. "He's been at two crime scenes the same night the murders took place, and . . . he *did* lie about our encounter."

"Uh-huh," I agree, relieved I'm not the only one seeing it. "The only thing I can't put together yet is why. Why would Quentin do it?"

Rafael thinks for a long moment, then clicks his tongue. "To be honest with you, I doubt he's ever read a book outside of the classroom." He tilts his head. "Or inside."

No kidding—he's always been baffled by my love for reading. "Movies are so much better" and whatnot. And what would be his motive? He might not be pleased with me, but he certainly doesn't hate me enough to frame me for murder.

"I don't see it, honestly. But if you think—"

"Nah." I wave the thought away. "I actually agree with you for once."

"Don't sound so surprised."

I watch the hint of a smirk playing on his lips and smile back, though it feels nothing like happiness. "Rafael Gray, always flirting."

"Only with you."

His finger lingers on my cheek, as if he can't quite let go, either, but then he drops it, and the loss of his touch feels like a physical blow. "Remember what you said in the letter, okay?"

"No romance ends without a happily ever after?"

He shakes his head. "Impossible."

Impossible.

"Bye, Gray," I whisper.

"Bye, Freckles," he says back.

I turn and walk away, each step heavier than the last, until I'm out of his sight. I don't look back, because I know if I do, I'll run to him, and this time I might not have the strength to leave.

He's right.

This is not the end.

the red herring

[trope]

the sneaky little narrative decoy designed to make you side-eye
the wrong suspect, often equipped with suspicious hobbies
(e.g., taxidermy) or a conveniently timed alibi gap; exists solely
to mislead readers who were *so sure* they'd cracked the case;
will inevitably turn out to be innocent—just really, *really* bad
at looking it

The courtroom feels smaller today.

My heart pounds against my ribs, and my hands won't stop shaking. I glance at the clock, then at the door, praying that Ethan will walk through it any second now. He has to. But every time I look, the door stays shut, and the knot in my stomach tightens.

Across the aisle, my grandparents sit stiffly, their expressions as cold and hard as ever. Their lawyer is smug, confidence oozing from his every pore. He knows, just as I do, that without Ethan's testimony, I don't stand a chance.

The judge has asked about him twice already, and each time, Steve has lied, saying Ethan's on his way, buying us more time. But there's doubt in the judge's eyes, like her patience is wearing thin.

My phone is clutched in my hand, and I try Ethan again, to no avail. Each unanswered call sends another wave of panic through me. I can't lose this. I can't lose him. Not after I gave up Rafael. Not after he left.

"Ms. Moore." The judge's voice cuts through the fog of my anxiety. "I'll ask this just one more time. Where is your brother?"

Steve jumps in before I can answer. "He's on his way, Your Honor. Just a little delayed."

The judge's expression is skeptical, her eyes narrowing slightly. "If he's not here soon, we'll have to move forward without him."

My throat is too tight to allow me to speak. Steve meets my gaze, his eyes urging me to stay calm, but I don't know what to do. I feel helpless, and this time, Rafael isn't here to make it better.

I'm all alone.

Just when I'm about to lose hope, the doors at the back of the courtroom creak open. I whip my head around, and there he is—Ethan, walking in with that familiar determined stride. Relief crashes over me as he steps past me, his focus entirely on the stand at the front of the courtroom. When his eyes finally land on me, he hesitates before stepping up to the stand.

"Sorry I'm late," he says as he faces the judge. There's an apology in his eyes when he glances at me again, but before I can process it, Steve clears his throat and approaches Ethan.

"Ethan, can you please tell the court about your relationship with your sister, Scarlett?"

My brother's gaze flicks to mine, a storm of emotions swirling in his eyes. "Yes, I can. But before I do, I'd like the judge to know something." He turns to her and swallows hard. "I . . . I'm gay."

I breathe out, not knowing whether to feel proud that he's come out or ashamed that he's basically been forced to. This is not what I expected, not what we planned. He deserves better than this. Better than having to do it in a courtroom, because of *them*.

"My sister knows this," Ethan continues, his voice gaining strength. "And she could have won this trial just by telling you the truth, which is that my grandparents don't accept my sexual orientation. They're homophobic. They've refused to let me come out, tried to keep me from my boyfriend, and now want to send me away so they won't have to face public judgment."

He looks directly at the judge. "I wanted to live with my sister even before this came up, but that's what caused the urgency. And my sister has known I'm gay, but she never said a word. She gave me the chance to come to her when I was ready, and she's done everything she could for me."

The courtroom fades away as I watch him. He's baring his soul here, and I can't imagine how difficult this is.

"And Rafael Gray? He helped me when he didn't even know me. He supported me and my sister, and with him, I finally saw her be selfish, like everyone should be once in a while. I saw her happy. I saw her open herself up to new things. I saw her be . . . *heroic*."

I shake my head, as if trying to tell him it's okay, that he doesn't have to do this.

"And instead of being happy for her"—Ethan's voice breaks, and he swipes at his eyes—"I screamed at her. I pushed her, and I told her I hated her."

He's crying now, his hands trembling as he looks at me. "I'm so sorry. You took me in even though nobody expected you to. You paused your life for me, told me one day we'd be here, and I just treated you so bad. I pushed you away because you *dared* to find some happiness."

"No, Ethan," I whisper. I want to run to him, to tell him he's forgiven, that I love him, but I'm afraid the judge will scold me like last time, and we've got too much on the line for that.

Ethan turns to the judge, his voice stronger now, though it still wavers with emotion. "Look at her."

The judge turns to me, her brows furrowing slightly as she studies my face. I know I look terrible. I haven't eaten or slept, and I'm barely holding it together.

"She broke things off with Rafael. My grandparents' lawyer twisted her life, her relationship, her work, and she didn't think about herself or the man she has feelings for. She only thought about me. And she's a mess, but she's here. She didn't go back to Rafael. She's fighting for me, even though I was a little bitch—"

"Language, Mr. Moore," the judge interrupts sternly.

Ethan flushes. "Sorry, Your Honor. What I meant is that my sister loves me, and I never need to *deserve* her love. It's not something she chooses to feel, something she can dole out. Even when it kills her, she still puts me first. That's why I want to live with her. Not just because she's okay with me being gay, but because she accepts *me*, no matter what. Because she's my role model, she's my family, and she's my hero."

The courtroom falls into a heavy silence, and the judge looks moved, her gaze softening as she regards him. "Thank you, Mr. Moore," she says quietly. "Are there any further questions for this witness?"

My grandparents' lawyer shakes his head, clearly rattled by Ethan's testimony. "No, Your Honor."

"In that case, we'll take a short recess and return with a decision."

As the judge stands and the courtroom stirs, Ethan leaves the stand and walks straight to me. I can't hold it in any longer. The moment he reaches me, I collapse into his arms, sobbing uncontrollably. He holds me tight, his voice gentle in my ear. "I'm so sorry, Scarlett. You've done everything for me, and I've been such an idiot. But it's okay now. We'll be okay no matter what."

His words are a lifeline, something solid to cling to in the storm of emotions. He strokes my hair, his tears wetting my shoulder. "Just this once, Scarlett," he murmurs. "Just this once, you can break down. I'll hold you up."

And for the first time, I let myself lean on him, let myself be weak. Ethan's definitely strong enough to hold me up.

"To Scarlett and Ethan, reunited at last!" Celeste says as she cheers.

Everyone raises their glass and drinks, and almost mechanically, so do I, watching the faces of people I love as they come to congratulate me.

We won.

It still doesn't seem real. I can almost feel Ethan's hand gripping mine, hear the judge say that the best interest of my brother lies in his being in my care. It was like my breath had been trapped in my chest for months, only to be released all at once. Ethan's tears of relief. The way my grandparents got out of there without so much as a glance our way.

We actually won. Ethan is now in my temporary custody, and until the judge sets a follow-up hearing, we're done. We live together, and no one can tell him how to live his life. He's free.

I watch him next to Jace, and despite the casual stance, I can tell they're flirting. I think I like his boyfriend—the way he looks at my brother. Maybe soon he'll feel like he can be more obvious about it.

"Congratulations again, Scarlett!" Jennifer from the bakery says as she approaches the table with food. I raise my glass in a silent thank-you, then let my eyes roam.

I know I should be thankful for this. Half the town must be squeezed at The Oak, and more are drinking outside. They all showed up for me, wanting to celebrate this moment, and all I can focus on is the one person who's missing. The one person who's gone.

Left this morning, Mrs. Prattle said. The new homeowners will be here in a couple of weeks.

"Scarlett!"

I turn around, locating Steve, who elbows his way through the crowd until he's in front of me. "Steve, my hero!" I cheer, cutting through the noise as he leans forward for a quick hug.

"Oh, please." He waves off the compliment. "The real hero was Ethan. What he did today was really brave."

"It really was. But seriously, without you—"

"Don't even mention it." He cuts me off before I can finish.

I persist. "Look, I know what Celeste said, but you deserve compensation. Let me—"

"Scarlett." His blue eyes glint with a hint of affection. "Please, forget about it, okay? Your mom . . . I could never accept money from you. Not for this."

I feel the lump in my throat rise. "At least let me buy you a drink," I say, then gesture to the tables piled high with food. "And take something to eat. The whole town's been cooking."

"Thank you, but I just came in to congratulate you and your brother." His smile quickly turns sour. "Between you and me, I'd rather stay as far away as possible from my wife and her boy toy."

His words land like a slap. *Her what?*

I glance over at Celeste, who's laughing with Theo and Paige at a table nearby as Quentin pours them drinks. He can't mean Theo, can he? Picturing him with Celeste feels less natural than seeing Sherlock with a labradoodle.

"Anyway, congratulations again."

"Thank you, Steve," I manage, hugging him one more time. As he walks toward my brother, my gaze flicks back to Celeste. Nah. There's absolutely no way she's having an affair with Theo.

"Hey, stranger."

I flinch at the voice, snapping out of my spiral to find Quentin standing beside me with a pitcher of beer. Like a flash before my eyes, I see the recording of Sherlock's camera that caught him tripping over the garden gnome. "Hey, hi," I say, straightening.

"Congratulations," he says, but it almost feels empty. "I didn't know you were doing all of this, but it's really cool. You must be happy."

"And relieved," I say. Rafael is right—Quentin can't be behind these murders. "Thank you for hosting us tonight."

He waves me off, then holds his hand out. "I found this the other day, and . . . I don't know." I look down, tentatively taking the framed picture. "I figured you might like to have it. Uncle John kept it in his office in the back."

I glance at the picture, my heart skipping a beat. It's my mom, my dad, Celeste, and Rafael's father, all smiling at The Oak, wearing matching gray T-shirts with what I can now tell is a tree printed on the front. I recognize them instantly, although the print isn't faded like it is now. "The broccoli shirt."

"Excuse me?"

I point at the picture. "My parents, they used to wear those shirts and do a silly little dance to get my brother to eat his vegetables. They called them the broccoli shirts."

"Oh." Quentin laughs, pointing at the picture. "Well, it's technically an oak tree, not broccoli. Apparently, there was a big snowstorm on opening day, so some of Uncle John's staff didn't show. Your parents and Celeste offered to help. He must've given them the shirts as a thank-you."

My stomach knots the moment his words register. The witness who saw the killer come out of Catherine's apartment described a gray shirt with a tree print on the front. Could they have meant *this* shirt?

"He never got around to making more for the employees." He wipes the table next to us. "Which, if you ask me, is a blessing, 'cause I can wear whatever I want."

I blink, nodding through his story. There are four shirts in this picture. Two of them are at my place; one I wore at Rafael's house. There's only one missing.

Celeste's.

I look up at Quentin, the blood freezing in my veins.

Between you and me, I'd rather stay as far away as possible from my wife's boy toy.

I thought Steve was looking at Theo, but Quentin was serving him a drink, wasn't he? Quentin. *Quentin* is Celeste's boy toy. That must be why he was so mysterious about seeing someone—because that someone is *technically* still married.

You wanna bet the two of them secretly meet at the Wildflower Inn?

"Scarlett, are you okay?"

"I, uh, yes. Yes, I'm sorry. I just . . ." I turn, making sure I still have eyes on Ethan as I hand Quentin back the picture. "I think I need a good night of sleep. The tension this week has been . . ."

"Oh, yeah. I get it."

I step back, heart thrumming. "See you, Quentin."

His voice calls for me again before I can take a step. I turn around, cautiously waiting for what he'll say next. "You didn't take the picture."

"Oh. Yes. Of course." I grip the frame. "Thank you."

"You got it." I can feel his eyes on me as I turn and walk away, but I ignore him, walking to Paige and Theo. Celeste's not with them anymore, and my pulse thrums in my ears as I reach Paige near the buffet table, then grab her arm. "Hey. I need you to take Ethan home."

She frowns, setting down her drink. "Right now? This party is for you."

"Right now." I swallow, tightening my hold on her arm. "Please."

She studies my face, and she must see something desperate in it, because she says, "Okay, yes. Of course."

Theo joins us, his brows knitting together. "What's going on? Are you okay?"

"I need to leave. Please go with Paige. Take Ethan and Jace, and stay at my place."

"Scarlett, you're scaring me. What's going on?" Paige says, but I'm already walking toward the exit, my heart pounding as I step into the cool night air.

What is happening is that I think I just figured out Quentin's motive.

37

the book boyfriend

[trope]

a fictional character so devastatingly perfect he makes real-life partners look like they forgot to take the chicken out of the freezer; known for his smoldering good looks, razor-sharp wit, and ability to spout heartfelt monologues that would make Shakespeare weep. warning: may cause *realistic* expectations and excessive rereading of favorite scenes

I push open the door to the Booked It office, my heart slamming against my ribs.

The space looks unfamiliar as I step inside. I've been here at night plenty, when all the lights are off, but it looks larger tonight. And isolated. If something happened here, nobody would hear it, would they? Not at this time of night.

It's the first time I've noticed it.

I take out my phone, but there are no missed calls. I tried reaching Rafael on my way here, but he hasn't picked up or gotten back to me. Maybe he didn't really mean it when he said he was a phone call away. Maybe he's busy getting settled wherever he is now. Whatever the truth is, I'm alone.

I turn the corner of the corridor, then quickly duck behind a desk. The light in Celeste's office is still on.

Slowly, I creep toward the door, my footsteps barely making a sound on the carpet. I peer through the partially open door, and there she is. Celeste, standing at her desk, fists pressed into the wood, lips moving in frantic whispers.

"I defended you," I say as she turns to me and brings a hand to her chest.

"Oh, geez, Scarlett. You scared me."

"I trusted you, Celeste. It made the most sense that it'd be you—you were the one with the most to gain from this. But I told Rafael there was no way you'd do it, that you'd kill people, all of it over a podcast."

She swallows, shoulders hunching. "What . . . what are you talking about?"

"I know about your *affair*. With Quentin."

"Oh." She clears her throat. "Are you upset? Jealous? Because, Scarlett, it's just a fling. In fact, I plan to end it. And you know I would have never done it if I'd known it'd hurt you."

She can't be serious, can she?

"Sherlock's cam caught Quentin coming out of Mrs. Brattle's house, dressed like the killer, knocking over the gnome. And I wondered why he lied about Rafael attacking him, but I get it now. He never thought he'd met the killer—he used that excuse in case Rafael accused *him* of being the killer. Why would anyone believe Rafael over our town's beloved Quentin?"

Celeste steps closer, but as she sees me reaching into my bag, she stops. "Wait, you think Quentin did this?"

"Oh, I'm pretty sure he did."

"But Vanessa was arrested. *She* was the murderer."

"Vanessa said she would never hurt anyone."

"And you believe her? She was *stalking* you."

Yes, but she didn't lie. She admitted she was stalking me. "Vanessa is sick, but she's not evil. She's not a killer—*you* are."

She shifts on her heels. "Scarlett, it's *me*. I'm your family. Your parents were my best friends."

"I know," I say, pain laced in my voice. "That's probably why it took me so long to see it. But it makes sense, doesn't it? You pretended not to want any attention drawn to the podcast, then posted that Reddit from my laptop when I left it at work."

She laughs, though it's humorless, and nervously brings a hand to the side of her head.

"Vanessa knew nothing about your visit to the chief of police, because you never went there. Did you?" My lips twist. "But you had an alibi for each murder. Rafael told me he tracked your car, Steve's, and nothing."

"Because it wasn't me," she insists, her voice rising.

"No. It wasn't *you* who slit Catherine's throat or who attacked Mallory with a machete."

She crosses her arms. "Okay, you know what? I think you're tired and you need to sleep." She scoffs. "You're not making any sense. Quentin, me—who's the killer, Scarlett?"

"Both of you."

Her brows knit together, and if anything, I'll give her credit for her acting skills. She really fooled both me and Rafael for so long. "What does that even mean?"

"It means that you're the brains and he's the muscle. You've taken the most gullible guy in town and turned him into your own murder machine."

"Scarlett, I'm not behind *any* of this!" she snaps. For a moment, I can see behind her mask—the panic, the awareness that this is the end—but quickly, she collects herself. "Look, I'm sure that there's an explanation for all of it, okay? Let's find Quentin, and—"

"Celeste, I'm only here because I wanted to give you the opportunity to come clean. But I've already called the police, and they're on their way here."

"The police? What—"

With a shake of my head, I turn around and start to walk.

"Scarlett, wait. Wait!"

When I turn back to her, she's breathing hard. "Let's just sit down and talk, okay?"

I observe her. She can't possibly think I'm stupid enough to stay here any longer. "You need time to get to your weapon so you can kill me, too?"

"*Kill*— Scarlett! You're like a daughter to me. I would never, *never* hurt you."

"But you're okay *framing* me?"

"No, I—"

"But you did. You used my laptop to post that Reddit, you ordered the flowers in my name, you even forged my signature."

"Because I knew the police would never suspect you! Your dad was a cop, and everyone in town loves you." Her eyes are desperate. "I knew they would exclude you immediately, but then Gray *had* to get involved, and that *idiot* cousin of his sent you the cat toy. I had *nothing* to do with that, Scarlett. I swear, I would have never . . . I did all of this for you, too, Scarlett. For us, for Booked It! We needed new listeners—we needed *something*, or we would have lost our jobs. Our whole lives."

I grimace, wondering if she can read the disappointment on my face. The disgust.

"Please, let's just sit down and—"

I turn on my heels and walk away.

"Wait! Rafael!"

I turn around.

She swallows, dabbing at the sweat on her forehead. "He showed up here. He was on to me, so I had to . . . I . . ."

Dread coils in my stomach, so sudden I feel the drop. I can't tell if she's being honest, but that would explain why he didn't answer my calls. Could it . . . could she . . .

"We need to do something about him, Scarlett. I need your help."

She's lying. She must be. But I can't walk away if there's *any* chance he could be hurt.

When her eyes dart to the right, so do mine, and I see dark shoes sticking out from beside the desk. I can't know for sure, but I imagine that's how being struck by lightning must feel.

"Rafael!" I cry out, my voice sharp, as I move to him.

"I had to . . . I had to. You understand, right?"

Celeste's voice is high-pitched, trembling with desperation, and when I turn around, I see she's now holding a gun. My eyes dart to Rafael, lying on the floor motionless. Blood spreads beneath him, and he's unnervingly still, as if he's asleep.

She shot him. She shot Rafael.

My hands shake violently as I reach out to touch him, my breath coming in shallow, frantic gasps. The sight of the dark, sticky pool beneath him makes my stomach churn as I struggle to find the source of the injury, my fingers fumbling over his body.

"Rafael!" I call, my voice cracking with fear. "Rafael, please . . ."

Celeste's voice cuts through the haze, cold and rational now. "He figured it out, and he was going to the police. Something about my perfume . . . how he smelled it on Quentin when they hugged goodbye or something. But I need to protect the podcast, right? Tell me you get it."

"Y-you shot him," I stammer.

"Only in the shoulder," she says, like that makes it okay.

My hands find the bullet wound on his shoulder, and I quickly pull off my cardigan, pressing it against the injury, trying desperately to stop the bleeding. "You shot him," I repeat, the awareness replaying in my mind like a nightmare I can't wake up from.

Celeste waves the gun. "Nowhere *important*, Scarlett."

I stare down at Rafael, my throat stinging. His shoulder isn't "nowhere important." It's the spot I bite when he makes me come, the place where I rest my head when everything overwhelms me. It's where I fall asleep, where I feel safe, where I've learned what love feels like. And now it's bleeding out beneath my hands.

I lean closer, listening for his breathing, feeling the soft rise and fall of his chest. Relief floods through me—he's still alive. But he's unconscious, and I have no idea how bad the damage is. I turn to Celeste, watching her blurry shape through the tears in my eyes. "Why is he passed out?"

"He hit his head on the desk when he fell," Celeste says. She brings the grip of the gun to her forehead, her chest heaving. "Is he not dead?"

I try to check his head for an injury, but I'm too afraid to move him, too terrified I might make it worse. I breathe out shakily, trying to collect myself, then reach for my phone in the back pocket of my jeans. But as I pull it out, Celeste's voice rises in a scream.

"Drop it!"

I freeze, my hand hovering over Rafael's body, the phone tight in my grasp, as Celeste takes a step closer, the gun trained on me. My mind races, my thoughts spiraling.

"I have to call an ambulance, Celeste," I say, trying as hard as I can to fight the panic. "He's going to die."

"He *has* to die, Scarlett," she says, her tone taking on an eerie calmness. "If he doesn't, Booked It is over. You love the podcast more than anything else."

My heart skips a beat, my blood running cold. She's lost it. She's willing to do whatever it takes to protect the podcast, and she thinks I am, too.

I have to play along, have to buy myself some time quickly.

I set the phone down slowly, my hands shaking so hard I can barely keep them steady. "Yes, I get it," I say, forcing the words out even though they taste like ash in my mouth. "Nobody can find out you were the killer, but we also can't let anyone else die. You did it, Celeste. The podcast is wildly successful now. Nobody else needs to get hurt."

Her eyes narrow, suspicion flickering across her face. "No—you're just saying that. He's a PI. He'll go to the police."

My heart hammers against my ribs. "No, I mean it. You'll leave, and I'll call the ambulance and convince Rafael not to say anything. We can still fix this. We can still save the podcast."

She hesitates, the gun wavering slightly in her hand. My eyes flick to Rafael, my heart aching as I see the blood still seeping from his wound. I have to keep it together, have to convince Celeste *fast*.

"Please, Celeste," I implore, my voice faltering. "Just go. We'll figure everything out. But I need to save him. *Please*."

I hold my breath, waiting for her response.

When a sudden noise echoes from somewhere in the building, her head snaps up. She glares at me, her eyes narrowing. "Don't say a word," she hisses between her teeth, her voice razor-sharp. "If I hear a single noise, I'll come back and kill him."

Before I can respond, she turns on her heel and storms out of the room, leaving me alone with Rafael. My heart races, pounding so loudly I'm sure she can hear it from wherever she is. Once I move my hand to Rafael's injury, I feel a sudden grip on my wrist. Dark gray eyes with golden flecks stare up at me.

"Rafael," I say, relief flooding me. "You're okay. You're—"

"You *have* to leave," he says, his voice weak but urgent. "Now."

"What? I'm not leaving you."

"You have to," he insists, his grip on my wrist tightening despite his obvious pain. "Drive away, *then* call the police. Do it now, before she decides not to let you go."

"Rafael, I'm *not* leaving you here," I say, shaking my head firmly. I look back at the door, then insist, "So tell me what to do."

His eyes flicker with frustration, and he gestures weakly with his free hand. "My gun," he says, eyes darting to his waist. "Take it, and give it to me."

I see the gun tucked into the waistband of his pants, on the same side as his injury. I reach for it, but when I try to hand it to him, he struggles to sit up and fails, slumping back down with a groan of pain.

That's when I see it—blood trickling from the back of his head, staining the carpet beneath him. My breath catches in my throat, and I instinctively pull him back down, my hand gently cradling his head. "Rafael, your head," I whimper.

He tries to speak, but the pain is too much. I can see it in his eyes—the frustration, the helplessness. I'm alone in this, and I have to do something.

I look down at the gun in my hand, the cold metal heavy and unfamiliar. I've never held a gun before, and now I might have to use it against someone I thought was my friend. My stomach twists at the thought, but I don't have a choice, do I?

Swallowing hard, I fumble with the safety, my fingers trembling as I slide it off. The soft click feels deafening in the silence, a point of no return.

Celeste is coming back, her footsteps echoing in the hallway, and I beg myself to stand. My heart leaps into my throat as I rise, holding the gun out in front of me with both hands.

When she enters the room, her eyes widen in shock. She raises her own gun, pointing it directly at me, and for a moment, we just stand there, staring at each other, our weapons aimed.

It's like time stands still.

"I can't let him die, Celeste," I beg. "Please, don't make me shoot you. *Please*."

Eyes set on her, I will her to understand, to see that I don't want to hurt her. My hands shake, every instinct screaming at me to run, to drop the gun and get out of here, but I can't. I can't leave Rafael.

After what feels like an eternity, her arm wavers, and slowly, she lowers her gun. Tears well up in her eyes, and her shoulders start shaking. "I can't shoot you, Scarlett. Just . . . just kill me and get it over with."

I lower my gun, too, taking a cautious step toward her. "I won't, Celeste," I say in between pants. "We can figure this out. Everything will be okay."

"No, it won't," she sobs. "I'll go to prison, and the podcast will fail. We're screwed, Scarlett. We're drowning in debt."

Drowning in debt? What?

"Celeste, listen to me," I say, closing the distance between us. "We'll figure it out. You've been there for me, and I'll be there for you. But first, we need to make sure no one else gets hurt."

I reach out and pull her into a hug, feeling her body shake against mine. As I let her go, my hand slips into my pocket, and in one quick movement, I press my Taser against her side and activate it.

She jerks, her body convulsing as the electric shock courses through her. I catch her as she crumples to the floor, my breath coming in rapid gasps as I delicately set her head down.

"Doesn't feel so pink now, does it?" I say as I drop the Taser and rush back to Rafael's side.

In an instant, I grab my phone, my fingers trembling as I dial 911. The operator answers, her voice steady and professional, but it feels distant, like I'm underwater.

"This is 911, what's your emergency?"

I try to speak, but my throat is so tight that it takes a moment before any words come out. "I— Th-there's been a shooting," I stammer, looking into Rafael's eyes. "My boyfriend, he's bleeding. We need an ambulance, please."

"Stay calm, ma'am. What's your location?"

"We're at—at the Booked It office, Willowbrook."

"Is the shooter still on the scene?" she asks, and I glance at Celeste's unconscious form, sprawled on the floor.

"She's . . . she's down. I tased her."

Thank *God* I stopped by my place to get it.

"Is she alive? Can you check—"

"No!" I nearly scream into the phone. "I don't care about her, and I'm not leaving my boyfriend. You have to save him, to—"

"Scarlett." He sets a calming hand on my thigh. "They're just making sure you're safe."

I take a shaky breath. "I'm—I'm sorry, but please, hurry. He's losing so much blood."

She reassures me that help is on the way and keeps asking questions about Rafael's condition, the location of his wounds, if he's conscious. I answer, but my eyes keep darting back to him, and his face is pale, his breathing shallow. It feels like hours before she finally says, "The ambulance is on its way, ma'am. Stay with him, and try to keep pressure on the wound."

"I will," I choke out. "Please, just hurry."

Rafael squeezes my hand, his grip weak but insistent. "Scarlett," he rasps. "You should go. Celeste could wake up."

I let out a laugh, though there's no humor in it. It's shaky, edged with panic. "If you think I'm leaving you, you're out of your mind."

His eyes search mine. "I know things went to shit, but I need to tell you something, Scarlett . . . I—"

"Don't you fucking dare," I cut him off, my voice sharp with fear. I know what he's going to say, and I can't bear to hear it. Not like this.

"Let me . . ." He tries again, his voice fainter this time.

"No," I snap, pressing harder on his injury, feeling the warm blood coat the cardigan and my hands. "You won't tell me you love me because you think you're dying."

"I don't just *think* I'm dying."

"No!" I shout, my voice cracking as I stare at the injury, as if I can keep him alive by sheer willpower. "You're not dying. You'll be fine. Everything will be fine."

"Scarlett," he says, his hand trembling as it grips my wrist. "I don't want this to be one of my regrets."

"You'll tell me at the hospital," I insist, barely holding it together. It feels like I'm going to vomit or pass out, like my body just wants to reject the situation altogether. Wants to escape it. "Once you're patched up and we talk about why you came here alone." There's a weight on my chest that makes it hard to breathe. "Spoiler alert: we're getting back together so I can dump you."

He chuckles, but it turns into a groan. His skin is cold, clammy, and his eyes are unfocused. He looks so fragile, so close to slipping away. It rips through me like a knife.

"This is all my fault," I sob, my voice trembling with guilt and fear. "If you'd never come back—"

"I don't regret you for a second, Freckles," he murmurs. "Not one."

His eyes flutter closed, and I panic, shaking him. "No, Rafael, don't fall asleep! The ambulance is coming. Please!"

His eyes open again. "It's okay."

"Stop saying it's okay! You're being *selfish*!" I cry as I watch that infuriatingly gentle smile that makes me want to scream and hold him tighter all at once. "No, stop looking at me like that. Ethan needs you. *I* need you. You're not leaving me, you hear me? You're going to be screamed at, and then you're going to grovel, and then we'll be together forever. I can't face everything alone. I can't get over you, Rafael."

"Okay." His voice is barely audible now. "You're right. Breathe."

"Don't tell me to breathe," I snap, even as I try to force air into my lungs. "I'm taking care of you, not the other way around." I choke back a sob. "The romance hero doesn't die at the end of the story. You promised me a love worthy of a romance book."

"I know. I'm sorry." I glare at him through my tears. "Or I would be sorry if . . . but I'm not."

"Right."

"But just in case . . ."

"Rafael . . ."

"If you don't want me to say it, then you do it, please."

I'm pressing down as hard as I can, but the bleeding won't stop. It's everywhere, and I don't even know if it's the shoulder wound or the injury on his head that's killing him. "No, no!" I plead, shaking my head frantically. "At the hospital, Rafael."

"Okay. But you know, right?"

I nod furiously, my tears falling faster. "I know."

"And you feel the same?"

"I do."

"Give me a kiss."

"No, Rafael."

"It's just a kiss."

"It's a goodbye kiss. I'm not giving you—"

"I promise, it's not a goodbye kiss. Just a kiss. Please."

I lean forward and kiss him, my lips trembling against his. They softly part, welcoming mine, but soon they stop moving, and when I pull back, he's still awake, but barely. He's looking up at the ceiling, his eyes distant.

"At least I'm the best version of myself," he mumbles.

"You are," I say, choking up. "You've always been. You're one of the best people I know, Rafael."

I hear the distant wail of ambulance sirens and feel a surge of relief, but when I look down at him, his eyes are closed. I shake him, but he doesn't respond. "No, no, no."

I lean the side of my face against his chest but I can't feel any movement, and then someone's pulling me away from behind.

I fight, desperate to stay with Rafael, but then I realize it's the paramedics. They're here, they're going to save him, and I watch as they try to reanimate him, my heart breaking with every second that passes. I'm crying and screaming at whoever's holding me to let me go, because all I can think about is that I didn't tell him the one thing he wanted to hear. That I love him.

"I'm sorry," I wail, my voice raw. "I'm sorry, I'm sorry, please," I repeat, as I'm taken out of the room, my world collapsing around me.

38

the happily ever after

[trope]

the quintessential rom-com finish line, where all misunderstandings, love triangles, and career dilemmas magically resolve; usually accompanied by a sweeping kiss, a slow fade to sparkly sunsets, and the promise that these two will never argue over Netflix shows or who left the milk out

I look over at Rafael, the steady rhythm of his breathing the only sound in the sterile hospital room. His head is bandaged, a stark white wrap against his dark hair, and his shoulder is covered, too, the dressing stained slightly. The machines beside him beep softly, a strange comfort that tells me he's still here, still fighting.

I sink back into the chair, my fingers trembling as I trace the tattoo on his left arm, the way I've been doing without pause for the last three days.

A quiet sob bubbles up in my chest, and I press the back of my hand to my mouth, trying to keep it in. I hate seeing him like this—

battered, vulnerable, almost lifeless in the bed. It's been three days, and it keeps hitting me just as hard. Under the dim hospital lights, he looks like a boy who's been through too much.

"I'm sorry." I'm not even sure why I'm apologizing, but I keep doing it. Maybe it's because I wasn't there for him when he *was* a boy going through too much, because I don't know how to make the past disappear for him. Maybe it's because I'm scared—scared of losing him, scared of not knowing if he'll ever wake up.

Maybe it's because it feels like I put him there.

I lean forward, resting my head on his stomach, my hand still brushing his side. "Just come back," I whisper. "Please."

"Hey," Paige says as she enters the room. With a glance at Rafael, she sighs. "Nothing new?"

I shake my head. The doctors said he suffered a traumatic head injury, and they're pretty confident he'll wake up once the swelling heals, but they can't say for sure. Nor can they say how much damage there'll be.

"He looks peaceful," she says as she stands at my side, then pulls some of my hair back. "Much better than you, for sure. When's the last time you took a shower?"

"Uh . . . two days ago."

"You really want him to wake up and find you like this?"

Though there's a humorous undertone to her voice, I don't bother forcing a smile out.

"He'll wake up, Scarlett."

I squeeze her hand when she gently grips my shoulder.

"But you really should take a shower. Eat something." She purses her lips. "Ethan said he's coming over after school. Maybe he could take your place for a couple of hours? Just enough for you to have lunch. Wash your hair."

"Is everything okay with him?" I ask, eyes still stuck to Rafael. His chest rising and falling is the only thing that's keeping me from breaking down. I need it to keep rising and falling.

"Yeah. Your grandparents dropped off all his stuff, and we've been working on his bedroom."

We've been in constant communication, and he comes to the hospital every afternoon. Still, I know this is unfair to him, too. *I* was supposed to be doing all that with him, not Paige. "But he's okay?"

"Trust me, he is. He's enjoying his alone time with Jace *plenty*. Right now, you need to think of yourself a little."

I firmly shake my head. "I can't leave his side."

"Scarlett . . ."

"I *can't*." I grip his hand, as if she'll forcibly drag me out of the room. The nurses have been trying to get me out every night, but I swear I'll bolt my feet to the floor before I agree to leave him alone in here. "He wanted to tell me he loved me, and I didn't let him. He begged me to tell him I loved him, and I wouldn't. And now . . ." Now we may never get to say those words. "I scrubbed my hands for half an hour, and the blood wouldn't leave, Paige. It just wouldn't. And his chest—his chest stopped moving, and his lips stopped moving, and I—"

"Scarlett . . ."

"I didn't tell him I loved him. That's all he wanted, and I didn't give it to him."

"Okay. You don't have to go." She moves closer. "Tomorrow, maybe."

Tomorrow. The implication is almost enough to break me. This is what our life will look like from now on, isn't it? For weeks, maybe months. Until I'll *have* to go. Find another job, because Booked It is obviously done, but the bills still need to be paid. Ethan needs to eat, and I need to be his guardian.

At some point, I'll have to leave Rafael here, all alone. Maybe hurting, though the doctors promise he's not. Defenseless, motionless. I'll have to move on like my life makes any sense without him in it.

But that day certainly isn't today. Or tomorrow.

"Maybe."

"Okay." There's some shuffling noise, then she holds out an envelope. "This is for you."

Tentatively, I grab the envelope and open it, trying to push away the sinking feeling I get once I let his hand go. "What is it?" I ask when all I see inside is money. "What is this for?"

"It's from—well, everyone. Whatever they could spare. So you can pay bills and buy food and whatever else you need while you're here."

My eyes sting and my nose burns. "I can't accept this."

"Not only can you, but you have to." She takes the envelope back. "In fact, I'll be using a chunk of this to pay your bills today and leave the rest at home, okay?"

Too tired to argue, I say, "Okay. Thank you."

She wraps her arm around me in a quick side hug.

"This is it, right? How love will destroy me? I thought it was our breakup—that no longer having him in my life was the strongest pain I could experience—but I should have known better."

Death. Grief. Loss.

That's what love really is.

"I'm sorry, you know? If it wasn't for me . . . I pushed you to fall in love, and—"

"I don't regret Rafael," I rush out. "Not for one second. Loving him is worth *any* pain."

I just wish it was me lying in this bed instead of him.

"He's your real-life book boyfriend, Scarlett." She presses a kiss to the side of my head. "Those *always* wake up."

Tears trickle down my cheeks.

"I'll text you later, okay?"

I turn with a smile over my shoulder until she leaves the room, and I'm finally alone with Rafael again. Maybe I should read to him some more. The doctors said he might hear it. Or maybe that's the sort of bullshit they say to people like me, hopelessly waiting for their loved ones to wake up.

I grab a noir Paige brought over yesterday, but I can't really focus, and to be honest, I'm kind of done with murder. Instead, I reach into my bag and take out *Hearts on Hold*. I've been reading it to him, annotating it the way he asked me to weeks ago. But once I reached the third-act breakup, I couldn't force myself to watch these two people hurt the same way I am hurting.

Still, it sounds better than murder, so I open to page 256 and read out loud: "Julie sat alone in the quiet of her apartment, her gaze fixed on the flickering candle in front of her, but her mind was far from the present. It kept drifting back to him—always back to him.

"Terrence. It felt like a lifetime ago when they were wrapped up in each other, when his touch felt like the safest place she could ever be. She could still see the way he'd watched her from across the room and made her heart skip a beat. She remembered how easily they'd fallen into step, how perfectly they'd fit, despite everything that should have kept them apart."

I glance up at him, then write on the corner of the page, "I thought the thing I'd miss the most about you would be your hugs or your voice. Both excellent, by the way. But it's your smile." I continue reading: "Even now, with all the hurt, she couldn't deny how much she had loved him. Still loved him. Because Terrence wasn't just the man she had lost—he was the man who had taught her what it meant to truly let someone in, even if that came at a price. He had shown her the love that terrified her because it forced her to confront parts of herself she'd kept buried for so long."

Wiping the tears off my face, I make another little note: "You know when I realized I loved you? When you made us breakfast in bed. And lunch. And we ate neither. I don't know why I didn't tell you back then, but I was sure of it."

I set the pen down. "Maybe that was the real heartbreak—not the loss of him but losing what they could have been. The future they could have had. But love, she realized, wasn't just about holding on. Sometimes it was about knowing when to let go."

I exhale; then, putting pen to paper, I scribble: "This is some bullshit. I'm not letting you go, now or ever."

"Well, come on. Keep going." The pen drops from my hand as I look up at Rafael, eyes barely open and a tired smile on his face. "I'm dying to know if these two end up together."

I lean against the cold hospital wall, arms crossed tightly over my chest, as I wait for the doctor to finish his visit. My heart races, my stomach churning with a mix of anxiety and hope. He's awake. Fully awake. I should feel relief, but all I can feel is more worry. Is he okay? Will he make a full recovery?

The door opens with a quiet click, and I straighten as Dr. Patel steps out into the hallway. His calm expression gives nothing away, but there's something in his eyes, something that feels like reassurance.

"He's awake."

Dr. Patel flips through the pages of Rafael's chart. "Yes, fully awake and coherent."

I release a shaky breath, relief flooding through me. But before I can let myself get lost in the joy of it, I ask the question that's been gnawing at me for days. "How . . . how is he?"

The doctor glances up at me, his tone steady but gentle. "Considering the trauma he experienced, he's doing exceptionally well. The head injury is serious, but there are no immediate signs of lasting cognitive damage."

A wave of gratitude crashes over me, but the way he says "immediate signs" plants a seed of doubt in my mind. "And long-term?" I ask, biting down on my lower lip. "What are we looking at?"

Dr. Patel pauses, as if choosing his words carefully. "Rafael will need time, both for physical healing and for us to fully assess any potential aftereffects. He'll likely experience some fatigue, maybe some memory lapses or headaches as his brain continues to heal. But from what we've seen so far, there's every reason to believe he'll make a full recovery."

I blink back tears, the pressure in my chest easing just enough for me to take a breath. "So . . . he's going to be okay?"

The doctor writes something down. "Yes. He'll need rest, rehabilitation, and patience, but he's on the right path."

I nod, my eyes stinging. "Thank you."

He tilts his head. "Scarlett, remember to take care of yourself, too. You're just as important as anything else in his recovery."

Right now, I don't care about anything else. He's awake. He's okay.

"You should go in."

I thank him, slip past him, and push open the door, heart thumping in my chest.

Rafael is propped up against the pillows, his face pale but his eyes sharp, awake, and focused. The sight of him, fully alert and alive, almost undoes me.

"Hey," I say tentatively.

"Hey," he rasps. His voice is rough, like gravel, but the familiar warmth in it soothes me like a balm.

I have no idea what to say. *How are you?* feels ridiculous. He's awake, yes, but I can't imagine the pain he must be in, the disorientation he must be experiencing. I wonder if anyone thought to offer him water. He must be thirsty. Or hungry. Do people wake up from comas starving? Should I ask if I can hug him? Or kiss him?

The thoughts pile up and then dissolve into nothing as I take a hesitant step forward. My hands tremble at my sides, and my breath comes in shallow bursts. I'm half afraid this is a dream, a cruel one I'll wake up from at any moment.

I glance at the tattooed skin peeking from the top of his hospital gown, my gaze trailing to his hand, open at his side with no rings—those are safely stored in the bedside table. Slowly, carefully, I take it in mine.

The second he squeezes back, a sob escapes my throat. He's awake. He's really awake. He's okay.

And I know exactly what I need to say.

"I love you."

His lips part slightly, and for a second, he just blinks at me. Then a slow, soft smile spreads across his face, like the sun breaking through a cloud.

"It's . . . Scarlett, right?"

My stomach drops into free fall.

He doesn't know who I am?

"Loves wontons, head always stuck in a book, face full of freckles?" he adds, his tone teasing.

"For fuck's sake." I exhale in relief as his laugh vibrates softly in the air. My hand itches to smack his chest, but I have to remind myself that he's injured. "Jokes? Really? After you've been in a coma for eight years?"

His smile falters for a split second, and I let out a chuckle, biting back the urge to cry again.

Shoulders relaxing, he laughs, the sound weak but so utterly *him* that it makes my heart swell. "*Mean.* Really, really mean."

"You started it."

His thumb brushes over the back of my hand, sending a quiet shiver through me. Then, with infinite care, he raises my hand to his lips, kissing the top. The gesture is so tender, so achingly familiar, I want to throw myself at him and bury my face in his chest.

My Rafael is back, and I'll *die* before I let him go again.

"Freckles," he says softly, intertwining our fingers and resting our hands on his lap. "I—"

"Is it true?" Ethan's voice booms from behind me, startling us both. I turn to see my brother standing in the doorway, his expression caught somewhere between disbelief and awe. "Holy shit. You're awake."

"Hey, man," Rafael says, his voice suddenly stronger, like he's summoning all his energy to reassure Ethan. "Have you been holding down the fort for me?"

I roll my eyes. "Oh, *he* holds down the fort?"

Ethan steps closer. "Shit, dude. You look like hell."

"Your sister doesn't think so."

I scoff, unable to hide my joy. He's joking. He's *himself*.

"Yeah, well, she has questionable taste," Ethan quips, pointing at the nightstand. "Did you show him yet?"

Rafael turns his head, wincing slightly, and I quickly squeeze his hand in comfort. Ethan grabs the folded copy of the *Whistle* from the table and sets it on Rafael's lap.

"'The Prodigal Son Turned Hero,'" Ethan reads aloud, his tone exaggerated. Rafael's brow furrows in confusion as Ethan snickers.

I grab the paper and shove it aside. "I can read that to you later. You should rest now."

"Was that my picture?"

Ethan grabs the paper again. "Yep. It's an article about you—how no one believed in you, and you saved everyone's asses. They might rename the main square after you."

Rafael turns to me, squinting. "That's not what happened. *You* caught the killer."

"And *you* caught a stalker I got credit for. Guess we're even."

"Scarlett . . ."

"I didn't lie. And besides, people needed to know what you've done, Rafael. Who you really are." I shrug, glancing away. "I didn't even do it for you. It's their loss they didn't see it before."

His eyes linger on mine, full of something I can't quite name.

Gratitude, maybe. Love, definitely. "What . . . what happened with that? Celeste and Quentin?"

"They've been arraigned, and both of them have pleaded guilty. Life without parole for him. She got life with the possibility of parole, which is . . ." I trail off, my chest tightening. *Unfair? Insane?*

"Well, he was the one who committed the murders," Rafael says.

"Because she manipulated him."

"Who cares?" Ethan groans from the corner. "They're both in prison, where they belong. And the second we were assigned a social worker, she's been flooded with letters and emails singing your praise from everyone in town."

Rafael turns to me sharply, his brows knitting together. "What?"

I open my mouth, but Ethan beats me to it. "All of a sudden, Chief Donovan said they didn't have enough evidence against you on that criminal trespass investigation, so that's gone too. I'm telling you. You're like the savior of Connecticut or something. The only reason half the town isn't in here groveling is that Scarlett forbade visits. But Mrs. Brattle is downstairs, and so is that old guy from the pharmacy. And—"

"Wait, so . . ." Rafael's voice falters as his eyes search mine, and I nod, my throat tightening. *So our relationship isn't a problem anymore.*

"Steve said no one can challenge my custody of Ethan, even if you're in my life," I say.

"Assuming you find a job," Ethan quips.

"I told you, Mrs. Brattle says they'll hire me at the newspaper."

"The newspaper?" Rafael asks, eyes jumping from Ethan to me. "What about the podcast?"

A pang of worry rises in me instantly. Is he confused? "Well, Celeste's . . . gone, Gray. And so is the podcast."

"Seriously, forget about those lunatics," Ethan interrupts, his eyes darting between me and Rafael like those of a spectator at a tennis match. "It's time for you two to DTR."

I glare at him, then turn back to Rafael, checking his expression.

"Ethan, can you give us a second?" he says, eyes never leaving mine.

My brother hesitates, his face twisting with mock concern. "Not to have sex, right? 'Cause you don't look like you should have sex."

Rafael's thumb brushes the top of my hand. "No, not to have sex. I'd like to tell your sister I love her."

The air shifts. I freeze, my breath catching in my chest. He said it. He actually *said it*. My heart thunders in my ears, drowning out everything else. *It counts. He said it. He loves me.*

"Oh. Okay," Ethan says before he steps toward the door. "I'll be outside."

The door closes with a soft click. I can't tell if the million machines around Rafael are still beeping, because I can't hear anything at all besides a loud ringing in my ears.

"Hi, Freckles." His voice is the kind of soft that makes my heart stumble in its rhythm.

"Hi, Gray."

He shakes his head slowly, as though marveling at something only he can see. "I have no memory of anything past what happened at Booked It, so how is it possible that I missed you so much?"

I cup his cheek. "Not as much as I missed you."

He gently tugs at my hand. "Give me a kiss."

My heart clenches, and I'm instantly reminded of the last time he asked me that. That gut-wrenching moment, the way I refused at first, my lips trembling as I fought back tears. I didn't want to kiss him then—not for the last time. But he's back now. He's here, and all I want is to kiss him for the rest of my life. To kiss him until my lips are raw, until time stops, until the world forgets to spin.

I lean forward, the space between us vanishing, but just as my lips are about to meet his, his voice breaks through the fragile quiet.

"Scarlett?"

I pause, my breath hitching. "Yes?"

"I know I've hurt you, but I'd really like a last chance." His smile widens, a little crooked, a little hopeful. It's the smile that's always undone me. "This time, I *know* I won't screw it up."

My heart flutters wildly. "You probably will," I say, my voice thick with emotion, a watery laugh breaking through. "So how about I don't give you a last chance?" I can see the question forming on his lips, but I press on. "How about I just give you *a* chance?"

His eyes close, his warm breath brushing over my lips.

"And then another," I add. "And then another. As many chances as you want."

He watches me, eyes brimming with relief, and slowly, he pulls me closer.

"I love you, Scarlett Moore," he whispers on my lips. "I want to watch you fall in love with one book after another until we're old and sore and our hair's gone silver. I want to build a life that looks like us—I want boring Tuesdays and chaotic Sundays, takeout dinners and late-night chats."

"Rafael," I cry against his lips. I was so scared I'd never get to hear his voice again, and now he's saying this. I don't think my heart can take it.

"I want to watch you chase dreams, change your mind, grow into new versions of yourself—and love every one of them."

He holds me close, his voice wavering like it's not close enough.

"I want this life with you. And the next. And every one after that. If there are a hundred versions of me, I want every single one to find you."

My chest is aching, breaking open, full of him.

And then he kisses me.

It feels like coming home. His hand cups my face, his thumb wiping away a stray tear, and I melt into him, every inch of me craving the closeness, the connection.

When we finally pull apart, he rests his forehead against mine.

"You know, I think I finally figured it out."

I sniffle. "What?"

"I need *you*. When I have you by my side, I'm the best version of myself."

I pull his hair back, savoring the feeling of his warm skin under my fingertips. "I'll take any version of you, Gray."

He cups my cheeks, thumbs swiping under my eyes. "Scarlett, about what you said, you know Celeste and Booked It have nothing to do with the podcast, right?"

"What do you mean?"

"Well, *you* are the podcast. Nobody who's ever listened to *Murders & Manuscripts* has done it because of Celeste. They want to hear *you*. And you have a sound engineer. Whatever equipment you need, we'll get. What's stopping you?"

Nothing, I guess. *My own podcast.* I've always been so comfortable at Booked It that I've never considered leaving, but the thought of launching my own venture seems exciting. "Maybe. I just . . . I'm not sure I want my *whole* life to revolve around murders."

I guess watching the man you love nearly bleed out in front of you will do that to a person.

"So don't. It's *your* podcast. Make it about whatever you want."

I huff out a single chuckle, but the thought takes shape in my mind. My own bookish podcast about whatever I want. "Mystery novels and smutty romance?"

He weakly claps. "We'll call it *Fuck, Marry, Kill*."

"Or . . ." I bite my lip, an idea taking shape. "*A Killer Kind of Romance*."

epilogue

[trope]

---

a final exhale at the end of the story; created to offer a glimpse of what "after" really looks like, reward hopeless romantics with proof that love didn't end at the last kiss, and let characters linger just a little longer in the light they fought for

And that's all for today's episode of A Killer Kind of Romance, *the podcast where we toy with the line between murder and happily ever after. Whether you're here for blood, butterflies, or both, I hope you found something worth obsessing over. Until next time, never fall for the man with too many secrets . . . unless he's got tattoos and a tragic backstory.*

I grin as the podcast comes to an end. My voice goes quiet, replaced by the chirping of birds outside the home office window.

Setting my pen beside the spiral notebook, I lean back in my chair and shoot Theo a message.

> **Scarlett**
> Episode is perfect. Still on for recording this Friday?

The next four episodes are *banging*. I've got two bestselling authors lined up, one chaotic influencer who writes fanfic, and a crime fiction editor I've been following for years. Sponsors are renewing, listener numbers are creeping up, and, best of all, the podcast finally pays the mortgage.

I stretch, and pad barefoot into the kitchen. The sun's bright, casting gold over the counter as I pull down two mismatched plates and start setting the table. Just as I reach for the silverware drawer, the front door creaks open.

"You're early," I call over my shoulder.

"And starving," comes a voice that's not Rafael's.

I turn just in time to see him toe off his shoes and shoot me a grin. Ethan.

I get another plate, happy to see he looks healthy and serene. We text often, but after having lived together for two whole years, it's not enough. "Didn't you move out? You know . . . for college and stuff?"

"I'm here for lunch," he says, heading straight for the fridge. "You've got podcast money now. That comes with a fully stocked pantry, yeah?"

I roll my eyes and toss a napkin at him. "Help yourself, parasite."

"Oh, and happy birthday, I guess."

I smile, pinching his arm.

He grabs a soda and slumps into the chair across from mine, throwing a look at the lasagna on the table. "You didn't make that, did you?"

"Nope. It's safe to eat, don't worry."

"Sorry. It's just, I'm still digesting the meatloaf from two months ago."

Funny. Unfortunately, also true. But I've learned my lesson—cooking isn't for me. "So how's Jace?" I ask, changing the topic.

"He's just passed his last exam." He blushes, but it's not out of awkwardness or shame—it's out of joy. He can't *wait* to see his boyfriend. "He'll be back in two weeks' time."

"Awww. Look at you. So smitten."

"Shut up. You should see your face every time Rafael is around. It's like he shits diamonds."

I shrug. "I'll admit I landed a pretty perfect man."

He huffs out a laugh. "Yeah, well. So did I."

The door opens and closes again, and then there's a groan. "I hope you're wearing an apron and nothing else, birthday girl!"

Ethan sets down the cracker that was halfway to his mouth. "Ugh, *gross.* I'm here—Ethan. Remember me?"

Rafael pops his head in. "Oh, yeah . . . *you*," he says, as if he'd forgotten who my brother was. He enters the kitchen and ruffles Ethan's hair. "I saw your car out front."

He circles around me and kisses me on the lips before he sits next to me. "How are you doing, Freckles?"

"I've missed you," I say, biting my lip.

About two weeks ago, Rafael got a proper office—a little place close to The Oak. And that was after he had to hire an assistant to help relieve him of admin tasks. I suspect it's just a matter of time before he will have to bring another PI in. People travel from out of town to see him—the detective who caught the Lit Killer.

The name stuck, of course.

For the past two weeks, I've missed him around the house. Working on one side of the couch while I write or read on the other end. Complaining about how I never use the home office he set up for me. Somehow the arguments always ending up with steamy make-out sessions against my rolling ladder.

"I've missed you, too." He brings my hand to his lips and kisses the top, and after Ethan's groan, he sets it back down on the table and turns to the food. "This looks good."

Ethan shakes his head. "Don't worry, she didn't make it."

Rafael chuckles, and eager to shut Ethan up, I hold up two plates and wait as they serve themselves. Sherlock joins us, meowing as he begs for food or attention.

Lunch goes by the way it usually does—with banter and chatter and the chaos that makes us the perfectly dysfunctional family we've been for the past three years. And as with every lunch since Ethan moved out, he stands right after the meal, says goodbye, and rushes back to his friends and his life.

"He looks good," Rafael says as he washes the dishes. He turns to look at me over his shoulder. "I mean, his sister looks better, but . . ."

"Yeah." I swat his ass with a dish towel. "He looks happy."

He holds out his hand, water dripping onto the kitchen rug, and I hand him the towel. When I don't let go, he smirks, tugging it to pull me closer. "God, getting an office was a mistake."

We kiss, his wet hand grazing my cheek.

"Hmm." I tug his hair. "The house feels empty without you."

"Do *you* feel *empty* without me?"

I huff on his lips, very much like a dog in heat. "Only all the time."

He pulls me closer. "Then we better get going, birthday girl. Are we taking my car or yours?"

"Going? Where?"

There's matching confusion on his face. "The lookout?" Noticing the blank look I'm giving him, he lets out a soft laugh. "The book you left in my office, Scarlett."

"I didn't leave anything in your office."

His chin jerks back. He heads to the entryway and pulls a small paperback from his jacket pocket. *The Art of Falling Slowly*—excellent fake-dating romance. I recognize it from the cover. "Look inside," he says. He hands it to me, and I flip to the first page.

Scarlett, it reads above the title. And beneath it: *Page 176, line 32.*

"What in the name . . ." I mutter, flipping through.

Rafael leans over and points. "I'll save you the counting."

Once they walked past the hill, the lookout loomed ahead.

"I—I don't understand."

"Me neither." His brow furrows. "I thought your name meant this was from you, but—"

"But whoever wrote this put my name *before* the message, not after."

"So maybe it's *for* you," Rafael says, echoing my thoughts. He takes the book from my hands, glaring at it like it's trying to hurt me. "Who the fuck would do this?"

Reminded of how the conversation started, I ask, "Where did you think we were going?"

"Hmm?" He's still flipping through the book like it might contain a hidden bomb.

"You said we better get going?"

"Oh. Yeah. When I thought this was *from* you, I assumed this line meant you wanted to go to the lookout by the rails."

Of course. I smile despite myself. On our first anniversary, we attempted a hike. Big mistake. By the time we were halfway up the trail, I was covered in mosquito bites and had tripped three times, and my feet felt like I was walking on hot coals. Rafael, ever the hero, pretended *he* was exhausted and suggested we find a place to have our picnic.

That's how we found the lookout—a grassy bluff past an overgrown trail, overlooking the abandoned train tracks and a sparkling stretch of river. It wasn't even on the map. We ate cold takeout and fought against a champagne bottle neither of us could open.

And yes—I ended up straddling him beneath the stars, jeans tugged down just far enough, one hand gripping his hair, the other bracing me against a tree root.

"What if that *is* the message?"

"You think someone's trying to send you to the lookout?" He shrugs. "Why? And who?"

I exhale, meeting his eyes. Only people close to us have heard this story—except for the spicy parts, which we kept for ourselves.

Oh boy, I'm getting flashbacks of the last time we asked ourselves these kinds of questions.

At the same time, we both say, "Someone we know."

Paige, maybe, or Stella, her girlfriend. Theo. Basically, the usual suspects.

"We *have* to go," I say, grabbing the keys.

He grimaces. "Do we? Because if there's a corpse at our lookout, I'm never calling it *our* lookout again."

"Come on," I say, already opening the door. "Let's go."

Panting, I stumble onto the patch of grass. If nothing else, this little adventure confirms what I thought—hiking and I will never be friends.

Rafael, looking maddeningly unbothered, crouches beside me and scans the area. "There's nothing here."

He's right. I turn in a slow circle, eyes sweeping across the clearing. Just wildflowers, tall swaying grass, too many bugs for my comfort, and that breathtaking view.

I drift toward the edge of the bluff and peer out, hoping there's something—anything—I'm missing. The town stretches in miniature below us, sun catching on rooftops, the river shimmering like a spilled bottle of mercury. The wind carries the scent of pine and something sweeter.

But there's nothing weird.

Rafael's arms wrap around me, his chest pressing against my back. "Not gonna lie, Freckles. I'm relieved as fuck. The last thing Willowbrook needs is another bookish serial killer."

I squeeze his arms and lean into him. I'm relieved, too, though a part of me kind of liked the thrill of it. Since he opened his own agency, I've never meddled in his PI work—playing detective that one time was enough—but this . . . this is fun. The two of us, solving whatever-this-is together.

"You okay?" he asks, his lips grazing my ear.

I keep my eyes on the view and inhale deeply, feeling my back expand against the solid weight of him. "Never been better, actually."

"Can you believe it's been two whole years since we came here?" There's a smile in his voice. I twist back to glance at him. "Actually, one year and . . ." He looks up, calculating. "Eleven months, twenty-four days . . . and eight hours?"

"Something like that," I say, laughing.

"Three years together. It feels like yesterday—but also forever?"

I nod. "I'm not sure I even remember my life before you."

"Afraid you're stuck with me now."

Oh, it could be worse. I could be hiking alone.

I start to turn back toward him when I see it. Just below the bluff, tucked into a narrow crevice between the roots of the same tree I once clung to while moaning Rafael's name. "There's a book."

Not just a book, actually. *Last First Kiss* is *the* best second-chance romance I've read this year. I told Rafael the hero from that book was the only man who would ever top him, and I stand by it.

"What?" He leans forward. "Oh, *damn*."

I crouch, but Rafael's quicker, reaching for it and holding it like it might bite.

"I'll open it," he says.

"Why?"

He shrugs. "It could explode."

I roll my eyes but know better than to argue.

He flips open the book, and his lips twist. "Scarlett," he reads. "Page seventy-seven, line twelve."

I step closer as he turns the pages. Together, we count down the lines until we find: *in the place she went to every time she needed to unwind.*

"The bookstore," he says without missing a beat.

I blink at him. "Wait . . . you think this is about me?"

He shrugs. "Want to spread your legs and check if the next clue's in there? 'Cause that's where *I* go when I need to unwind."

My face heats as I grab the book out of his hands and flip to the first page. The handwriting isn't familiar, and half the town could guess I spend money at the bookstore any time life mildly inconveniences me.

"So . . . bookstore?" I say.

He nods. "Bookstore."

Goddamn it. Hiking *again*.

———————

I'm practically lifeless by the time we step into the bookstore, my feet dragging behind me. Rafael, still looking as fresh as if he just rolled out of bed, follows me in and exhales.

"Lots of books in here," he says, glancing around the shop. "How are we supposed to find the right one?"

Good question.

"Scarlett, hi!" Dana calls from behind the counter. "We just got some new arrivals. I set a few aside for you."

"Did you?" I ask, suddenly reinvigorated. She waves me over and starts pulling out a stack of books. She's already mid-description of the first one—a historical forbidden romance—when Rafael steps up and kisses the side of my head.

"I'll take a look around."

Right. I forgot why we were here.

"Oh, I can—"

"Stay," he says, smiling, like watching me around books is better than seeing me naked. "Have fun." Then, to Dana, he adds, holding out his card, "Whatever she's getting—it's on me."

He walks off, and Dana lowers the book.

"Wow, Scarlett. Does he happen to have a brother or something?"

"Sorry. He's one of a kind."

She lets out a low whistle. "That I believe."

We go through the pile, and I'm not even ashamed to say I'm taking all of them home. He offered, didn't he? And he always does—which is why he had to build me another bookshelf. It's only polite that I fill it.

After thanking her, I wander back to him. I can already tell from his expression that he hasn't found anything.

"There's gotta be another clue, right?" he says, rubbing his jaw. "Something we missed?" When I smile, he smiles back. "Yes, I'm invested now."

I scan the shelves, my mind spinning.

If this is about me, then the book has to be here. But if this is about *me* . . . then why was the first book in *his* office?

I turn down the aisle, Rafael trailing behind, and stop in front of the romance section.

"This is where we were, right?"

"What?"

"When we read *The Love Alibi* together? It was . . ." I look around and tug him closer. "Right here."

"Okay?"

I turn toward the shelf—and there it is. A copy of *The Love Alibi* staring back at me.

I pick it up as Rafael mumbles, "Holy shit" beside me. Flipping to the first page, I find my name again. *Scarlett.* Then: *Page 276, line 22.*

"Seriously?" Rafael groans. "How many of these are we doing?"

He takes the book, flips through, and reads aloud, "There's coffee on the counter, and the whiskey's in the fridge."

"Hmm . . . The Oak?" I say. "Maybe it's a reference to the night we got whiskey and coffee—"

"—and you ended up drinking both." When I chuckle, he takes my hand. "Worth a try."

I follow him to the counter, and holding the book out to Dana, he asks me, "How'd you know it would be there? The book?"

"Because I don't think this is about me," I say as Dana starts scanning the stack. "I think it's about *us*."

"*Us*?" Rafael blinks, thoughtful. "Hey, Dana, did anything weird happen around here in the past twenty-four hours?"

"The past twenty-four hours?" I say before Dana can answer.

"It rained on Tuesday. The book at the lookout would've been soaked if it had been put there before that."

Right. God, his brain is so hot.

Dana furrows her brow. "Weird? Not really, no."

"No break-ins? Shady customers?"

"The most excitement I get in here is Scarlett," she says with a smile. Then her expression shifts. "Although . . . Mrs. Brattle came by this morning. She usually only visits on weekends. Looked kind of frantic, said she was late for her post-Pilates gossip."

"Mrs. Brattle?" I echo. Sure, she knows everything, but I can't imagine her setting this up. Or hiking all the way up to the lookout with her bad back.

"Thanks, Dana," I say as Rafael grabs the bag of books with an "Oof."

We step out of the shop, tuck the books into the trunk of his car, and decide to walk to The Oak. The sun's high, the air is finally bearable after a long winter, and . . . God, we haven't done this in forever, have we?

"It's good to be out," I say, sliding my hand into his.

"We've been busy, huh? These past few months?"

So busy. Between the podcast taking off and spending weekends helping Paige get her event-planning business off the ground, I haven't had a second to breathe.

I glance up at him, brows knitting. "Oh my God, are you mad at me?"

"Excuse me?"

"I've been so busy, and . . . did I put our relationship on the back burner? Are you unhappy? Oh my God, are you break—"

"Whoa, Freckles." He stops short, gently hooking two fingers under my chin to tip my face toward his. "All I said was 'We've been busy.'"

"But you meant *I've* been busy."

"No, I've been pulling late nights, too," he says, rubbing his hand down my arm. "But we have lunch together almost every day. I order takeout for you every Friday night. We spend nearly every evening together, and I get to tuck you in when you fall asleep reading on the couch." He smiles. "I love your podcast. I love that you help everyone. And I love you. I only ask that you come back home every day and let me squeeze you in my sleep."

"Deal," I say—way too fast. On the rare nights he's away for a case, I can barely sleep. I *need* him in my bed.

He nudges his nose against mine. "Come on. This prank—or *whatever* it is—can't last forever, can it?"

The Oak is just five minutes away, and we're grateful to slip inside, out of the heat.

The bar smells like wood and warm bread. After Quentin's arrest the place closed for a bit, but the mayor eventually convinced him to sign over power of attorney. Now Josh runs it, and everyone loves him—mostly because he hasn't quite figured out proper serving sizes.

"Welcome, welcome!" Josh calls as he darts behind the bar to serve Steve, who gives us a cheery wave. "I've got your book—no worries."

I frown. "You've got our what?"

"Your book!" Josh bends, rummaging under the counter before presenting us with a worn paperback. *Love, Late Fees, and Other Disasters* is printed across the front. "You left it here, didn't you?"

"I—what? No!" I whirl toward Rafael, who raises an eyebrow. "I didn't!"

Rafael looks back at Josh. "Did you actually see her drop it off?"

"Well, no," Josh admits, handing Rafael the book. "But her name's on the first page, so I set it aside."

"Thanks, Josh," Rafael murmurs, already flipping through the pages.

"I don't get it," I say, scanning the room as if I'll see someone recording us or something. "Why is someone taking us on this book hunt? And why these places? Or better yet . . . what are we supposed to find at the end?"

"Hmm. I'm not sure I get this one." Rafael turns the book and shows me a highlighted line:

> *Finally, they'd said it. And it was over—it had to be—but they both knew it just meant they'd have to find each other again.*

I remember this scene. Both main characters had ulterior motives when they started dating each other, but they ended up falling in love. The fallout was brutal, written in the most excruciatingly painful way. I *loved* it.

I shake my head. "I don't get it either, but I think the next location is the last one."

"*It was over,*" he echoes, thoughtful. "You might be right."

Great. But where? There's no clear clue this time—the line's just about feelings.

"A place where . . . things end?" I say aloud. "Or where you *find* something again?"

"And it's about us," he adds, quietly.

A sudden ache blooms in my chest. I remember those three awful days at the hospital being unsure if Rafael would ever wake up. But I never believed it was over. I was ready to be there forever if I had to be.

"Wait—hold on," I gasp, locking eyes with his. I can almost still see the guilt and pain flashing in his eyes when I told him I wished he'd never come back. I regret it to this day. "They'd *finally said it,*" I quote, pointing to the line. "And then it was over. But they had to *find each other* again."

"Uh-huh," he says slowly, still not putting it together.

"It's the library," I breathe. "That's where we told each other the truth. I thought you might've been the killer. You were investigating me."

"And once it all came out, we lost each other—only to find each other again." His eyes widen with a soft laugh. "Holy shit, Freckles. Are you looking for a job? I could use another PI."

"Sorry, I'm fully booked." After stealing a kiss, I tug on his hand. "Come on. We have to go."

We wave a quick goodbye and run out of The Oak. Quickly, we make it over the bridge and past the school, and the library comes into view. Even with the memory of Rafael pointing a gun at me there, this is still my favorite place in the whole town.

We enter, breathing hard from the quick jog, and I nod a silent "Hello" at every familiar face. The silence here is different from anywhere else. It's reverent, filled with knowledge, with art.

Rafael leans closer, his breath warm against my ear. "Another place that, if I may say so, has one major drawback."

"Tons of books?"

He smirks. "Exactly."

I keep my voice low. "But the clue is about us, right? About that night?"

He hums, pointing ahead. "We were in the psychology section."

"Appropriate," I murmur, trailing after him. He's carrying the stack of books-slash-clues—if that were an Olympic sport, he'd bring home the gold—and he's got his usual magnetic charm that turns every head in the room. "You know what's weird?"

"*Everything*. Everything about this is extremely weird."

"No, I mean . . . today's my birthday."

He gasps, then theatrically smacks his forehead. "Oh, shit. Is it?"

"Funny." I shoot him a look. "This is kind of a treasure hunt, isn't it?"

His teasing grin fades into something softer. "And your mom used to plan one for every birthday." He cups my face. "So . . . this is not creepy. It's kind of sweet?"

"Yeah, kind of." My gaze lingers on the books in his arms.

The Art of Falling Slowly

Last First Kiss

The Love Alibi

Love, Late Fees, and Other Disasters

I squint at the covers. These are some of my favorite books—

specifically, the ones Rafael annotated for me. It's been a constant over the past three years: whenever I thought he might enjoy something, I told him to read it. He did, every time. And he left behind notes in the margins. Thoughts, jokes, cute and flirty lines. It's still one of my favorite acts of love.

It can't be by chance, but there isn't a single other person in the world who would know which books he annotated for me, is there? *I* certainly can't remember telling anyone.

"Here," he says, stopping at the spot where I almost tased him—and where, in return, he pointed a gun at me. "I guess we're looking for a pastel cover?"

"A pink one." I scan the shelf. "*Only Ever You.*"

He tilts his head, but doesn't question it before he turns and starts searching the spines. And then I see it—a bright pink one, wedged behind his elbow.

I step forward and pull it out.

I always tell Rafael this is the book that fully completed my transition into being a romance reader. The one no other has ever topped. Which is funny, considering it revolves around the trope I had sworn I'd never get behind: arranged marriage.

I flip to the first page. There it is—my name, scribbled at the top, followed by the usual page and line number: Page 48, line 10.

"Did you notice," I ask, my voice light as I thumb through it, "that these are all books you annotated for me?" Page 47, 48. I scroll through the lines until I reach the tenth one. "Who would know that besides me and . . ."

Turn around.

"You," I whisper. I blink, my back straightening before I turn.

Instead of Rafael's face, I'm met with a ring. A ring with a black diamond—small and discreet, exactly the kind I'd buy for myself. A ring sitting on velvet in a red box.

I swear I see white for a moment, like a flash-bang of emotion detonating before my eyes.

Then my gaze shifts past the ring to the man holding it. Tall. Tattooed. Beautiful. Kneeling. Looking up at me with a soft, uncharacteristically nervous smile.

"Freckles."

"Holy motherfucking shitballs," I say, my hands shaking.

He opens his mouth, then closes it again. "Nice."

"Sorry, I—this was you? This whole . . ."

Of course it was him.

He brought me on this adventure. Got us away, just the two of us. Sent me on a scavenger hunt for my birthday. Gave me mystery and meaning and nostalgia and *us*. He gave me everything I didn't need to ask for—and now he's giving me this.

"Did you have fun?" he asks.

My voice breaks and my vision blurs. "So much fun."

"Oh, don't cry, Freckles. Not before my speech."

Speech? No. I don't think I can survive a speech.

He smiles, preparing. "Scarlett Moore, I love you. I've loved you since the day you knocked down your own birthday cake without even noticing. And I *knew* I was going to marry you the day you wrote me a rambling letter that vaguely smelled like vomit."

Oof. My romance skills have improved since, but . . . whatever.

"All those years I was gone, I lived in limbo. Just waiting for Thursday nights, for your podcast. To hear the way your voice would shift when you were tired, or passionate, or pretending not to be nervous. I held on to that. Your laugh. The way your voice dipped when you were feeling something big." He swallows. "I wanted to come back—but I knew that when I did, I'd have to fight to be happy. Because Willowbrook would always be haunted by the ghost of my father's abuse. And I'd always have to live with that."

He looks up at me like I'm the light at the end of every tunnel he's ever walked down, and I press my lips together, fighting the overwhelming urge to throw my arms around him.

"But I was so wrong, Scarlett, because when I finally came back . . . you rewrote entire chapters. Changed the settings. Helped me complete my story arc." He grins when I can't help but let out a wet chuckle. "This town isn't haunted anymore. That bookstore? It's not just the place where I used to buy schoolbooks and piss off my dad because they were too expensive. It's where we read together for the first time. And The Oak? Not my father's bar anymore—it's where I met your friends for the first time. Where you tried to make me feel like I belonged."

I swipe at my eyes, my lips trembling so hard I can't speak.

"You're everywhere, Scarlett. You're everything. And for the rest of my life, I want to keep collecting moments with you. Create new memories." He clears his throat, shifting slightly on one knee. "And since this is your favorite place, I'd like to make a new memory. So from today on, this library can stop being the place where I almost lost you . . . and start being the place where I asked you to be mine forever."

The tears spill freely now, and I'm so grateful he's done with his speech—because if he said one more word, I might actually collapse.

"So, Scarlett Moore—girl of wontons, books, and freckles—will you marry me?"

I sob, nodding so hard my neck cramps up and the moment stutters. "Yes. *Yes*. I love you—s-so much." I can't find words, not the right ones, but I see it in his eyes as he rises and kisses me.

He knows.

He knows he's more than I ever let myself dream of. That I fell in love with his soul, not in spite of his shadows but because of how he chose to fight through them. That I loved him before I even understood what love really was. On a cellular level. In some other life, maybe even in all of them.

And in this life—he *is* what I know as love.

He *knows*. I can feel it in the way his tongue brushes mine, in the smile he leaves on my lips, in the way his fingers tremble just slightly as he slips the ring onto my finger. In the quiet, reverent way he whispers, "I love you, too," his forehead resting against mine.

But I should say something. Anything. So in between hiccups and sniffles, I wrap my arms around him and bury my face in his neck.

"God, Rafael Gray. I'm *so* glad you're not a serial killer."

acknowledgments

Every good murder mystery has a suspect list, and this book is no exception. Here are the partners in crime and masterminds who made *A Killer Kind of Romance* possible.

First, my partner, Caroline. Thank you for loving me through the late-night writing binges, the "I'll come to bed after one more chapter" lies, and the caffeine-fueled meltdowns. You kept me grounded, fed, and (mostly) sane.

My family and friends, especially Mary, Steph, Claire, Lucca, Amanda, Paola, and so many others. Thank you for being my anchor and my cheerleaders. This book exists because of your patience and encouragement.

My critique partners and beta readers: Oksana, Amanda, Leanne, Catherine, Claudia, and Erin. Thank you for reading messy drafts, for telling me what worked and (bravely) what didn't, and for sharing your brilliant insights. Your feedback sharpened this story into something I could never have managed alone.

My editor, Carrie, who pushed the story to be the best version of itself while still letting it sound like *me*. My agents, Caitlin and Suzie, who believed in my messy drafts and championed this book from day one.

My fellow authors and writing community, particularly Laura, Heather, Rebecca, and Eliza. You make this often lonely job feel like a team sport. Your encouragement, memes, and mutual venting sessions about edits and deadlines kept me afloat.

The indie bookstores that take a chance on my books and give them a home on their shelves—you keep stories alive and communities thriving. I'm honored every time I see my work among your selections.

The artists I've been lucky enough to work with. Thank you for taking my messy words and turning them into something beautiful and tangible. You gave these stories their face and spirit before anyone read a single page.

Oksana and Madison: You've been my sanity and my safe place. Thank you for listening to endless rants about characters who don't exist and for always reminding me that I could do this even when I doubted myself. Your belief in me is stitched into every page of this book.

Elodie, I could thank you for so many things, I wouldn't even know where to start, so I'll just thank you for being the kind of friend who stops listening to voice messages midway through to call me instead. I love you.

And my dog, Nordik, who forced me to take walks when I felt stuck.

Finally, to my readers—whether you've been with me since my

debut or you picked up this book on a whim—thank you. Thank you for letting my characters live in your heads and hearts, for sending me messages that made me tear up, for posting reviews, and for recommending my books to friends.

You are the reason I get to keep doing this.

about the author

LETIZIA LORINI is a *USA Today* bestselling author of heartwarming books with high cackling potential. An Italian writer currently based in a Scandinavian country, she lives with her partner and their fluffy Japanese Spitz. She also has a degree in sociology and one in criminology, speaks three languages, and drinks the daily recommended dose of coffee before breakfast. Find out more at LetiziaLorini.com.